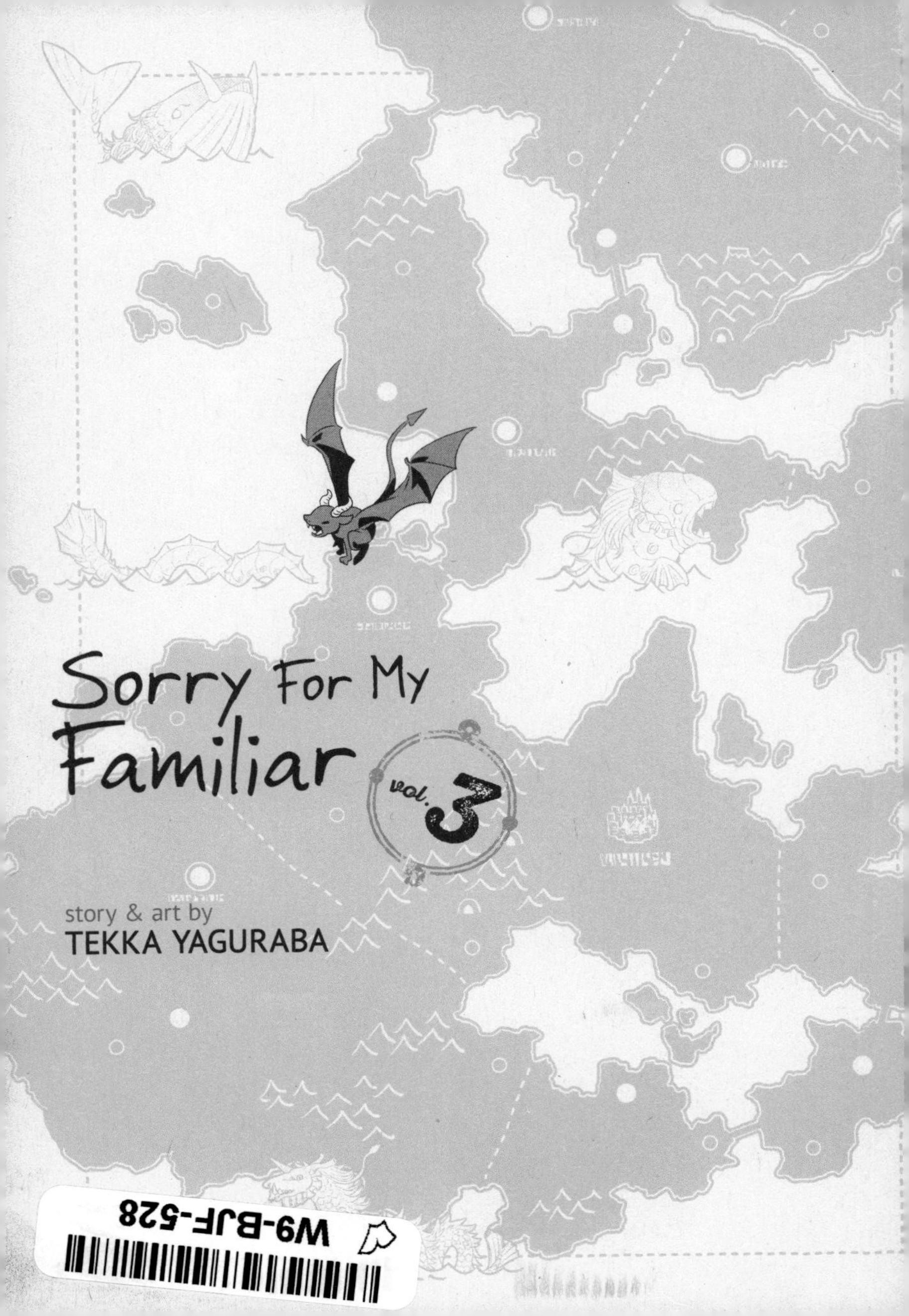

Sorry For My Familiar

vol. 3

story & art by
TEKKA YAGURABA

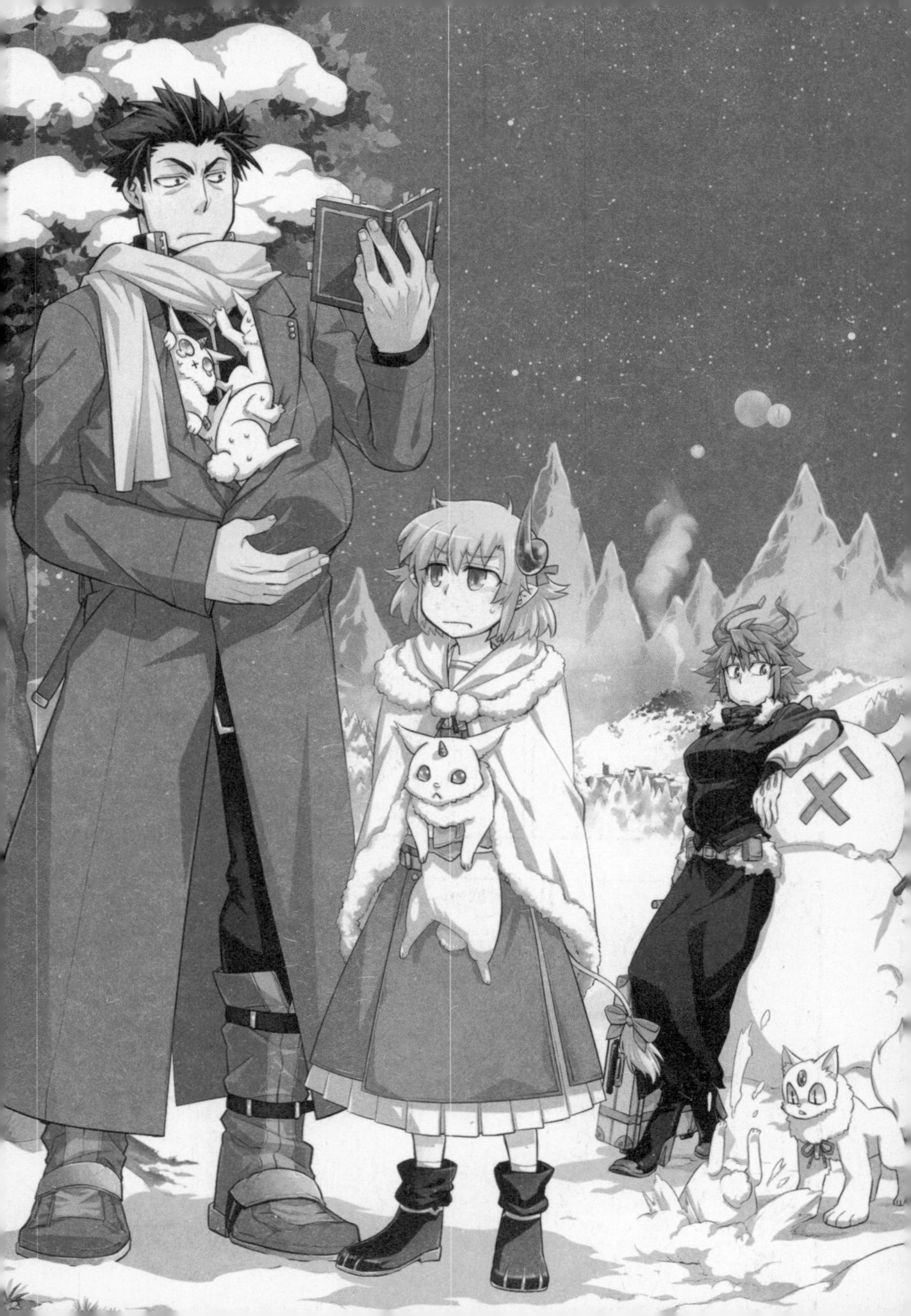

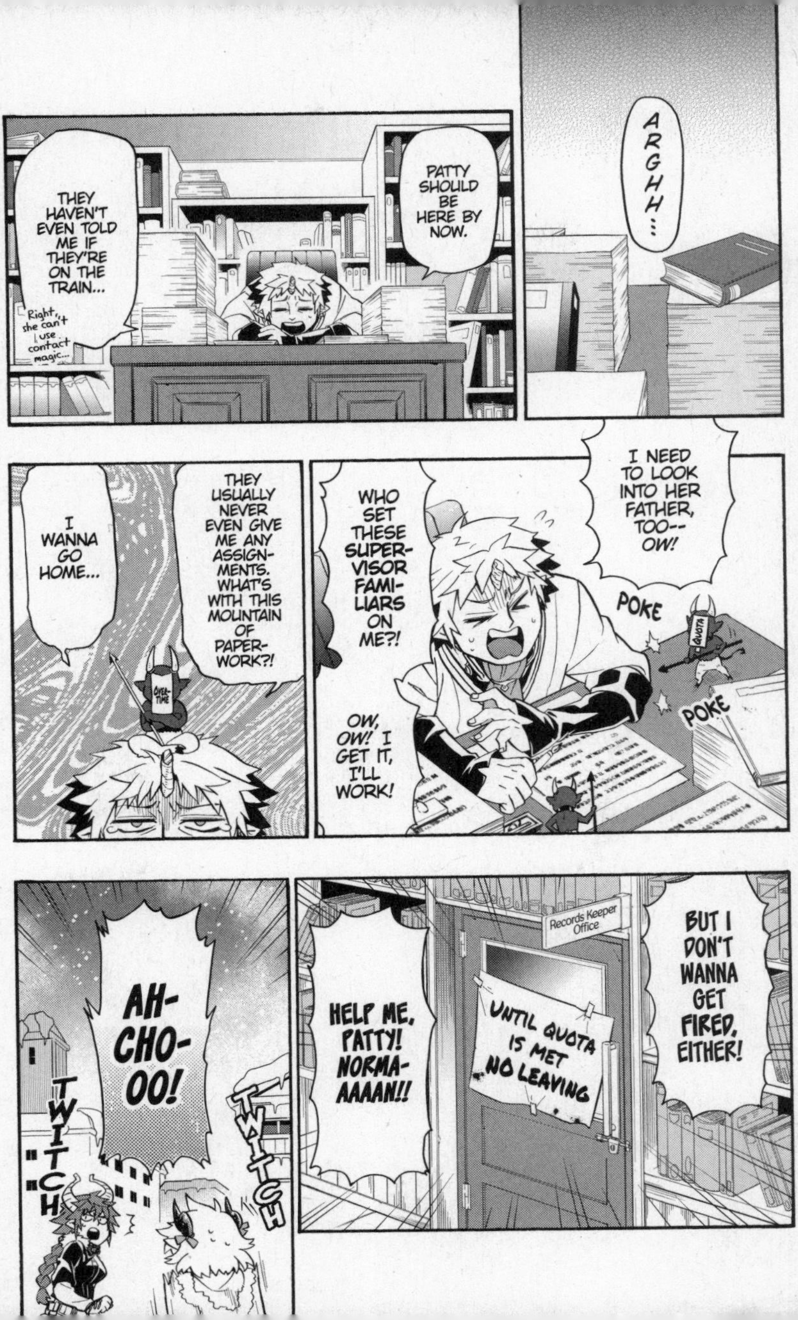
ARGHH...
PATTY SHOULD BE HERE BY NOW.
THEY HAVEN'T EVEN TOLD ME IF THEY'RE ON THE TRAIN...
Right, she can't use contact magic...
I NEED TO LOOK INTO HER FATHER, TOO--OW!
WHO SET THESE SUPER-VISOR FAMI-LIARS ON ME?!
POKE
QUOTA
POKE
OW, OW! I GET IT, I'LL WORK!
THEY USUALLY NEVER EVEN GIVE ME ANY ASSIGN-MENTS. WHAT'S WITH THIS MOUNTAIN OF PAPER-WORK?!
I WANNA GO HOME...
OVER-TIME
BUT I DON'T WANNA GET FIRED, EITHER!
Records Keeper Office
UNTIL QUOTA IS MET NO LEAVING
HELP ME, PATTY! NORMA-AAAAN!!
AH-CHO-OO!
TWITCH
TWITCH

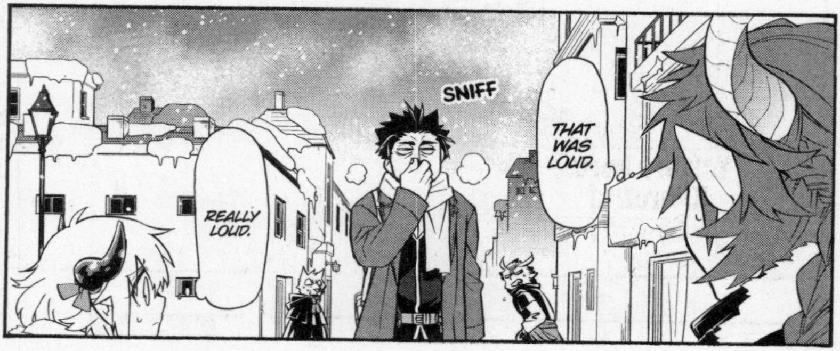
THAT WAS LOUD.
SNIFF
REALLY LOUD.

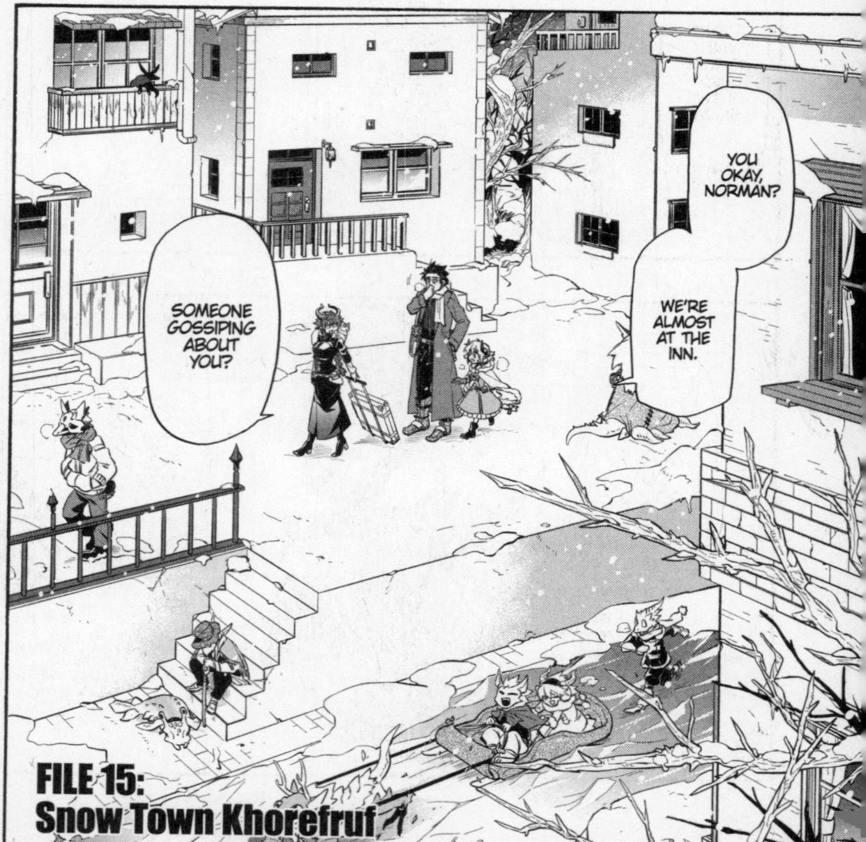
YOU OKAY, NORMAN?
WE'RE ALMOST AT THE INN.
SOMEONE GOSSIPING ABOUT YOU?

FILE 15: Snow Town Khorefruf

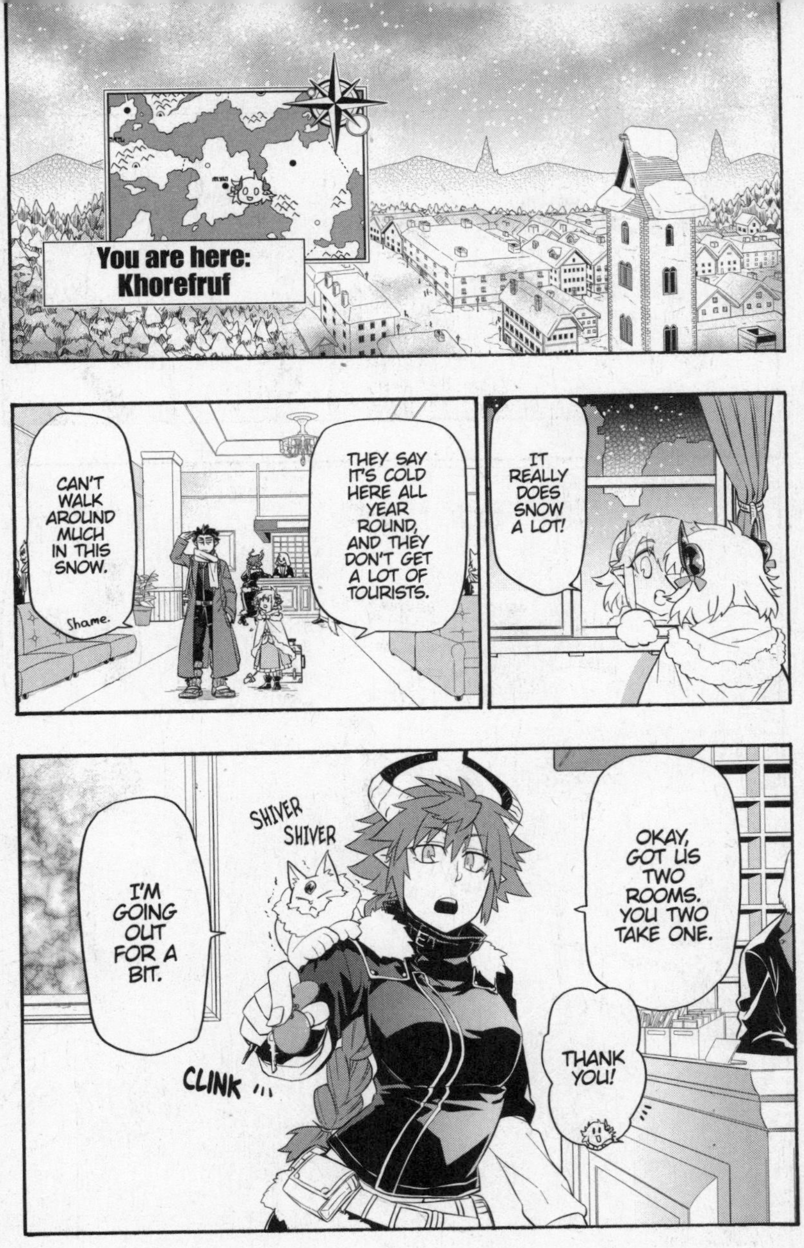
You are here: Khorefruf
IT REALLY DOES SNOW A LOT!
THEY SAY IT'S COLD HERE ALL YEAR ROUND, AND THEY DON'T GET A LOT OF TOURISTS.
CAN'T WALK AROUND MUCH IN THIS SNOW.
Shame.
OKAY, GOT US TWO ROOMS. YOU TWO TAKE ONE.
THANK YOU!
SHIVER SHIVER
I'M GOING OUT FOR A BIT.
CLINK

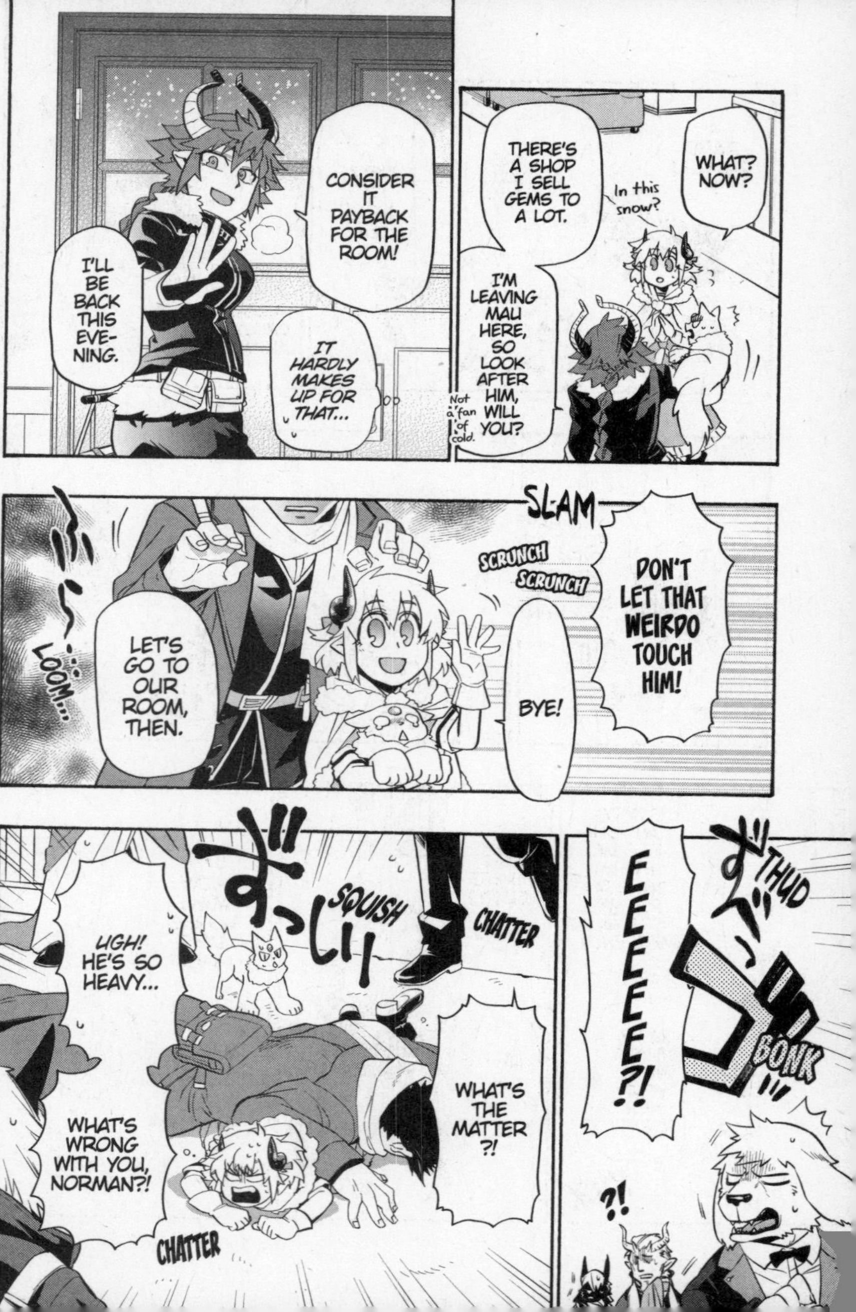
WHAT? NOW?
In this snow?
THERE'S A SHOP I SELL GEMS TO A LOT.
I'M LEAVING MAU HERE, SO LOOK AFTER HIM, WILL YOU?
Not a fan of cold.
CONSIDER IT PAYBACK FOR THE ROOM!
IT HARDLY MAKES UP FOR THAT...
I'LL BE BACK THIS EVE-NING.
SL-AM
DON'T LET THAT WEIRDO TOUCH HIM!
SCRUNCH
SCRUNCH
BYE!
LET'S GO TO OUR ROOM, THEN.
LOOM...
THUD
EEEEEE?!
BONK
?!
SQUISH
CHATTER
UGH! HE'S SO HEAVY...
WHAT'S THE MATTER?!
WHAT'S WRONG WITH YOU, NORMAN?!
CHATTER

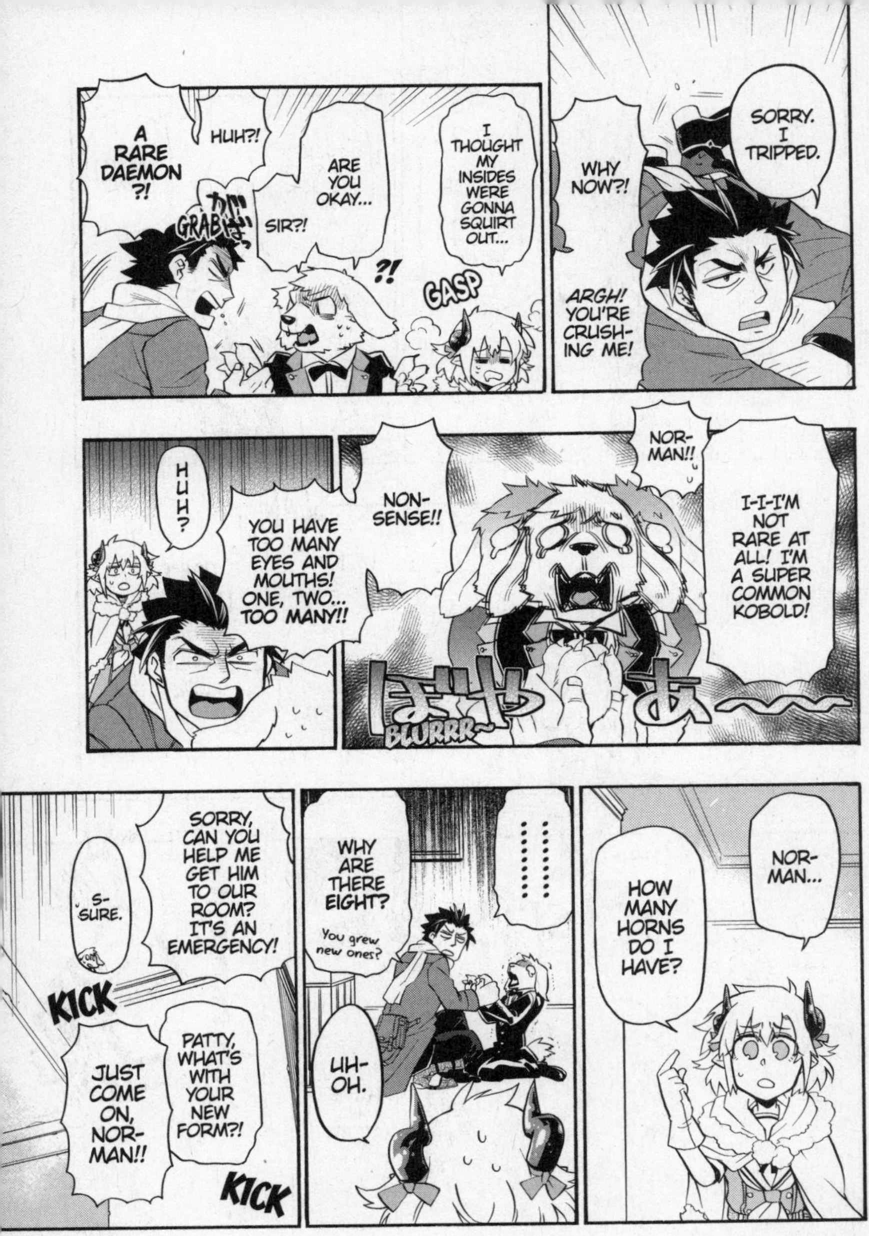
SORRY. I TRIPPED.
WHY NOW?!
ARGH! YOU'RE CRUSHING ME!
I THOUGHT MY INSIDES WERE GONNA SQUIRT OUT...
ARE YOU OKAY...
SIR?!
HUH?!
A RARE DAEMON?!
GRAB
?!
GASP
NOR-MAN!!
I-I-I'M NOT RARE AT ALL! I'M A SUPER COMMON KOBOLD!
NON-SENSE!!
BLURRR~
HUH?
YOU HAVE TOO MANY EYES AND MOUTHS! ONE, TWO... TOO MANY!!
NOR-MAN...
HOW MANY HORNS DO I HAVE?
......
WHY ARE THERE EIGHT?
You grew new ones?
UH-OH.
SORRY, CAN YOU HELP ME GET HIM TO OUR ROOM? IT'S AN EMERGENCY!
S-SURE.
KICK
PATTY, WHAT'S WITH YOUR NEW FORM?!
JUST COME ON, NOR-MAN!!
KICK

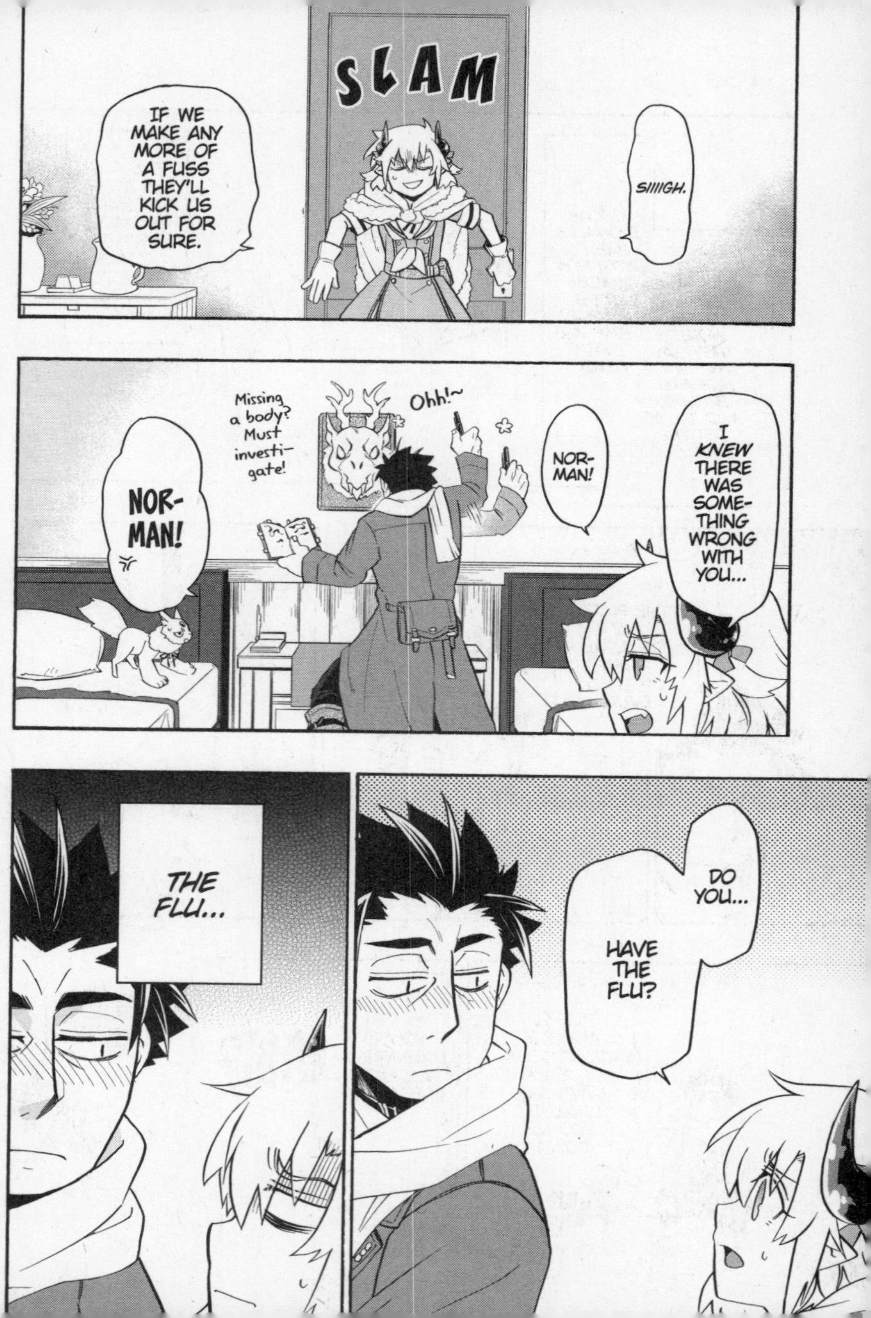
SLAM
SIIIGH.
IF WE MAKE ANY MORE OF A FUSS THEY'LL KICK US OUT FOR SURE.
I *KNEW* THERE WAS SOMETHING WRONG WITH YOU...
NOR-MAN!
Ohh!~
Missing a body? Must investi-gate!
NOR-MAN!
DO YOU...
HAVE THE FLU?
THE FLU...

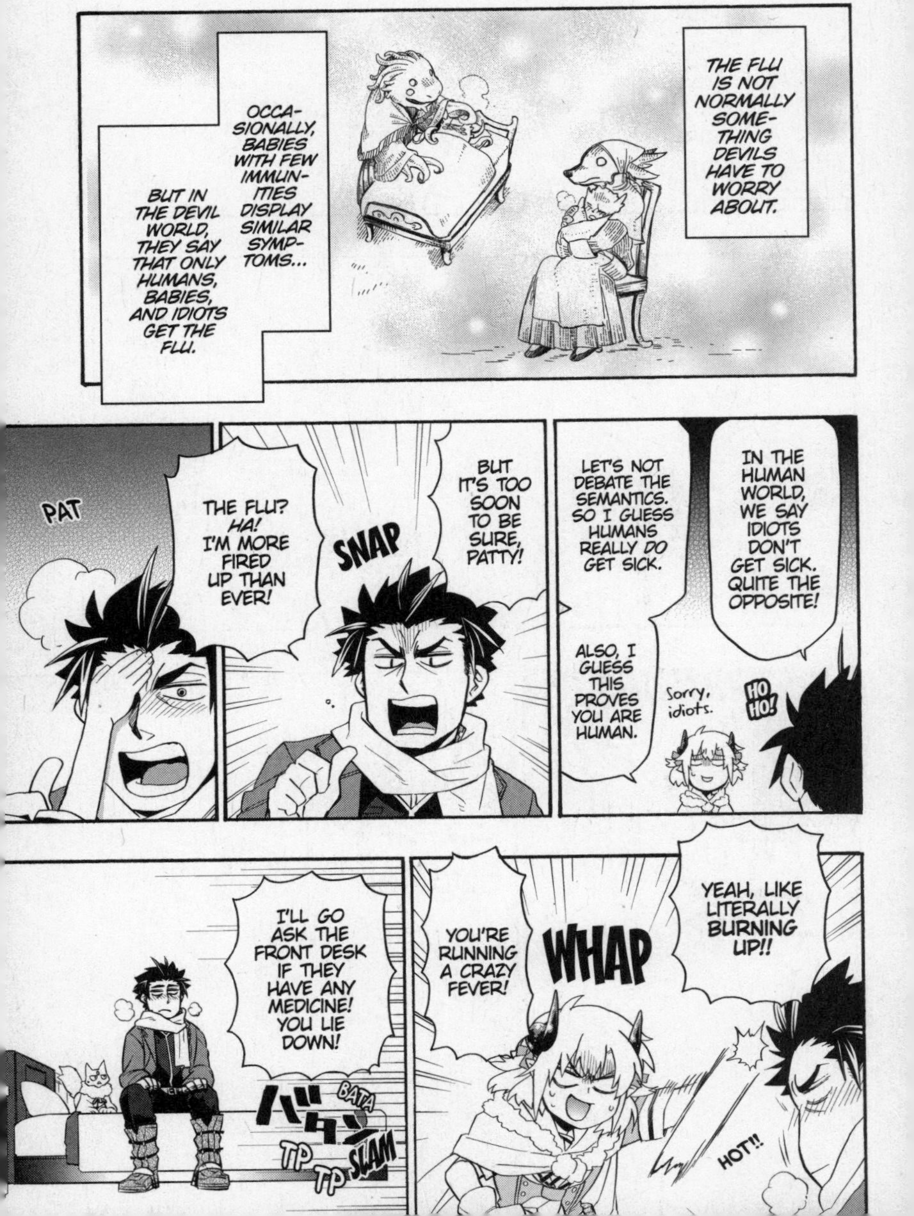
THE FLU IS NOT NORMALLY SOMETHING DEVILS HAVE TO WORRY ABOUT.
OCCASIONALLY, BABIES WITH FEW IMMUNITIES DISPLAY SIMILAR SYMPTOMS...
BUT IN THE DEVIL WORLD, THEY SAY THAT ONLY HUMANS, BABIES, AND IDIOTS GET THE FLU.
IN THE HUMAN WORLD, WE SAY IDIOTS DON'T GET SICK. QUITE THE OPPOSITE!
HO HO!
LET'S NOT DEBATE THE SEMANTICS. SO I GUESS HUMANS REALLY *DO* GET SICK.
ALSO, I GUESS THIS PROVES YOU ARE HUMAN.
Sorry, idiots.
BUT IT'S TOO SOON TO BE SURE, PATTY!
SNAP
THE FLU? *HA!* I'M MORE FIRED UP THAN EVER!
PAT
YEAH, LIKE LITERALLY BURNING UP!!
WHAP
YOU'RE RUNNING A CRAZY FEVER!
HOT!!
I'LL GO ASK THE FRONT DESK IF THEY HAVE ANY MEDICINE! YOU LIE DOWN!
バタン
BATA
SLAM
TP TP

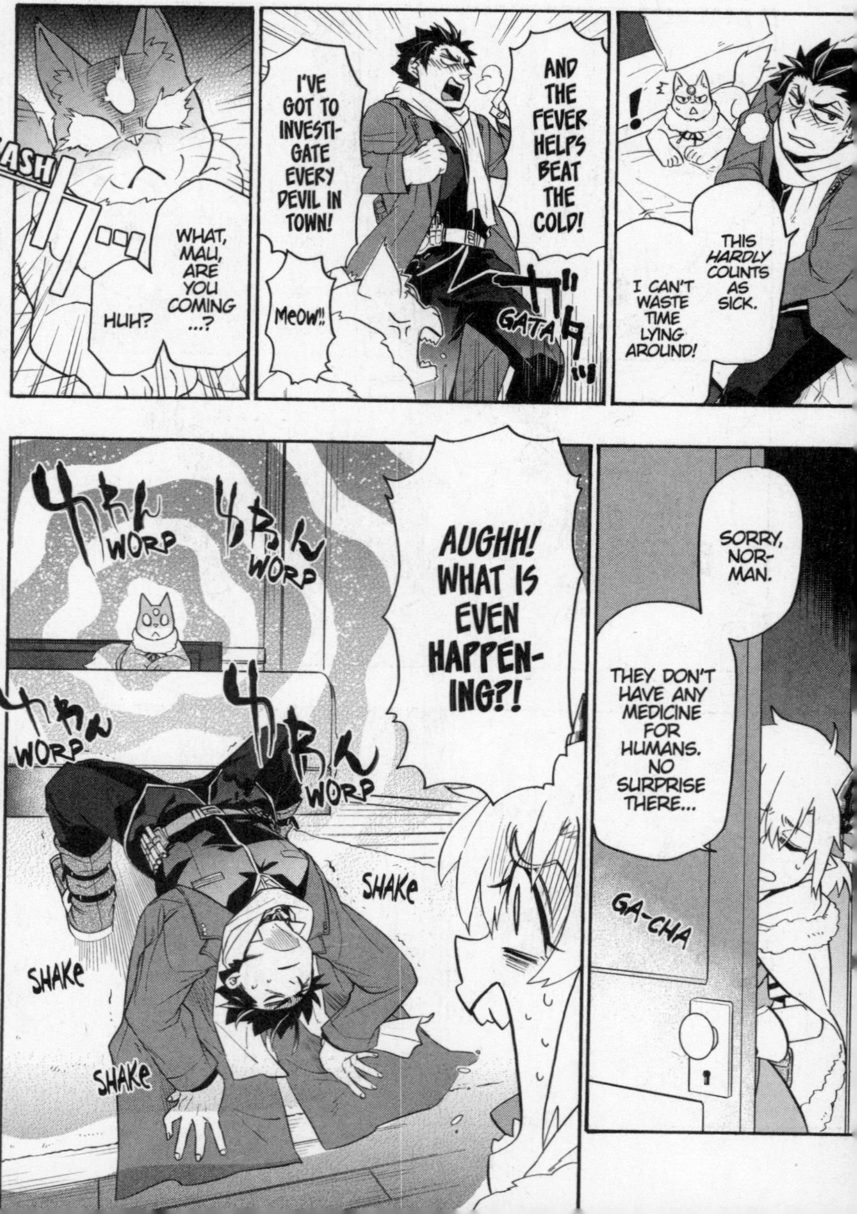

THIS HARDLY COUNTS AS SICK.
I CAN'T WASTE TIME LYING AROUND!
AND THE FEVER HELPS BEAT THE COLD!
I'VE GOT TO INVESTI-GATE EVERY DEVIL IN TOWN!
GATA
Meow!!
FLASH
WHAT, MAU, ARE YOU COMING ...?
HUH?
SORRY, NOR-MAN.
THEY DON'T HAVE ANY MEDICINE FOR HUMANS. NO SURPRISE THERE...
GA-CHA
AUGHH! WHAT IS EVEN HAPPEN-ING?!
WORP
WORP
WORP
WORP
SHAKE
SHAKE
SHAKE

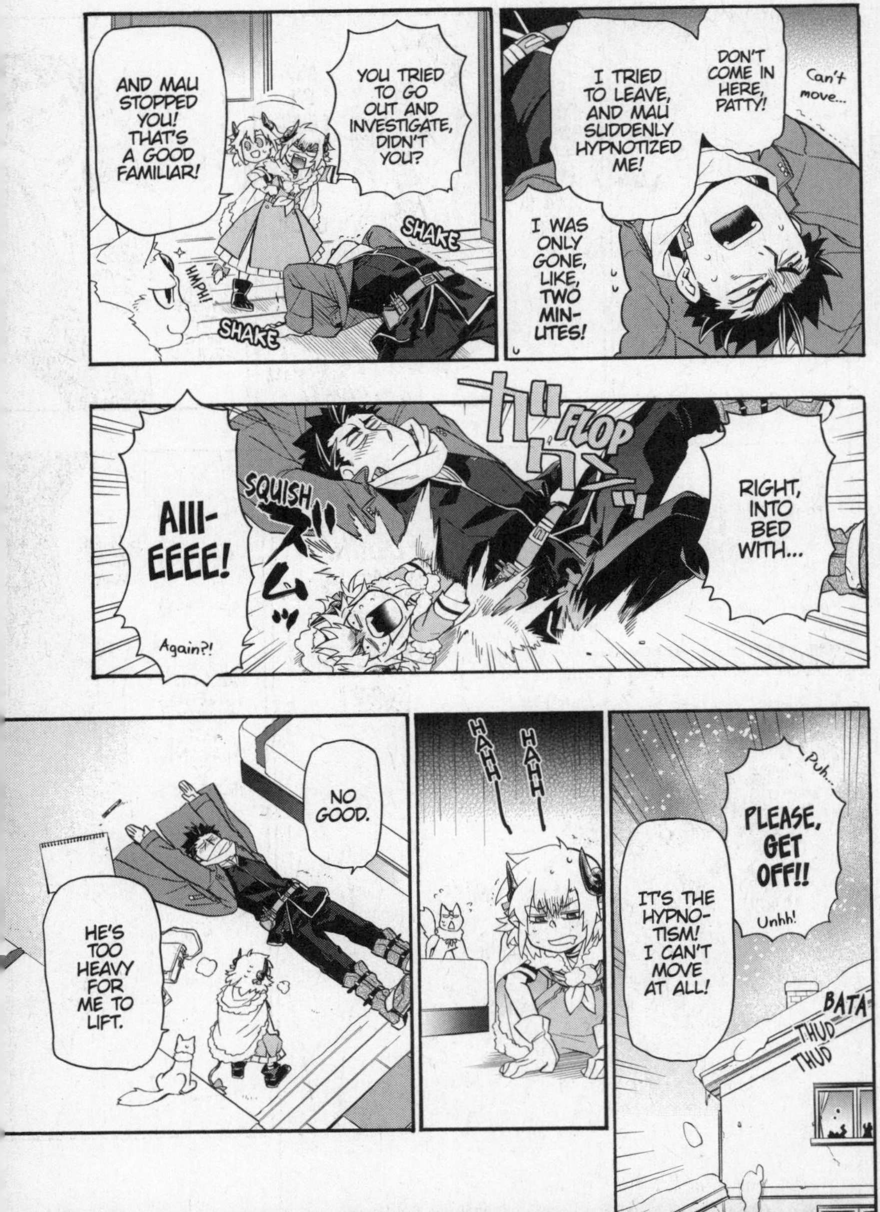
DON'T COME IN HERE, PATTY!
Can't move...
I TRIED TO LEAVE, AND MAU SUDDENLY HYPNOTIZED ME!
I WAS ONLY GONE, LIKE, TWO MINUTES!
YOU TRIED TO GO OUT AND INVESTIGATE, DIDN'T YOU?
AND MAU STOPPED YOU! THAT'S A GOOD FAMILIAR!
SHAKE
HMPH!
SHAKE
RIGHT, INTO BED WITH...
FLOP
SQUISH
AIII-EEEE!
Again?!
Puh...
PLEASE, GET OFF!!
Unhh!
IT'S THE HYPNO-TISM! I CAN'T MOVE AT ALL!
BATA
THUD
THUD
HAHH
HAHH
NO GOOD.
HE'S TOO HEAVY FOR ME TO LIFT.

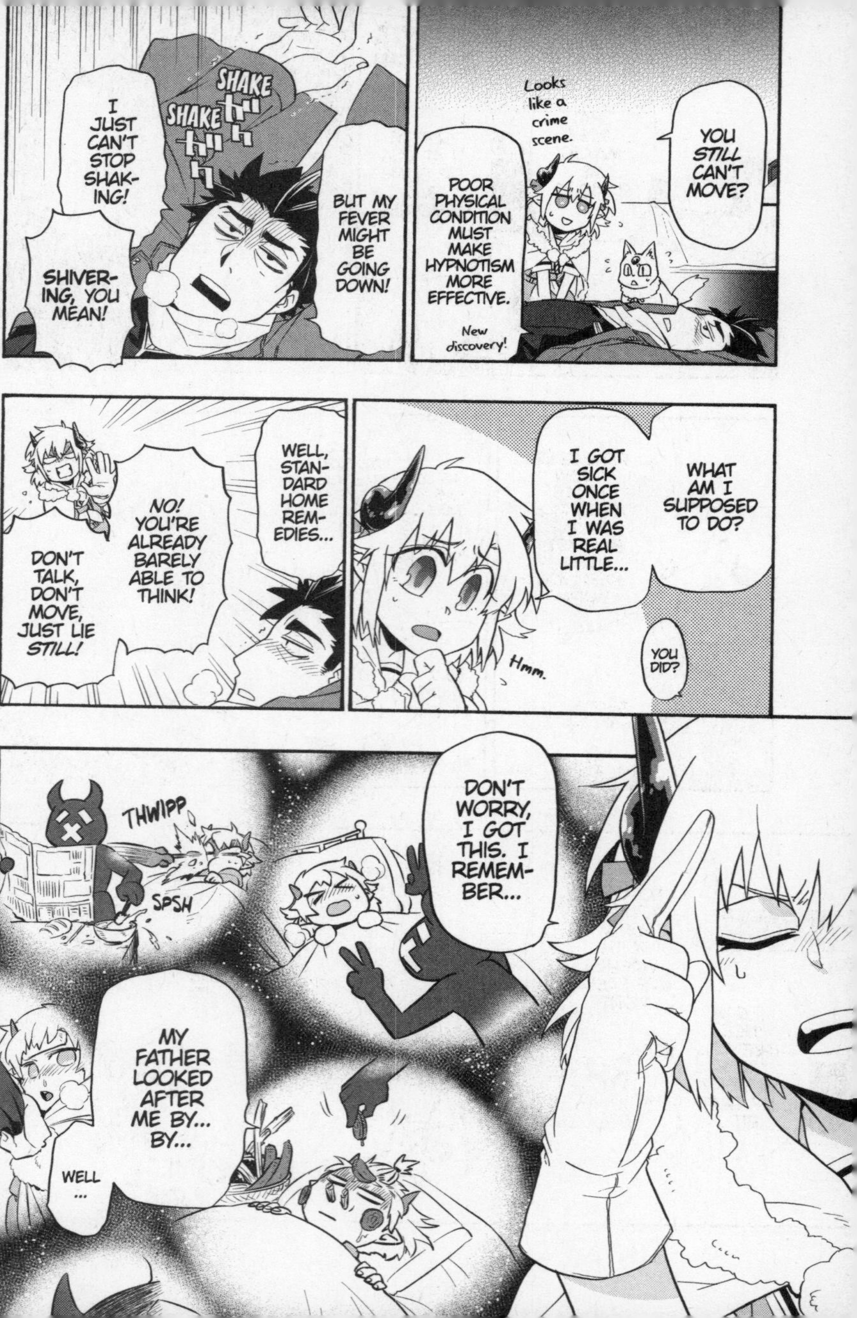
YOU STILL CAN'T MOVE?
Looks like a crime scene.
POOR PHYSICAL CONDITION MUST MAKE HYPNOTISM MORE EFFECTIVE.
New discovery!
BUT MY FEVER MIGHT BE GOING DOWN!
SHAKE
SHAKE
I JUST CAN'T STOP SHAKING!
SHIVERING, YOU MEAN!
WHAT AM I SUPPOSED TO DO?
I GOT SICK ONCE WHEN I WAS REAL LITTLE...
YOU DID?
Hmm.
WELL, STANDARD HOME REMEDIES...
NO! YOU'RE ALREADY BARELY ABLE TO THINK!
DON'T TALK, DON'T MOVE, JUST LIE STILL!
DON'T WORRY, I GOT THIS. I REMEMBER...
THWIPP
SPSH
MY FATHER LOOKED AFTER ME BY... BY...
WELL ...

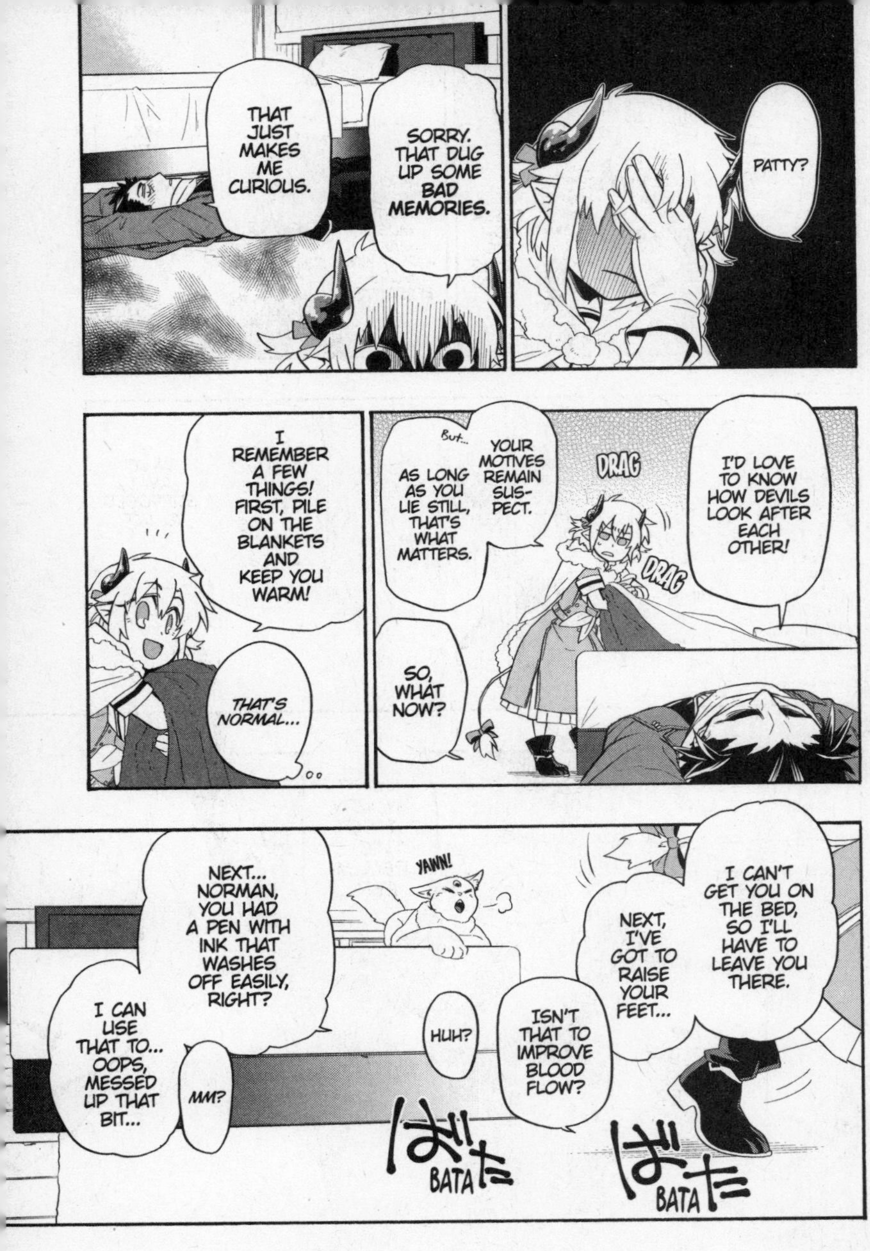
PATTY?
SORRY. THAT DUG UP SOME BAD MEMORIES.
THAT JUST MAKES ME CURIOUS.
I'D LOVE TO KNOW HOW DEVILS LOOK AFTER EACH OTHER!
DRAG
DRAG
YOUR MOTIVES REMAIN SUS-PECT.
But...
AS LONG AS YOU LIE STILL, THAT'S WHAT MATTERS.
SO, WHAT NOW?
I REMEMBER A FEW THINGS! FIRST, PILE ON THE BLANKETS AND KEEP YOU WARM!
THAT'S NORMAL...
I CAN'T GET YOU ON THE BED, SO I'LL HAVE TO LEAVE YOU THERE.
NEXT, I'VE GOT TO RAISE YOUR FEET...
ISN'T THAT TO IMPROVE BLOOD FLOW?
ばた BATA
ばた BATA
HUH?
YAWN!
NEXT... NORMAN, YOU HAD A PEN WITH INK THAT WASHES OFF EASILY, RIGHT?
MM?
I CAN USE THAT TO... OOPS, MESSED UP THAT BIT...

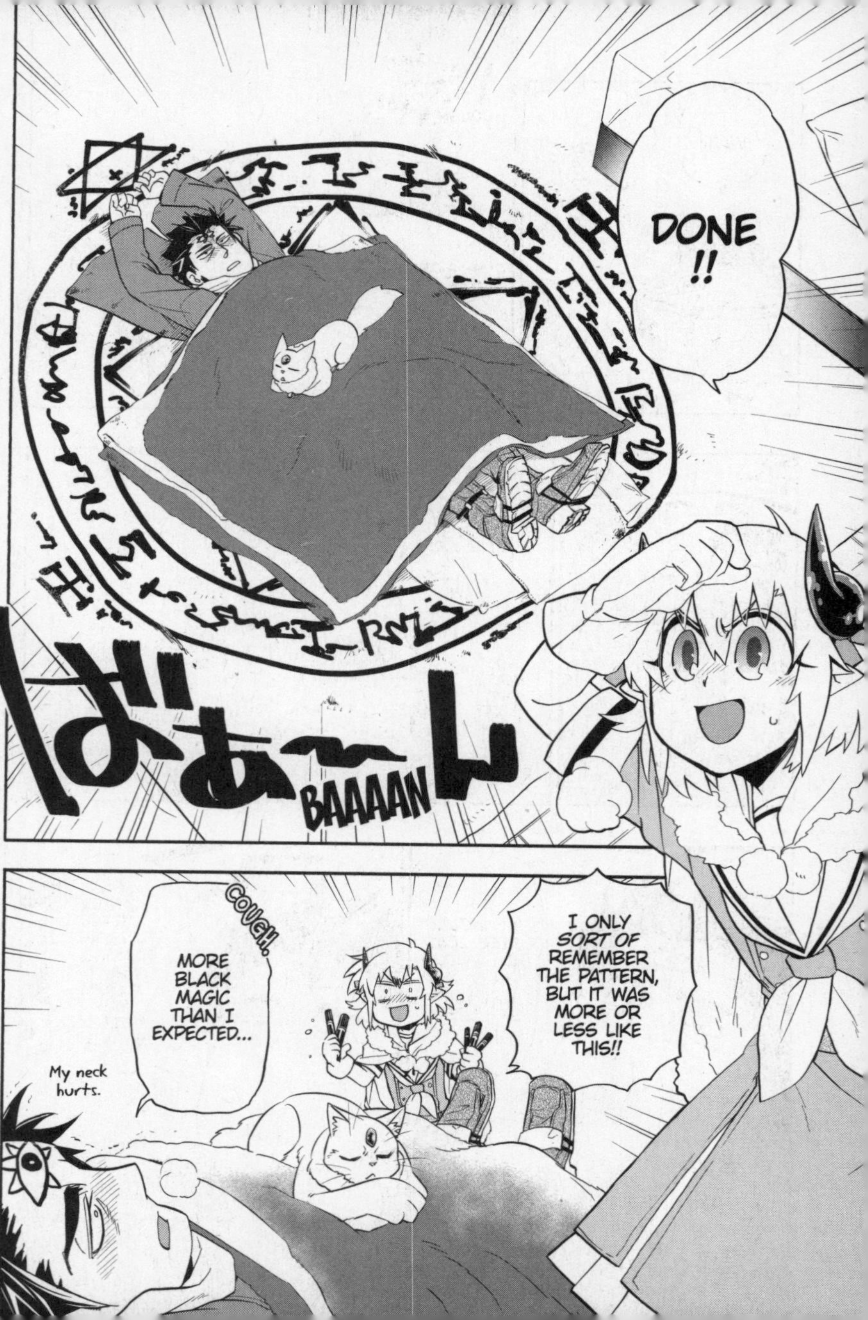
DONE!!
ばあ〜ん
BAAAAN
I ONLY SORT OF REMEMBER THE PATTERN, BUT IT WAS MORE OR LESS LIKE THIS!!
COUGH!
MORE BLACK MAGIC THAN I EXPECTED...
My neck hurts.

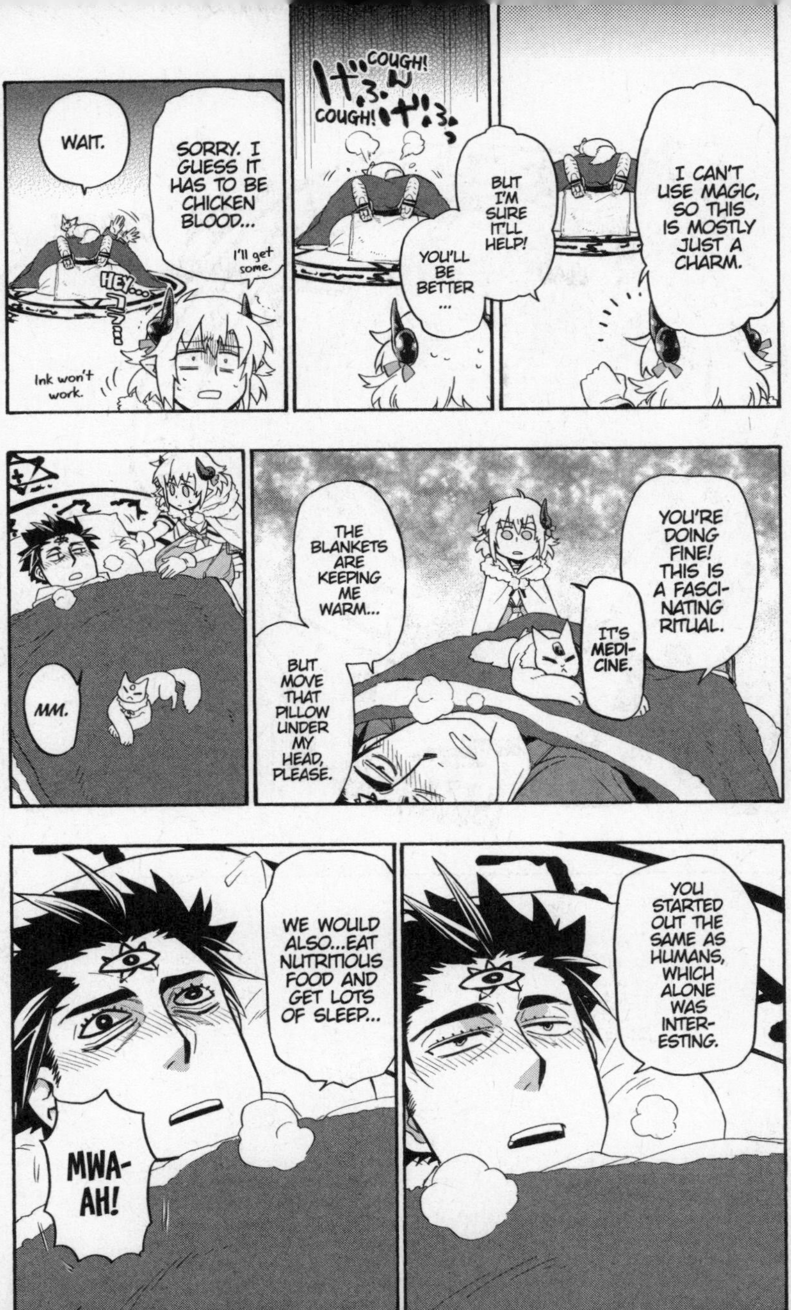
I CAN'T USE MAGIC, SO THIS IS MOSTLY JUST A CHARM.
COUGH!
COUGH!
BUT I'M SURE IT'LL HELP!
YOU'LL BE BETTER ...
SORRY. I GUESS IT HAS TO BE CHICKEN BLOOD...
I'll get some.
WAIT.
HEY...
Ink won't work.
YOU'RE DOING FINE! THIS IS A FASCINATING RITUAL.
IT'S MEDICINE.
THE BLANKETS ARE KEEPING ME WARM...
BUT MOVE THAT PILLOW UNDER MY HEAD, PLEASE.
MM.
YOU STARTED OUT THE SAME AS HUMANS, WHICH ALONE WAS INTERESTING.
WE WOULD ALSO...EAT NUTRITIOUS FOOD AND GET LOTS OF SLEEP...
MWA-AH!

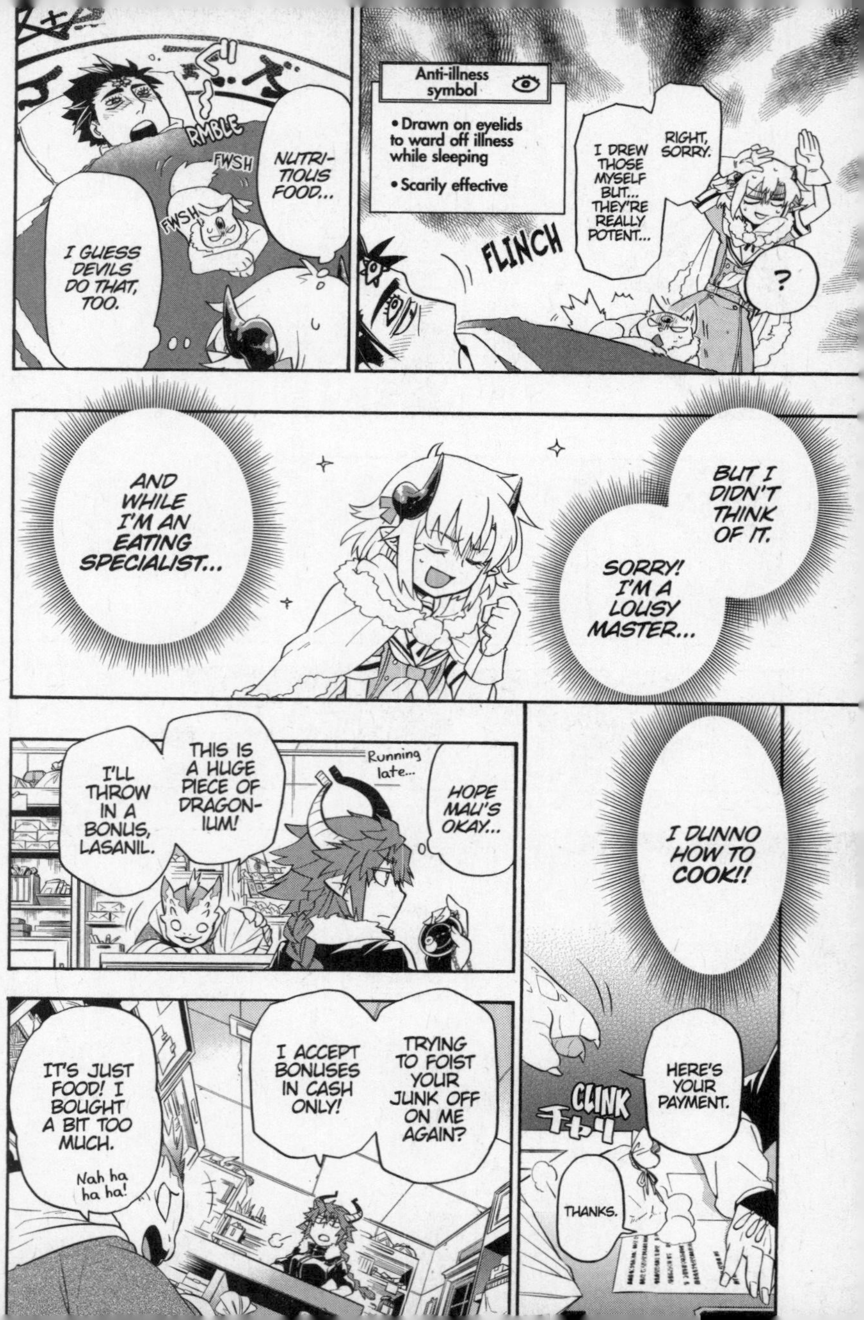
RIGHT, SORRY.
I DREW THOSE MYSELF BUT... THEY'RE REALLY POTENT...
Anti-illness symbol
• Drawn on eyelids to ward off illness while sleeping
• Scarily effective
?
FLINCH
RMBLE
NUTRITIOUS FOOD...
FWSH
FWSH
I GUESS DEVILS DO THAT, TOO.
BUT I DIDN'T THINK OF IT.
SORRY! I'M A LOUSY MASTER...
AND WHILE I'M AN EATING SPECIALIST...
I DUNNO HOW TO COOK!!
HERE'S YOUR PAYMENT.
CLINK
THANKS.
HOPE MAU'S OKAY...
Running late...
THIS IS A HUGE PIECE OF DRAGONIUM!
I'LL THROW IN A BONUS, LASANIL.
TRYING TO FOIST YOUR JUNK OFF ON ME AGAIN?
I ACCEPT BONUSES IN CASH ONLY!
IT'S JUST FOOD! I BOUGHT A BIT TOO MUCH.
Nah ha ha ha!

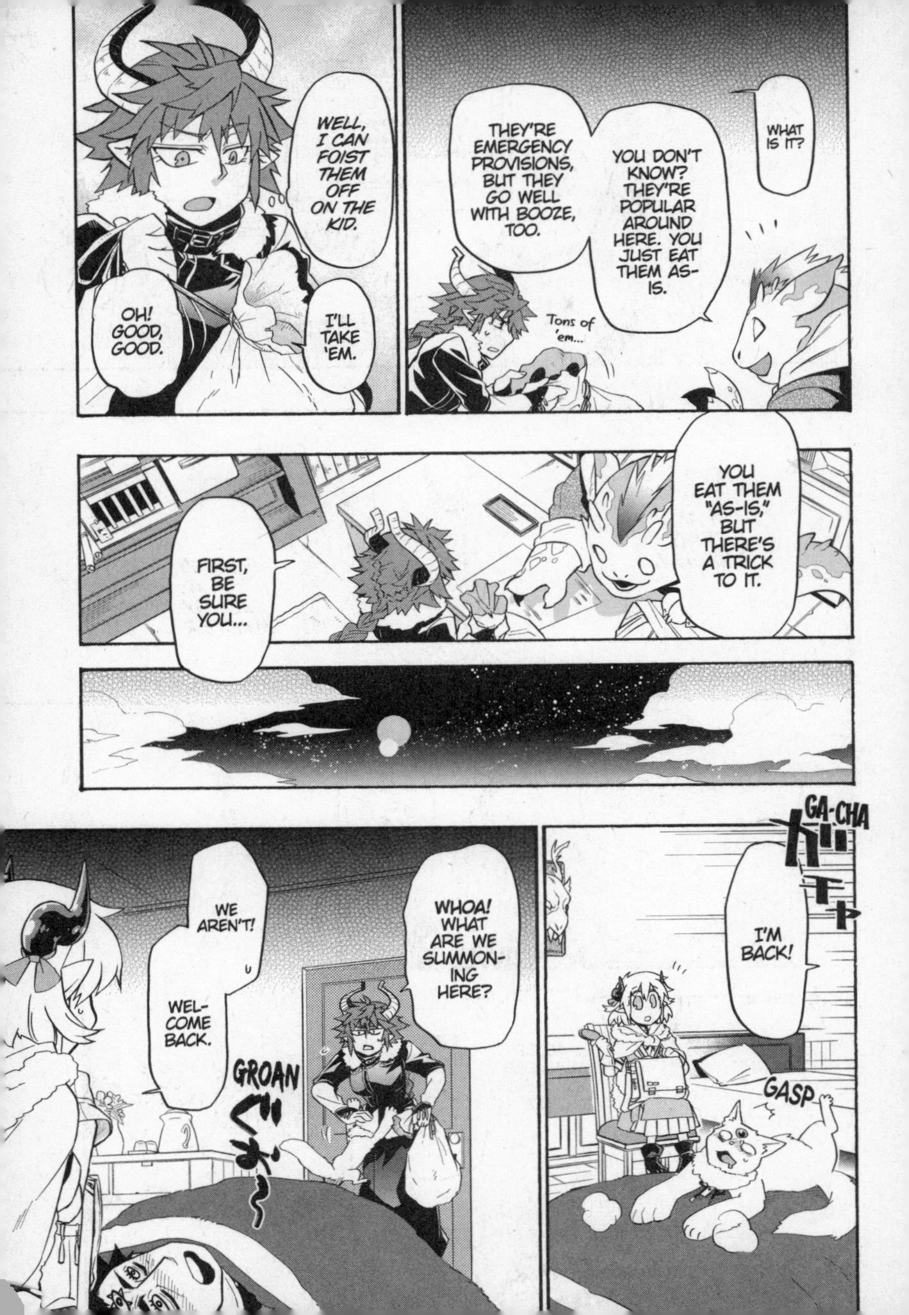
WHAT IS IT?
YOU DON'T KNOW? THEY'RE POPULAR AROUND HERE. YOU JUST EAT THEM AS-IS.
THEY'RE EMERGENCY PROVISIONS, BUT THEY GO WELL WITH BOOZE, TOO.
Tons of 'em...
WELL, I CAN FOIST THEM OFF ON THE KID.
I'LL TAKE 'EM.
OH! GOOD, GOOD.
YOU EAT THEM "AS-IS," BUT THERE'S A TRICK TO IT.
FIRST, BE SURE YOU...
GA-CHA
I'M BACK!
GASP
WHOA! WHAT ARE WE SUMMONING HERE?
WE AREN'T!
WEL-COME BACK.
GROAN

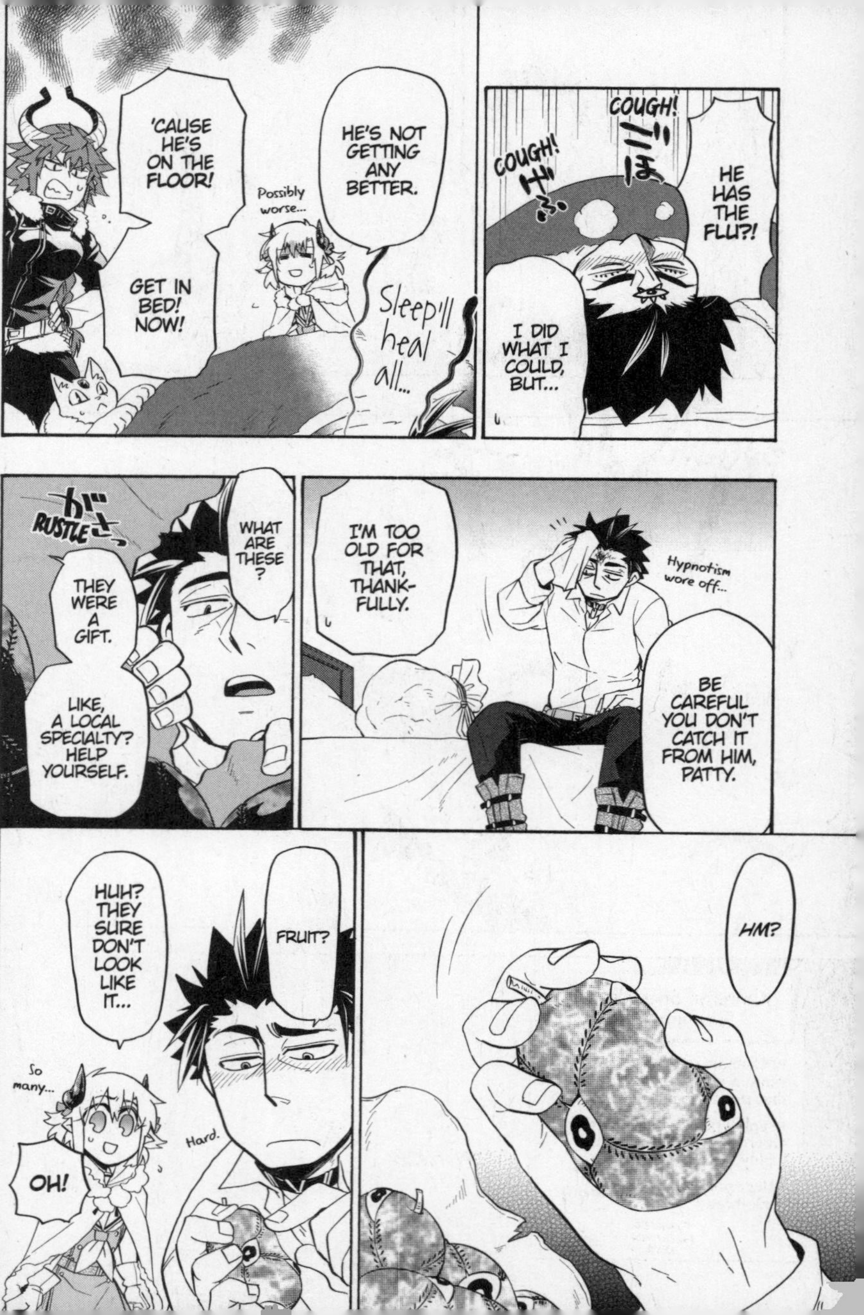
COUGH!
HE HAS THE FLU?!
COUGH!
I DID WHAT I COULD, BUT...
HE'S NOT GETTING ANY BETTER.
Possibly worse...
Sleep'll heal all...
'CAUSE HE'S ON THE FLOOR!
GET IN BED! NOW!
BE CAREFUL YOU DON'T CATCH IT FROM HIM, PATTY.
Hypnotism wore off...
I'M TOO OLD FOR THAT, THANKFULLY.
WHAT ARE THESE?
RUSTLE
THEY WERE A GIFT.
LIKE, A LOCAL SPECIALTY? HELP YOURSELF.
HM?
FRUIT?
HUH? THEY SURE DON'T LOOK LIKE IT...
So many...
Hard.
OH!

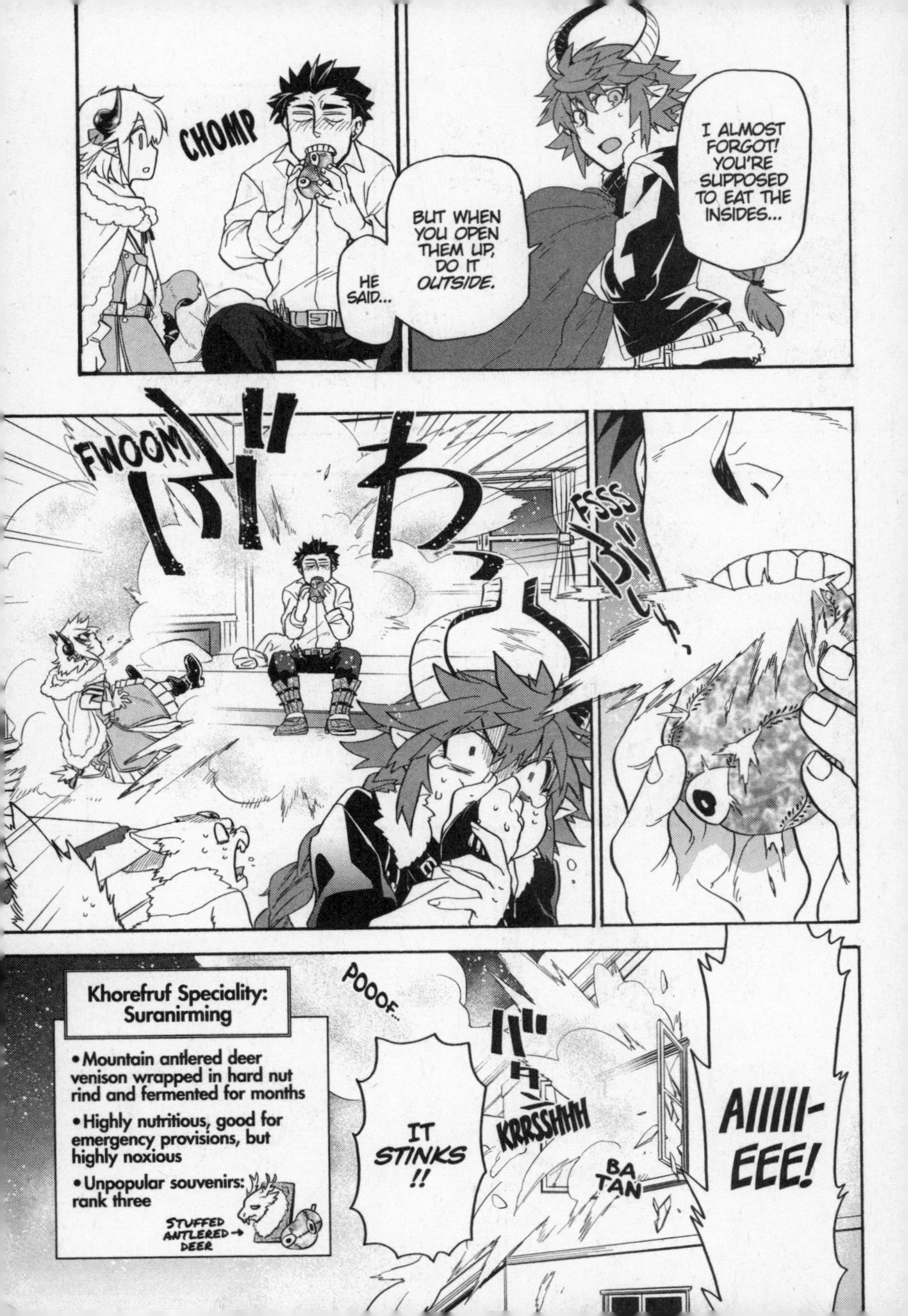
I ALMOST FORGOT! YOU'RE SUPPOSED TO EAT THE INSIDES...
BUT WHEN YOU OPEN THEM UP, DO IT OUTSIDE.
HE SAID...
CHOMP
FSSS
FWOOM
AIIIII-EEE!
BA TAN
KRRSSHHH
IT STINKS!!
POOOF...
Khorefruf Speciality: Suranirming
•Mountain antlered deer venison wrapped in hard nut rind and fermented for months
•Highly nutritious, good for emergency provisions, but highly noxious
•Unpopular souvenirs: rank three
STUFFED ANTLERED DEER

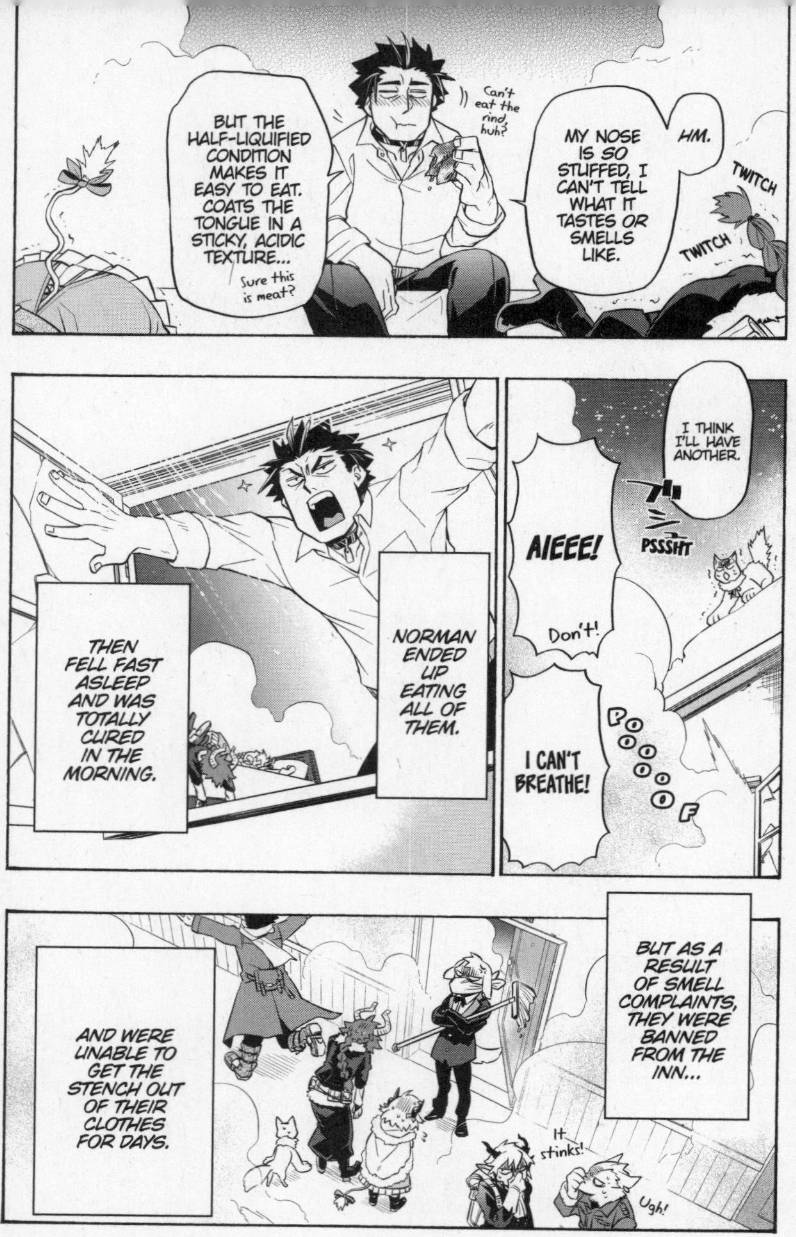
HM.
TWITCH
TWITCH
MY NOSE IS SO STUFFED, I CAN'T TELL WHAT IT TASTES OR SMELLS LIKE.
Can't eat the rind, huh?
BUT THE HALF-LIQUIFIED CONDITION MAKES IT EASY TO EAT. COATS THE TONGUE IN A STICKY, ACIDIC TEXTURE...
Sure this is meat?
I THINK I'LL HAVE ANOTHER.
PSSSHT
AIEEE!
Don't!
POOOOOF
I CAN'T BREATHE!
NORMAN ENDED UP EATING ALL OF THEM.
THEN FELL FAST ASLEEP AND WAS TOTALLY CURED IN THE MORNING.
BUT AS A RESULT OF SMELL COMPLAINTS, THEY WERE BANNED FROM THE INN...
AND WERE UNABLE TO GET THE STENCH OUT OF THEIR CLOTHES FOR DAYS.
It stinks!
Ugh!

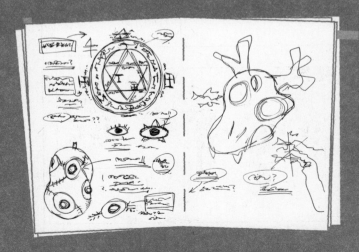

Sorry For My Familiar

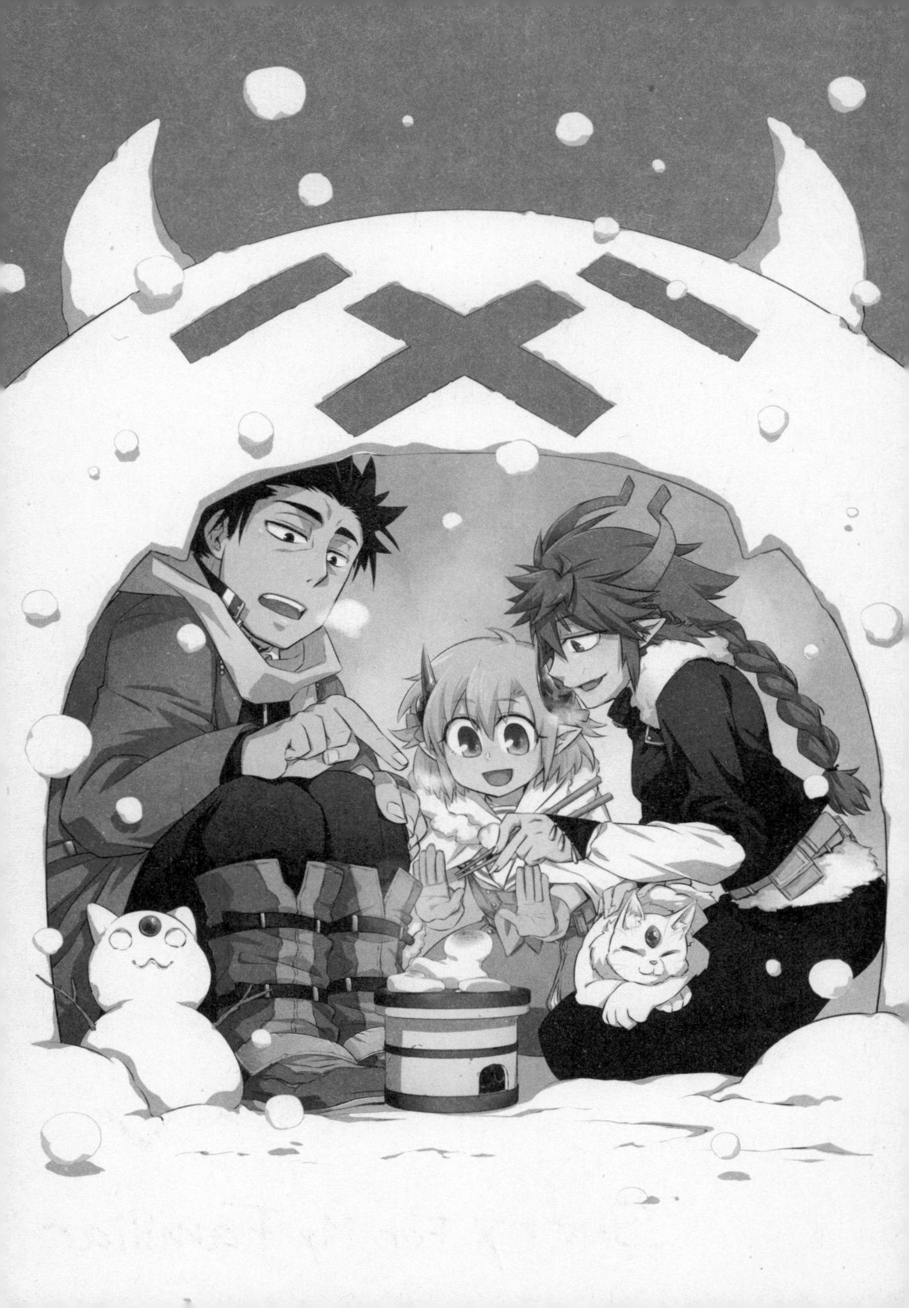

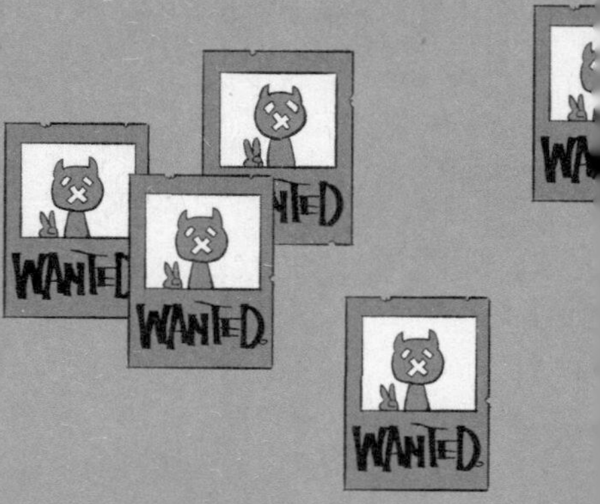
WANTED
WANTED
WANTED
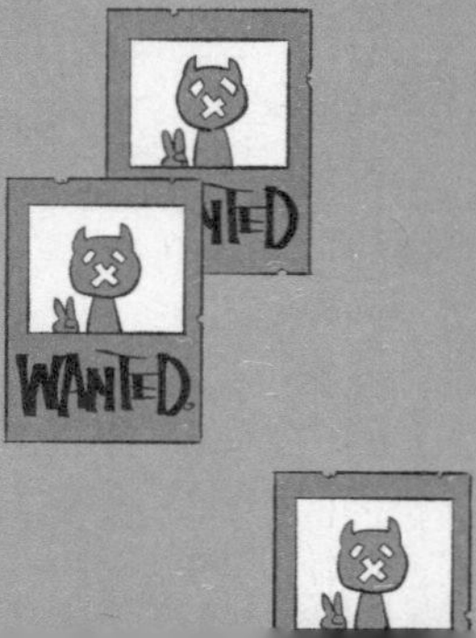
WANTED

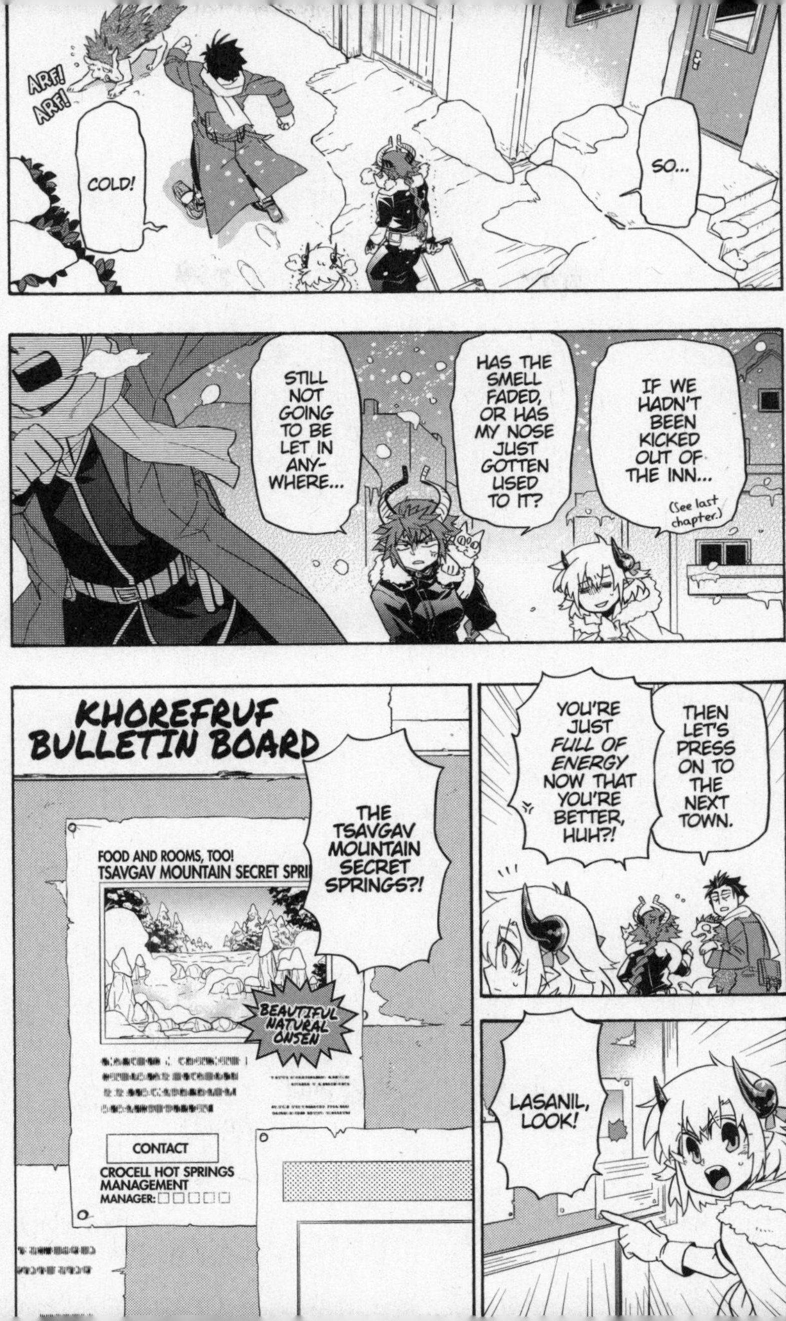
SO...
COLD!
ARF! ARF!
IF WE HADN'T BEEN KICKED OUT OF THE INN...
(See last chapter.)
HAS THE SMELL FADED, OR HAS MY NOSE JUST GOTTEN USED TO IT?
STILL NOT GOING TO BE LET IN ANY-WHERE...
THEN LET'S PRESS ON TO THE NEXT TOWN.
YOU'RE JUST FULL OF ENERGY NOW THAT YOU'RE BETTER, HUH?!
LASANIL, LOOK!
KHOREFRUF BULLETIN BOARD
THE TSAVGAV MOUNTAIN SECRET SPRINGS?!
FOOD AND ROOMS, TOO!
TSAVGAV MOUNTAIN SECRET SPRI
BEAUTIFUL NATURAL ONSEN
CONTACT
CROCELL HOT SPRINGS MANAGEMENT
MANAGER: □□□□□

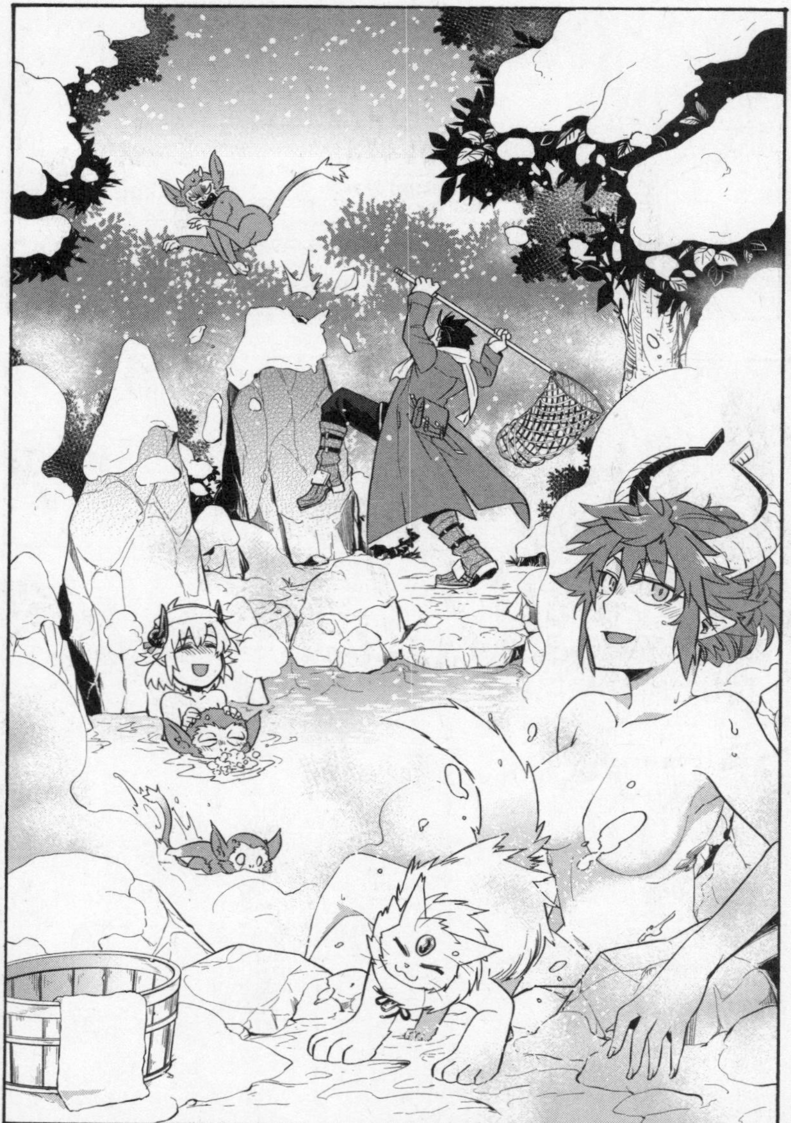

FILE 16: Tsavgav Mountain

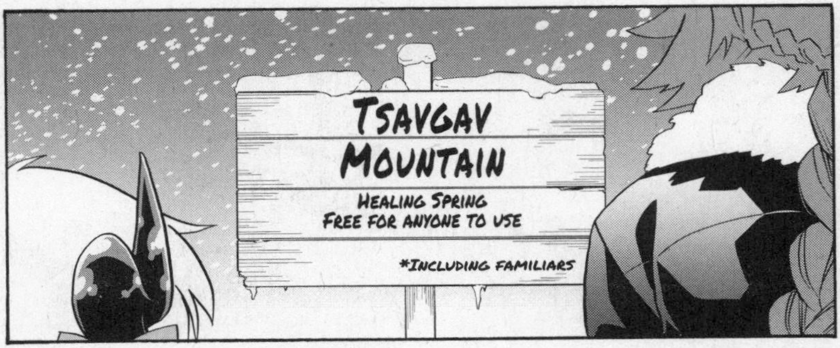
TSAVGAV MOUNTAIN
HEALING SPRING
FREE FOR ANYONE TO USE
*INCLUDING FAMILIARS

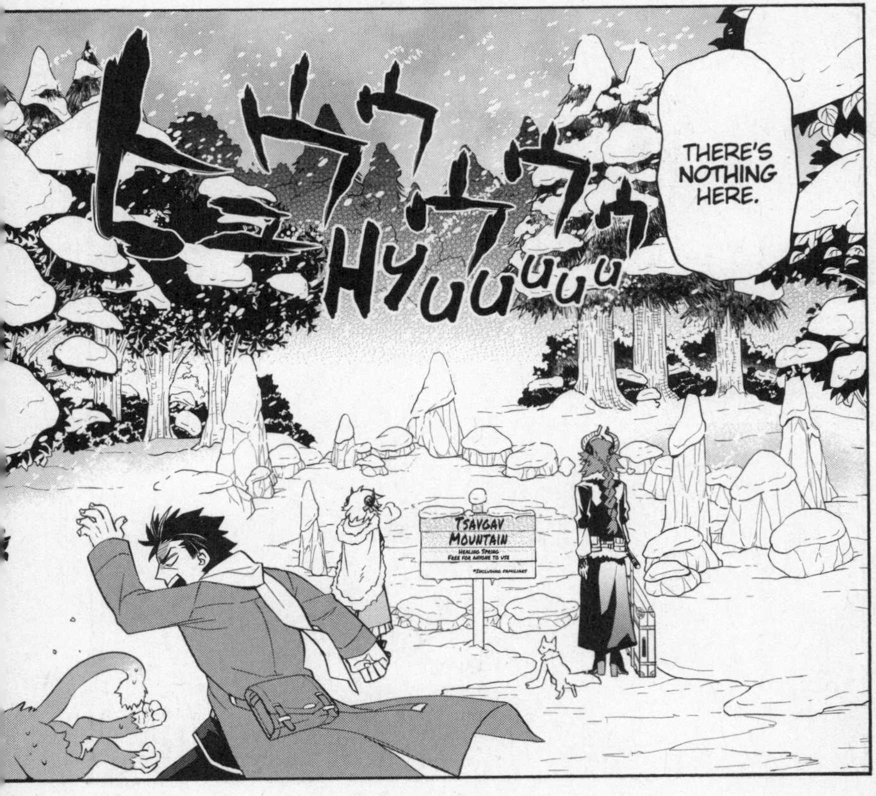
THERE'S NOTHING HERE.
HYUUUUU
TSAVGAV MOUNTAIN

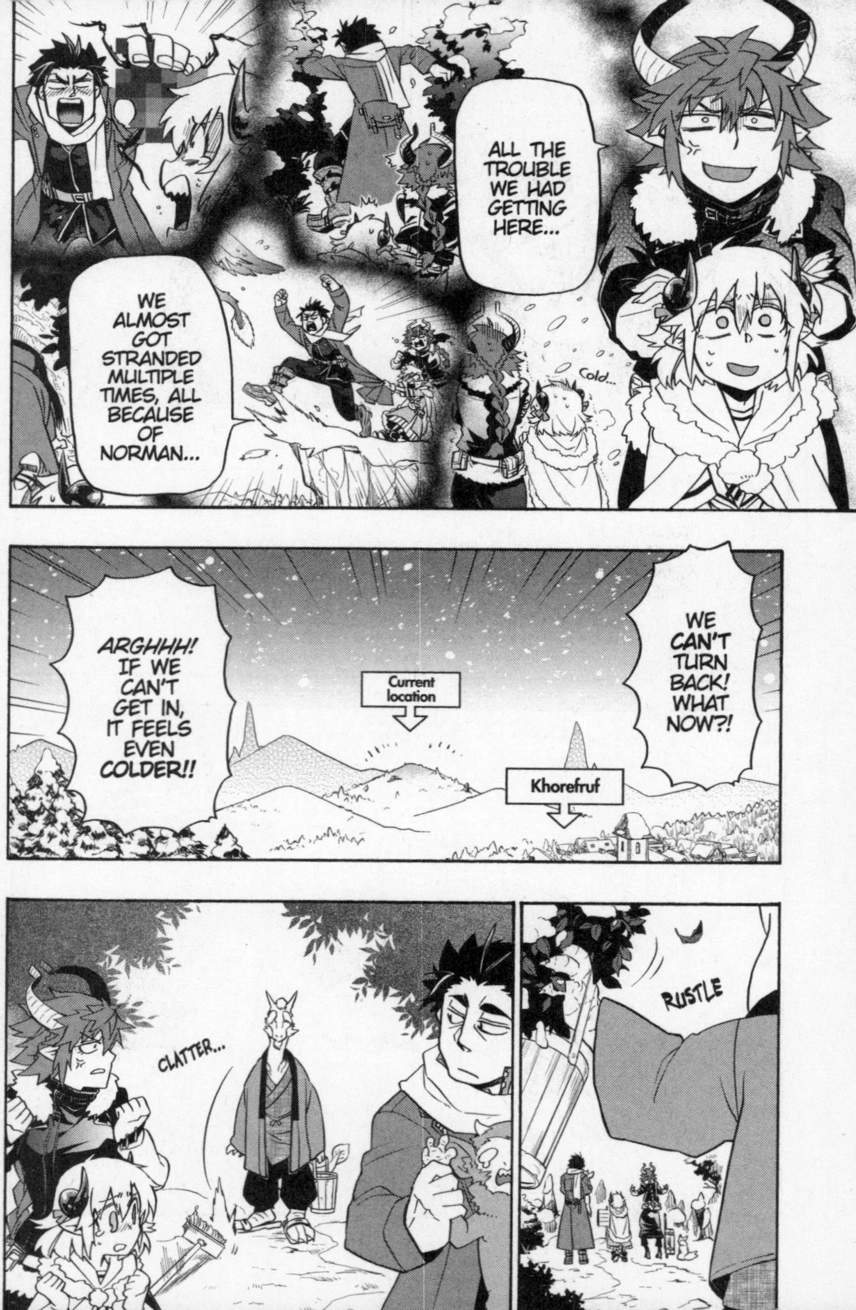
ALL THE TROUBLE WE HAD GETTING HERE...
Cold...
WE ALMOST GOT STRANDED MULTIPLE TIMES, ALL BECAUSE OF NORMAN...
WE CAN'T TURN BACK! WHAT NOW?!
Current location
Khorefruf
ARGHHH! IF WE CAN'T GET IN, IT FEELS EVEN COLDER!!
RUSTLE
CLATTER...

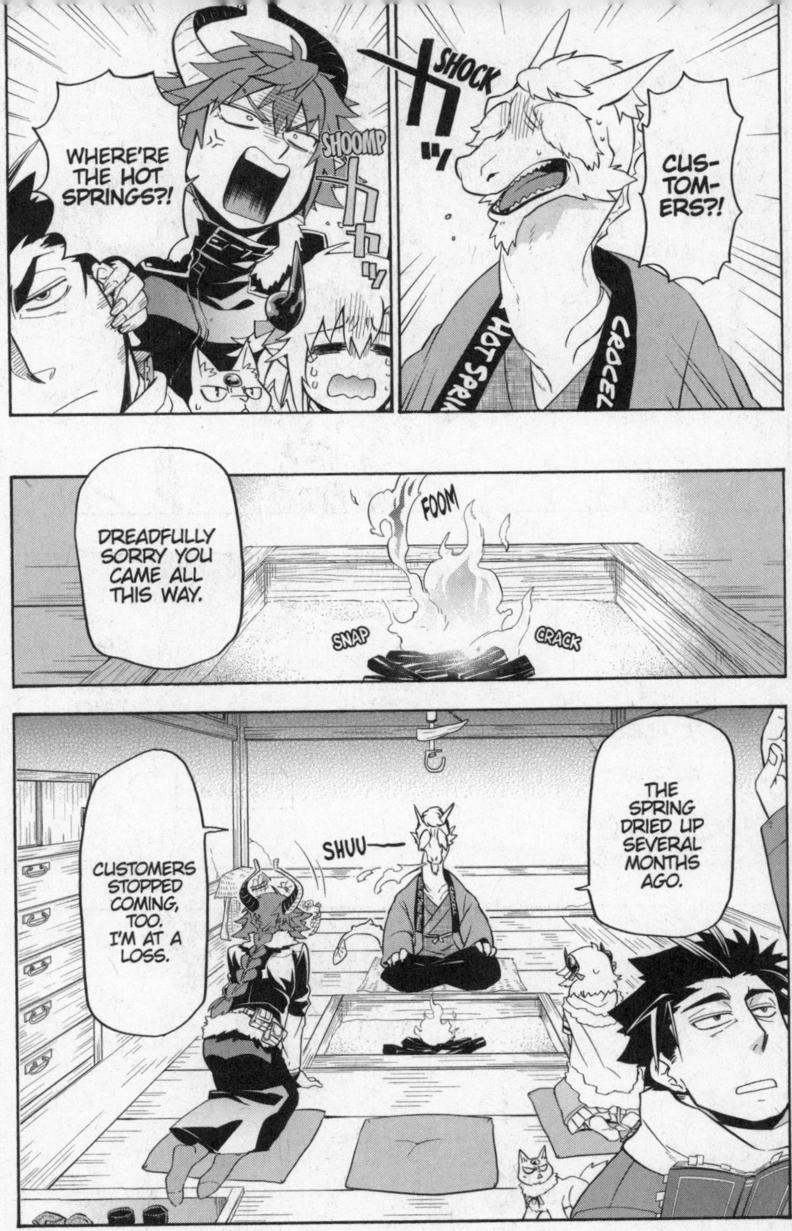
SHOCK
CUS-TOM-ERS?!
CROCEL
SHOOMP
WHERE'RE THE HOT SPRINGS?!
FOOM
DREADFULLY SORRY YOU CAME ALL THIS WAY.
CRACK
SNAP
THE SPRING DRIED UP SEVERAL MONTHS AGO.
SHUU—
CUSTOMERS STOPPED COMING, TOO. I'M AT A LOSS.

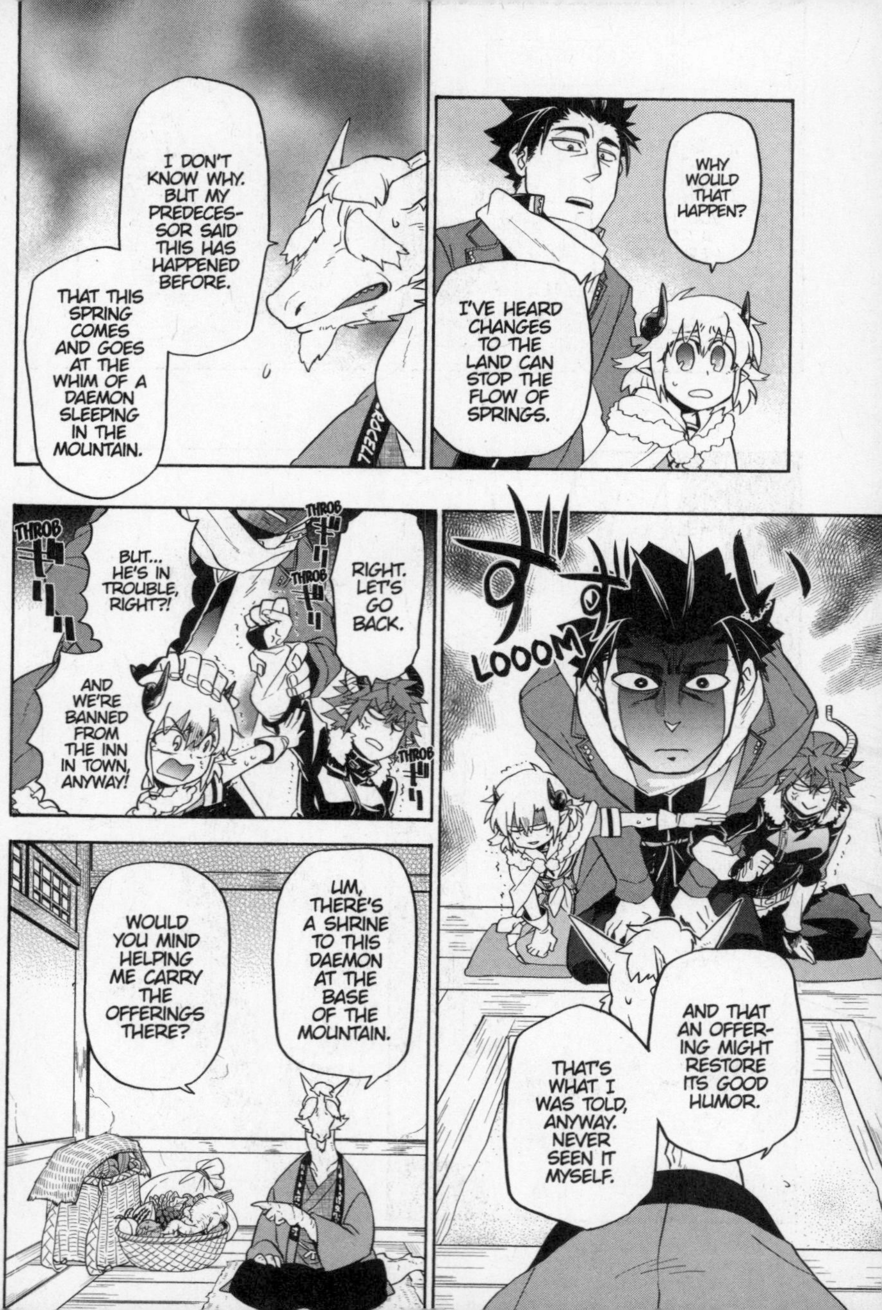
WHY WOULD THAT HAPPEN?
I'VE HEARD CHANGES TO THE LAND CAN STOP THE FLOW OF SPRINGS.
I DON'T KNOW WHY. BUT MY PREDECES-SOR SAID THIS HAS HAPPENED BEFORE.
THAT THIS SPRING COMES AND GOES AT THE WHIM OF A DAEMON SLEEPING IN THE MOUNTAIN.
LOOOM
AND THAT AN OFFER-ING MIGHT RESTORE ITS GOOD HUMOR.
THAT'S WHAT I WAS TOLD, ANYWAY. NEVER SEEN IT MYSELF.
THROB
THROB
THROB
THROB
RIGHT. LET'S GO BACK.
BUT... HE'S IN TROUBLE, RIGHT?!
AND WE'RE BANNED FROM THE INN IN TOWN, ANYWAY!
UM, THERE'S A SHRINE TO THIS DAEMON AT THE BASE OF THE MOUNTAIN.
WOULD YOU MIND HELPING ME CARRY THE OFFERINGS THERE?

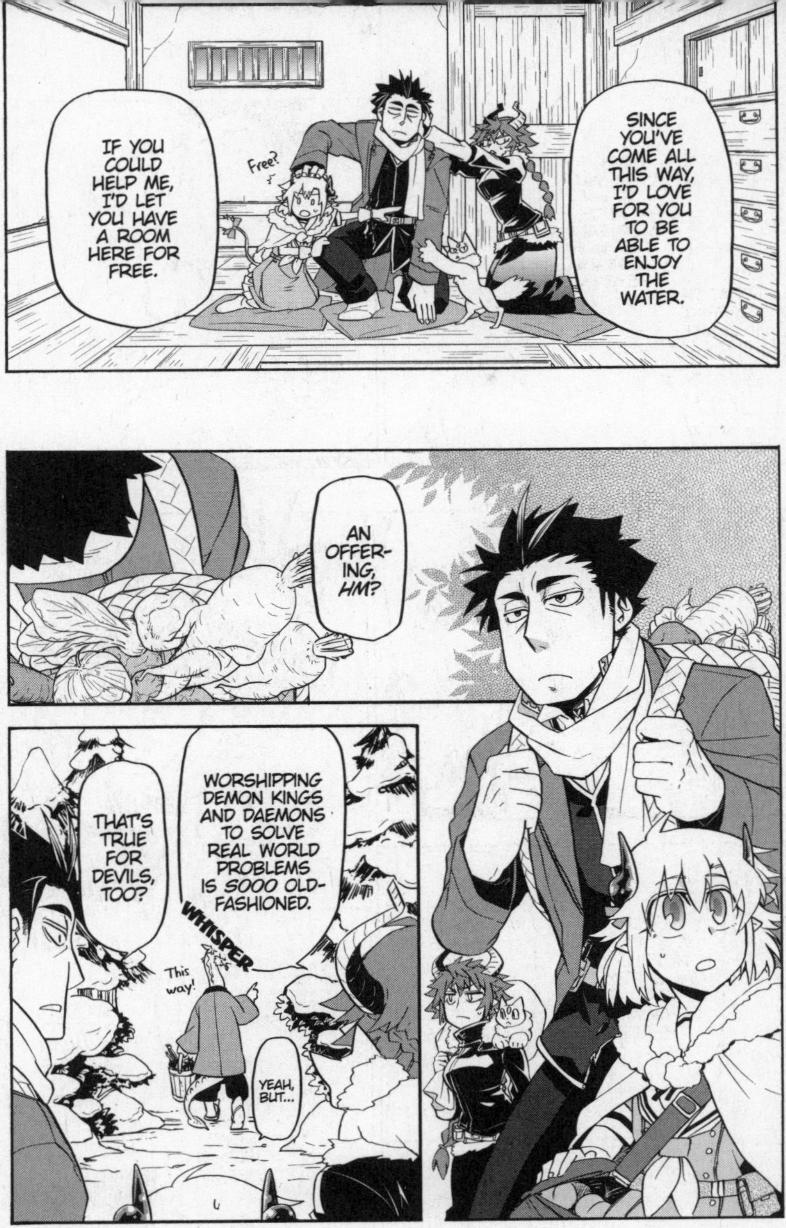
SINCE YOU'VE COME ALL THIS WAY, I'D LOVE FOR YOU TO BE ABLE TO ENJOY THE WATER.
IF YOU COULD HELP ME, I'D LET YOU HAVE A ROOM HERE FOR FREE.
Free?
AN OFFERING, HM?
WORSHIPPING DEMON KINGS AND DAEMONS TO SOLVE REAL WORLD PROBLEMS IS SOOO OLD-FASHIONED.
WHISPER
THAT'S TRUE FOR DEVILS, TOO?
This way!
YEAH, BUT...

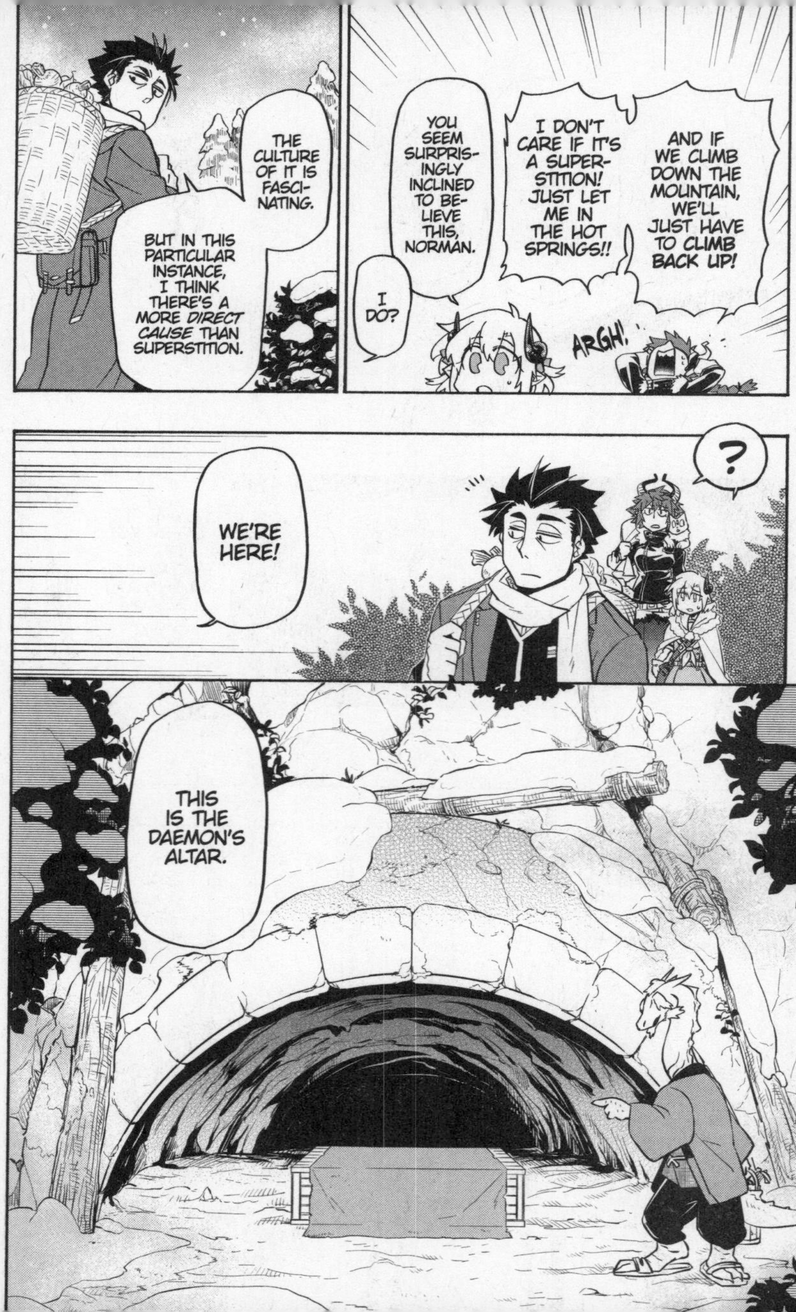
AND IF WE CLIMB DOWN THE MOUNTAIN, WE'LL JUST HAVE TO CLIMB BACK UP!
I DON'T CARE IF IT'S A SUPERSTITION! JUST LET ME IN THE HOT SPRINGS!!
YOU SEEM SURPRISINGLY INCLINED TO BELIEVE THIS, NORMAN.
ARGH!
I DO?
THE CULTURE OF IT IS FASCINATING.
BUT IN THIS PARTICULAR INSTANCE, I THINK THERE'S A MORE *DIRECT CAUSE* THAN SUPERSTITION.
?
WE'RE HERE!
THIS IS THE DAEMON'S ALTAR.

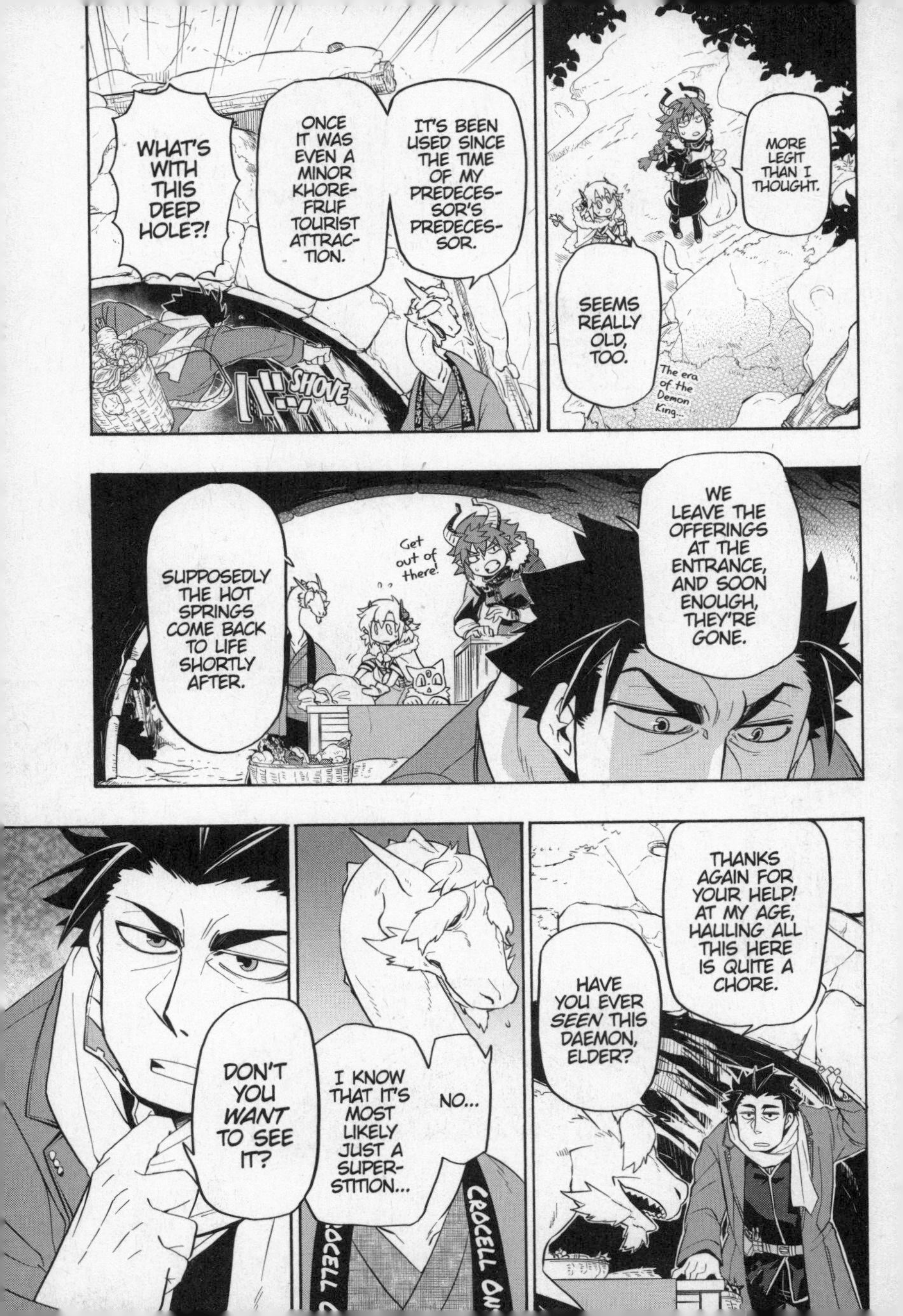
MORE LEGIT THAN I THOUGHT.
SEEMS REALLY OLD, TOO.
The era of the Demon King...
IT'S BEEN USED SINCE THE TIME OF MY PREDECES-SOR'S PREDECES-SOR.
ONCE IT WAS EVEN A MINOR KHORE-FRUF TOURIST ATTRAC-TION.
WHAT'S WITH THIS DEEP HOLE?!
SHOVE
WE LEAVE THE OFFERINGS AT THE ENTRANCE, AND SOON ENOUGH, THEY'RE GONE.
Get out of there!
SUPPOSEDLY THE HOT SPRINGS COME BACK TO LIFE SHORTLY AFTER.
THANKS AGAIN FOR YOUR HELP! AT MY AGE, HAULING ALL THIS HERE IS QUITE A CHORE.
HAVE YOU EVER SEEN THIS DAEMON, ELDER?
NO...
I KNOW THAT IT'S MOST LIKELY JUST A SUPER-STITION...
DON'T YOU WANT TO SEE IT?

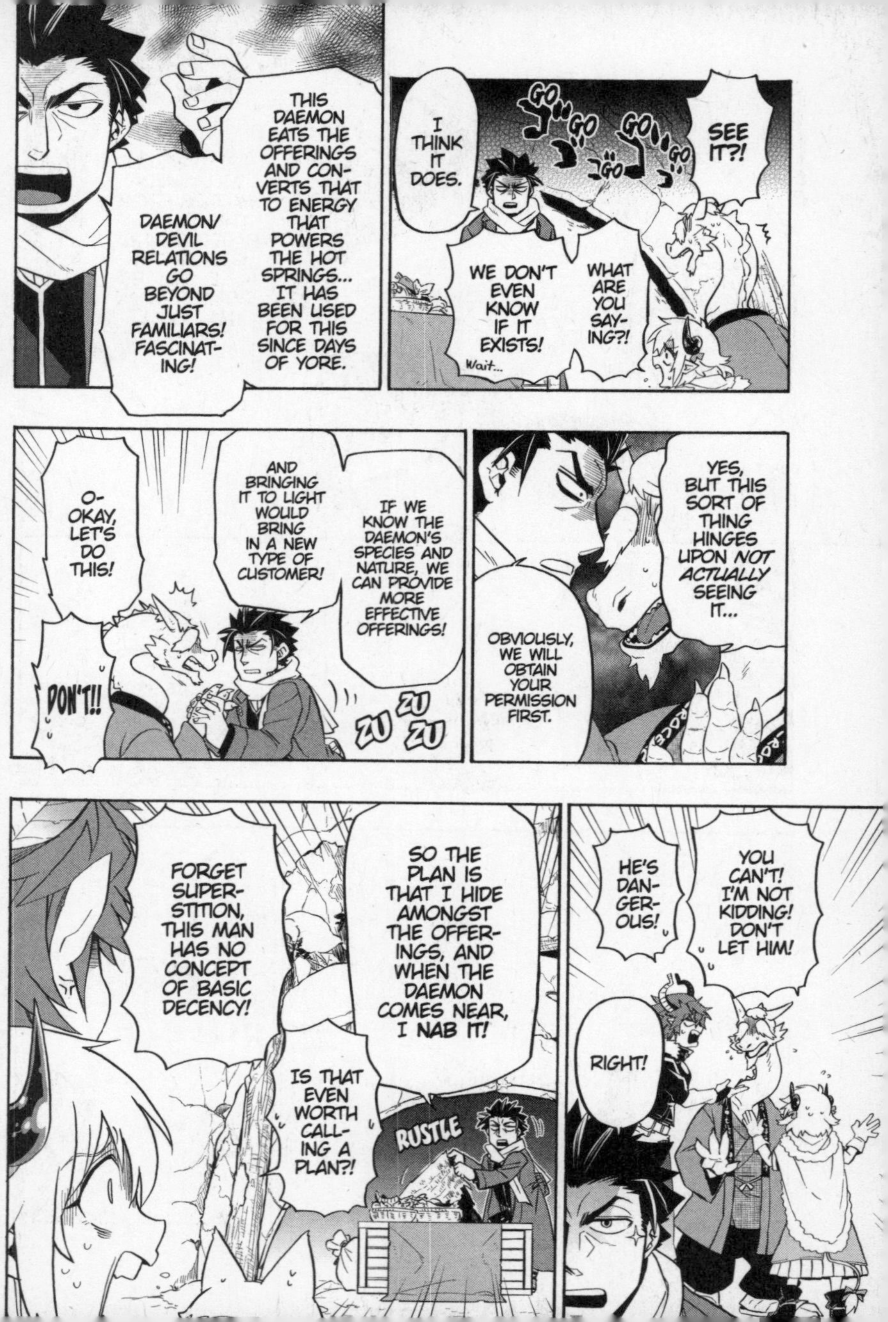
SEE IT?!
GO GO GO GO GO GO
I THINK IT DOES.
WHAT ARE YOU SAYING?!
WE DON'T EVEN KNOW IF IT EXISTS!
Wait...
THIS DAEMON EATS THE OFFERINGS AND CONVERTS THAT TO ENERGY THAT POWERS THE HOT SPRINGS... IT HAS BEEN USED FOR THIS SINCE DAYS OF YORE.
DAEMON/DEVIL RELATIONS GO BEYOND JUST FAMILIARS! FASCINATING!
YES, BUT THIS SORT OF THING HINGES UPON *NOT ACTUALLY* SEEING IT...
OBVIOUSLY, WE WILL OBTAIN YOUR PERMISSION FIRST.
IF WE KNOW THE DAEMON'S SPECIES AND NATURE, WE CAN PROVIDE MORE EFFECTIVE OFFERINGS!
AND BRINGING IT TO LIGHT WOULD BRING IN A NEW TYPE OF CUSTOMER!
O-OKAY, LET'S DO THIS!
DON'T!!
ZU ZU ZU ZU
YOU CAN'T! I'M NOT KIDDING! DON'T LET HIM!
HE'S DANGEROUS!
RIGHT!
SO THE PLAN IS THAT I HIDE AMONGST THE OFFERINGS, AND WHEN THE DAEMON COMES NEAR, I NAB IT!
FORGET SUPERSTITION, THIS MAN HAS NO CONCEPT OF BASIC DECENCY!
IS THAT EVEN WORTH CALLING A PLAN?!
RUSTLE

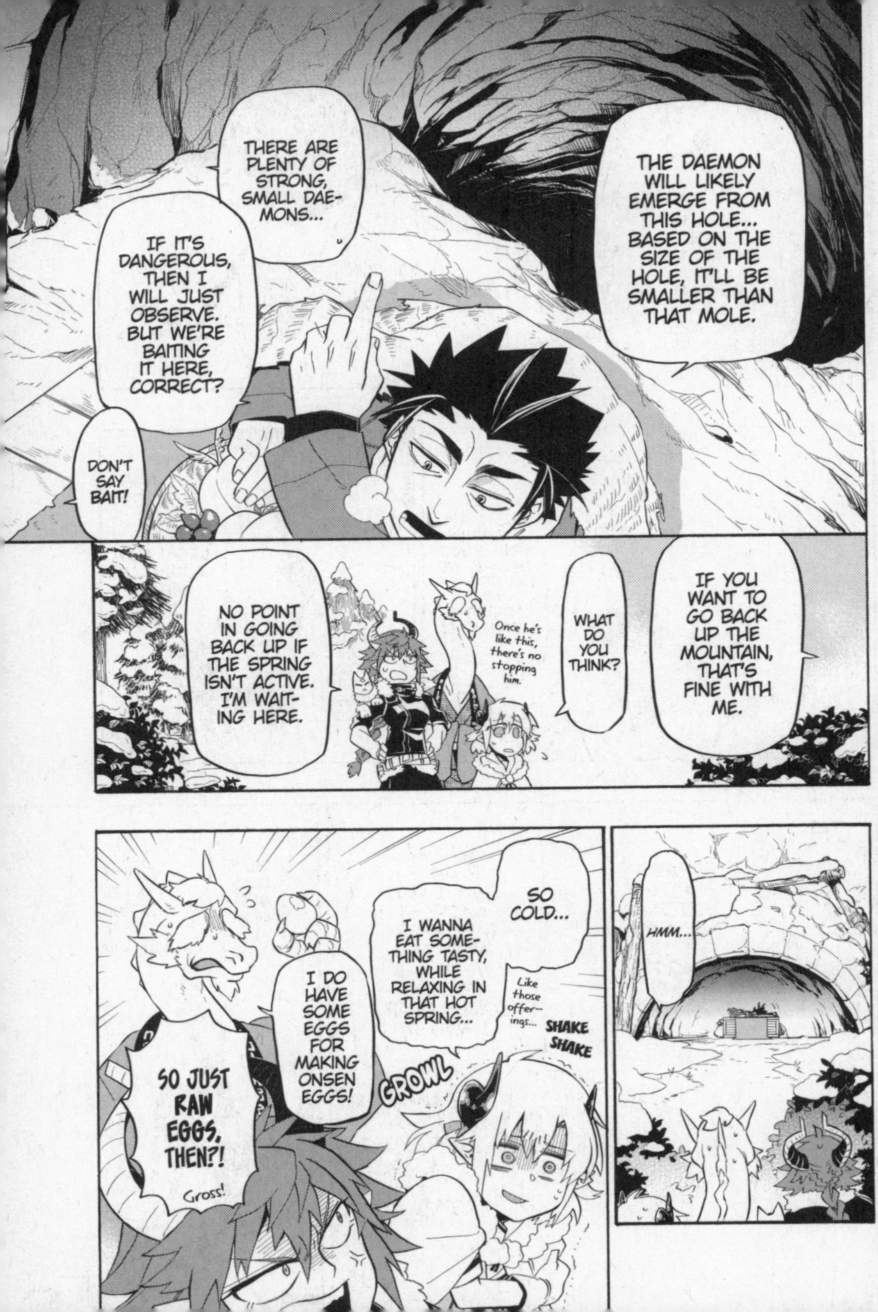
THE DAEMON WILL LIKELY EMERGE FROM THIS HOLE... BASED ON THE SIZE OF THE HOLE, IT'LL BE SMALLER THAN THAT MOLE.
THERE ARE PLENTY OF STRONG, SMALL DAE-MONS...
IF IT'S DANGEROUS, THEN I WILL JUST OBSERVE. BUT WE'RE BAITING IT HERE, CORRECT?
DON'T SAY BAIT!
IF YOU WANT TO GO BACK UP THE MOUNTAIN, THAT'S FINE WITH ME.
WHAT DO YOU THINK?
Once he's like this, there's no stopping him.
NO POINT IN GOING BACK UP IF THE SPRING ISN'T ACTIVE. I'M WAIT-ING HERE.
HMM...
SO COLD...
I WANNA EAT SOME-THING TASTY, WHILE RELAXING IN THAT HOT SPRING...
Like those offer-ings...
SHAKE SHAKE
GROWL
I DO HAVE SOME EGGS FOR MAKING ONSEN EGGS!
SO JUST RAW EGGS, THEN?!
Gross!

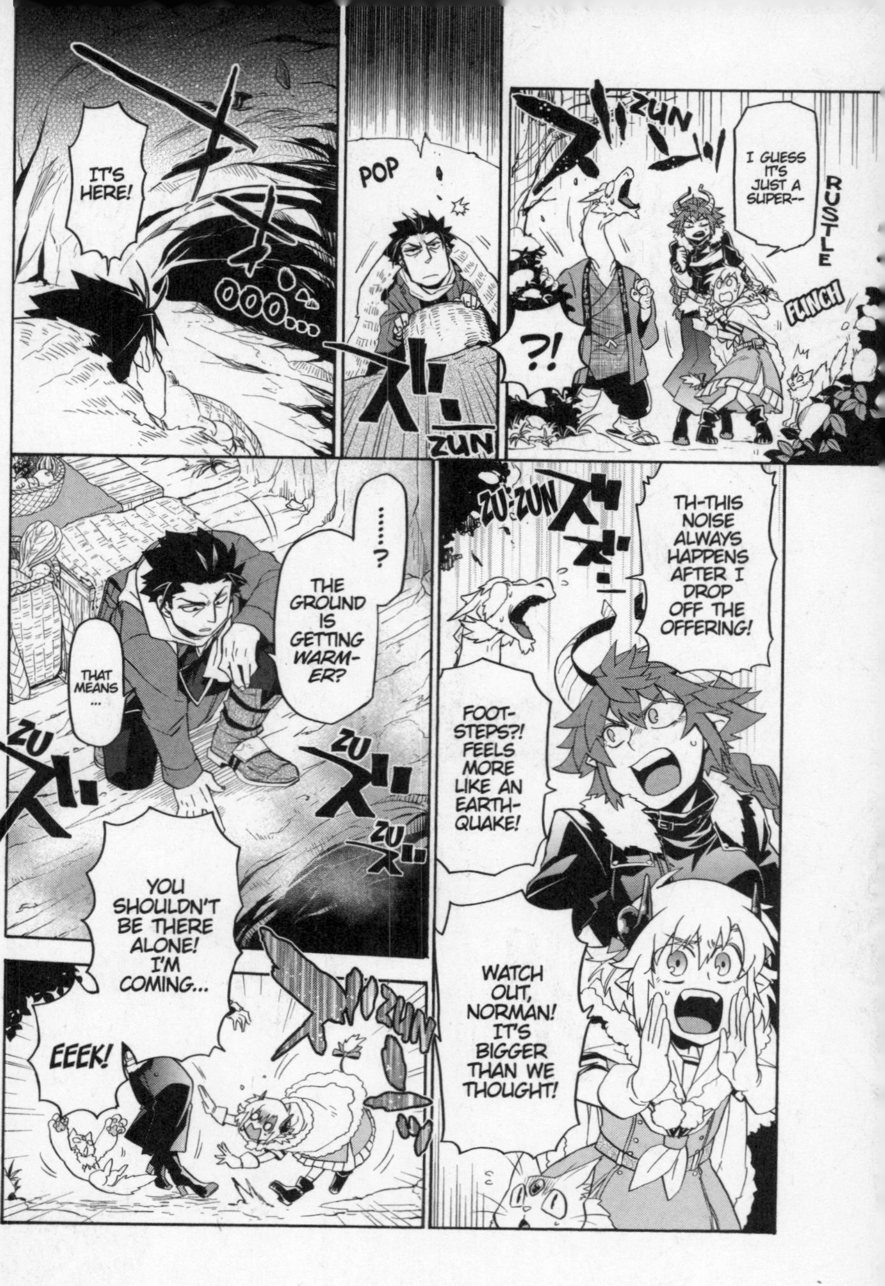
I GUESS IT'S JUST A SUPER--
RUSTLE
ZUN
FLINCH
?!
POP
ZUN
IT'S HERE!
OOO...
TH-THIS NOISE ALWAYS HAPPENS AFTER I DROP OFF THE OFFERING!
ZU-ZUN
FOOT-STEPS?! FEELS MORE LIKE AN EARTH-QUAKE!
WATCH OUT, NORMAN! IT'S BIGGER THAN WE THOUGHT!
......?
THE GROUND IS GETTING WARM-ER?
THAT MEANS ...
ZU
ZU
ZU
YOU SHOULDN'T BE THERE ALONE! I'M COMING...
ZUN
EEEK!

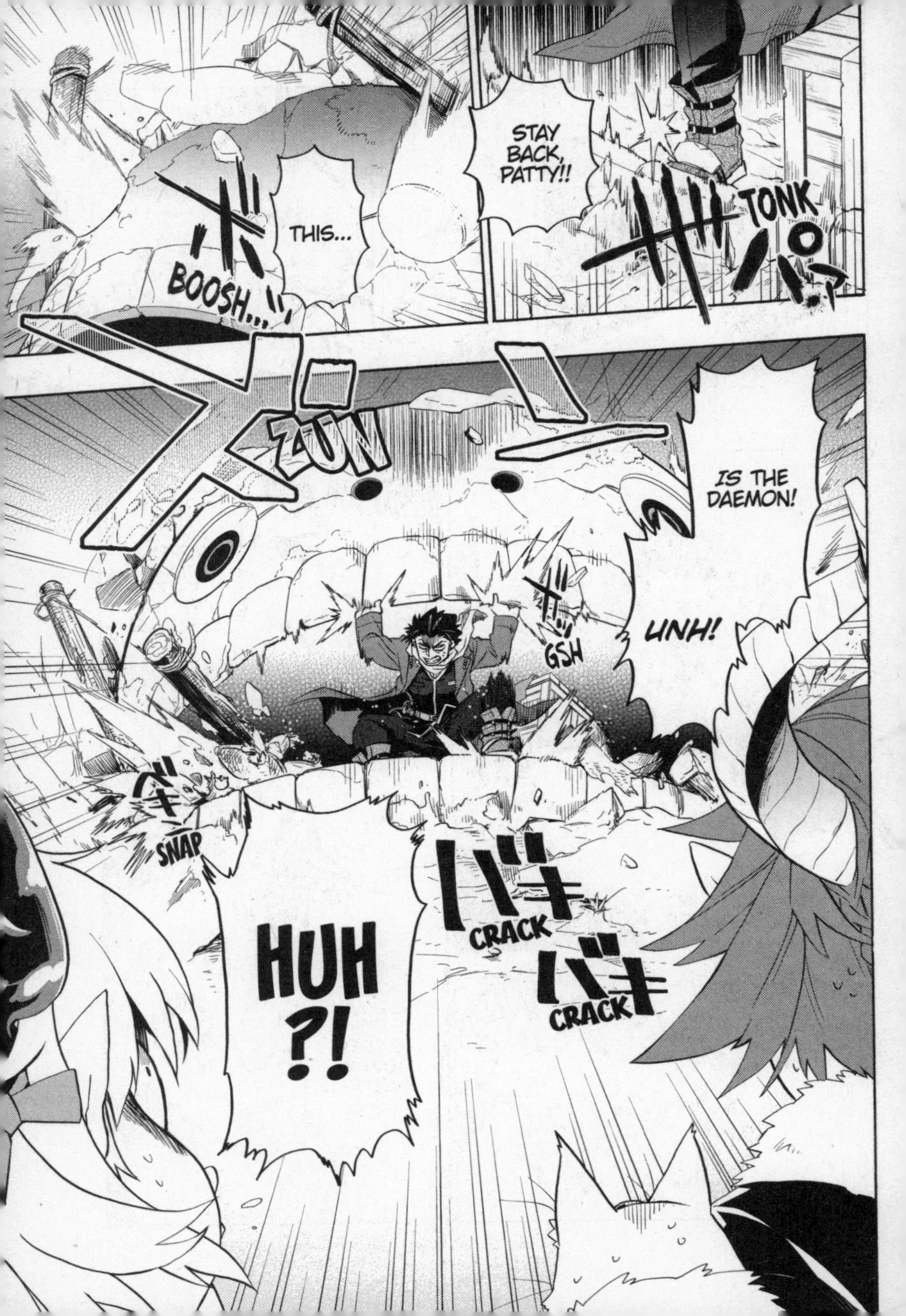

STAY BACK, PATTY!!
TONK
THIS...
BOOSH...
IS THE DAEMON!
ZUN
UNH!
GSH
SNAP
CRACK
CRACK
HUH ?!

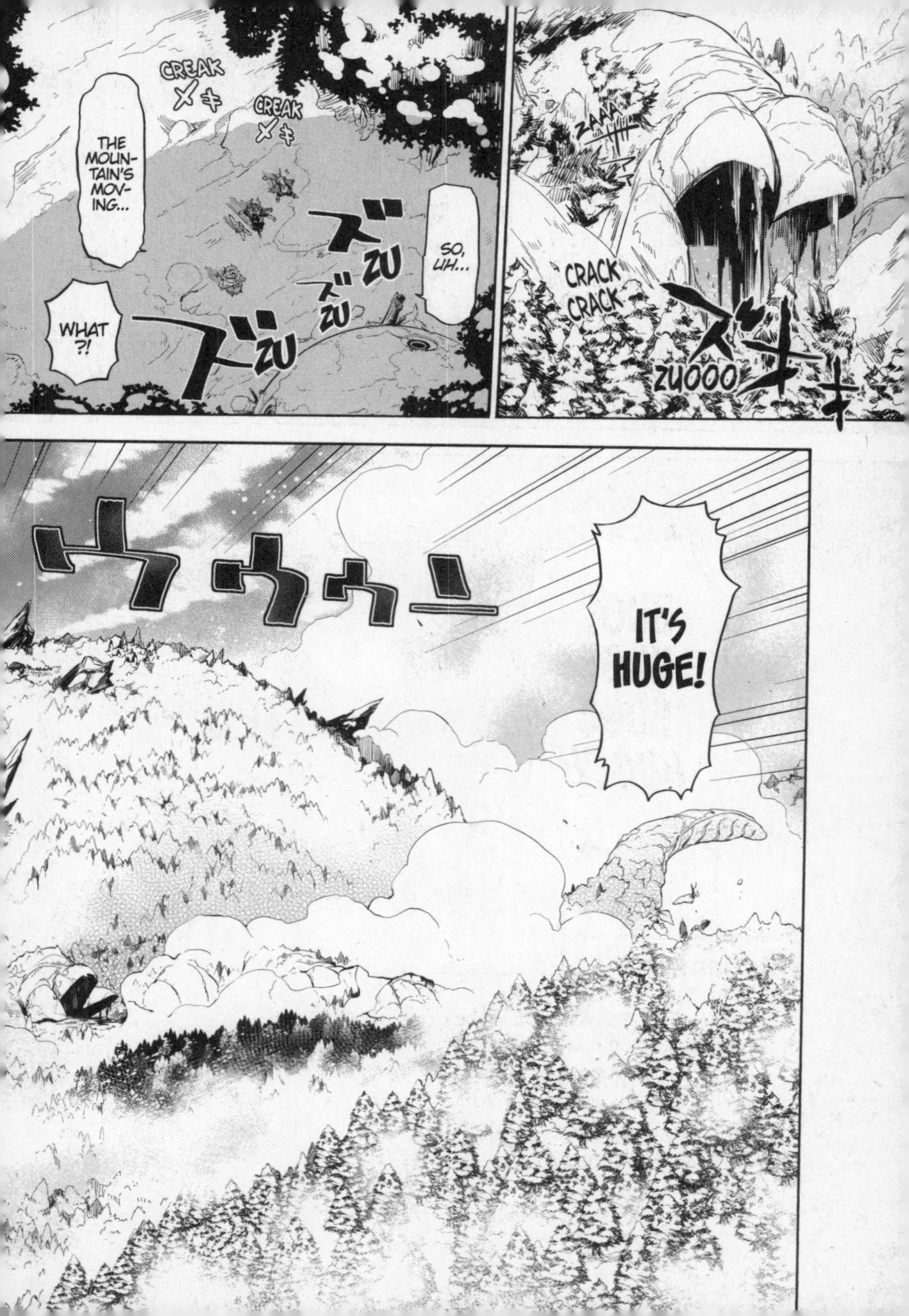
ZAAA
CRACK CRACK
ZUOOO
CREAK
メキ
CREAK
メキ
THE MOUNTAIN'S MOVING...
SO, UH...
ZU
ZU
ZU
WHAT?!
IT'S HUGE!
ウウウー

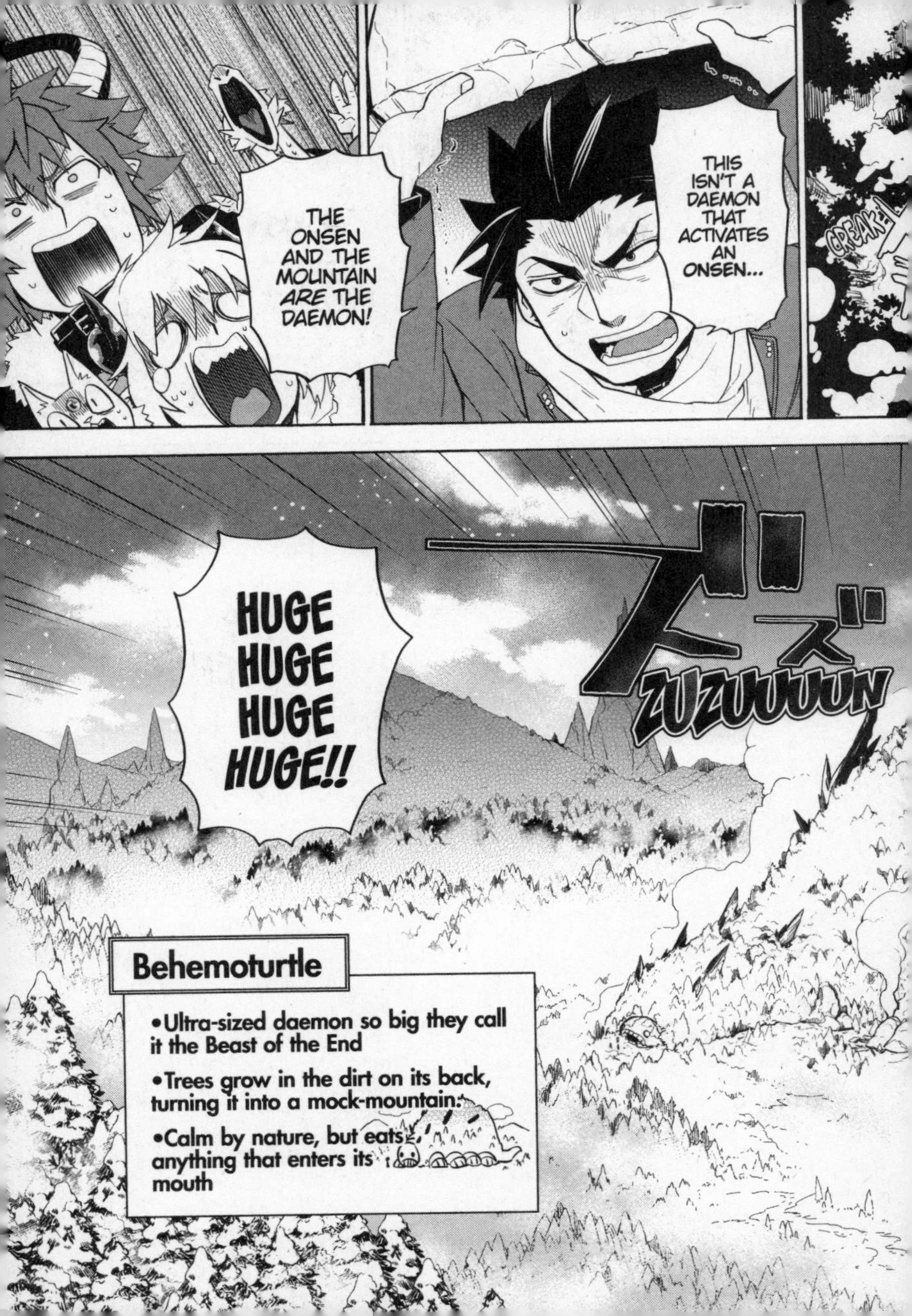
CREAK!!
THIS ISN'T A DAEMON THAT ACTIVATES AN ONSEN...
THE ONSEN AND THE MOUNTAIN *ARE* THE DAEMON!
ZUZUUUUN
HUGE HUGE HUGE *HUGE!!*
Behemoturtle
•Ultra-sized daemon so big they call it the Beast of the End
•Trees grow in the dirt on its back, turning it into a mock-mountain.
•Calm by nature, but eats anything that enters its mouth

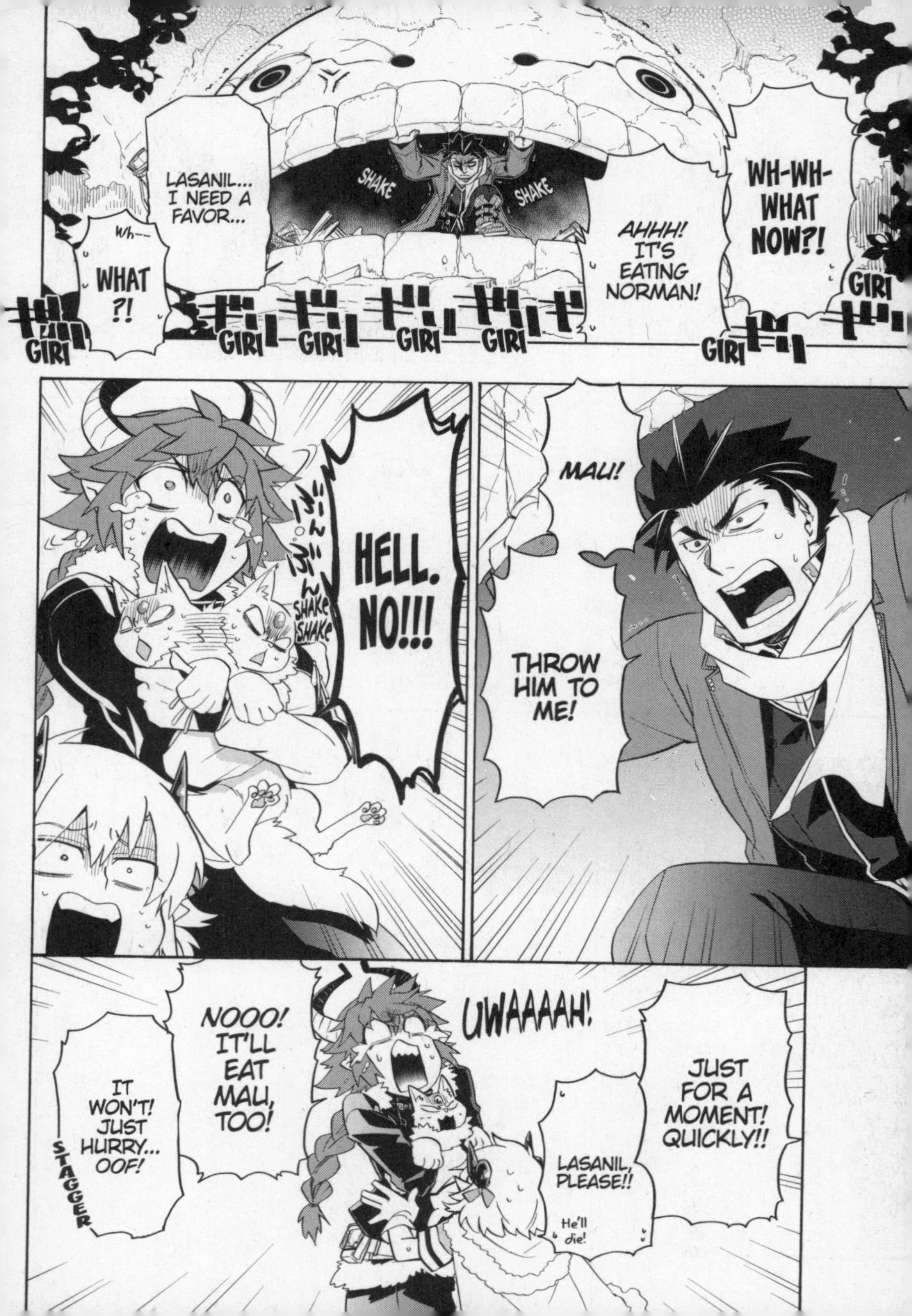
WH-WH-WHAT NOW?!
GIRI
AHHH! IT'S EATING NORMAN!
SHAKE
SHAKE
LASANIL... I NEED A FAVOR...
Wh--
WHAT ?!
GIRI
GIRI
GIRI
GIRI
GIRI
GIRI
MAU!
THROW HIM TO ME!
HELL. NO!!!
SHAKE SHAKE
JUST FOR A MOMENT! QUICKLY!!
LASANIL, PLEASE!!
He'll die!
UWAAAAH!
NOOO! IT'LL EAT MAU, TOO!
IT WON'T! JUST HURRY... OOF!
STAGGER

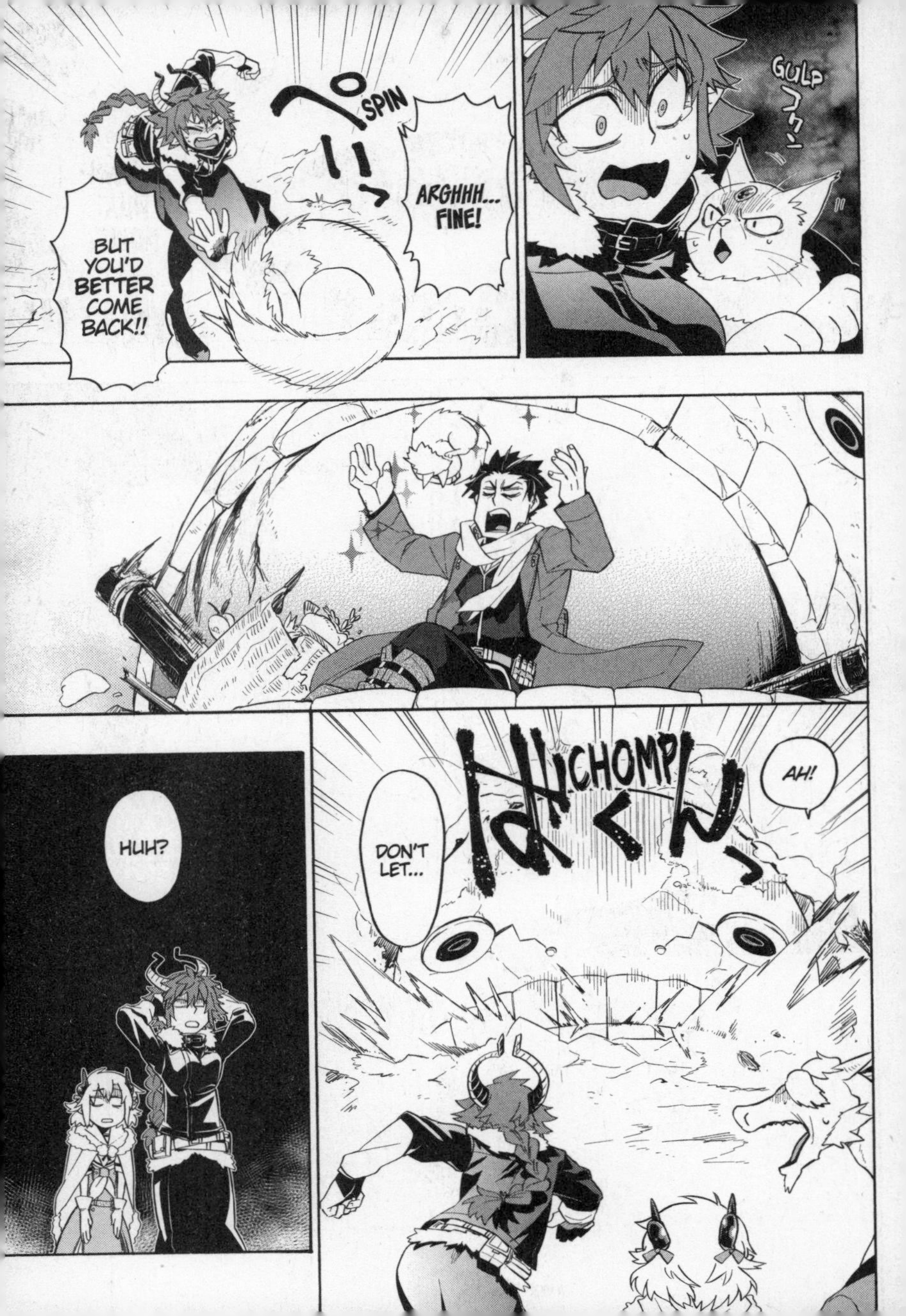
GULP
ゴクン
ARGHHH... FINE!
SPIN
BUT YOU'D BETTER COME BACK!!
AH!
CHOMP
DON'T LET...
HUH?

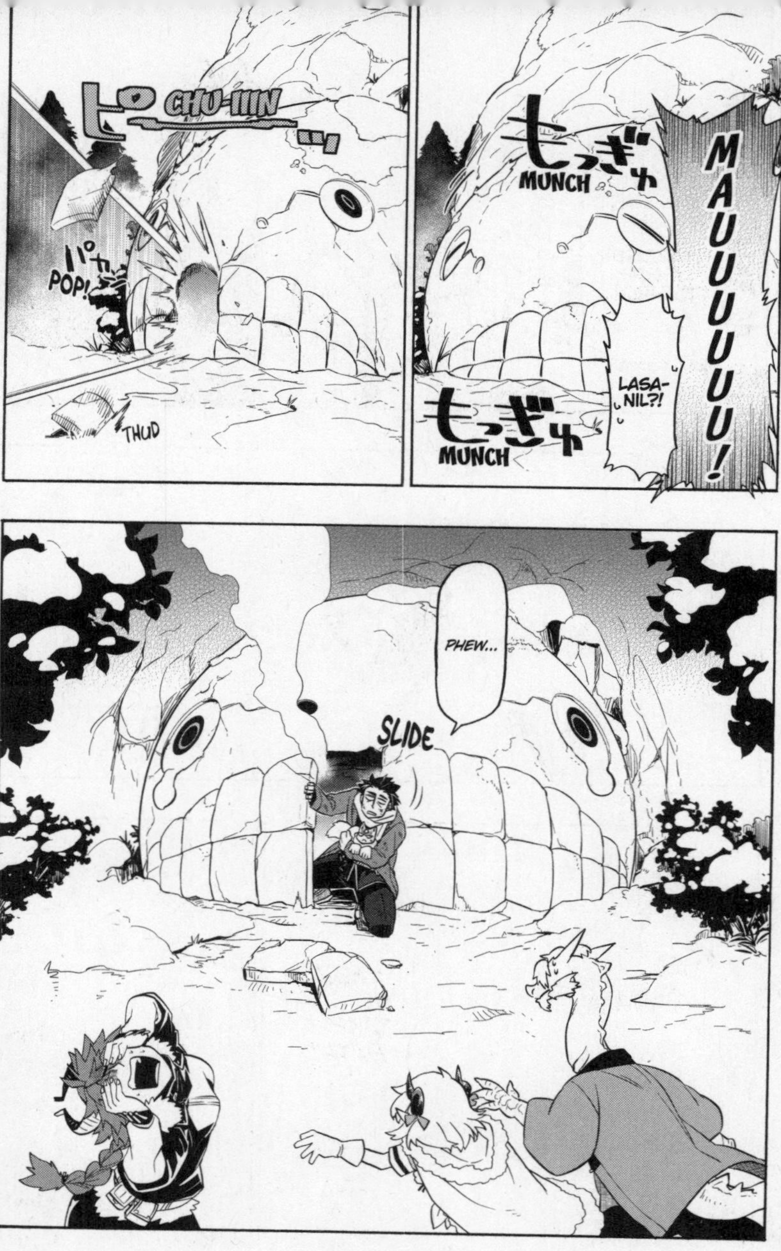
MAUUUUUUU!
LASA-NIL?!
もっぎゃ
MUNCH
もっぎゃ
MUNCH
CHU-IIIN
POP!
THUD
SLIDE
PHEW...

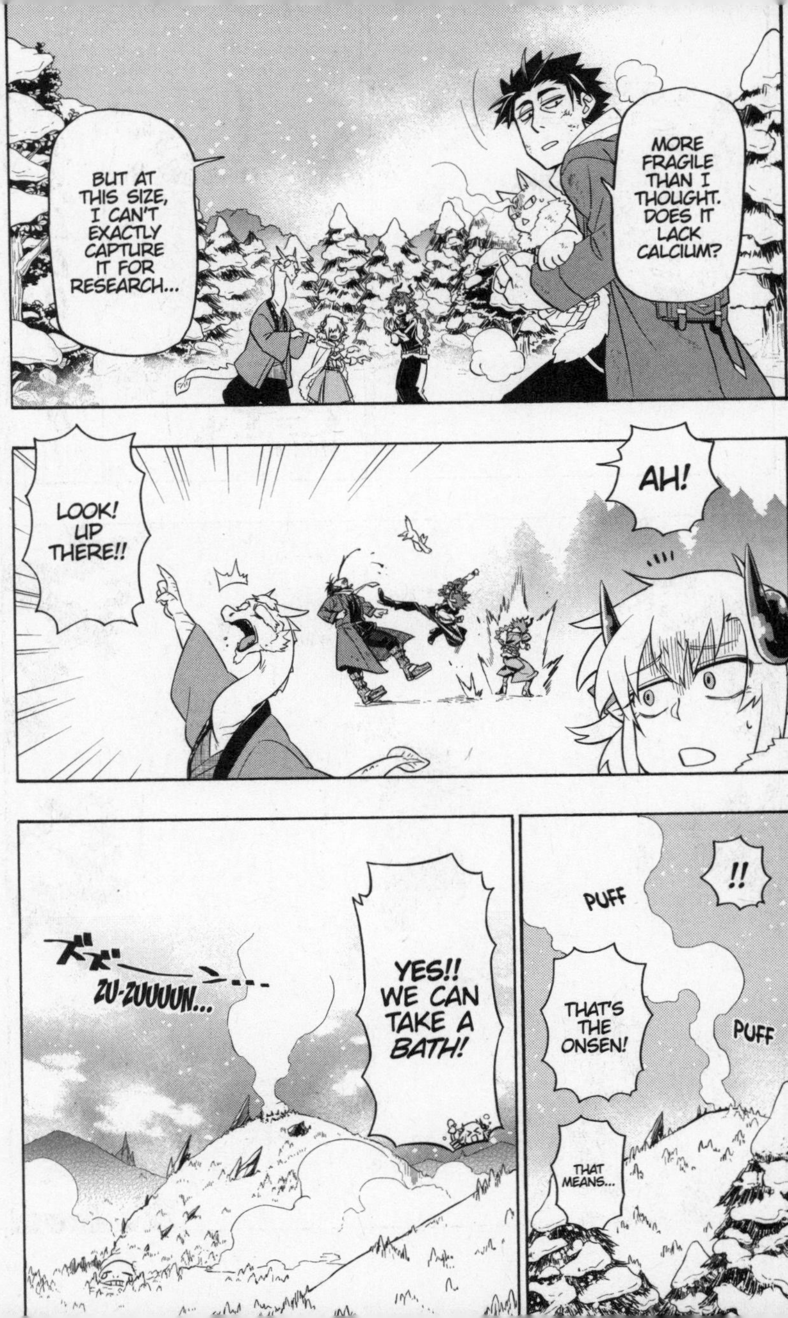
MORE FRAGILE THAN I THOUGHT. DOES IT LACK CALCIUM?
BUT AT THIS SIZE, I CAN'T EXACTLY CAPTURE IT FOR RESEARCH...
AH!
LOOK! UP THERE!!
!!
PUFF
THAT'S THE ONSEN!
PUFF
THAT MEANS...
YES!! WE CAN TAKE A BATH!
ズズ——ン...
ZU-ZUUUUN...

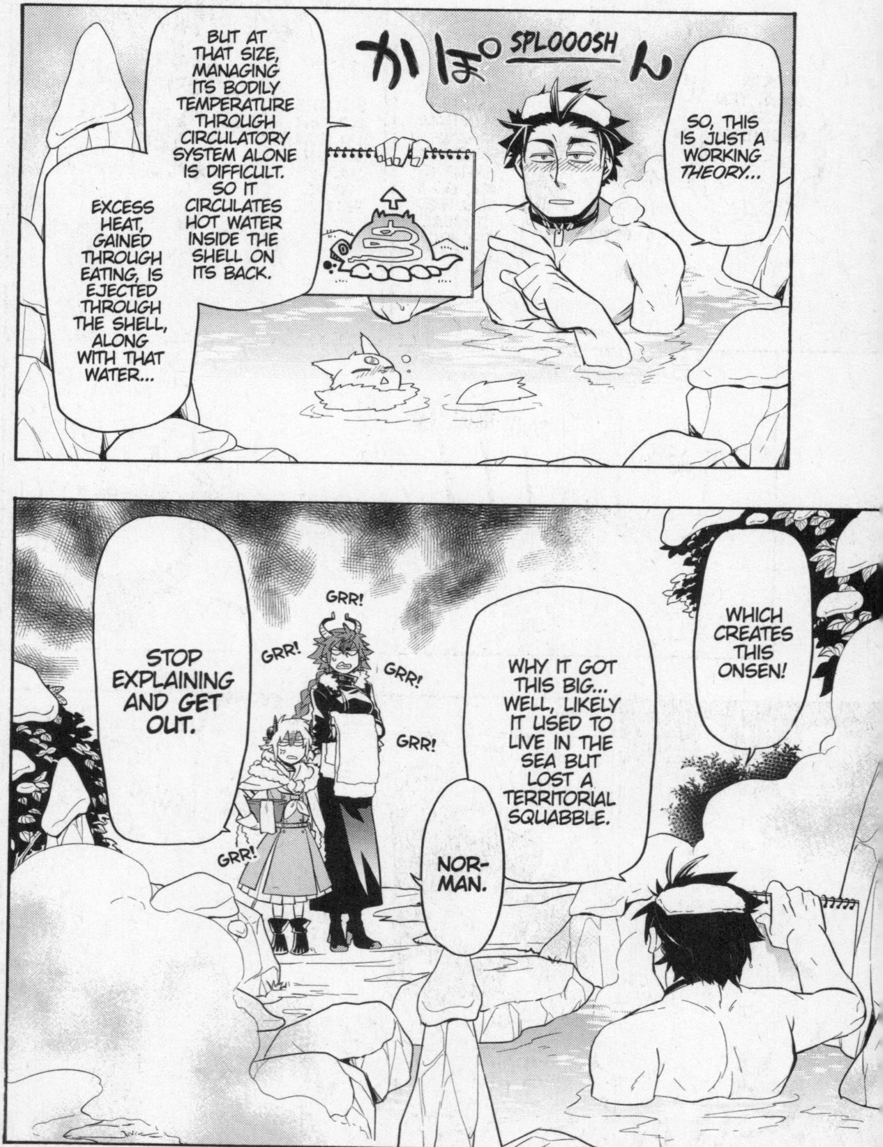
SO, THIS IS JUST A WORKING *THEORY*...
かぽ SPLOOOSH ん
BUT AT THAT SIZE, MANAGING ITS BODILY TEMPERATURE THROUGH CIRCULATORY SYSTEM ALONE IS DIFFICULT. SO IT CIRCULATES HOT WATER INSIDE THE SHELL ON ITS BACK.
EXCESS HEAT, GAINED THROUGH EATING, IS EJECTED THROUGH THE SHELL, ALONG WITH THAT WATER...
WHICH CREATES THIS ONSEN!
WHY IT GOT THIS BIG... WELL, LIKELY IT USED TO LIVE IN THE SEA BUT LOST A TERRITORIAL SQUABBLE.
NOR-MAN.
GRR!
GRR!
GRR!
GRR!
GRR!
STOP EXPLAINING AND GET OUT.

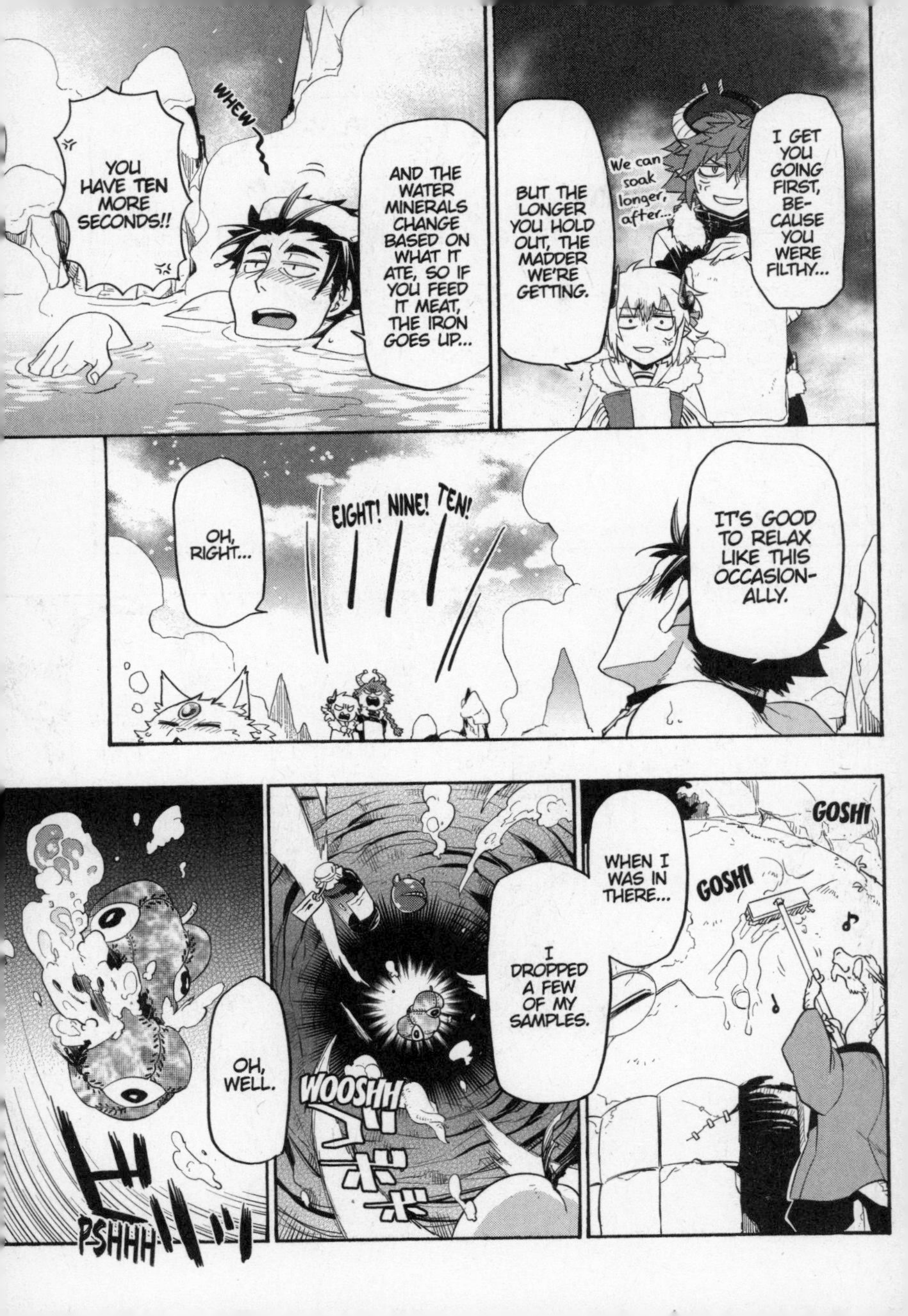
I GET YOU GOING FIRST, BECAUSE YOU WERE FILTHY...
We can soak longer, after...
BUT THE LONGER YOU HOLD OUT, THE MADDER WE'RE GETTING.
AND THE WATER MINERALS CHANGE BASED ON WHAT IT ATE, SO IF YOU FEED IT MEAT, THE IRON GOES UP...
WHEW
YOU HAVE TEN MORE SECONDS!!
IT'S GOOD TO RELAX LIKE THIS OCCASIONALLY.
EIGHT! NINE! TEN!
OH, RIGHT...
GOSHI
GOSHI
WHEN I WAS IN THERE...
I DROPPED A FEW OF MY SAMPLES.
WOOSHH
OH, WELL.
PSHHH

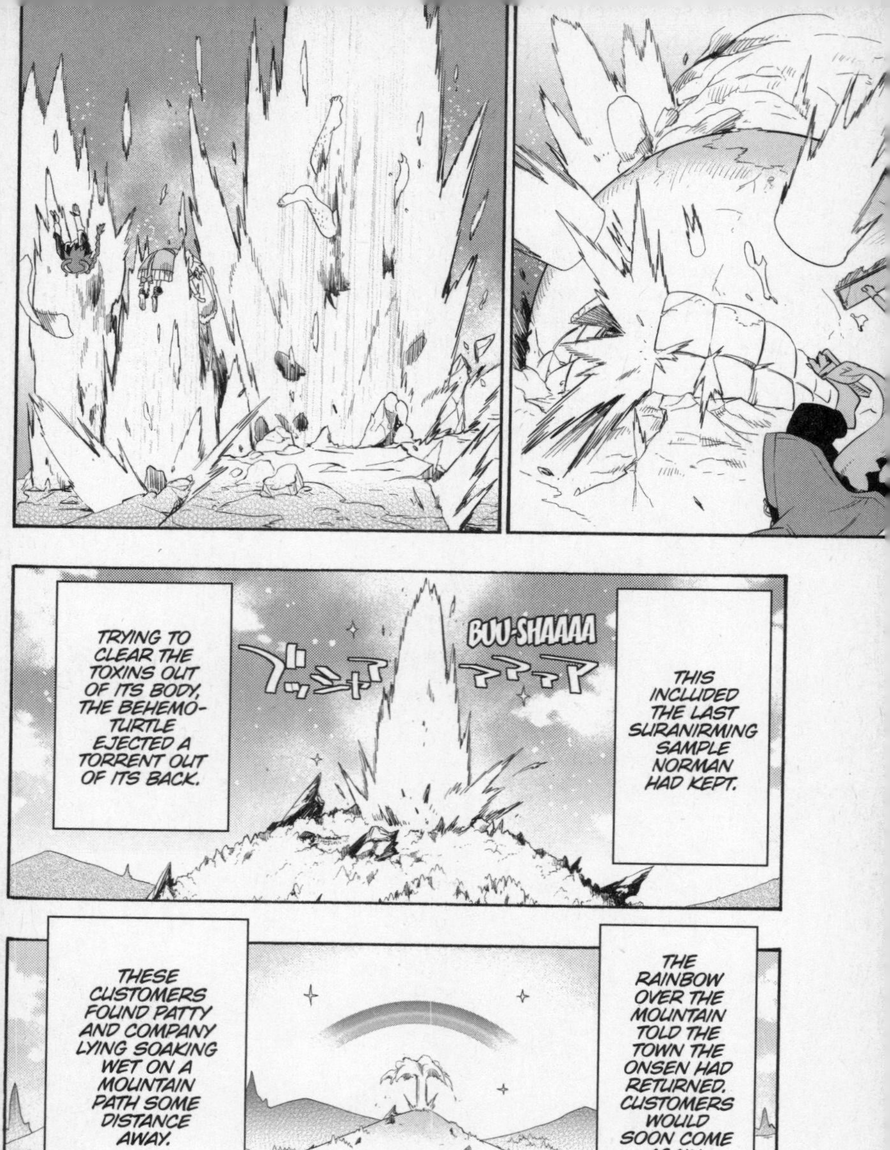
TRYING TO CLEAR THE TOXINS OUT OF ITS BODY, THE BEHEMO-TURTLE EJECTED A TORRENT OUT OF ITS BACK.
BUU-SHAAAA
THIS INCLUDED THE LAST SURANIRMING SAMPLE NORMAN HAD KEPT.
THE RAINBOW OVER THE MOUNTAIN TOLD THE TOWN THE ONSEN HAD RETURNED. CUSTOMERS WOULD SOON COME AGAIN.
THESE CUSTOMERS FOUND PATTY AND COMPANY LYING SOAKING WET ON A MOUNTAIN PATH SOME DISTANCE AWAY.

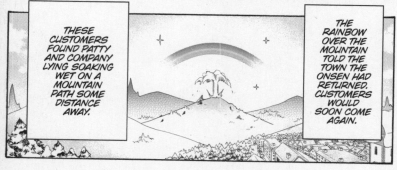

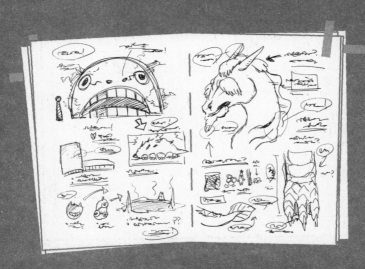

Sorry For My Familiar

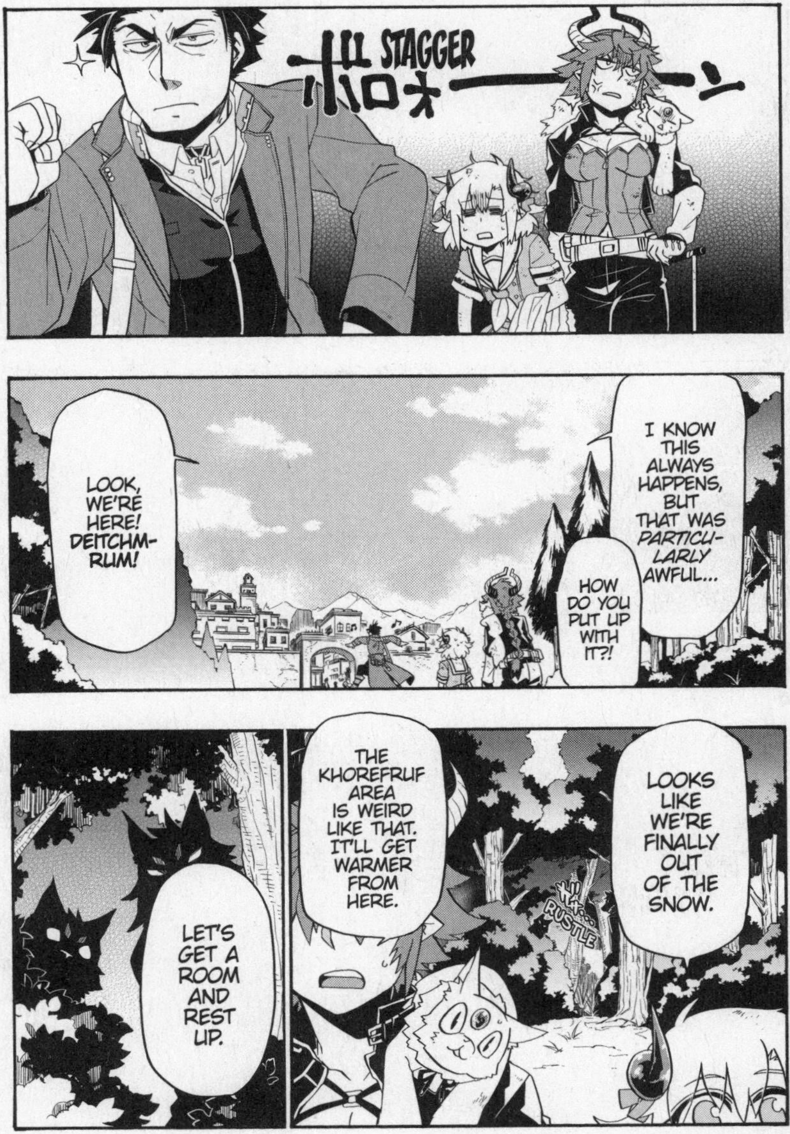

STAGGER
ボロォーーーン
I KNOW THIS ALWAYS HAPPENS, BUT THAT WAS *PARTICULARLY* AWFUL...
HOW DO YOU PUT UP WITH IT?!
LOOK, WE'RE HERE! DEITCHMRUM!
LOOKS LIKE WE'RE FINALLY OUT OF THE SNOW.
RUSTLE
THE KHOREFRUF AREA IS WEIRD LIKE THAT. IT'LL GET WARMER FROM HERE.
LET'S GET A ROOM AND REST UP.

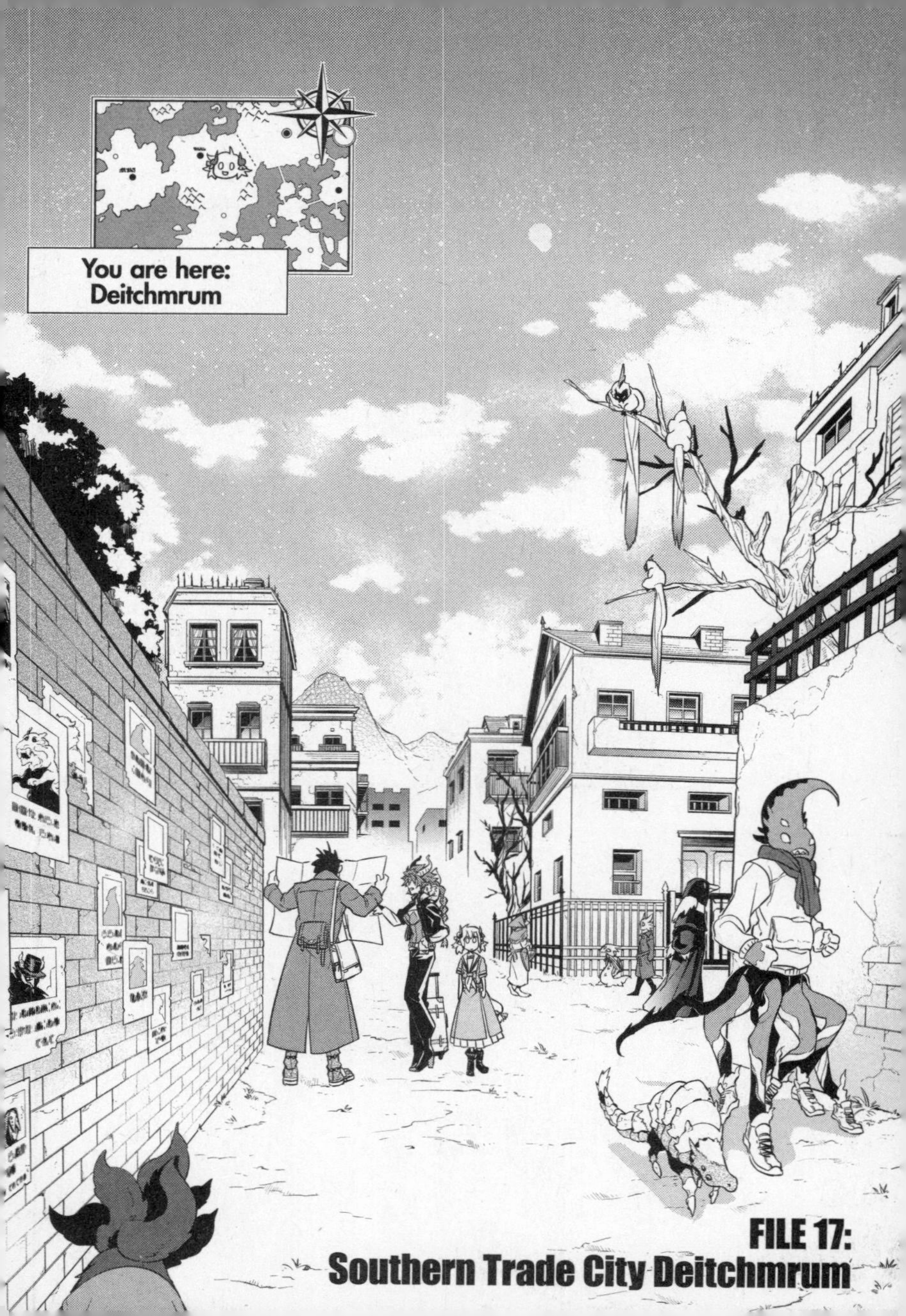
You are here:
Deitchmrum
FILE 17:
Southern Trade City Deitchmrum

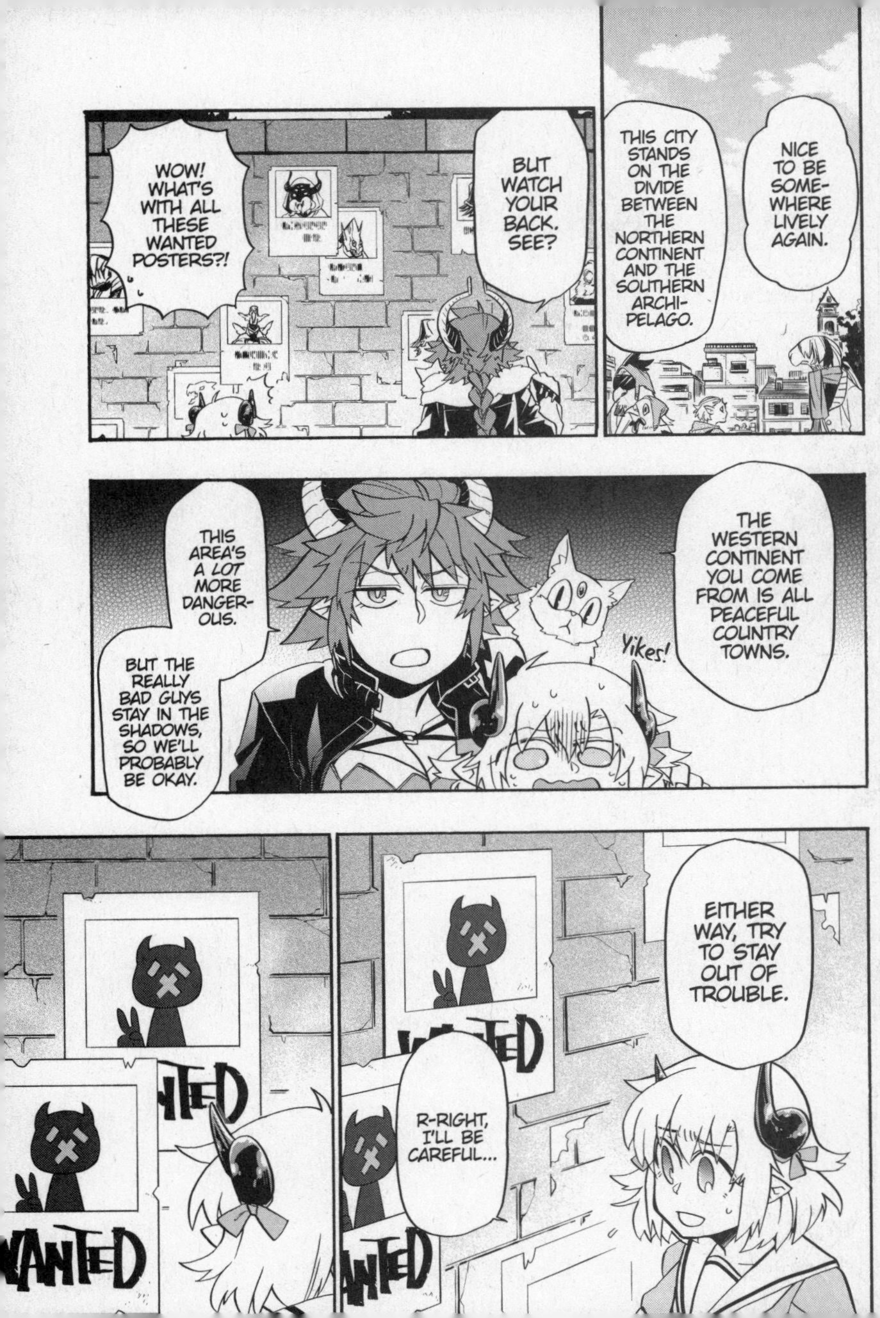
NICE TO BE SOME-WHERE LIVELY AGAIN.
THIS CITY STANDS ON THE DIVIDE BETWEEN THE NORTHERN CONTINENT AND THE SOUTHERN ARCHI-PELAGO.
BUT WATCH YOUR BACK. SEE?
WOW! WHAT'S WITH ALL THESE WANTED POSTERS?!
THE WESTERN CONTINENT YOU COME FROM IS ALL PEACEFUL COUNTRY TOWNS.
Yikes!
THIS AREA'S A LOT MORE DANGER-OUS.
BUT THE REALLY BAD GUYS STAY IN THE SHADOWS, SO WE'LL PROBABLY BE OKAY.
EITHER WAY, TRY TO STAY OUT OF TROUBLE.
R-RIGHT, I'LL BE CAREFUL...

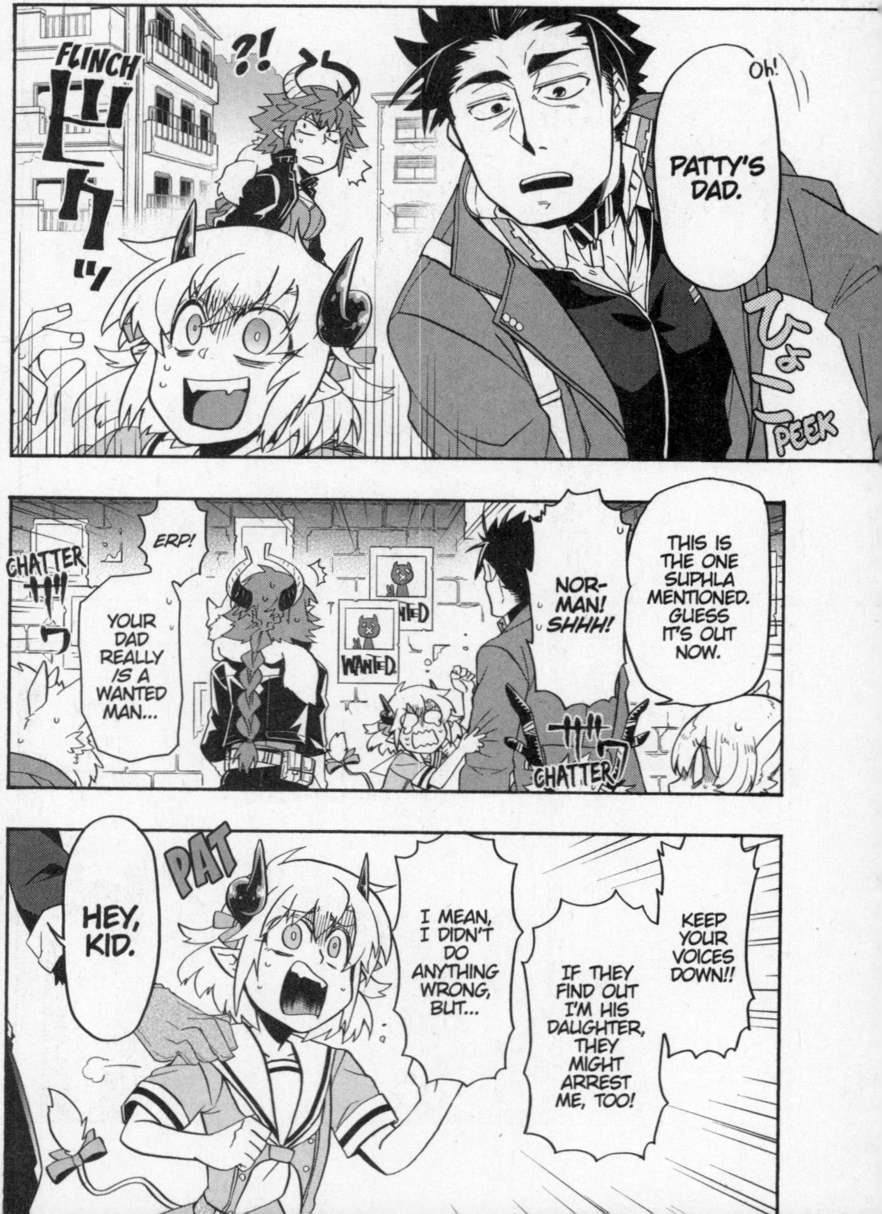
Oh!
PATTY'S DAD.
PEEK
?!
FLINCH
THIS IS THE ONE SUPHLA MENTIONED. GUESS IT'S OUT NOW.
NOR-MAN! SHHH!
CHATTER
WANTED
WANTED
ERP!
YOUR DAD REALLY IS A WANTED MAN...
CHATTER
KEEP YOUR VOICES DOWN!!
IF THEY FIND OUT I'M HIS DAUGHTER, THEY MIGHT ARREST ME, TOO!
I MEAN, I DIDN'T DO ANYTHING WRONG, BUT...
PAT
HEY, KID.

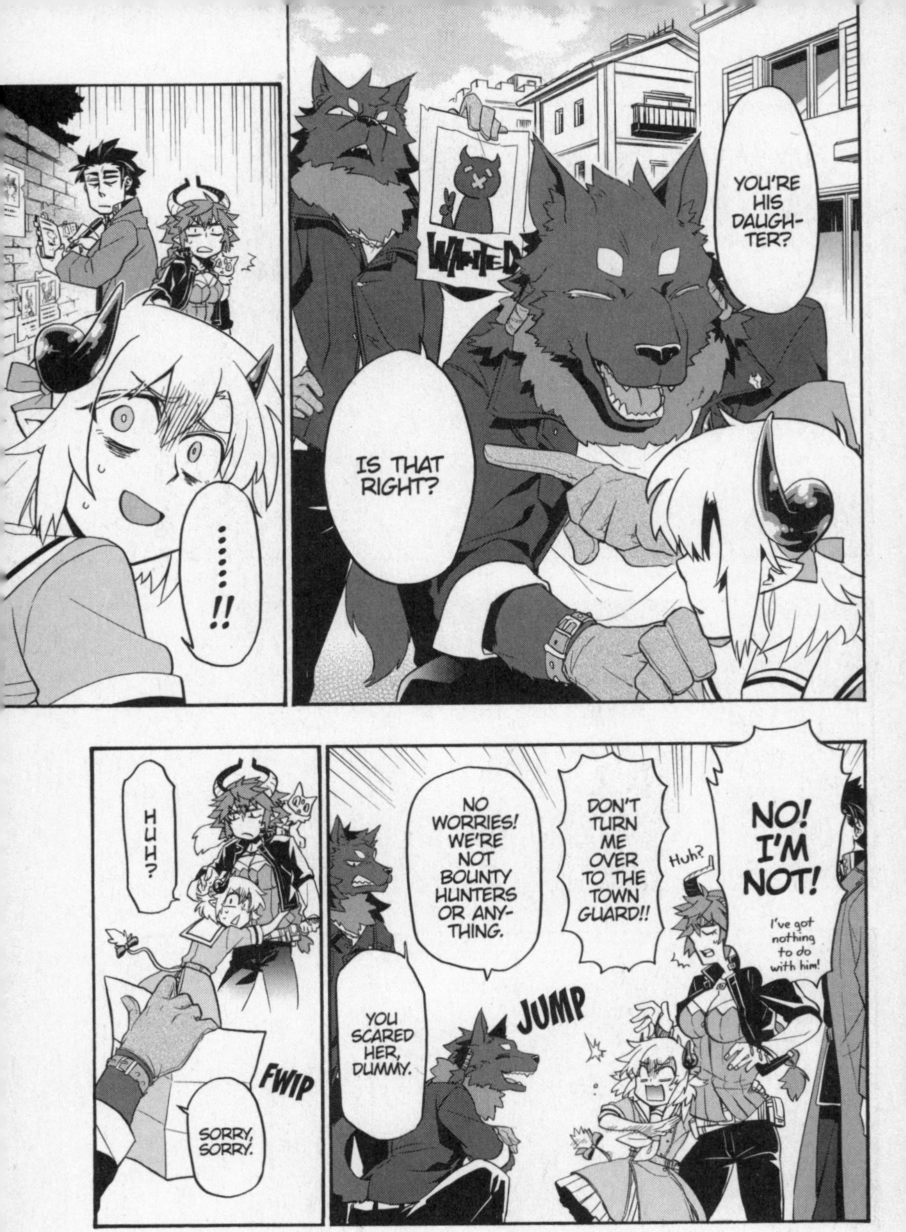
WANTED
YOU'RE HIS DAUGHTER?
IS THAT RIGHT?
......!!
NO! I'M NOT!
I've got nothing to do with him!
Huh?
DON'T TURN ME OVER TO THE TOWN GUARD!!
NO WORRIES! WE'RE NOT BOUNTY HUNTERS OR ANYTHING.
JUMP
YOU SCARED HER, DUMMY.
HUH?
FWIP
SORRY, SORRY.

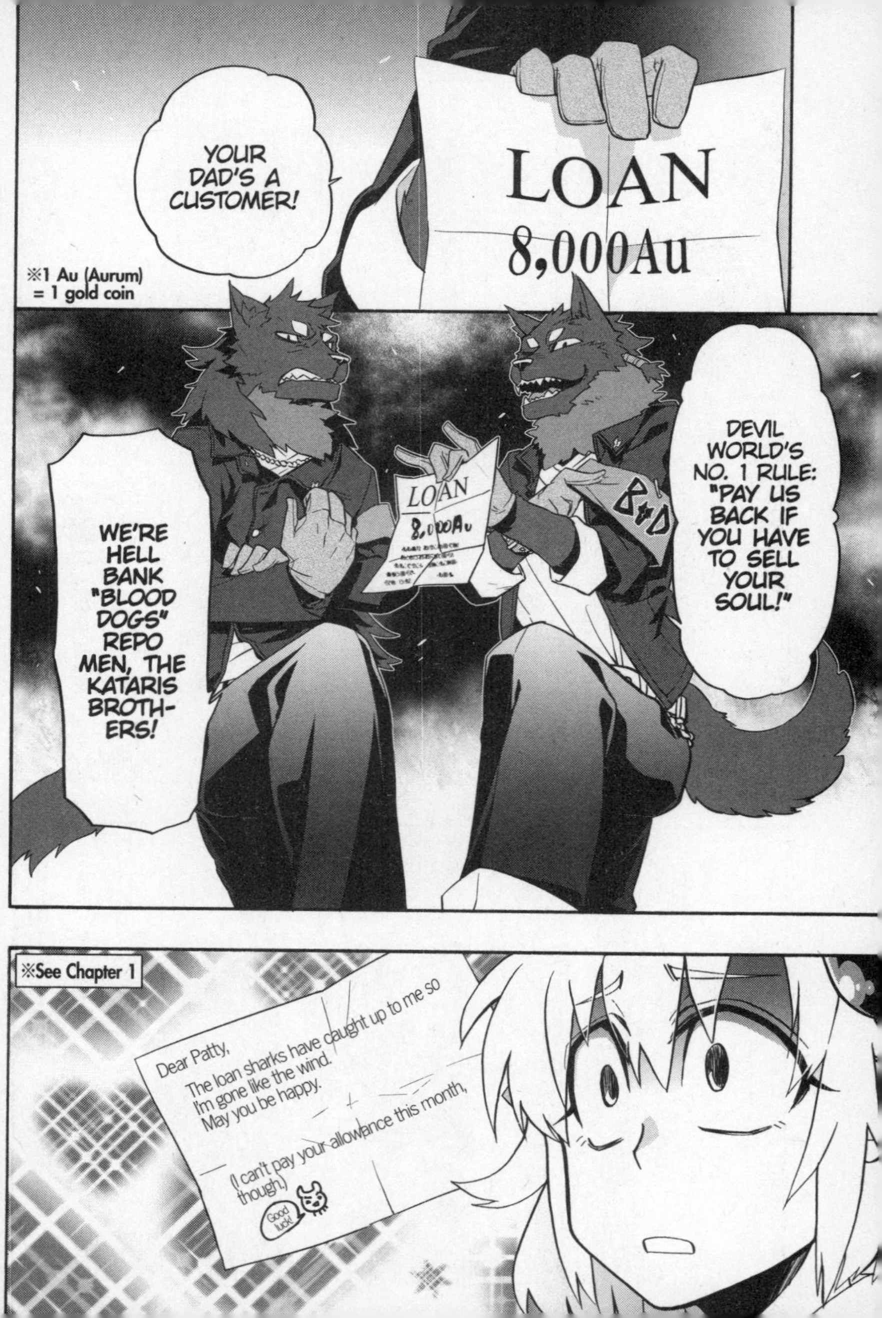
LOAN
8,000Au
YOUR DAD'S A CUSTOMER!
※1 Au (Aurum) = 1 gold coin
DEVIL WORLD'S NO. 1 RULE: "PAY US BACK IF YOU HAVE TO SELL YOUR SOUL!"
LOAN
8,000Au
B+D
WE'RE HELL BANK "BLOOD DOGS" REPO MEN, THE KATARIS BROTHERS!
※See Chapter 1
Dear Patty,
The loan sharks have caught up to me so I'm gone like the wind.
May you be happy.
(I can't pay your allowance this month, though.)
Good luck!

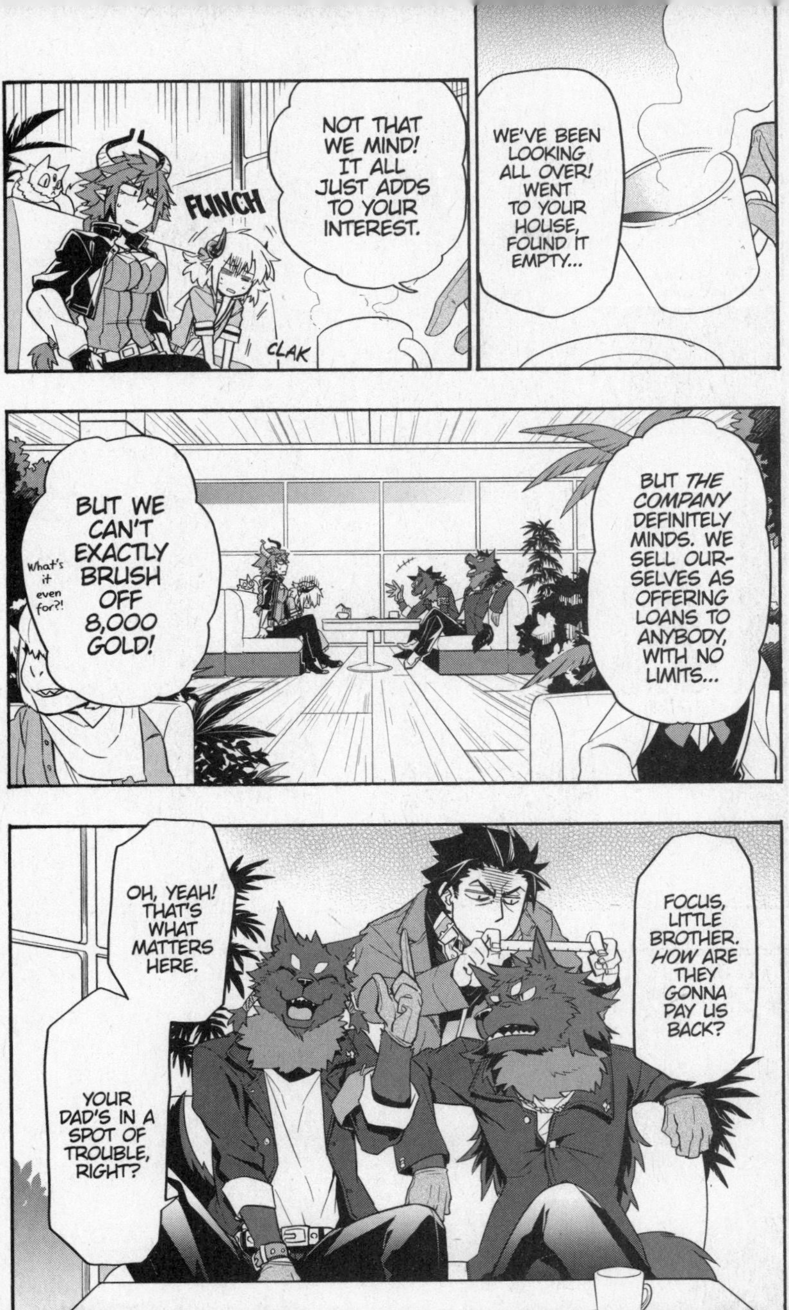
WE'VE BEEN LOOKING ALL OVER! WENT TO YOUR HOUSE, FOUND IT EMPTY...
NOT THAT WE MIND! IT ALL JUST ADDS TO YOUR INTEREST.
FLINCH
CLAK
BUT THE COMPANY DEFINITELY MINDS. WE SELL OURSELVES AS OFFERING LOANS TO ANYBODY, WITH NO LIMITS...
BUT WE CAN'T EXACTLY BRUSH OFF 8,000 GOLD!
What's it even for?!
FOCUS, LITTLE BROTHER. HOW ARE THEY GONNA PAY US BACK?
OH, YEAH! THAT'S WHAT MATTERS HERE.
YOUR DAD'S IN A SPOT OF TROUBLE, RIGHT?

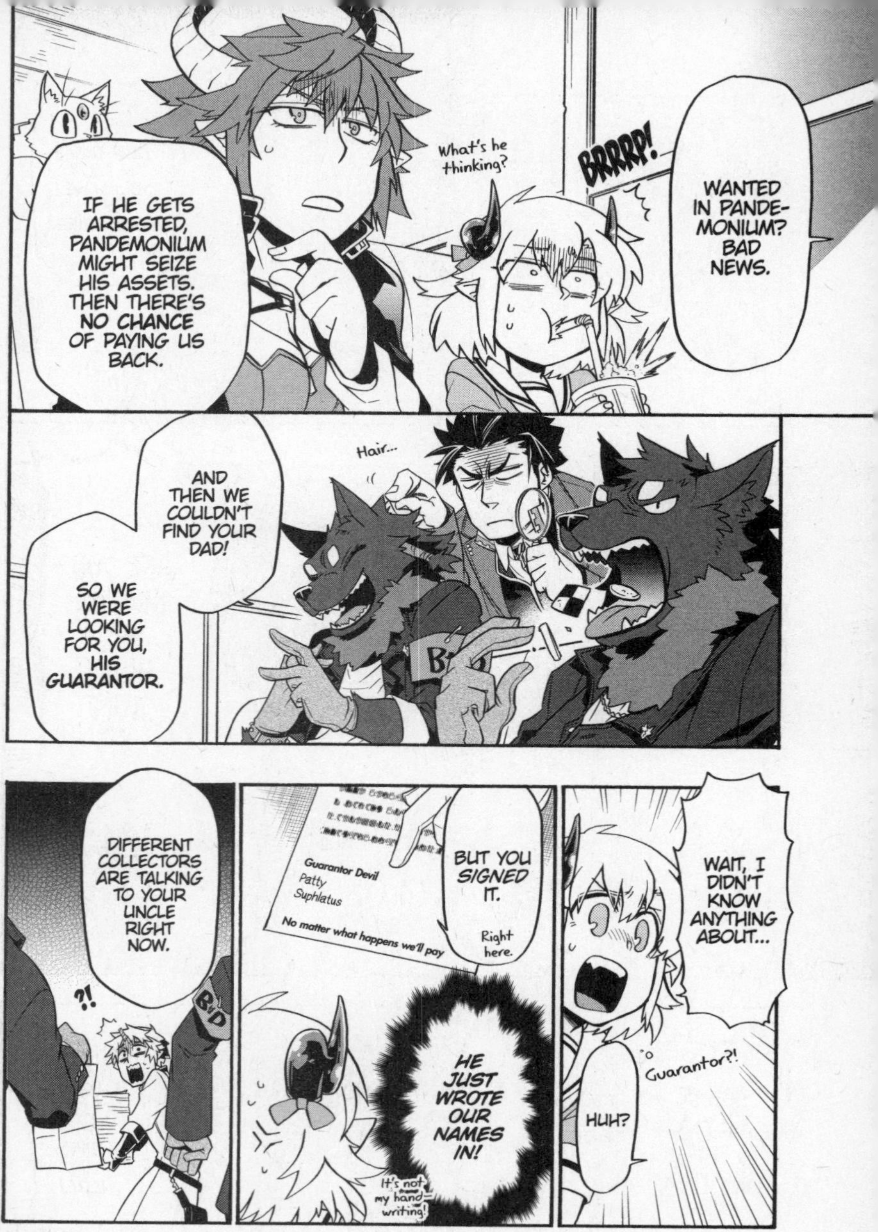
BRRRP!
WANTED IN PANDEMONIUM? BAD NEWS.
What's he thinking?
IF HE GETS ARRESTED, PANDEMONIUM MIGHT SEIZE HIS ASSETS. THEN THERE'S NO CHANCE OF PAYING US BACK.
Hair...
AND THEN WE COULDN'T FIND YOUR DAD!
SO WE WERE LOOKING FOR YOU, HIS GUARANTOR.
WAIT, I DIDN'T KNOW ANYTHING ABOUT...
Guarantor?!
HUH?
BUT YOU SIGNED IT.
Right here.
Guarantor Devil
Patty
Suphlatus
No matter what happens we'll pay
HE JUST WROTE OUR NAMES IN!
It's not my handwriting!
DIFFERENT COLLECTORS ARE TALKING TO YOUR UNCLE RIGHT NOW.
?!

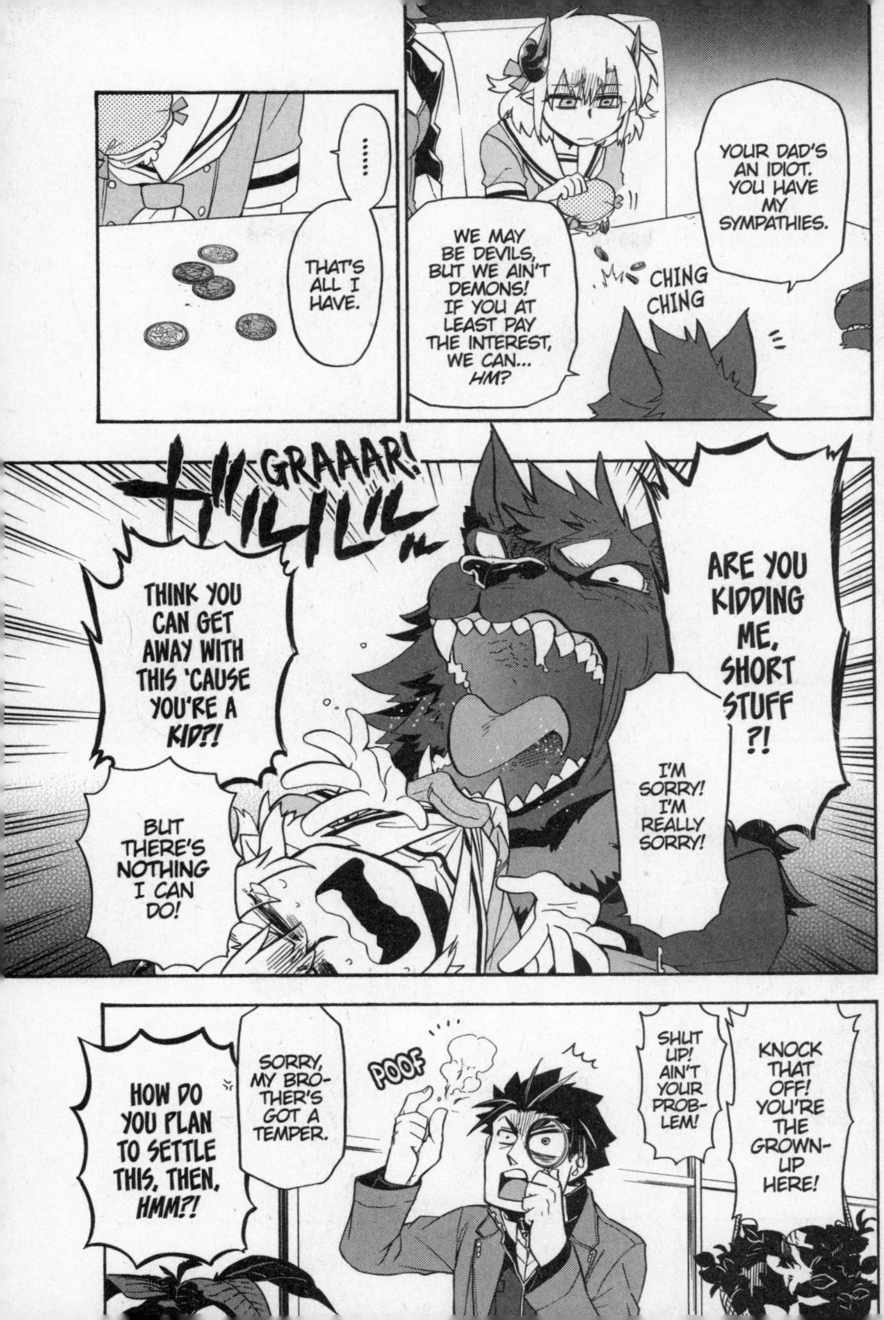
YOUR DAD'S AN IDIOT. YOU HAVE MY SYMPATHIES.
CHING CHING
WE MAY BE DEVILS, BUT WE AIN'T DEMONS! IF YOU AT LEAST PAY THE INTEREST, WE CAN... HM?
......
THAT'S ALL I HAVE.
GRAAAR!
ARE YOU KIDDING ME, SHORT STUFF?!
THINK YOU CAN GET AWAY WITH THIS 'CAUSE YOU'RE A KID?!
I'M SORRY! I'M REALLY SORRY!
BUT THERE'S NOTHING I CAN DO!
KNOCK THAT OFF! YOU'RE THE GROWN-UP HERE!
SHUT UP! AIN'T YOUR PROBLEM!
POOF
SORRY, MY BRO-THER'S GOT A TEMPER.
HOW DO YOU PLAN TO SETTLE THIS, THEN, HMM?!

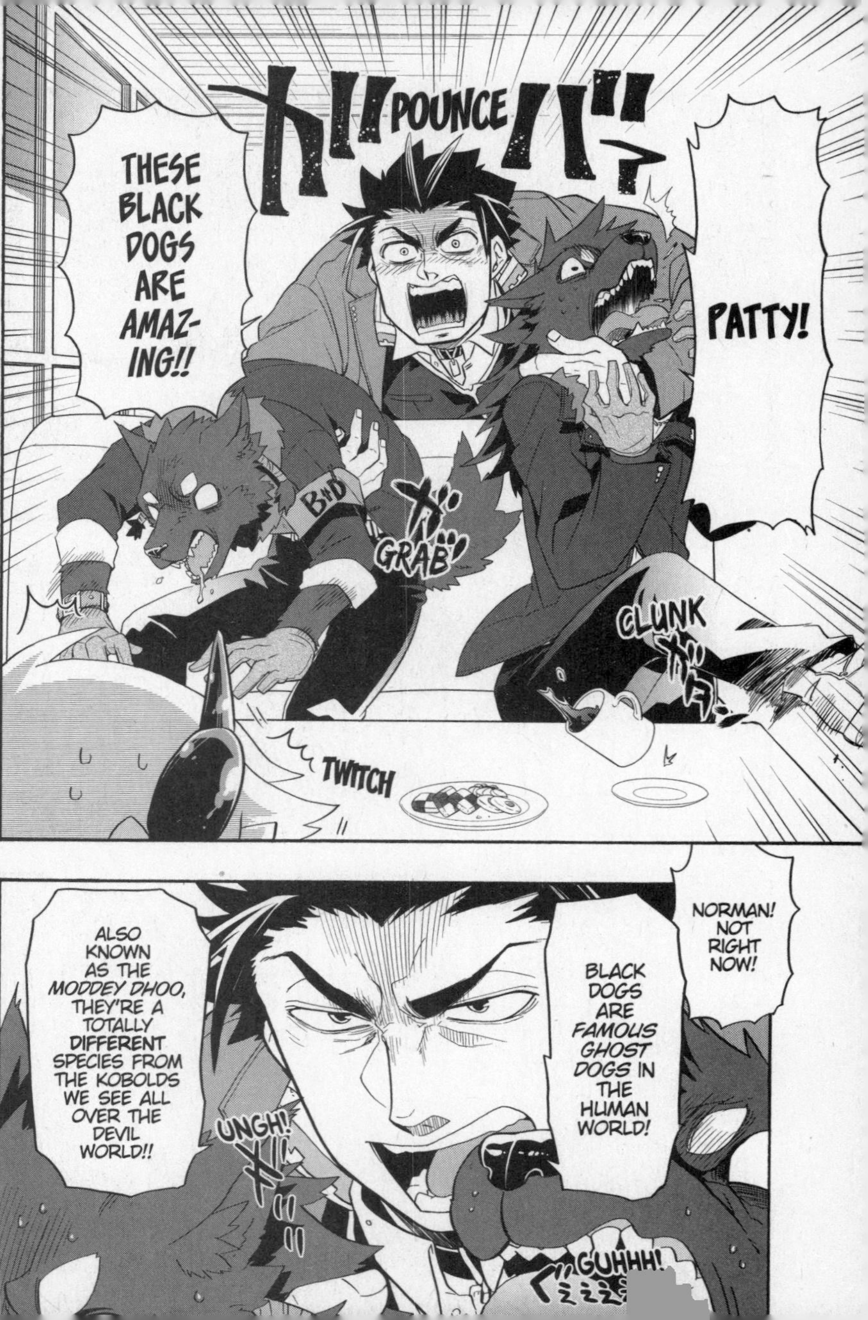
POUNCE
PATTY!
THESE BLACK DOGS ARE AMAZ-ING!!
GRAB
CLUNK
TWITCH
NORMAN! NOT RIGHT NOW!
BLACK DOGS ARE FAMOUS GHOST DOGS IN THE HUMAN WORLD!
ALSO KNOWN AS THE *MODDEY DHOO*, THEY'RE A TOTALLY DIFFERENT SPECIES FROM THE KOBOLDS WE SEE ALL OVER THE DEVIL WORLD!!
UNGH!
GUHHH!

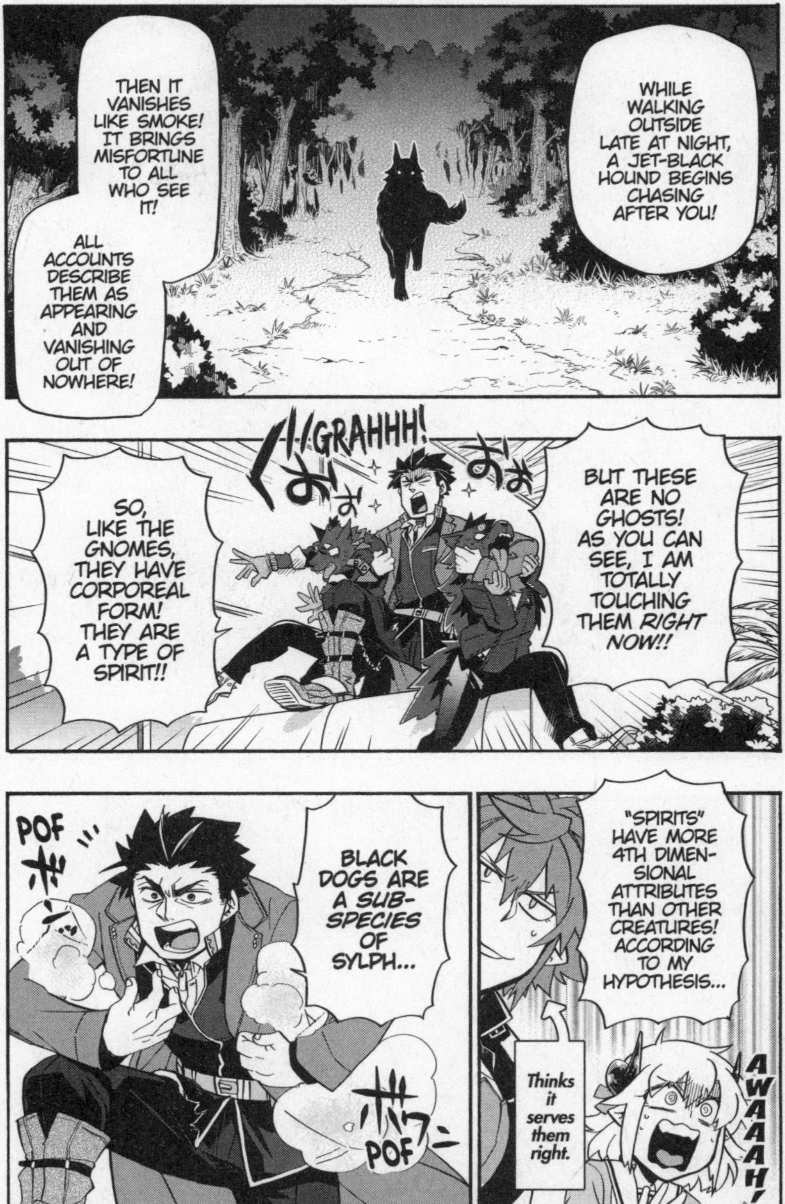
WHILE WALKING OUTSIDE LATE AT NIGHT, A JET-BLACK HOUND BEGINS CHASING AFTER YOU!
THEN IT VANISHES LIKE SMOKE! IT BRINGS MISFORTUNE TO ALL WHO SEE IT!
ALL ACCOUNTS DESCRIBE THEM AS APPEARING AND VANISHING OUT OF NOWHERE!
BUT THESE ARE NO GHOSTS! AS YOU CAN SEE, I AM TOTALLY TOUCHING THEM *RIGHT NOW!!*
GRAHHH!
SO, LIKE THE GNOMES, THEY HAVE CORPOREAL FORM! THEY ARE A TYPE OF SPIRIT!!
"SPIRITS" HAVE MORE 4TH DIMENSIONAL ATTRIBUTES THAN OTHER CREATURES! ACCORDING TO MY HYPOTHESIS...
Thinks it serves them right.
AWAAAAH!
BLACK DOGS ARE A *SUB-SPECIES* OF SYLPH...
POF
POF

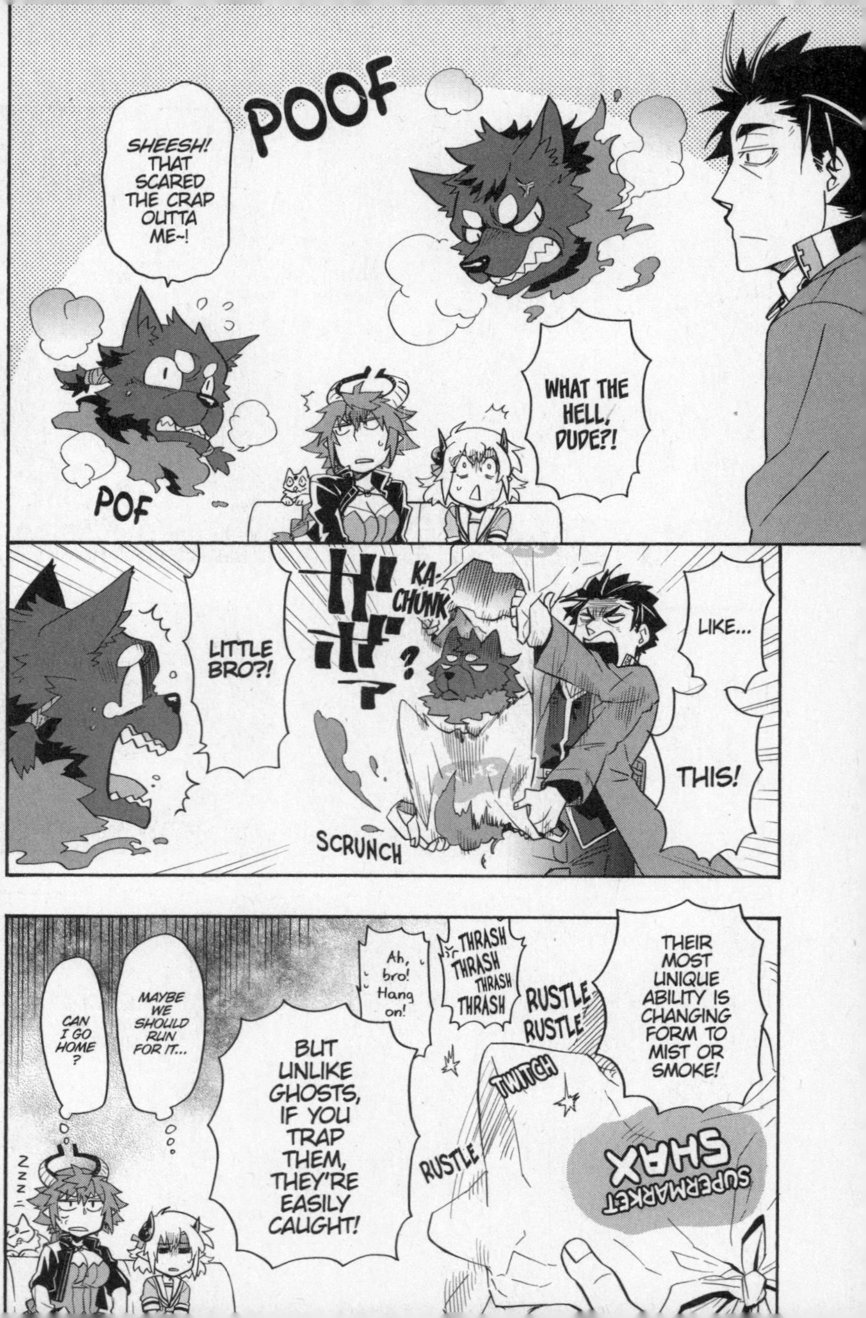
POOF
SHEESH! THAT SCARED THE CRAP OUTTA ME~!
WHAT THE HELL, DUDE?!
POF
LIKE...
KA-CHUNK
THIS!
SCRUNCH
LITTLE BRO?!
THEIR MOST UNIQUE ABILITY IS CHANGING FORM TO MIST OR SMOKE!
THRASH THRASH THRASH THRASH
RUSTLE RUSTLE
Ah, bro! Hang on!
TWITCH
SUPERMARKET SHAX
BUT UNLIKE GHOSTS, IF YOU TRAP THEM, THEY'RE EASILY CAUGHT!
RUSTLE
MAYBE WE SHOULD RUN FOR IT...
CAN I GO HOME?

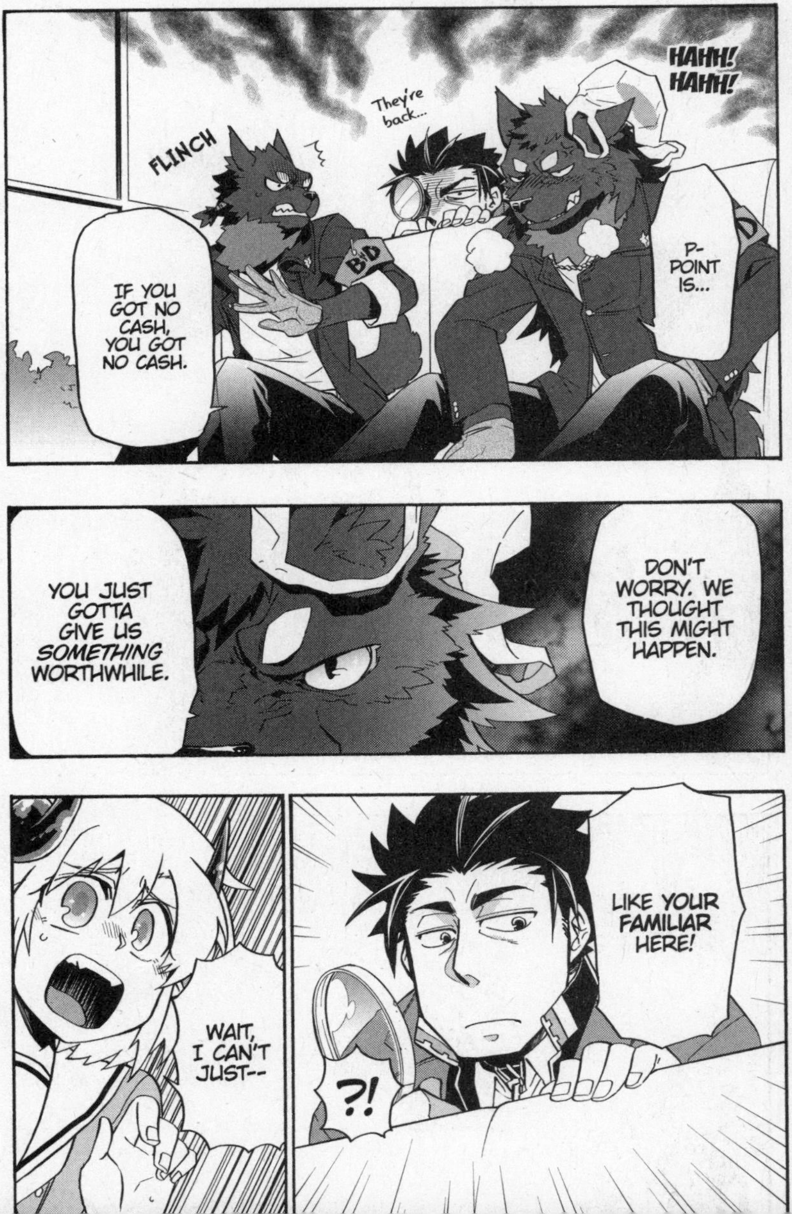
HAHH! HAHH!
P-POINT IS...
They're back...
FLINCH
IF YOU GOT NO CASH, YOU GOT NO CASH.
DON'T WORRY. WE THOUGHT THIS MIGHT HAPPEN.
YOU JUST GOTTA GIVE US SOMETHING WORTHWHILE.
LIKE YOUR FAMILIAR HERE!
?!
WAIT, I CAN'T JUST--

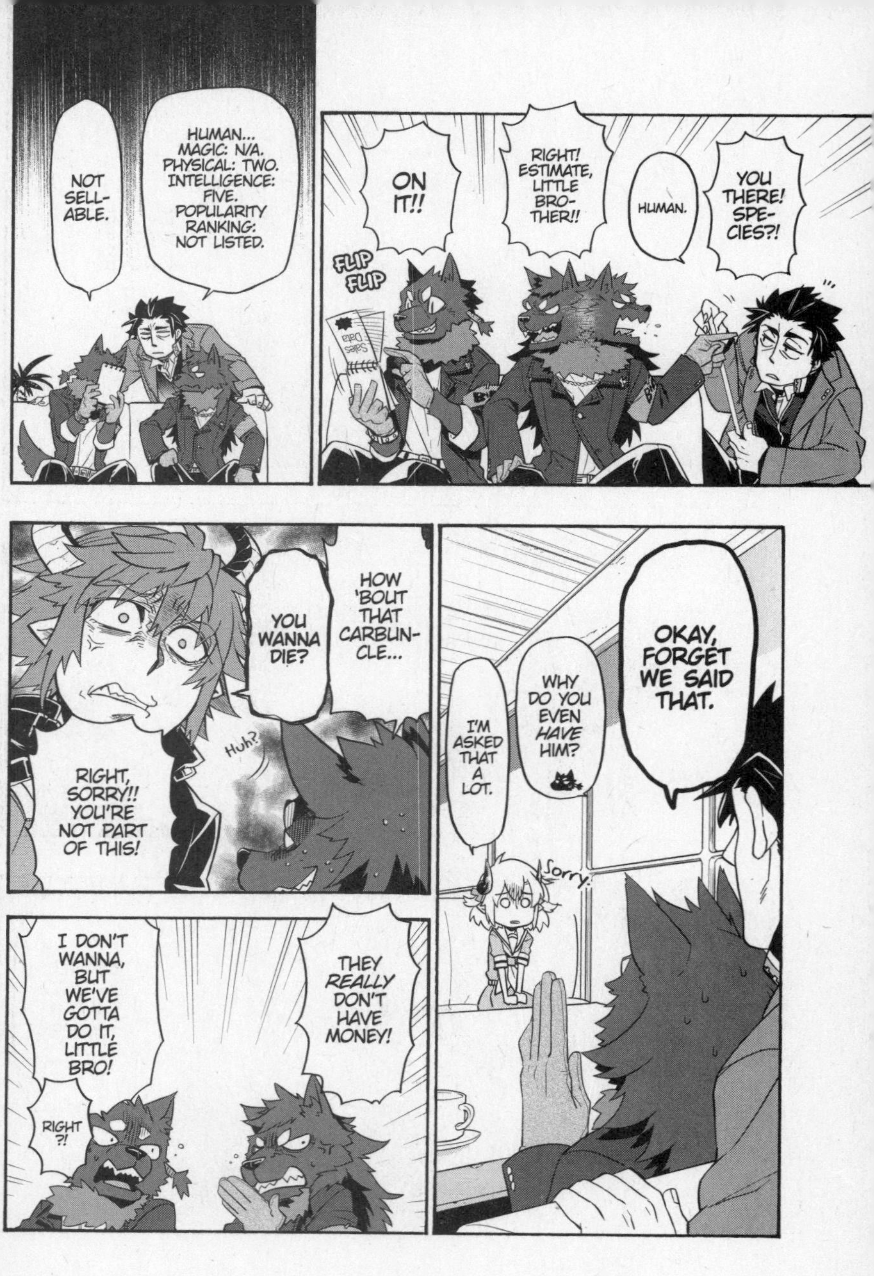
YOU THERE! SPE-CIES?!
HUMAN.
RIGHT! ESTIMATE, LITTLE BRO-THER!!
ON IT!!
FLIP FLIP
HUMAN... MAGIC: N/A. PHYSICAL: TWO. INTELLIGENCE: FIVE. POPULARITY RANKING: NOT LISTED.
NOT SELL-ABLE.
OKAY, FORGET WE SAID THAT.
WHY DO YOU EVEN *HAVE* HIM?
I'M ASKED THAT A LOT.
Sorry.
HOW 'BOUT THAT CARBUN-CLE...
YOU WANNA DIE?
Huh?
RIGHT, SORRY!! YOU'RE NOT PART OF THIS!
THEY *REALLY* DON'T HAVE MONEY!
I DON'T WANNA, BUT WE'VE GOTTA DO IT, LITTLE BRO!
Huh
RIGHT ?!

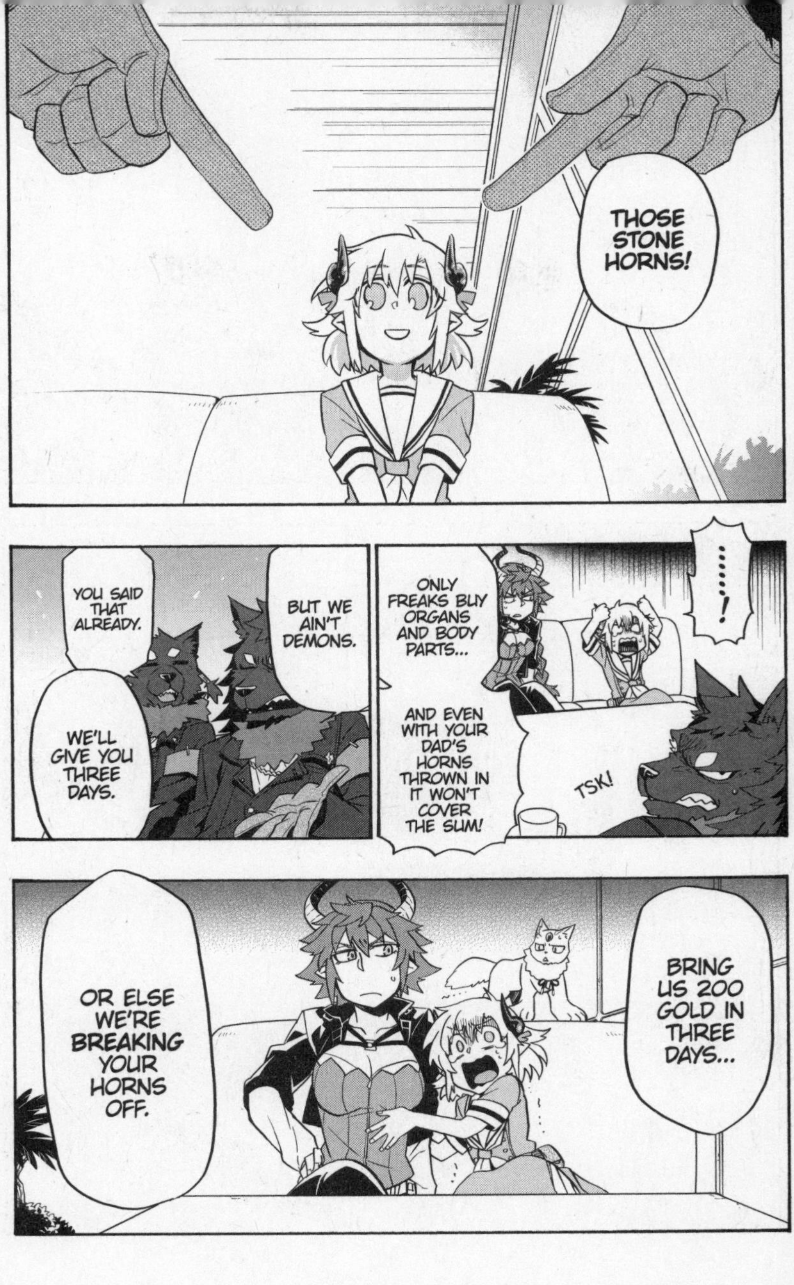
THOSE STONE HORNS!
.....!
ONLY FREAKS BUY ORGANS AND BODY PARTS...
AND EVEN WITH YOUR DAD'S HORNS THROWN IN IT WON'T COVER THE SUM!
TSK!
BUT WE AIN'T DEMONS.
YOU SAID THAT ALREADY.
WE'LL GIVE YOU THREE DAYS.
BRING US 200 GOLD IN THREE DAYS...
OR ELSE WE'RE BREAKING YOUR HORNS OFF.

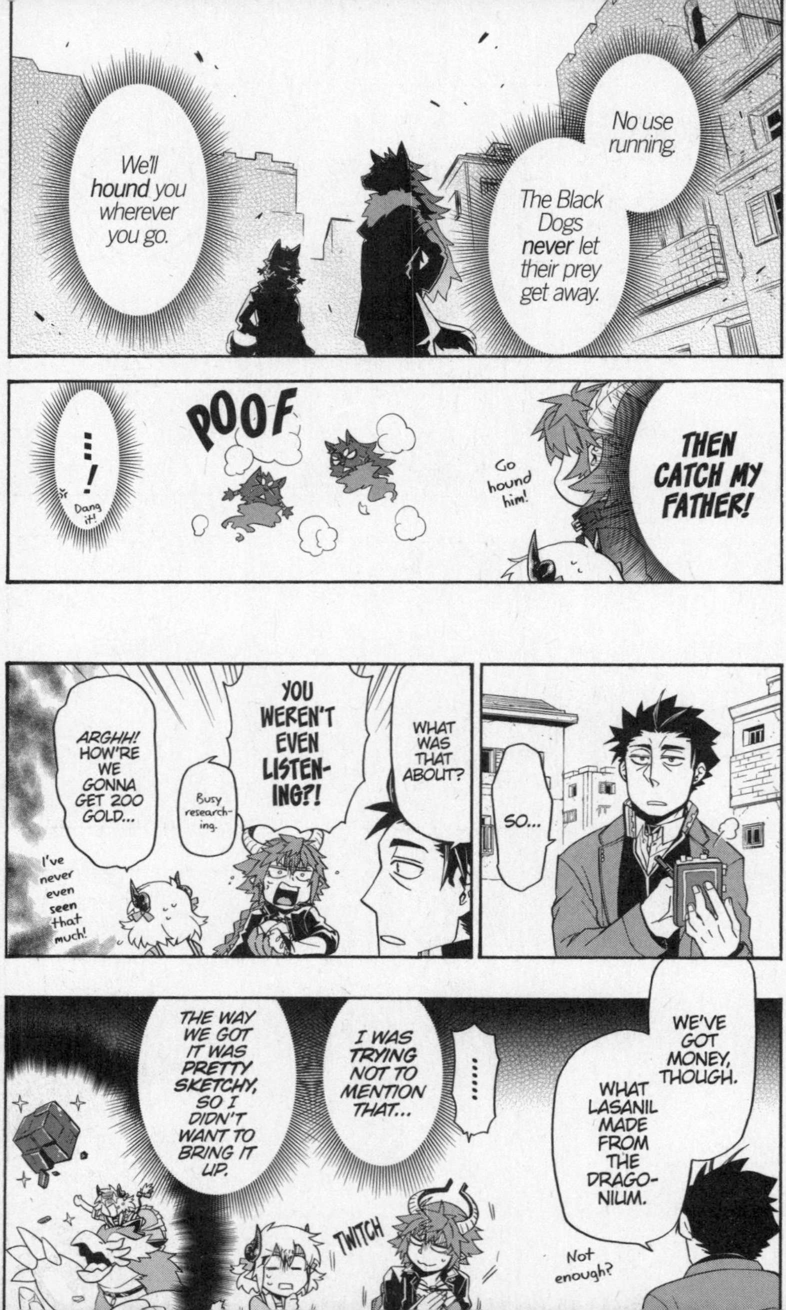
No use running.
The Black Dogs never let their prey get away.
We'll hound you wherever you go.
THEN CATCH MY FATHER!
Go hound him!
POOF
...!
Dang it!
SO...
WHAT WAS THAT ABOUT?
YOU WEREN'T EVEN LISTEN-ING?!
Busy research-ing.
ARGHH! HOW'RE WE GONNA GET 200 GOLD...
I've never even seen that much!
WE'VE GOT MONEY, THOUGH.
WHAT LASANIL MADE FROM THE DRAGO-NIUM.
Not enough?
......
I WAS TRYING NOT TO MENTION THAT...
THE WAY WE GOT IT WAS PRETTY SKETCHY, SO I DIDN'T WANT TO BRING IT UP.
TWITCH

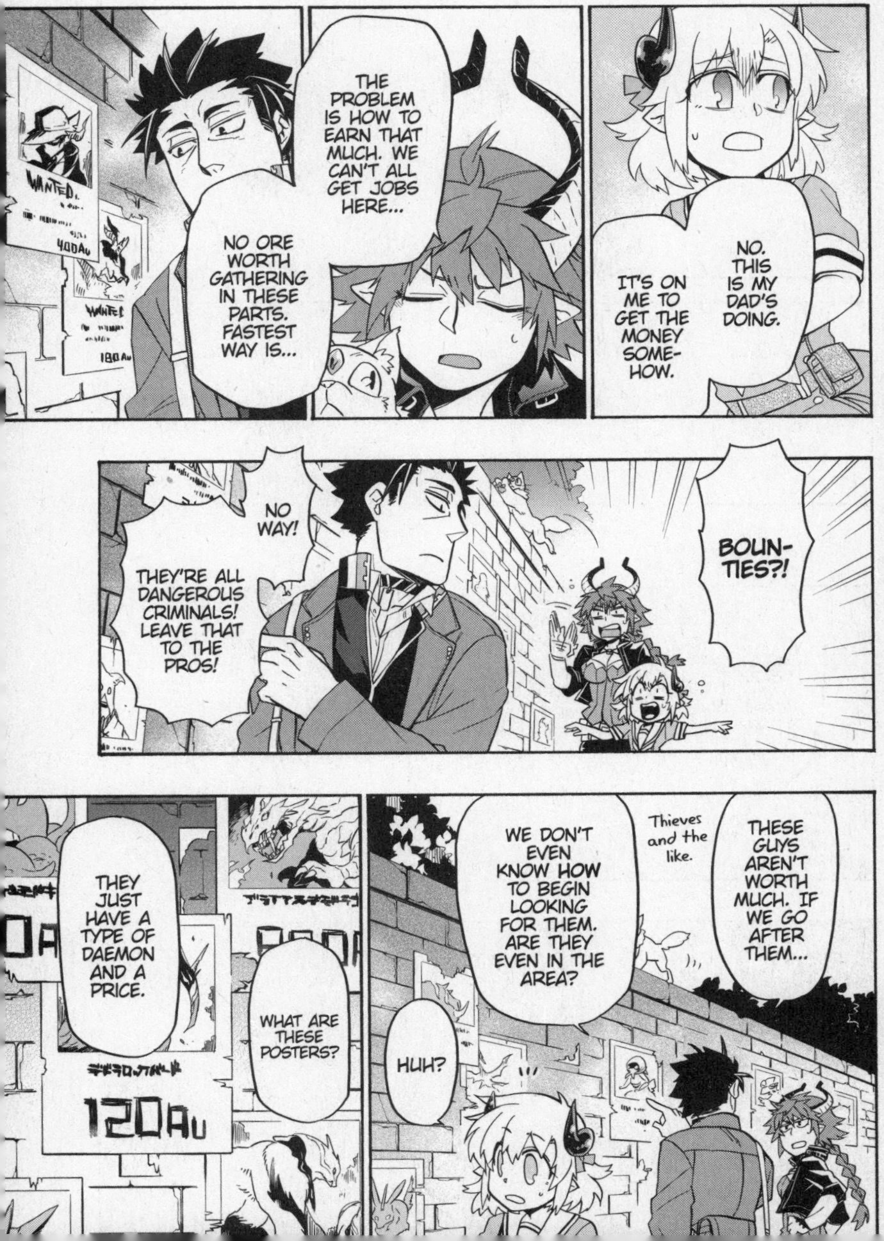
NO. THIS IS MY DAD'S DOING.
IT'S ON ME TO GET THE MONEY SOME-HOW.
THE PROBLEM IS HOW TO EARN THAT MUCH. WE CAN'T ALL GET JOBS HERE...
NO ORE WORTH GATHERING IN THESE PARTS. FASTEST WAY IS...
WANTED.
400Au
180Au
BOUN-TIES?!
NO WAY!
THEY'RE ALL DANGEROUS CRIMINALS! LEAVE THAT TO THE PROS!
THESE GUYS AREN'T WORTH MUCH. IF WE GO AFTER THEM...
Thieves and the like.
WE DON'T EVEN KNOW HOW TO BEGIN LOOKING FOR THEM. ARE THEY EVEN IN THE AREA?
HUH?
WHAT ARE THESE POSTERS?
THEY JUST HAVE A TYPE OF DAEMON AND A PRICE.
120Au

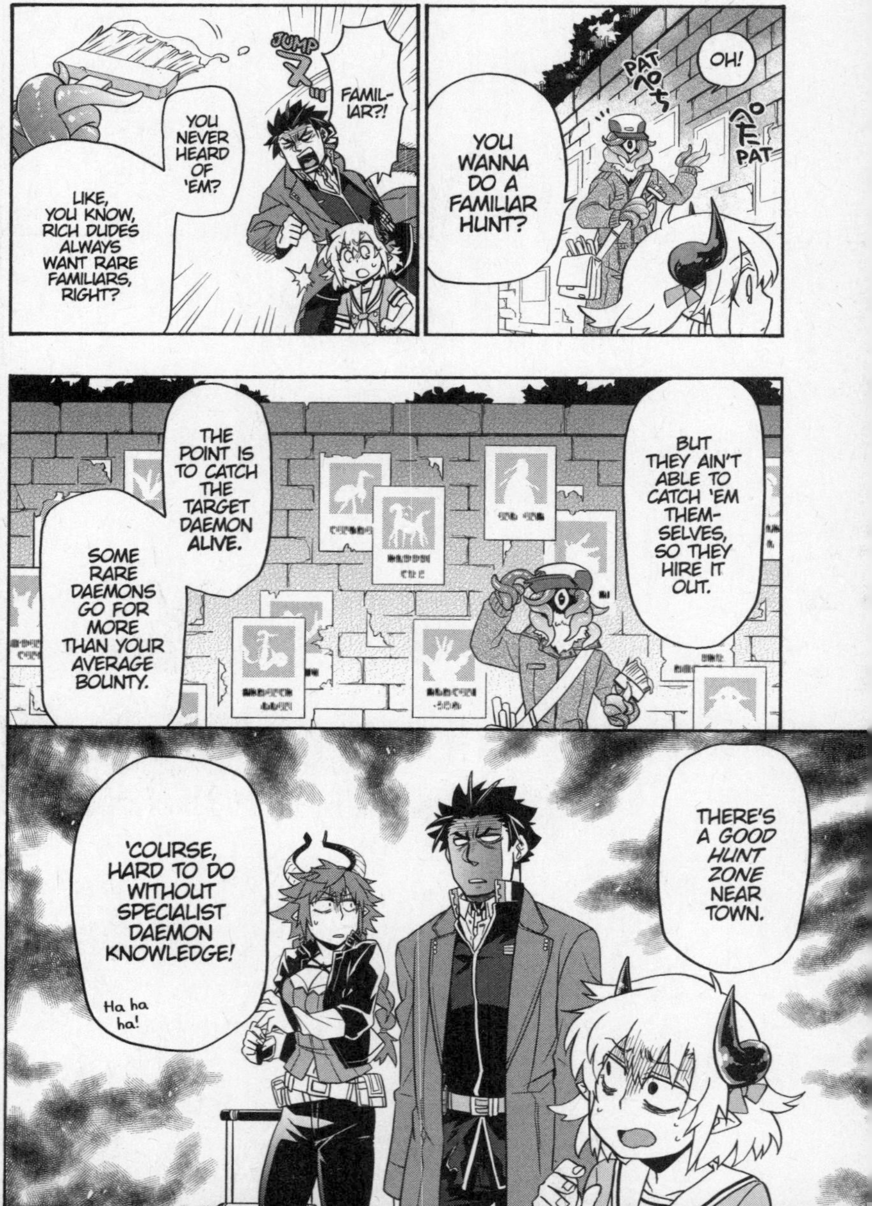
OH!
PAT
PAT
YOU WANNA DO A FAMILIAR HUNT?
JUMP
FAMILIAR?!
YOU NEVER HEARD OF 'EM?
LIKE, YOU KNOW, RICH DUDES ALWAYS WANT RARE FAMILIARS, RIGHT?
BUT THEY AIN'T ABLE TO CATCH 'EM THEMSELVES, SO THEY HIRE IT OUT.
THE POINT IS TO CATCH THE TARGET DAEMON ALIVE.
SOME RARE DAEMONS GO FOR MORE THAN YOUR AVERAGE BOUNTY.
THERE'S A GOOD HUNT ZONE NEAR TOWN.
'COURSE, HARD TO DO WITHOUT SPECIALIST DAEMON KNOWLEDGE!
Ha ha ha!

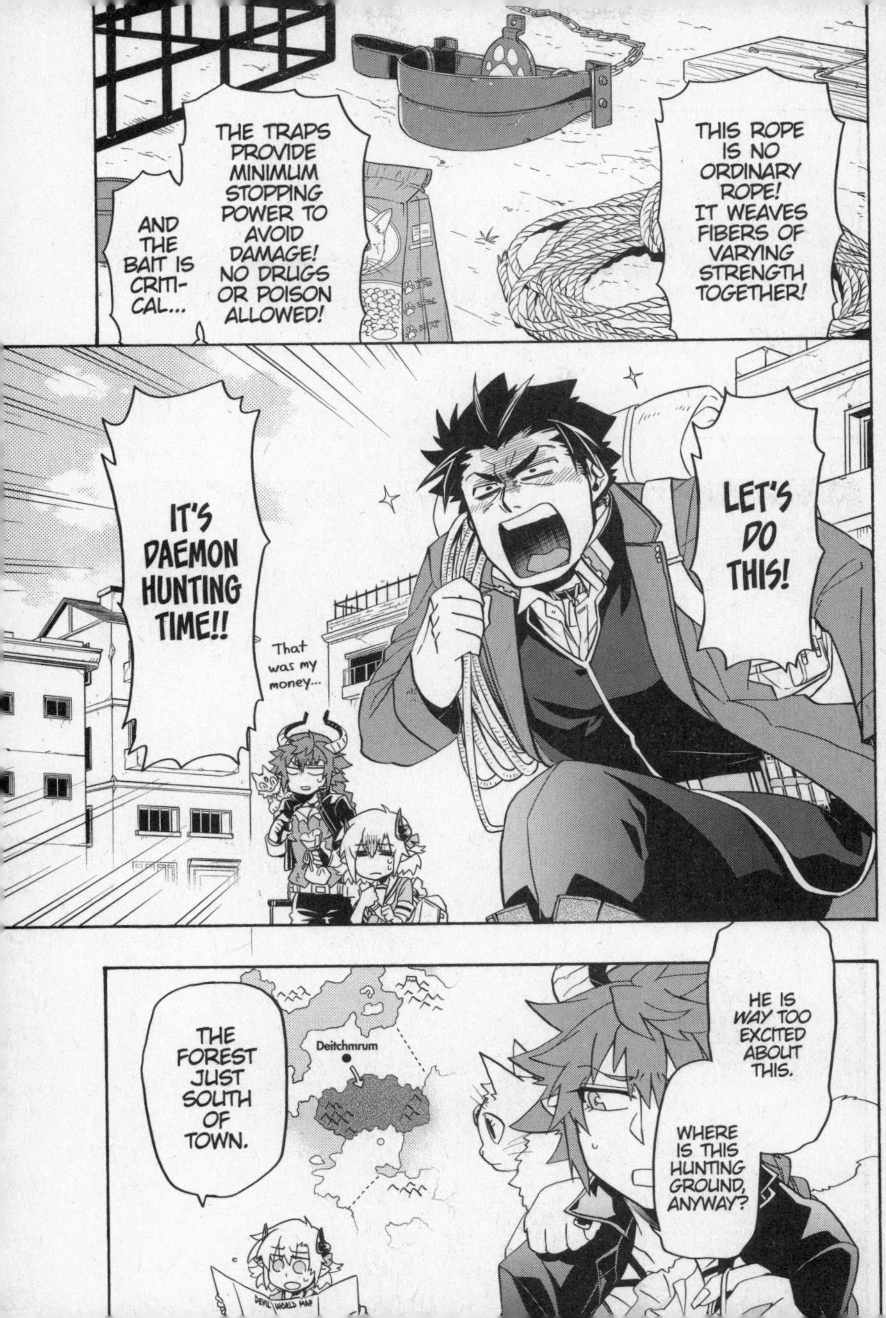
THIS ROPE IS NO ORDINARY ROPE! IT WEAVES FIBERS OF VARYING STRENGTH TOGETHER!
THE TRAPS PROVIDE MINIMUM STOPPING POWER TO AVOID DAMAGE! NO DRUGS OR POISON ALLOWED!
AND THE BAIT IS CRITI-CAL...
LET'S DO THIS!
IT'S DAEMON HUNTING TIME!!
That was my money...
HE IS WAY TOO EXCITED ABOUT THIS.
WHERE IS THIS HUNTING GROUND, ANYWAY?
THE FOREST JUST SOUTH OF TOWN.
Deitchmrum
DEVIL WORLD MAP

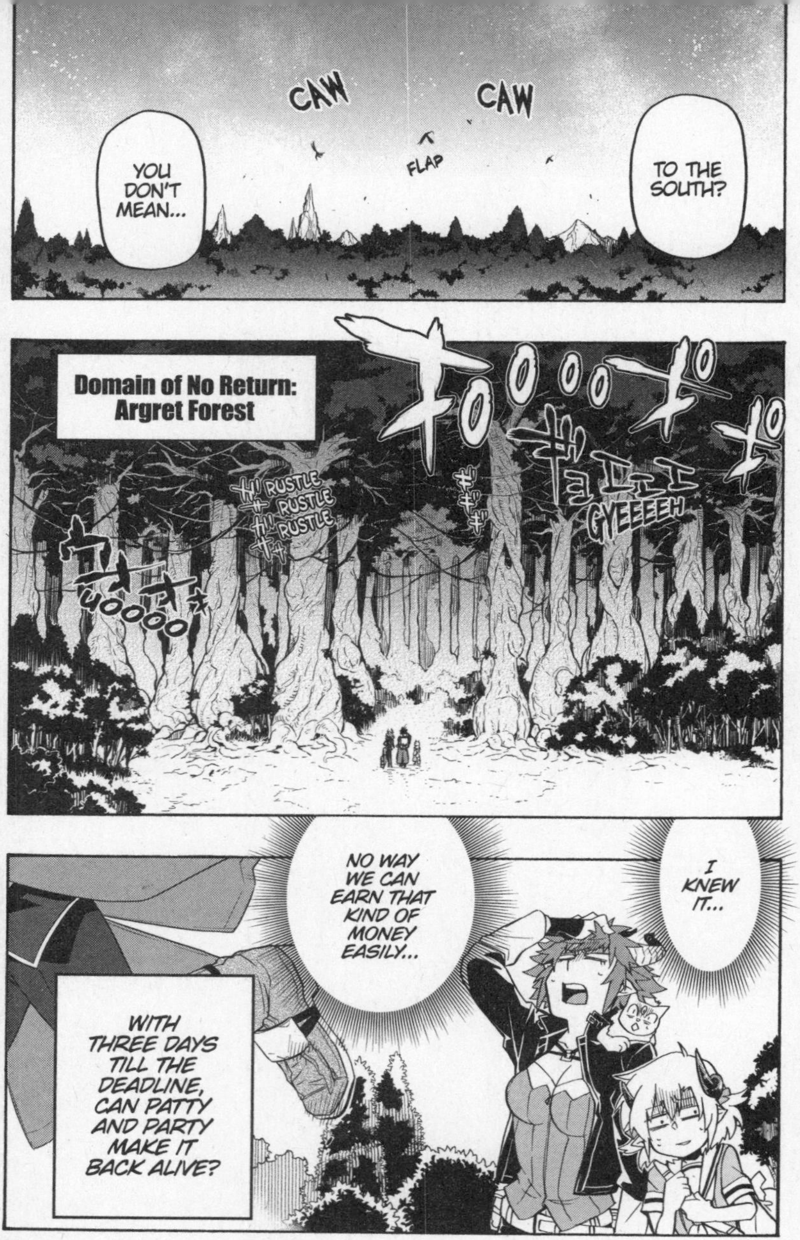
CAW
CAW
TO THE SOUTH?
FLAP
YOU DON'T MEAN...
Domain of No Return: Argret Forest
GYEEEEH
RUSTLE RUSTLE RUSTLE
UOOOOO
I KNEW IT...
NO WAY WE CAN EARN THAT KIND OF MONEY EASILY...
WITH THREE DAYS TILL THE DEADLINE, CAN PATTY AND PARTY MAKE IT BACK ALIVE?

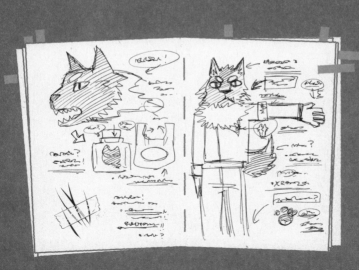

Sorry For My Familiar

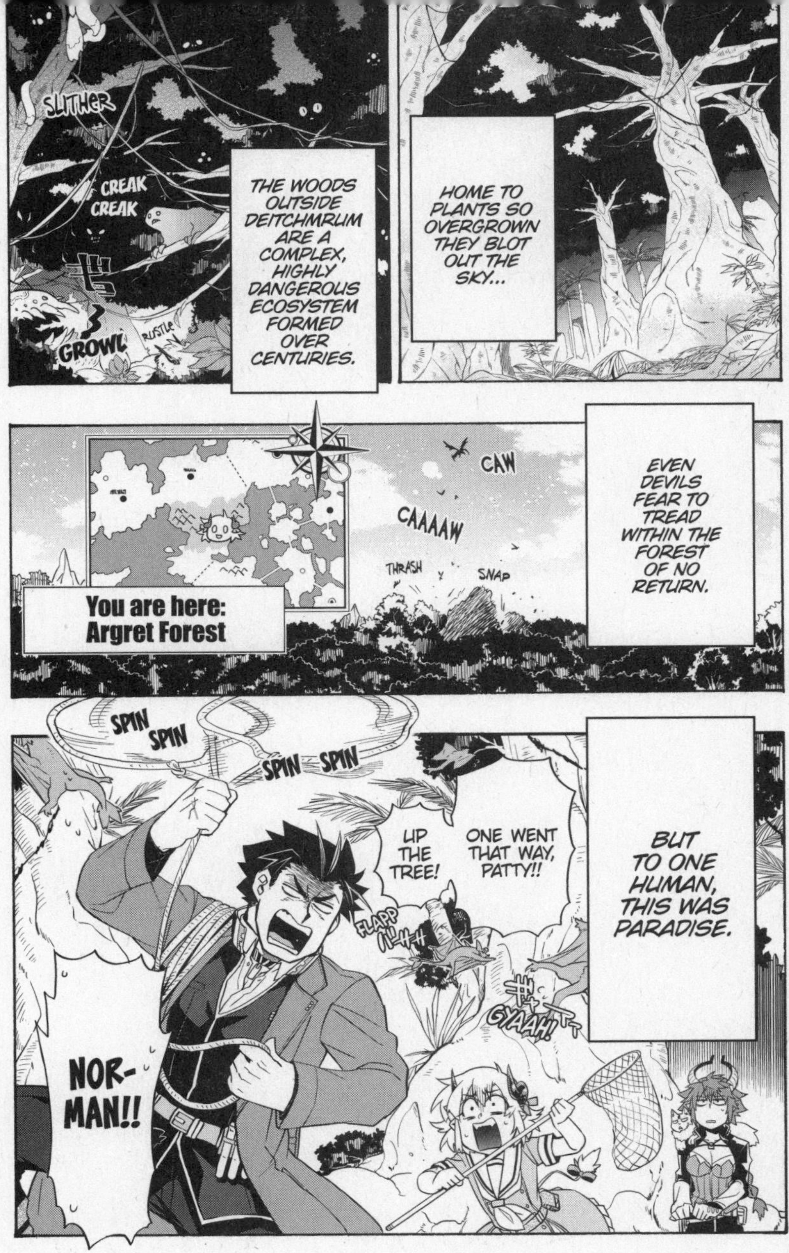
SLITHER
CREAK
CREAK
GROWL
RUSTLE
THE WOODS OUTSIDE DEITCHMRUM ARE A COMPLEX, HIGHLY DANGEROUS ECOSYSTEM FORMED OVER CENTURIES.
HOME TO PLANTS SO OVERGROWN THEY BLOT OUT THE SKY...
EVEN DEVILS FEAR TO TREAD WITHIN THE FOREST OF NO RETURN.
CAW
CAAAAW
SNAP
THRASH
You are here: Argret Forest
BUT TO ONE HUMAN, THIS WAS PARADISE.
ONE WENT THAT WAY, PATTY!!
UP THE TREE!
FLAPP
GYAAH!
SPIN
SPIN
SPIN
SPIN
NOR-MAN!!

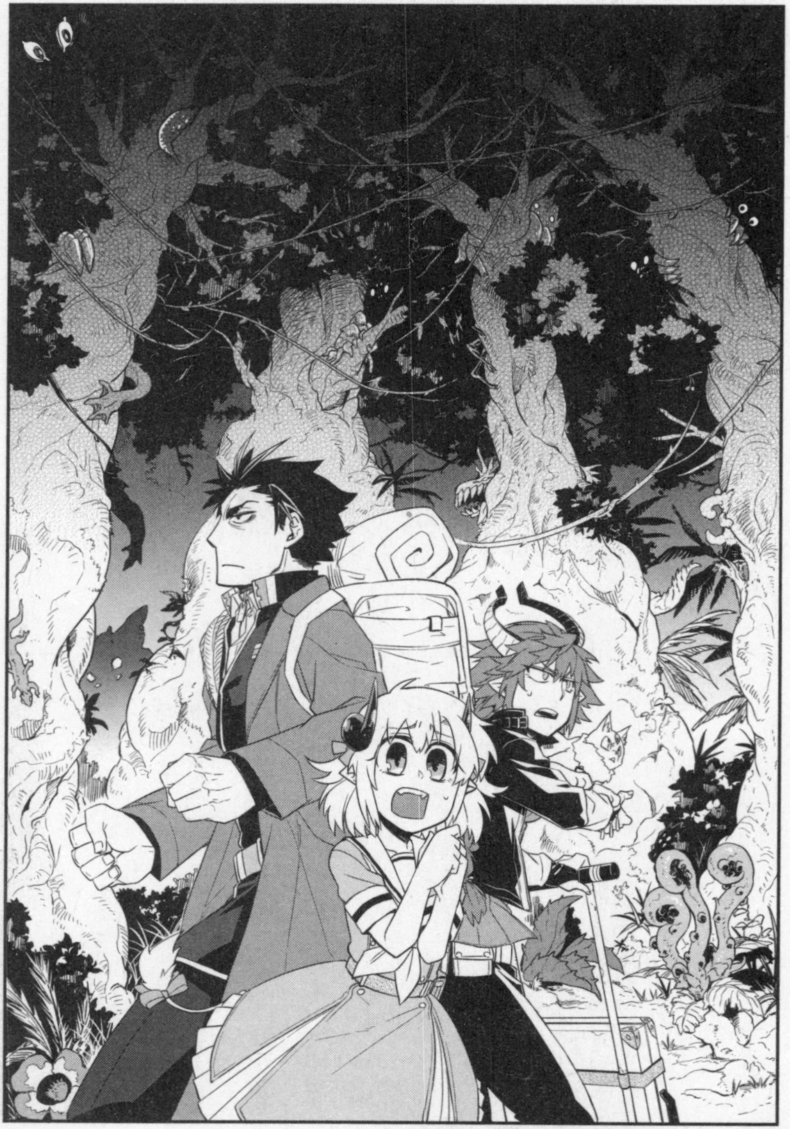

FILE 18: Argret Forest ①

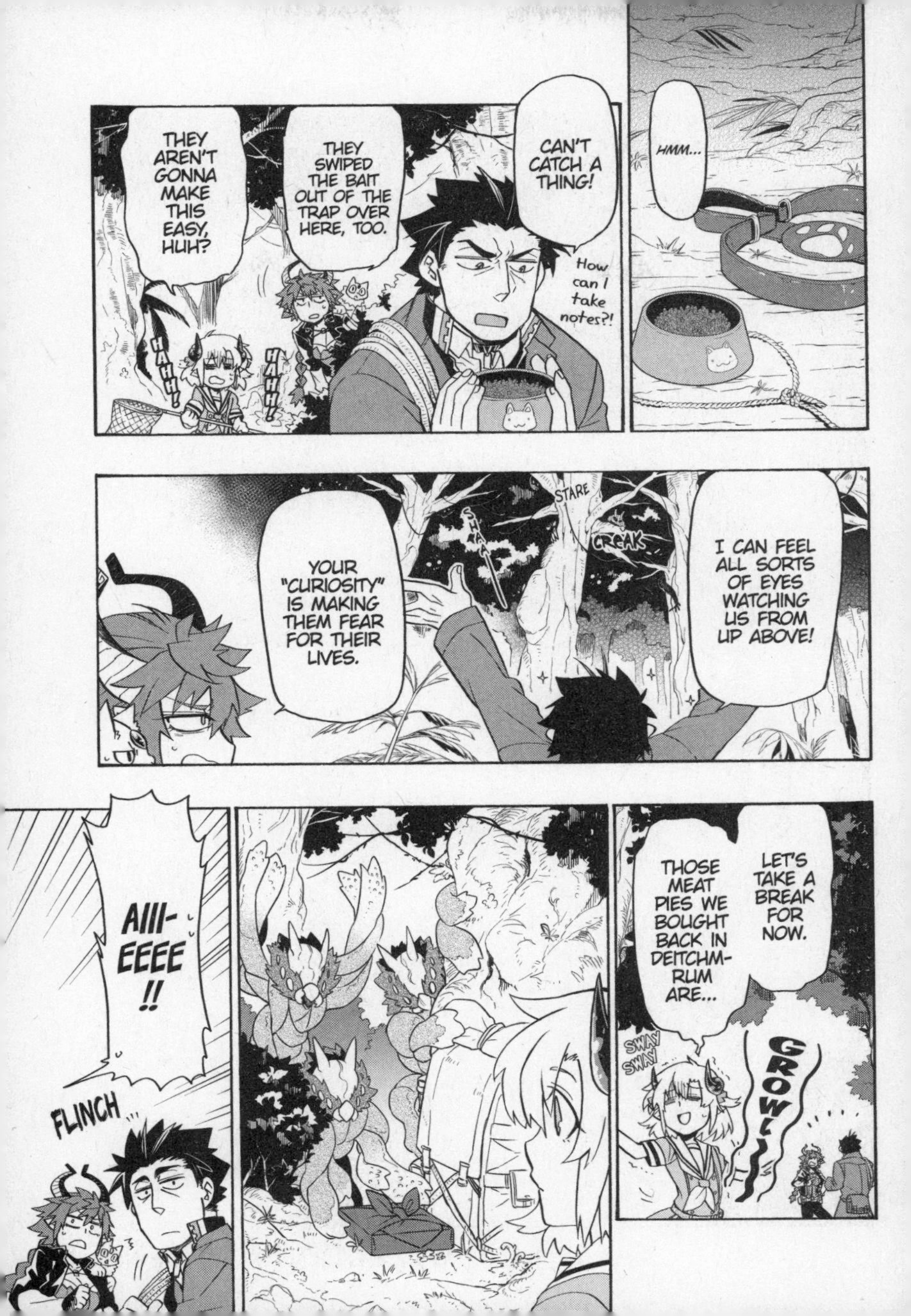
HMM...
CAN'T CATCH A THING!
How can I take notes?!
THEY SWIPED THE BAIT OUT OF THE TRAP OVER HERE, TOO.
THEY AREN'T GONNA MAKE THIS EASY, HUH?
HAHH!
HAHH!
I CAN FEEL ALL SORTS OF EYES WATCHING US FROM UP ABOVE!
STARE
CREAK
SHAA
YOUR "CURIOSITY" IS MAKING THEM FEAR FOR THEIR LIVES.
LET'S TAKE A BREAK FOR NOW.
THOSE MEAT PIES WE BOUGHT BACK IN DEITCHM-RUM ARE...
SWAY SWAY
GROWL
AIII-EEEE!!
FLINCH

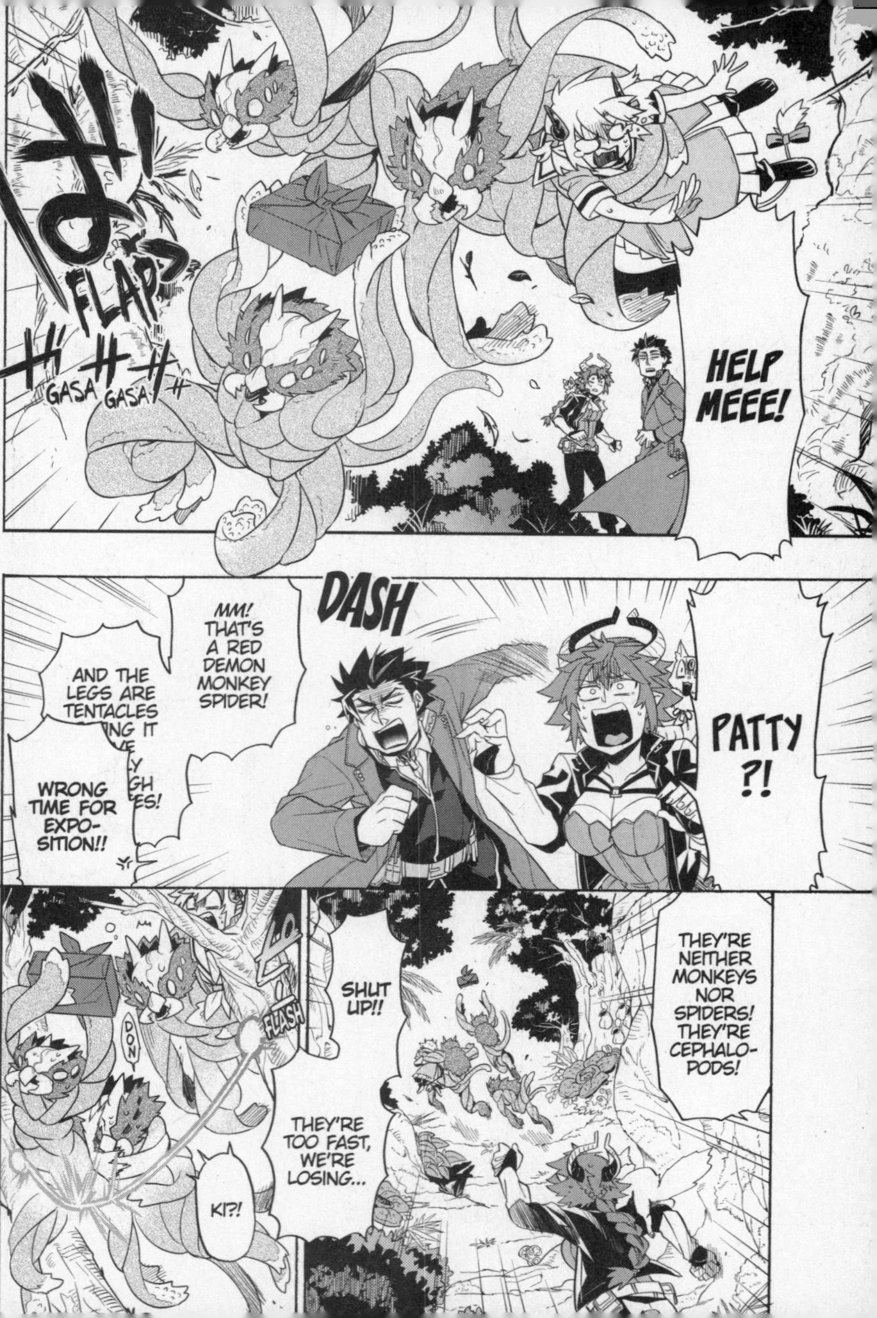
HELP MEEE!
FLAP
GASA GASA
PATTY ?!
DASH
MM! THAT'S A RED DEMON MONKEY SPIDER!
AND THE LEGS ARE TENTACLES
WRONG TIME FOR EXPO-SITION!!
THEY'RE NEITHER MONKEYS NOR SPIDERS! THEY'RE CEPHALO-PODS!
SHUT UP!!
THEY'RE TOO FAST, WE'RE LOSING...
FLASH
DON
KI?!

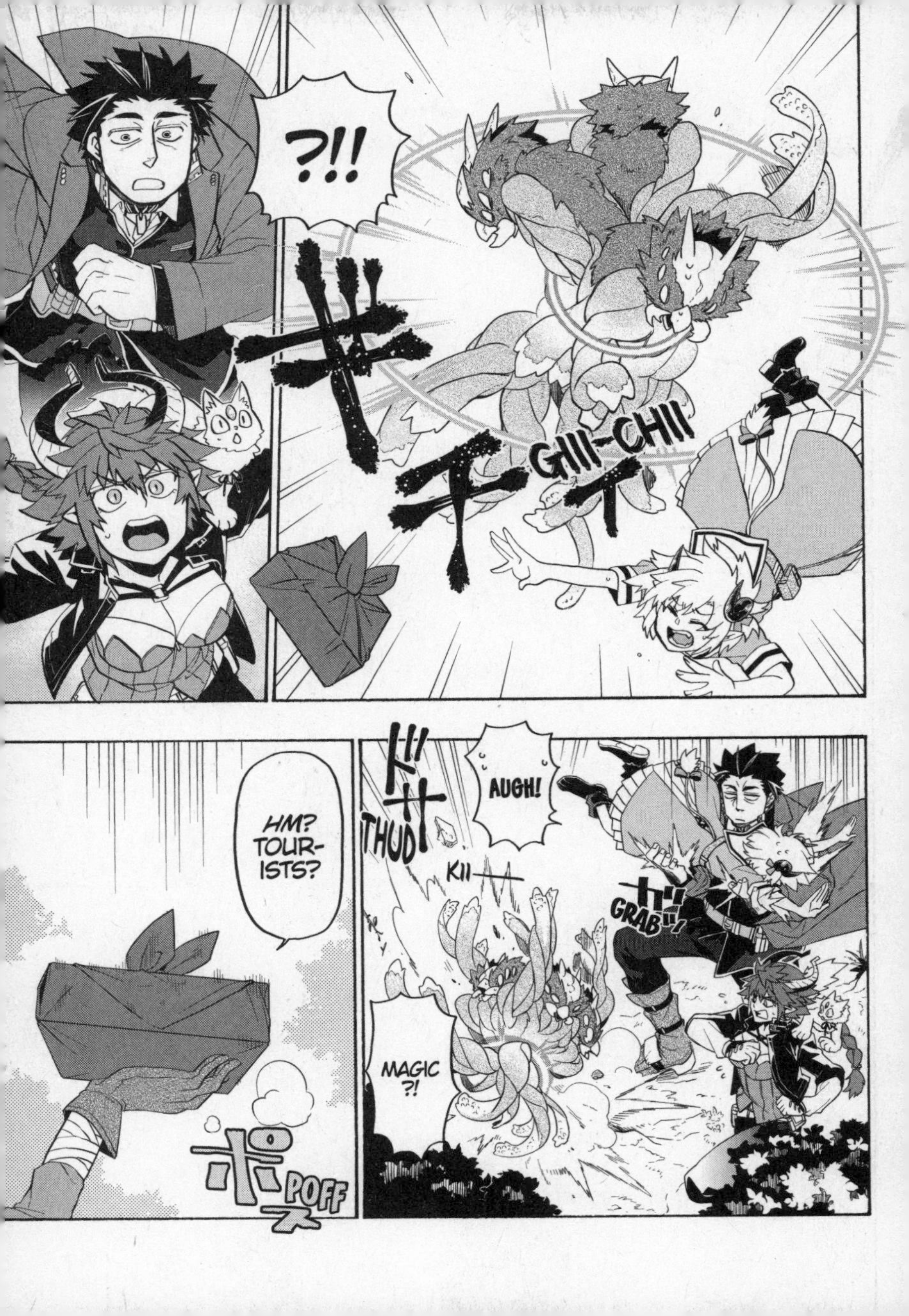
GIII-CHIII
?!!
AUGH!
THUD
KII—
GRAB
MAGIC ?!
HM? TOURISTS?
POFF

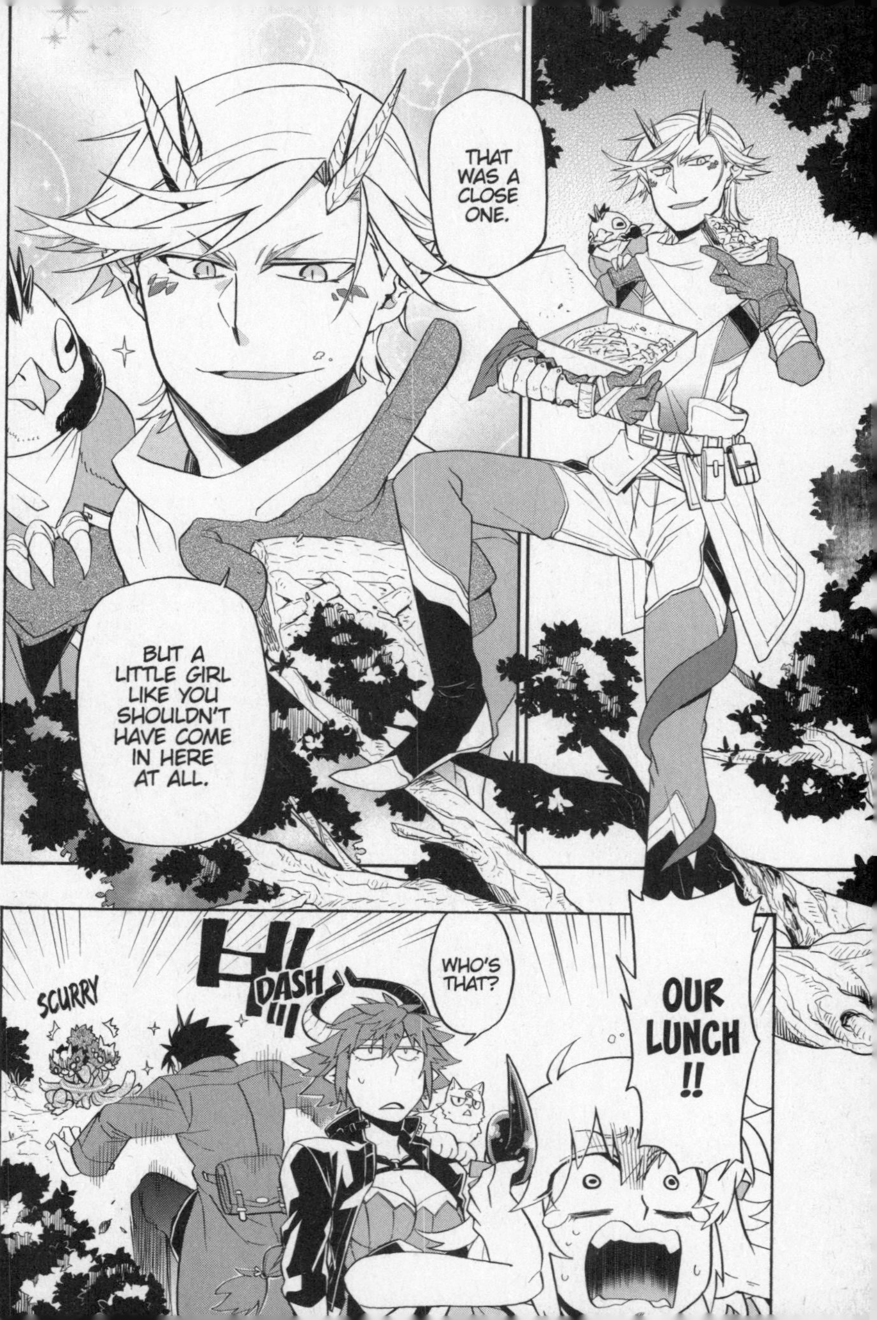
THAT WAS A CLOSE ONE.
BUT A LITTLE GIRL LIKE YOU SHOULDN'T HAVE COME IN HERE AT ALL.
OUR LUNCH!!
WHO'S THAT?
DASH
SCURRY

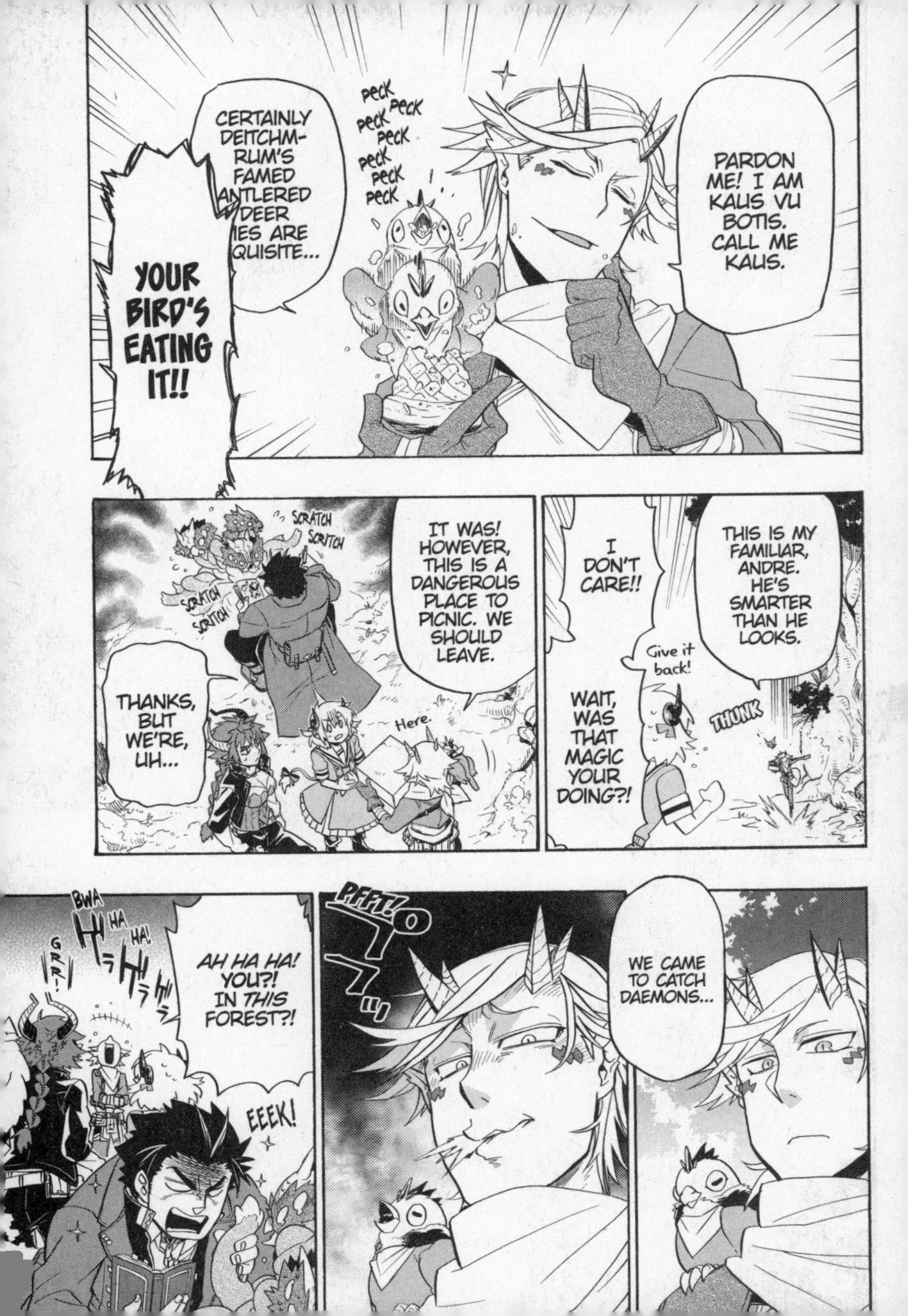
PARDON ME! I AM KAUS VU BOTIS. CALL ME KAUS.
peck peck peck peck peck peck peck
CERTAINLY DEITCHM-RUM'S FAMED ANTLERED DEER IES ARE QUISITE...
YOUR BIRD'S EATING IT!!
THIS IS MY FAMILIAR, ANDRE. HE'S SMARTER THAN HE LOOKS.
THUNK
I DON'T CARE!!
Give it back!
WAIT, WAS THAT MAGIC YOUR DOING?!
IT WAS! HOWEVER, THIS IS A DANGEROUS PLACE TO PICNIC. WE SHOULD LEAVE.
SCRATCH SCRATCH
SCRATCH SCRATCH
THANKS, BUT WE'RE, UH...
Here.
WE CAME TO CATCH DAEMONS...
PFFT!
AH HA HA! YOU?! IN *THIS* FOREST?!
BWA HA HA!
GRR!
EEEK!

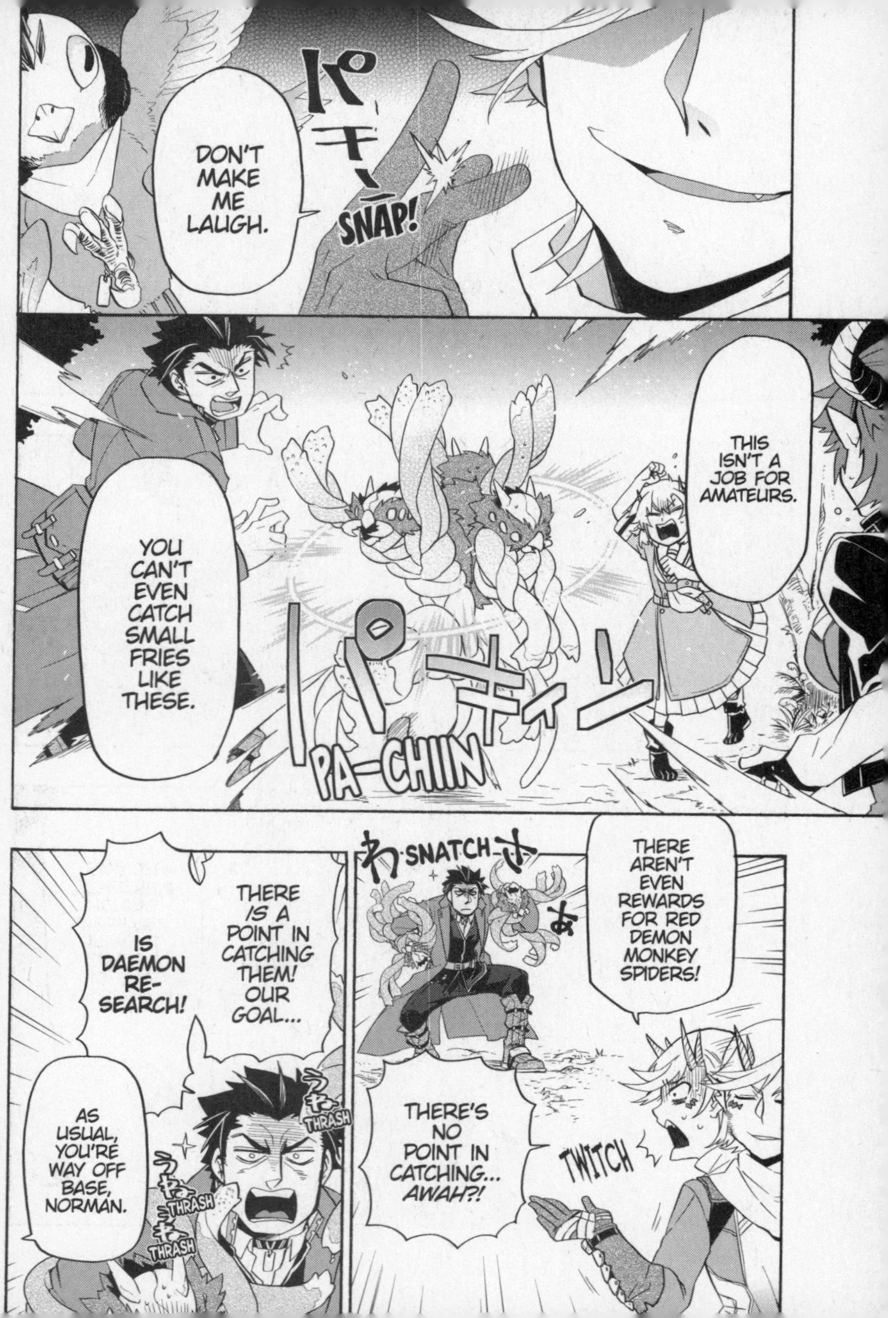
SNAP!
DON'T MAKE ME LAUGH.
THIS ISN'T A JOB FOR AMATEURS.
PA-CHIIN
YOU CAN'T EVEN CATCH SMALL FRIES LIKE THESE.
THERE AREN'T EVEN REWARDS FOR RED DEMON MONKEY SPIDERS!
SNATCH
TWITCH
THERE'S NO POINT IN CATCHING... AWAH?!
THERE IS A POINT IN CATCHING THEM! OUR GOAL...
IS DAEMON RE-SEARCH!
THRASH
THRASH
THRASH
AS USUAL, YOU'RE WAY OFF BASE, NORMAN.

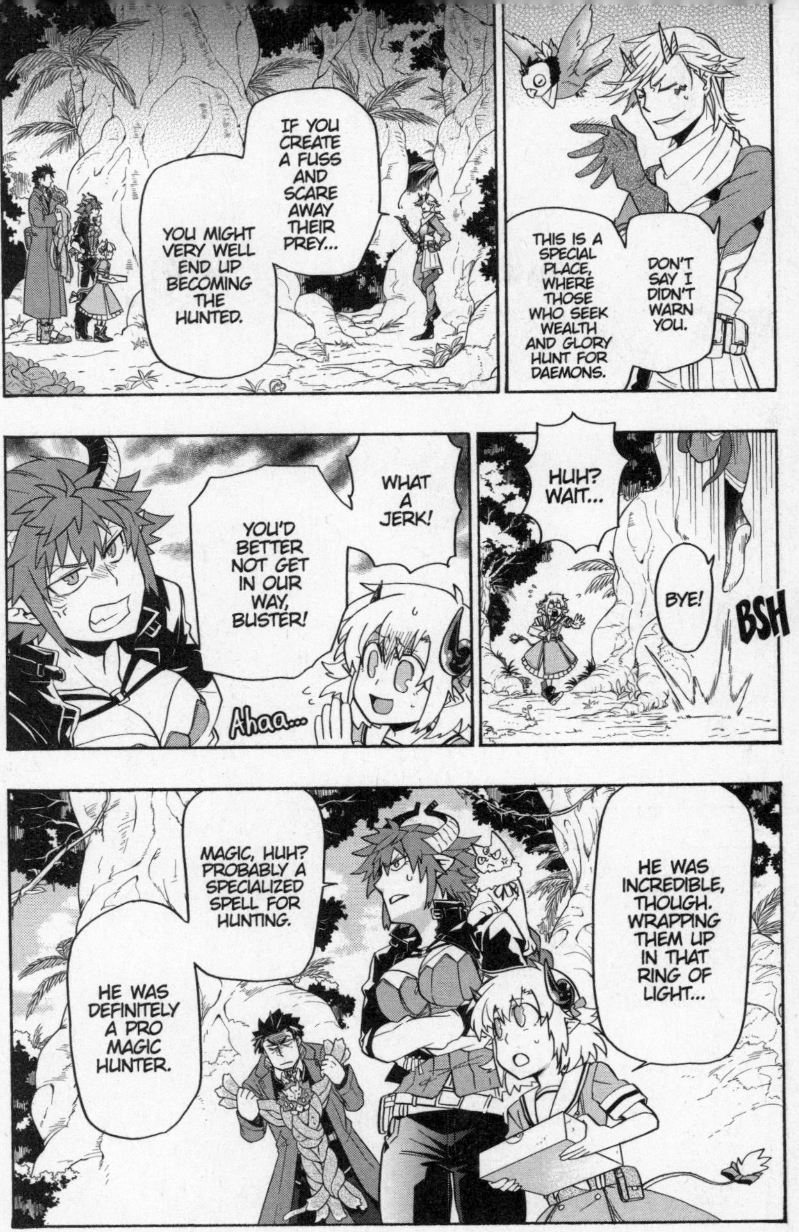
THIS IS A SPECIAL PLACE, WHERE THOSE WHO SEEK WEALTH AND GLORY HUNT FOR DAEMONS.
DON'T SAY I DIDN'T WARN YOU.
IF YOU CREATE A FUSS AND SCARE AWAY THEIR PREY...
YOU MIGHT VERY WELL END UP BECOMING THE HUNTED.
HUH? WAIT...
BYE!
BSH
WHAT A JERK!
YOU'D BETTER NOT GET IN OUR WAY, BUSTER!
Ahaa...
HE WAS INCREDIBLE, THOUGH. WRAPPING THEM UP IN THAT RING OF LIGHT...
MAGIC, HUH? PROBABLY A SPECIALIZED SPELL FOR HUNTING.
HE WAS DEFINITELY A PRO MAGIC HUNTER.

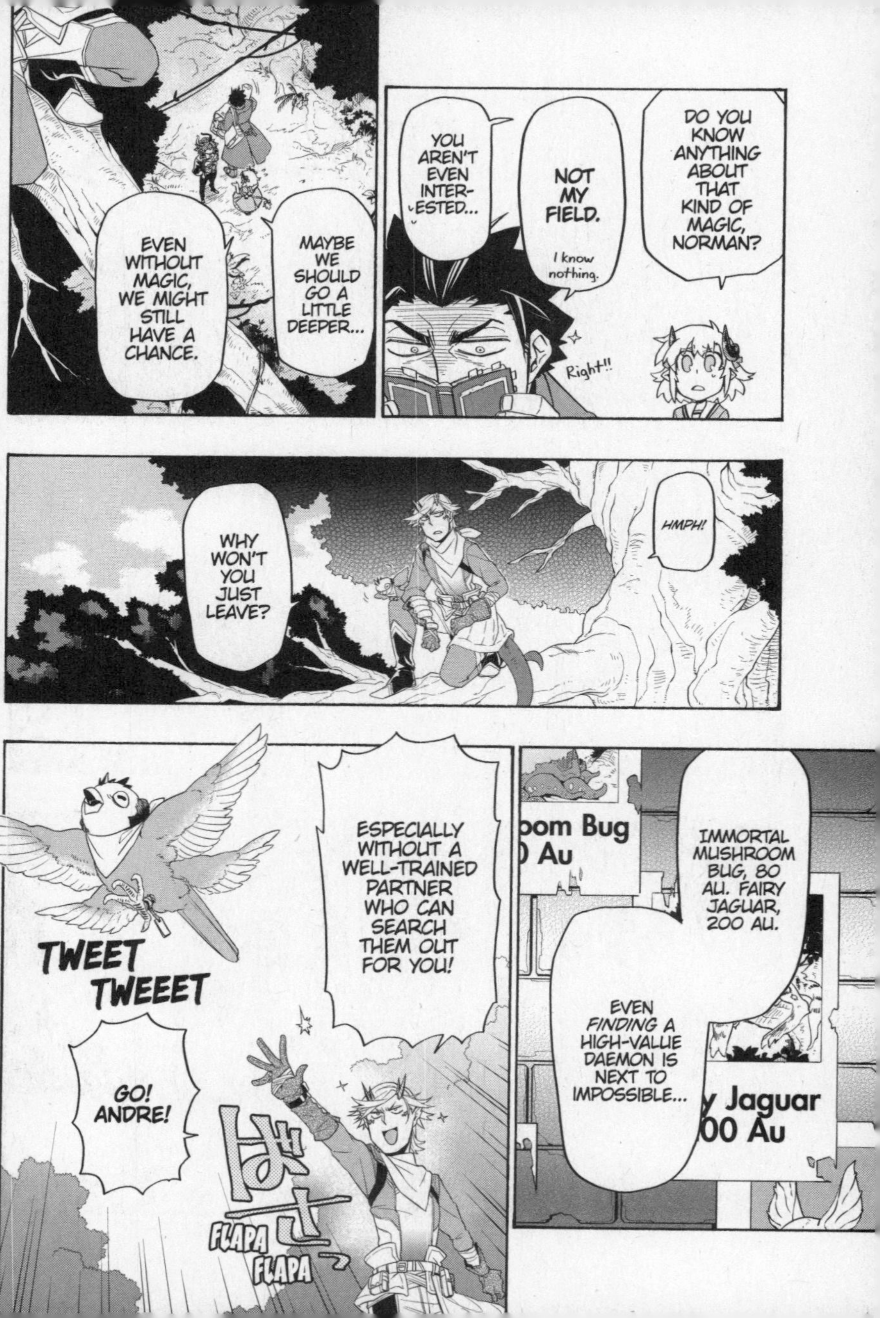
DO YOU KNOW ANYTHING ABOUT THAT KIND OF MAGIC, NORMAN?
NOT MY FIELD.
I know nothing.
YOU AREN'T EVEN INTER-ESTED...
Right!!
MAYBE WE SHOULD GO A LITTLE DEEPER...
EVEN WITHOUT MAGIC, WE MIGHT STILL HAVE A CHANCE.
HMPH!
WHY WON'T YOU JUST LEAVE?
oom Bug
0 Au
IMMORTAL MUSHROOM BUG, 80 AU. FAIRY JAGUAR, 200 AU.
EVEN FINDING A HIGH-VALUE DAEMON IS NEXT TO IMPOSSIBLE...
y Jaguar
00 Au
ESPECIALLY WITHOUT A WELL-TRAINED PARTNER WHO CAN SEARCH THEM OUT FOR YOU!
TWEET TWEEET
GO! ANDRE!
ばさっ
FLAPA FLAPA

YANK

Squawk!

FWIP

Tagged...

WHOOPS. THIS IS A FAMILIAR.

THAT WORKED BETTER THAN EXPECTED. MM?

?!

DA-DA-DA

DAN

THUD

Andre!

SORRY. HE JUST LOOKED REALLY EASY TO CATCH.

SNATCH

WHAT ARE YOU DOING TO MY PART-NER?!

DON'T YOU DARE TOUCH ANDRE AGAIN!!

Because he's not wild.

Eeeee...

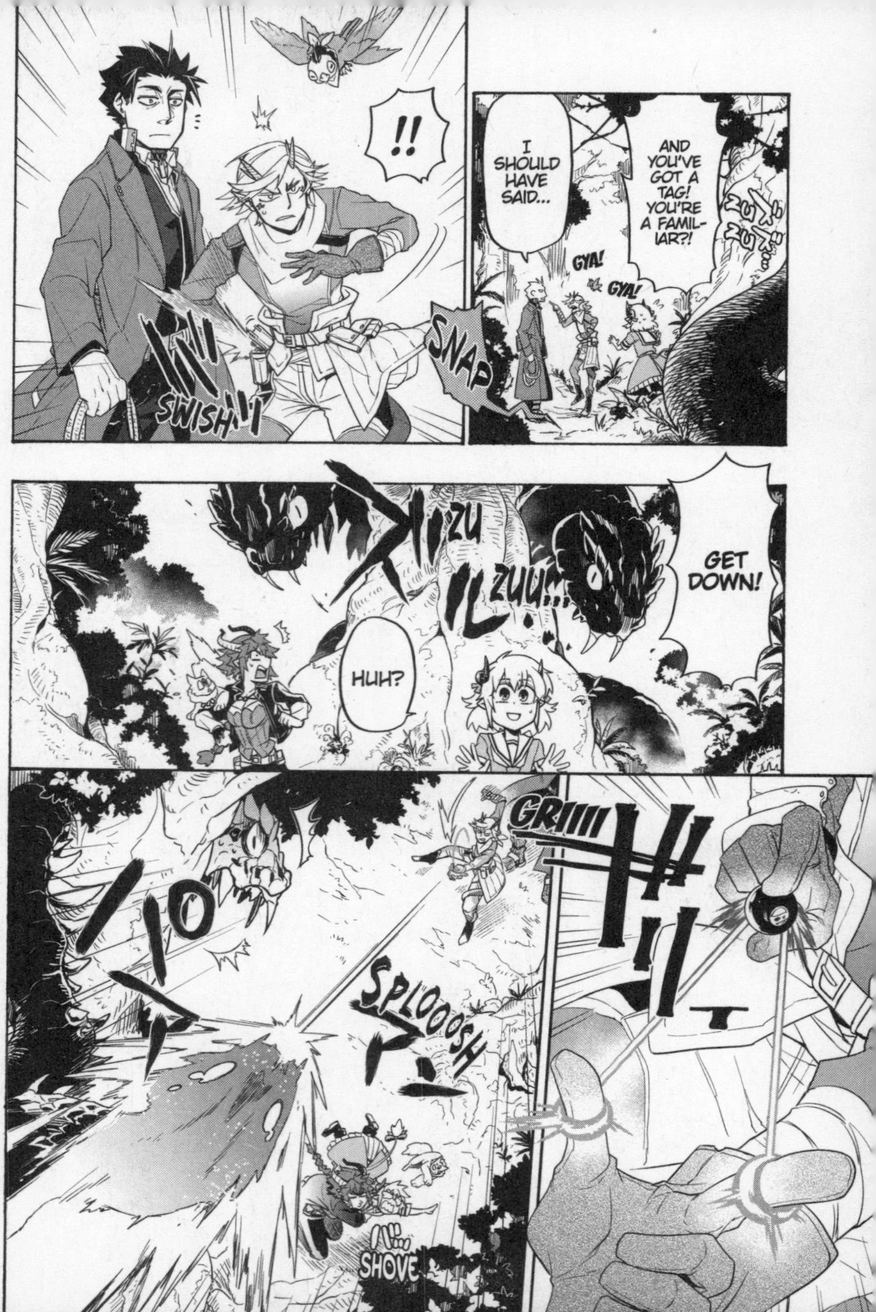
AND YOU'VE GOT A TAG! YOU'RE A FAMILIAR?!
I SHOULD HAVE SAID...
GYA!
GYA!
!!
SNAP
SWISH
GET DOWN!
ZU
ZUU...
HUH?
GRIIII
SPLOOOSH
SHOVE

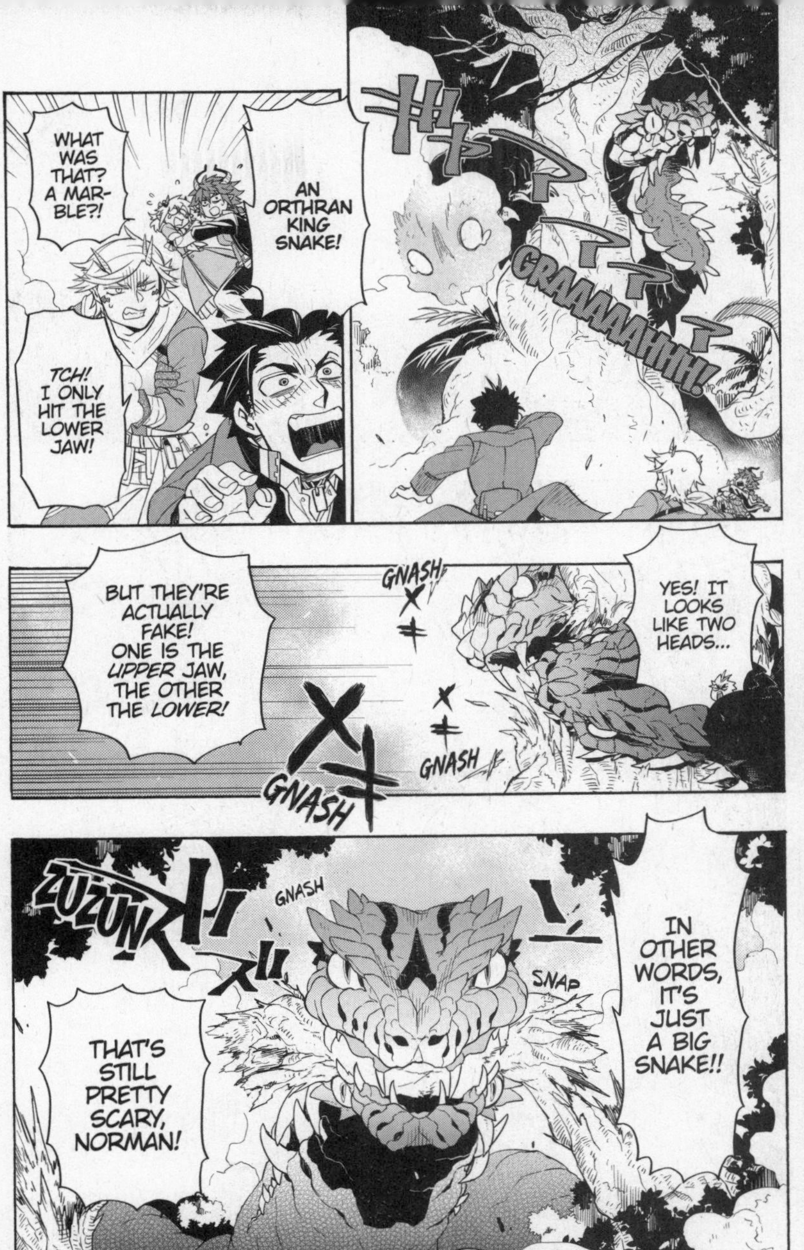
GRAAAAAAHHHH!
AN ORTHRAN KING SNAKE!
WHAT WAS THAT? A MARBLE?!
TCH! I ONLY HIT THE LOWER JAW!
YES! IT LOOKS LIKE TWO HEADS...
GNASH
GNASH
BUT THEY'RE ACTUALLY FAKE! ONE IS THE *UPPER JAW*, THE OTHER THE *LOWER*!
GNASH
IN OTHER WORDS, IT'S JUST A BIG SNAKE!!
SNAP
GNASH
ZUZUN
THAT'S STILL PRETTY SCARY, NORMAN!

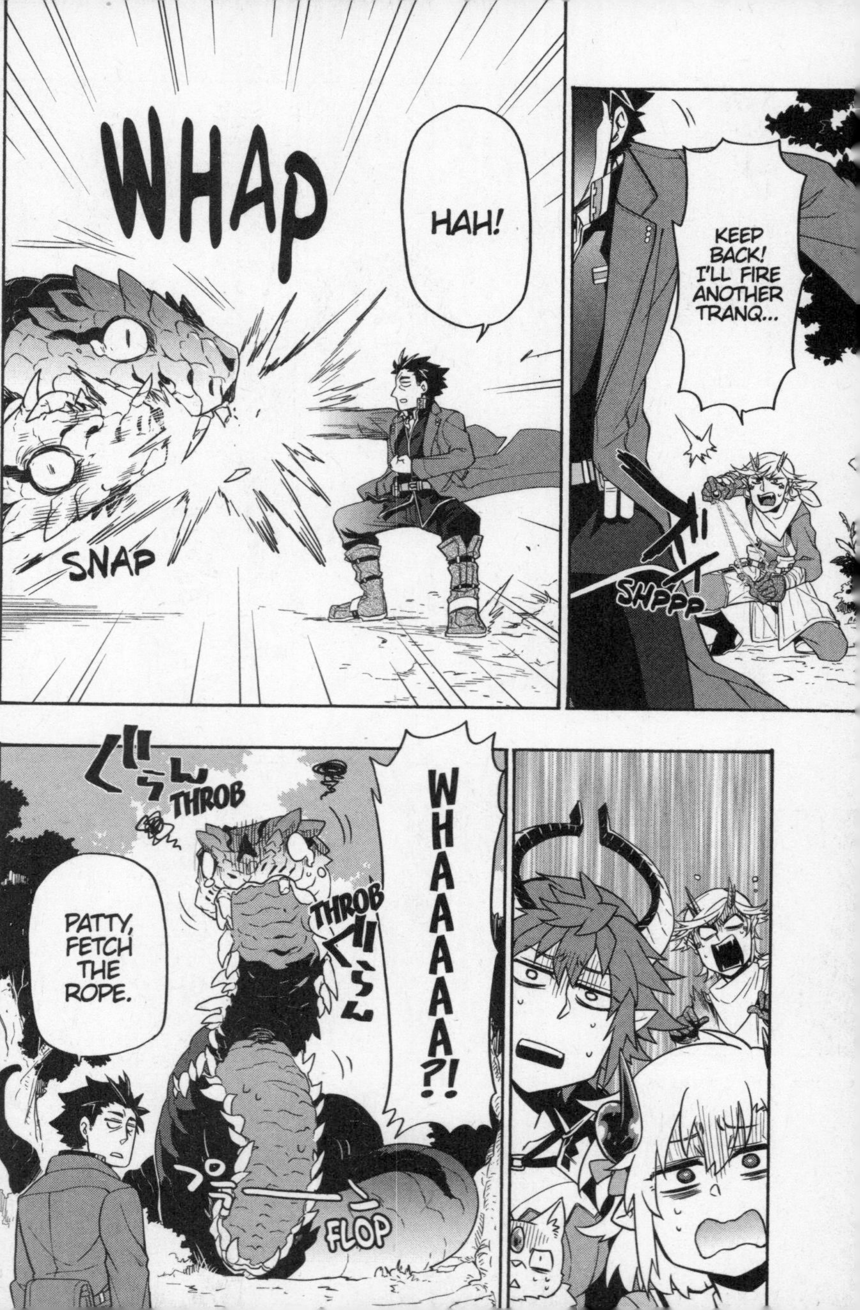
KEEP BACK! I'LL FIRE ANOTHER TRANQ...
SHPPP
WHAP
HAH!
SNAP
WHAAAAAAA?!
THROB
THROB
PATTY, FETCH THE ROPE.
FLOP

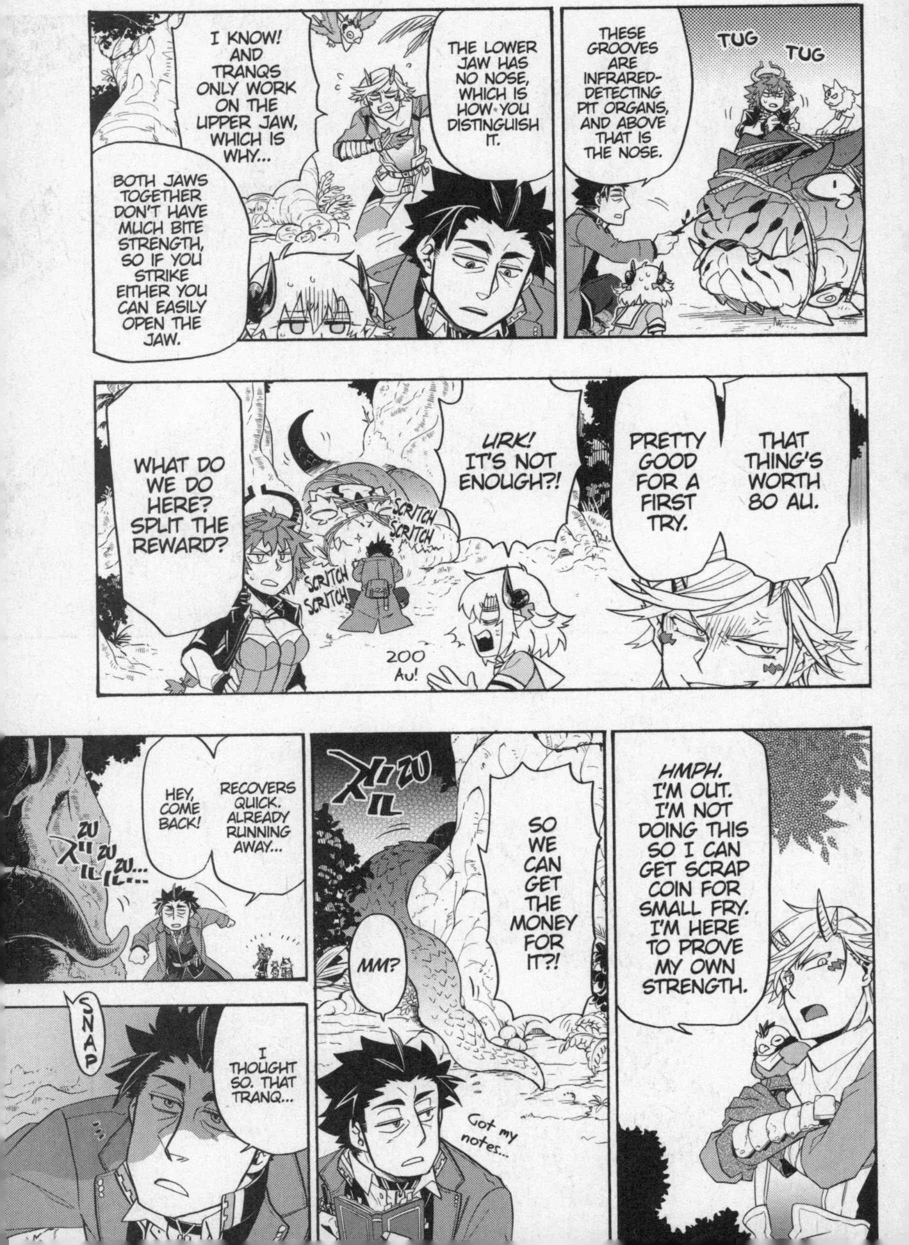
TUG
TUG
THESE GROOVES ARE INFRARED-DETECTING PIT ORGANS, AND ABOVE THAT IS THE NOSE.
THE LOWER JAW HAS NO NOSE, WHICH IS HOW YOU DISTINGUISH IT.
I KNOW! AND TRANQS ONLY WORK ON THE UPPER JAW, WHICH IS WHY...
BOTH JAWS TOGETHER DON'T HAVE MUCH BITE STRENGTH, SO IF YOU STRIKE EITHER YOU CAN EASILY OPEN THE JAW.
THAT THING'S WORTH 80 AU.
PRETTY GOOD FOR A FIRST TRY.
URK! IT'S NOT ENOUGH?!
200 Au!
SCRITCH SCRITCH
SCRITCH SCRITCH
WHAT DO WE DO HERE? SPLIT THE REWARD?
HMPH. I'M OUT. I'M NOT DOING THIS SO I CAN GET SCRAP COIN FOR SMALL FRY. I'M HERE TO PROVE MY OWN STRENGTH.
ZU ZU
SO WE CAN GET THE MONEY FOR IT?!
MM?
Got my notes...
RECOVERS QUICK. ALREADY RUNNING AWAY...
HEY, COME BACK!
ZU ZU ZU...
SNAP
I THOUGHT SO. THAT TRANQ...

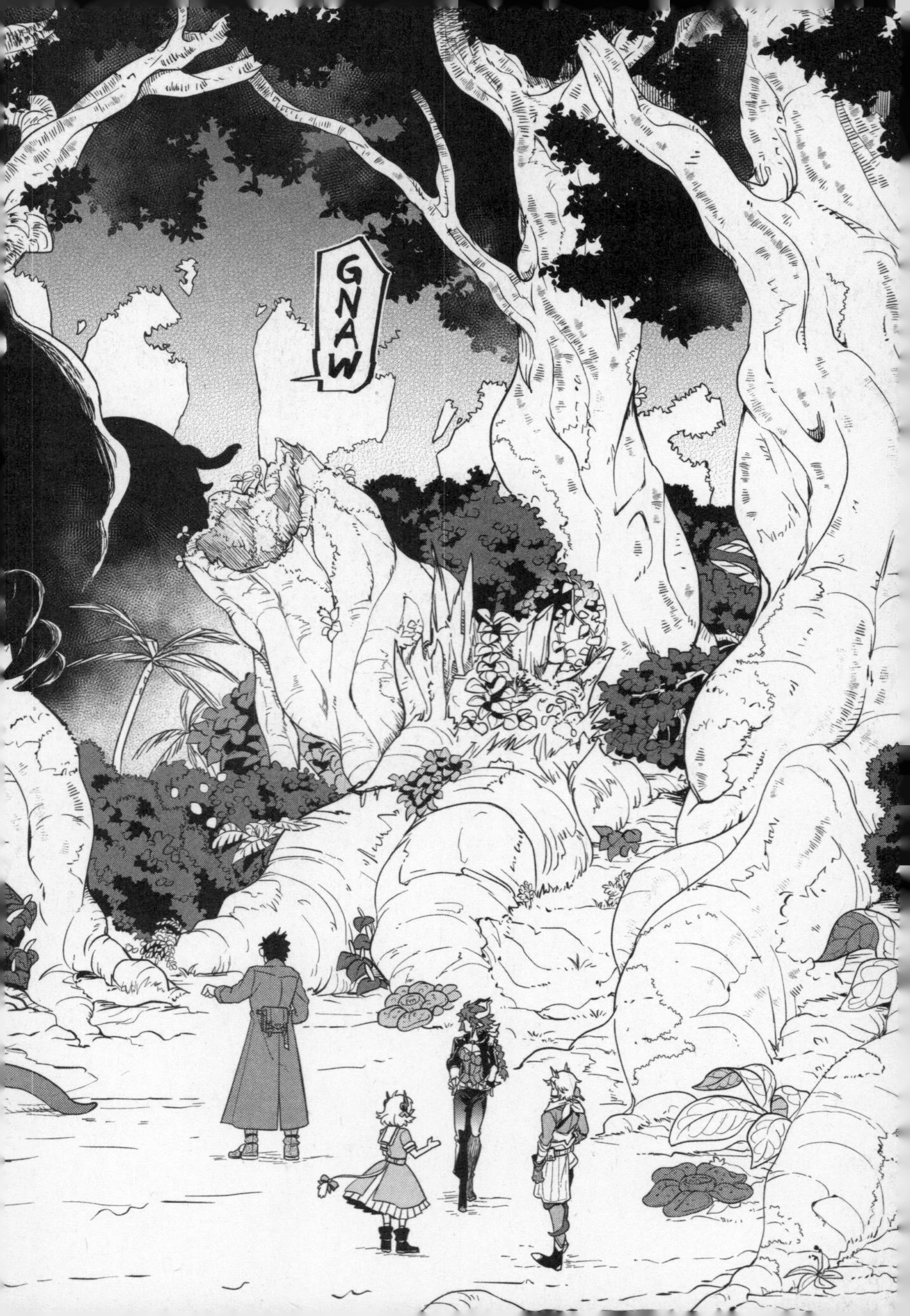
GNAW

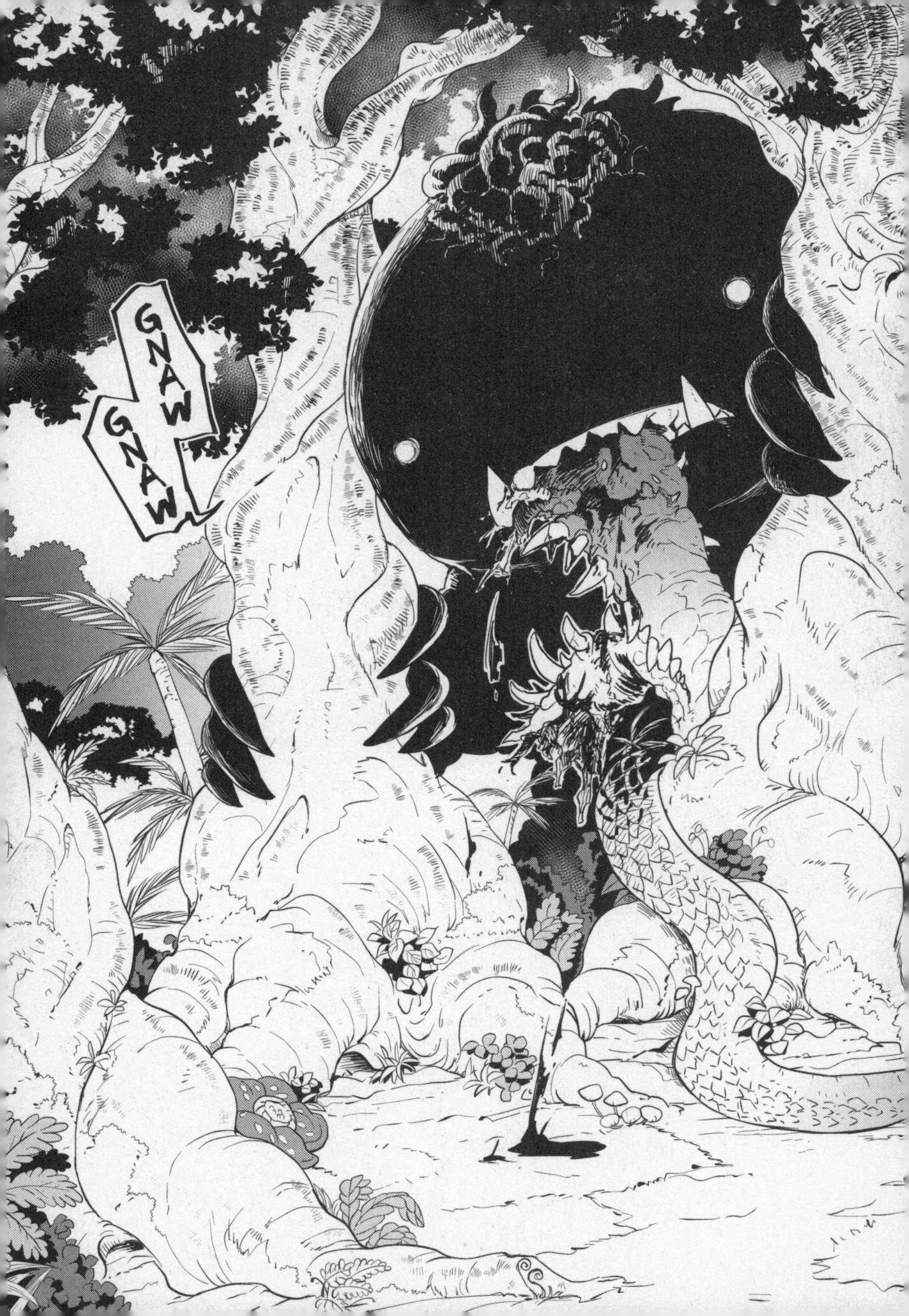
GNAW GNAW

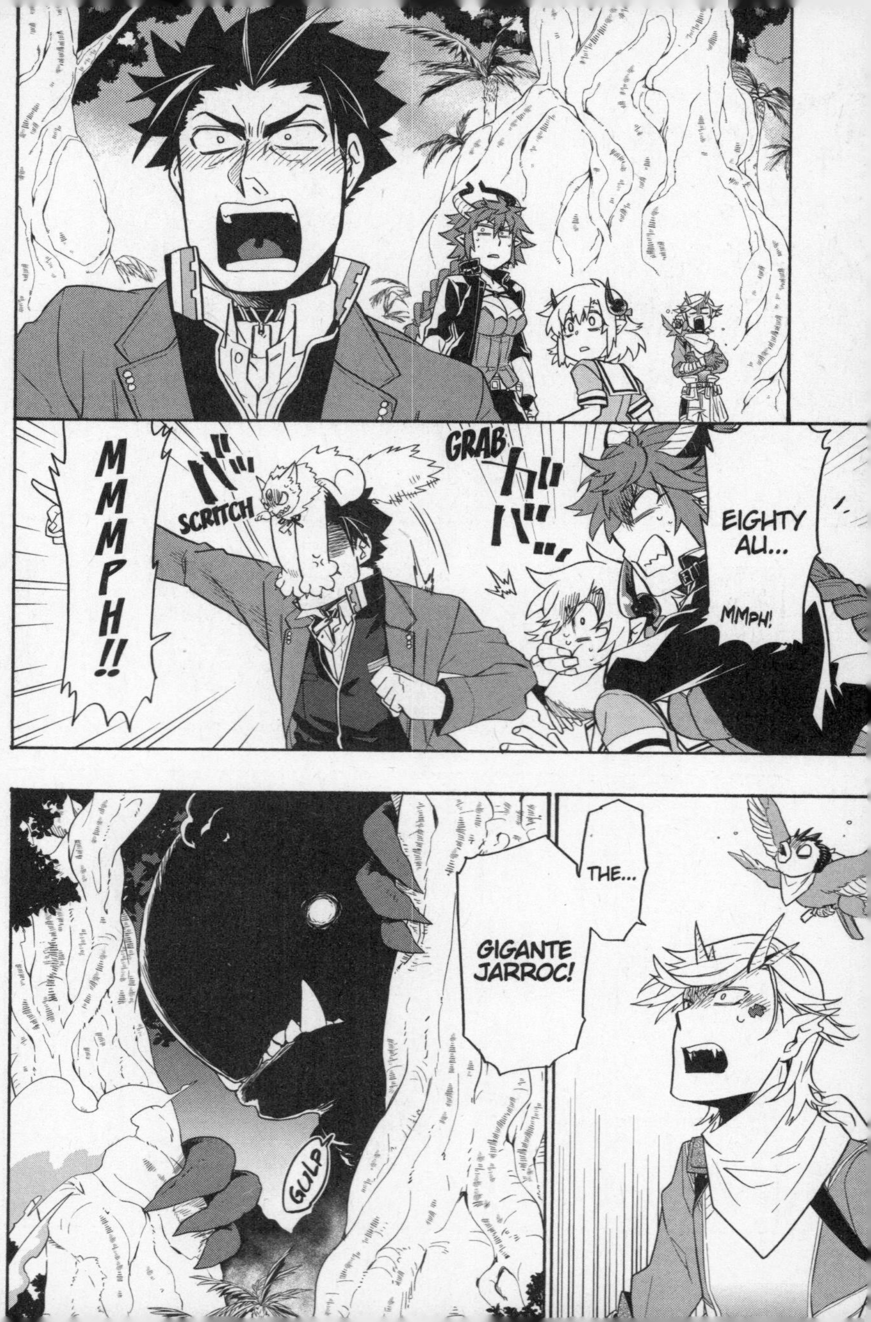
EIGHTY AU...
MMPH!
GRAB
SCRITCH
MMMPH!!
THE...
GIGANTE JARROC!
GULP

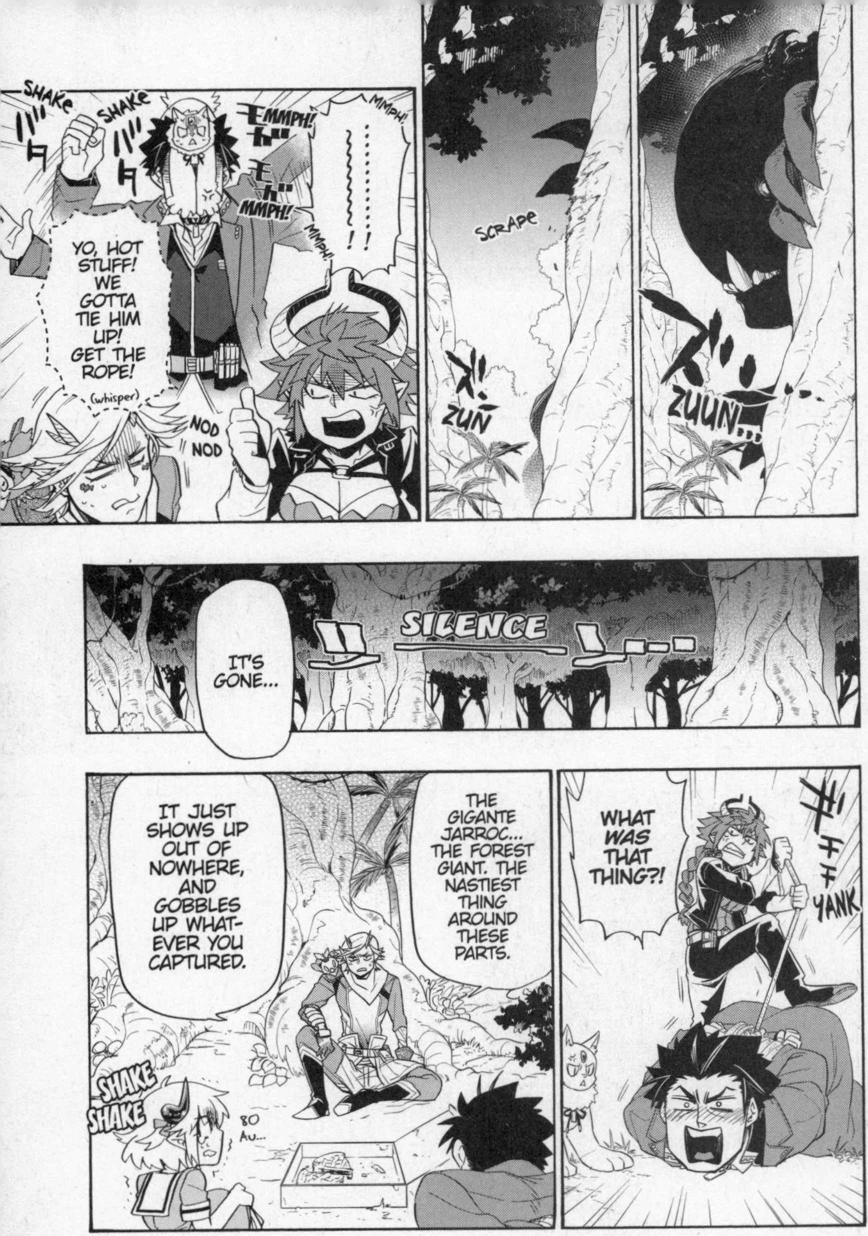
ZUUN...
SCRAPE
ZUN
SHAKE
SHAKE
EMMPH!
MMPH!
MMPH!
MMPH!
............!!
YO, HOT STUFF! WE GOTTA TIE HIM UP! GET THE ROPE!
(whisper)
NOD NOD
SILENCE
IT'S GONE...
WHAT WAS THAT THING?!
YANK
THE GIGANTE JARROC... THE FOREST GIANT. THE NASTIEST THING AROUND THESE PARTS.
IT JUST SHOWS UP OUT OF NOWHERE, AND GOBBLES UP WHATEVER YOU CAPTURED.
SHAKE SHAKE
80 AU...

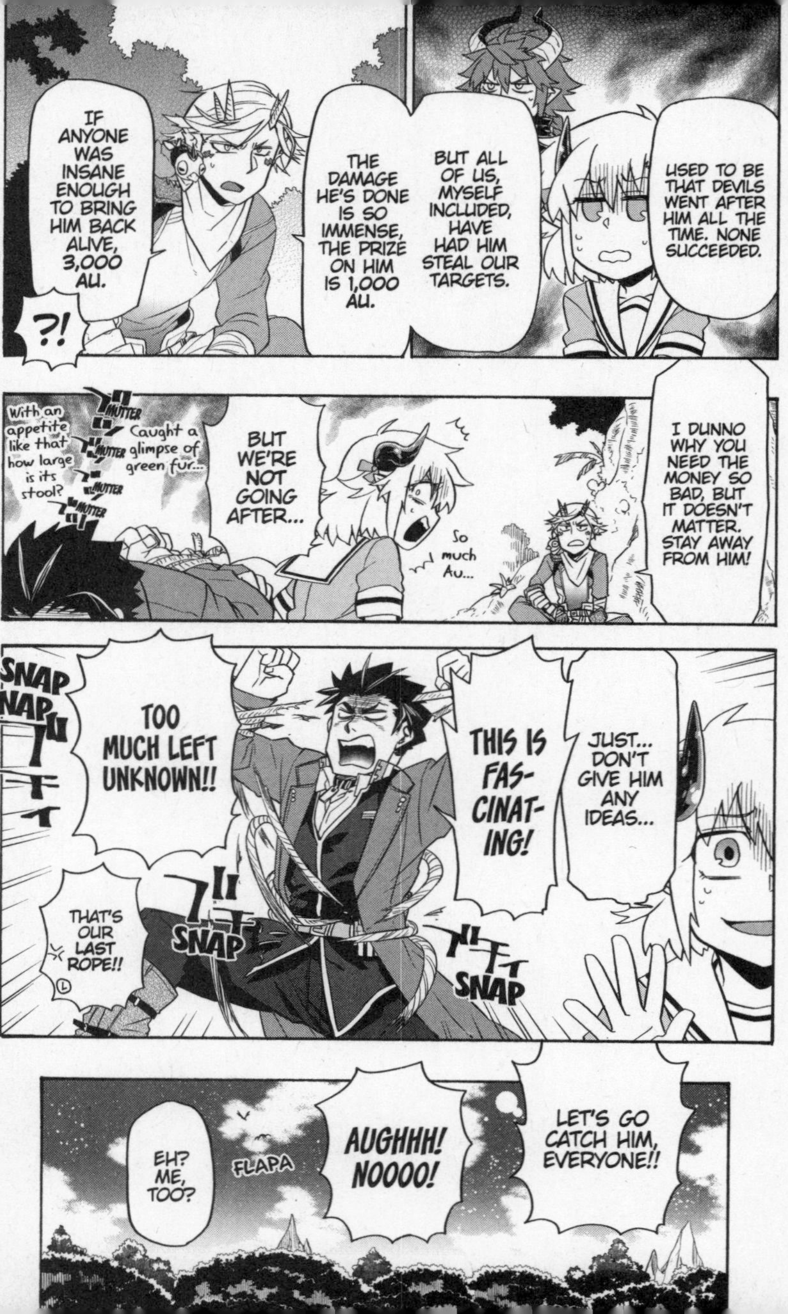
USED TO BE THAT DEVILS WENT AFTER HIM ALL THE TIME. NONE SUCCEEDED.
BUT ALL OF US, MYSELF INCLUDED, HAVE HAD HIM STEAL OUR TARGETS.
THE DAMAGE HE'S DONE IS SO IMMENSE, THE PRIZE ON HIM IS 1,000 AU.
IF ANYONE WAS INSANE ENOUGH TO BRING HIM BACK ALIVE, 3,000 AU.
?!
I DUNNO WHY YOU NEED THE MONEY SO BAD, BUT IT DOESN'T MATTER. STAY AWAY FROM HIM!
So much Au...
BUT WE'RE NOT GOING AFTER...
Caught a glimpse of green fur...
With an appetite like that how large is its stool?
MUTTER
MUTTER
MUTTER
MUTTER
JUST... DON'T GIVE HIM ANY IDEAS...
THIS IS FAS-CINAT-ING!
TOO MUCH LEFT UNKNOWN!!
SNAP
SNAP
SNAP
THAT'S OUR LAST ROPE!!
SNAP
LET'S GO CATCH HIM, EVERYONE!!
AUGHHH! NOOOO!
FLAPA
EH? ME, TOO?

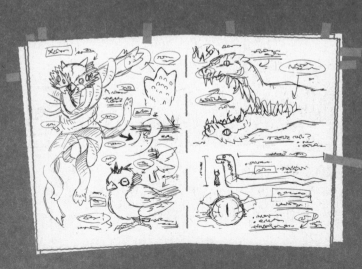

Sorry For My Familiar

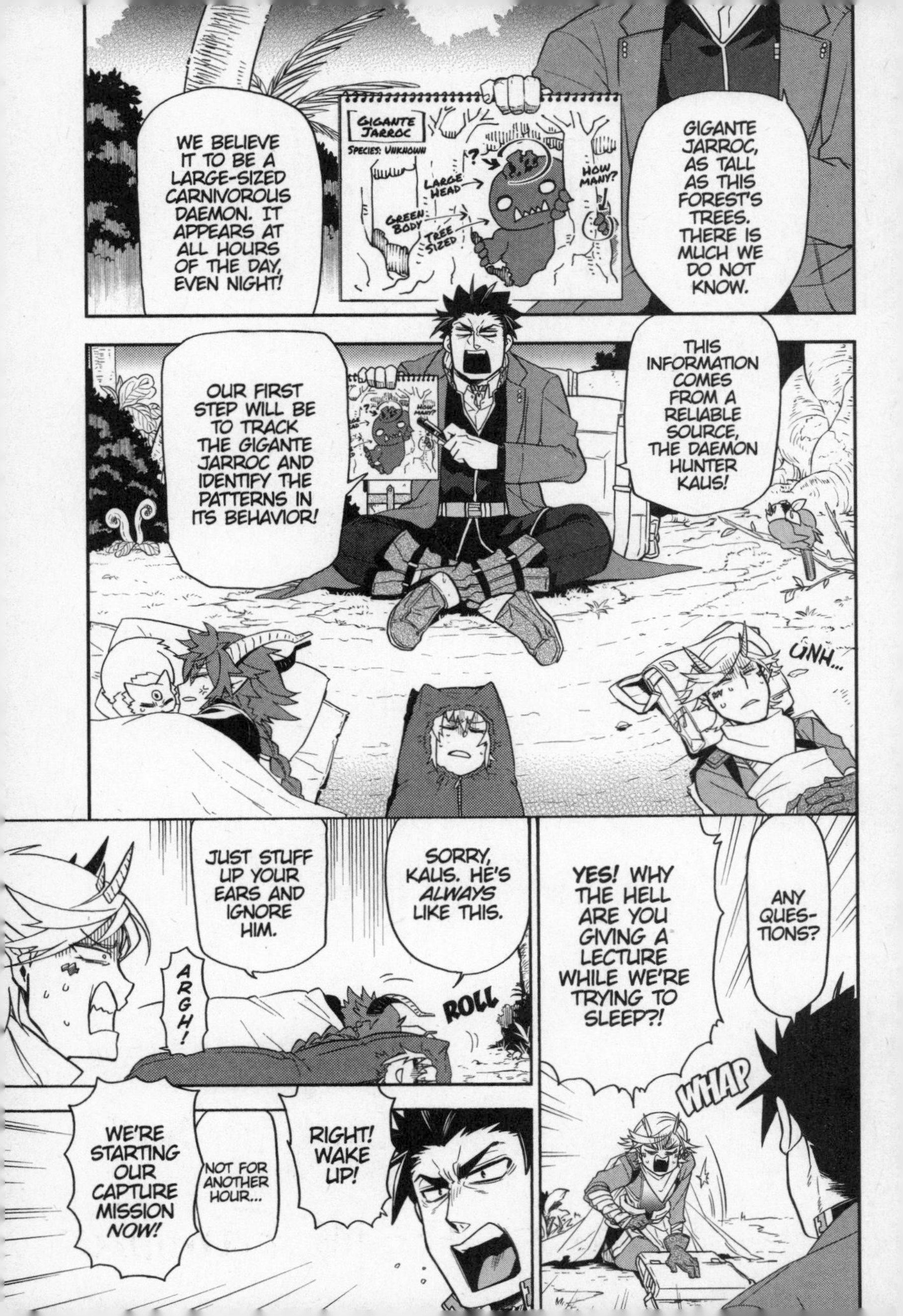
GIGANTE JARROC, AS TALL AS THIS FOREST'S TREES. THERE IS MUCH WE DO NOT KNOW.
GIGANTE JARROC
SPECIES: UNKNOWN
?
HOW MANY?
LARGE HEAD
GREEN BODY
TREE SIZED
WE BELIEVE IT TO BE A LARGE-SIZED CARNIVOROUS DAEMON. IT APPEARS AT ALL HOURS OF THE DAY, EVEN NIGHT!
THIS INFORMATION COMES FROM A RELIABLE SOURCE, THE DAEMON HUNTER KAUS!
OUR FIRST STEP WILL BE TO TRACK THE GIGANTE JARROC AND IDENTIFY THE PATTERNS IN ITS BEHAVIOR!
UNH...
ANY QUES-TIONS?
YES! WHY THE HELL ARE YOU GIVING A LECTURE WHILE WE'RE TRYING TO SLEEP?!
WHAP
SORRY, KAUS. HE'S *ALWAYS* LIKE THIS.
JUST STUFF UP YOUR EARS AND IGNORE HIM.
ROLL
ARGH!
RIGHT! WAKE UP!
NOT FOR ANOTHER HOUR...
WE'RE STARTING OUR CAPTURE MISSION *NOW!*

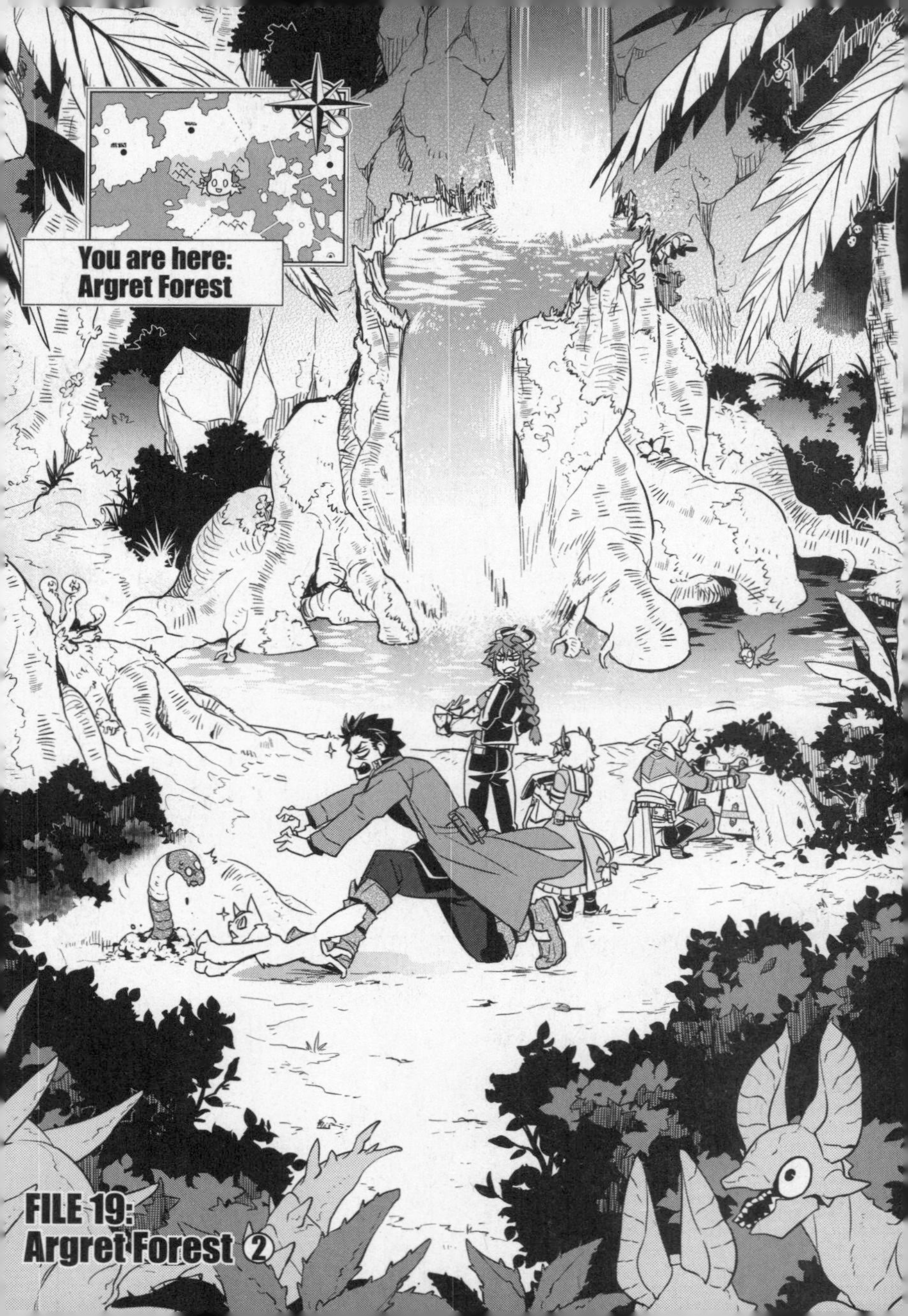
You are here:
Argret Forest
FILE 19:
Argret Forest ②

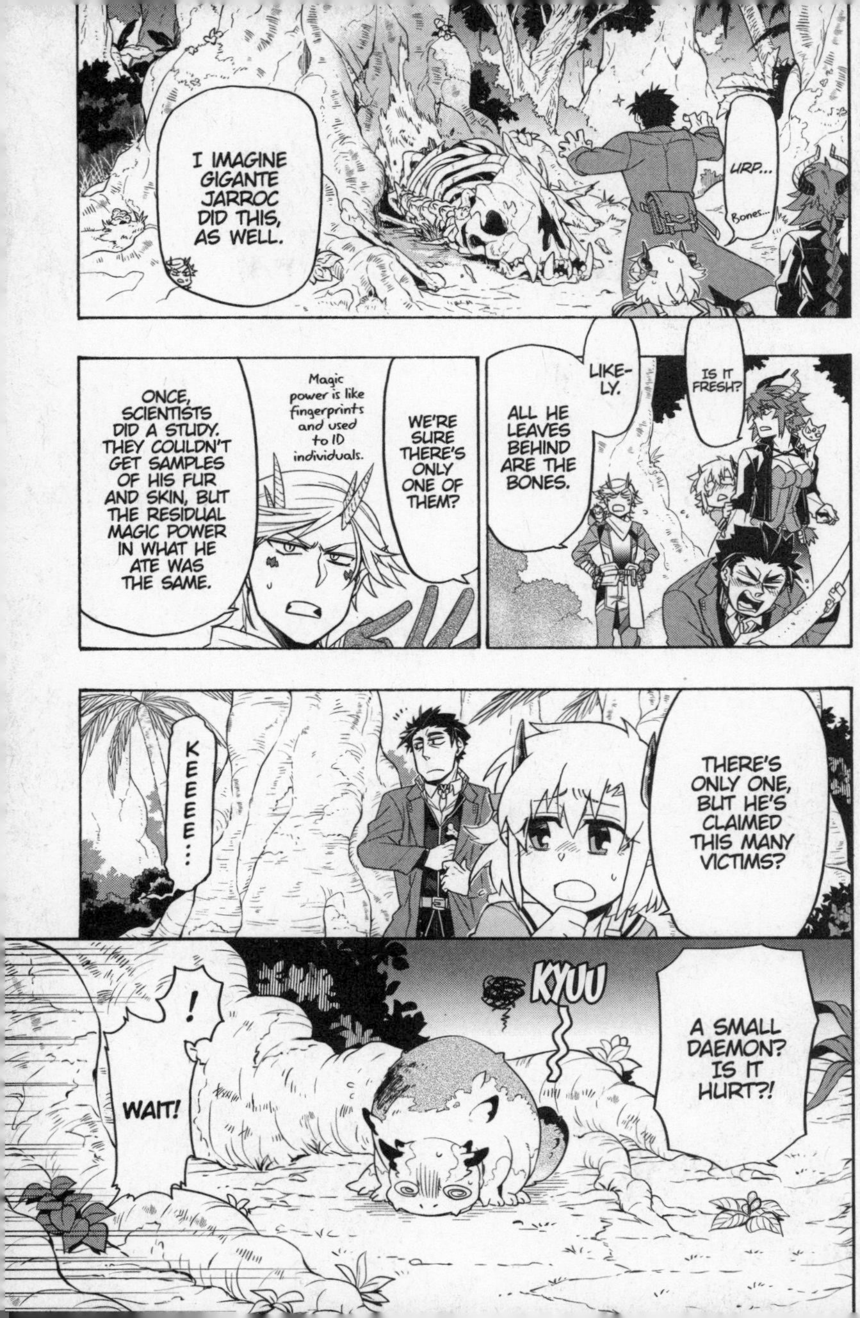
URP...
Bones...
I IMAGINE GIGANTE JARROC DID THIS, AS WELL.
IS IT FRESH?
LIKE-LY.
ALL HE LEAVES BEHIND ARE THE BONES.
WE'RE SURE THERE'S ONLY ONE OF THEM?
Magic power is like fingerprints and used to ID individuals.
ONCE, SCIENTISTS DID A STUDY. THEY COULDN'T GET SAMPLES OF HIS FUR AND SKIN, BUT THE RESIDUAL MAGIC POWER IN WHAT HE ATE WAS THE SAME.
THERE'S ONLY ONE, BUT HE'S CLAIMED THIS MANY VICTIMS?
KEEEE...
A SMALL DAEMON? IS IT HURT?!
KYUU
!
WAIT!

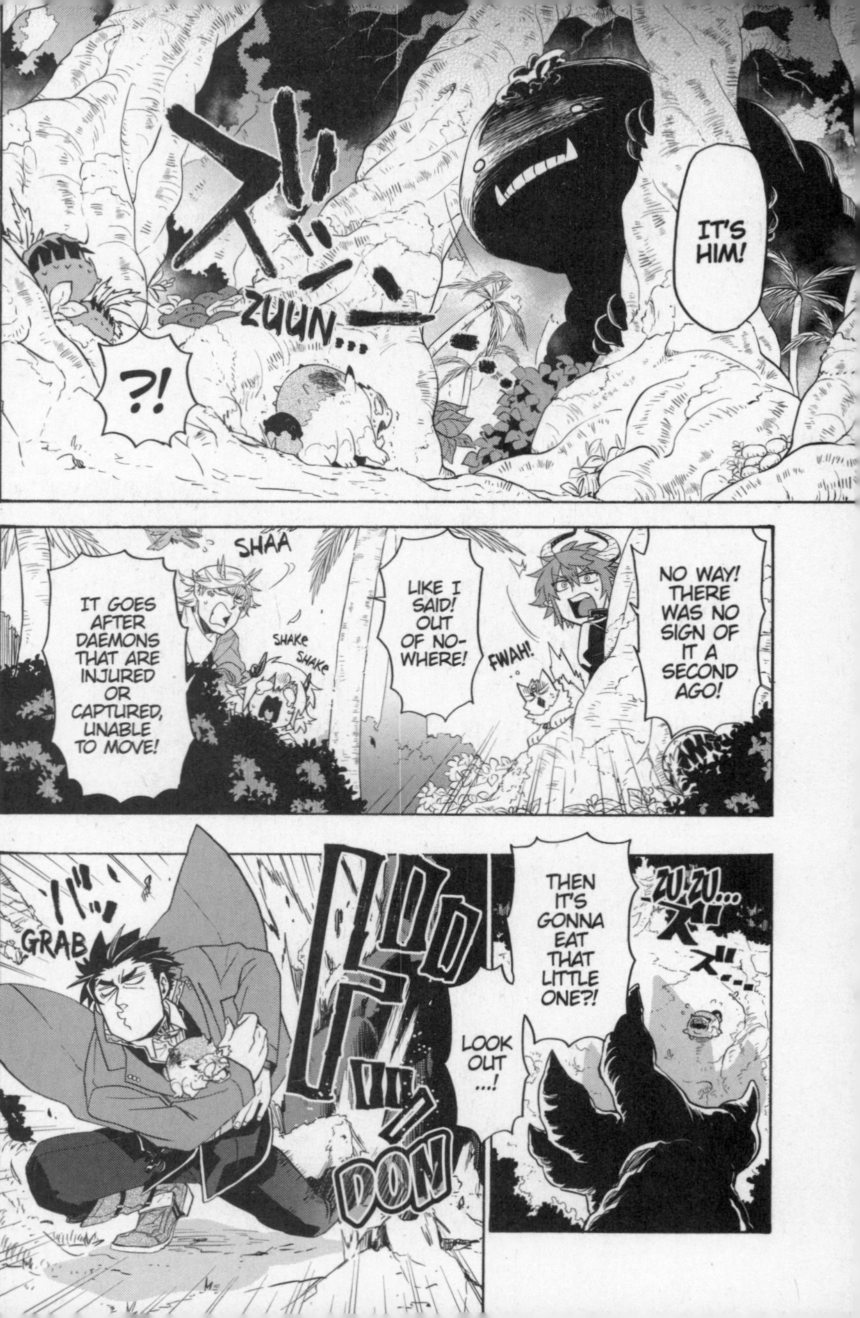
IT'S HIM!
ZUUN...
?!
NO WAY! THERE WAS NO SIGN OF IT A SECOND AGO!
FWAH!
LIKE I SAID! OUT OF NO-WHERE!
SHAKE SHAKE
SHAA
IT GOES AFTER DAEMONS THAT ARE INJURED OR CAPTURED, UNABLE TO MOVE!
ZU ZU...
THEN IT'S GONNA EAT THAT LITTLE ONE?!
LOOK OUT ...!
DON
GRAB

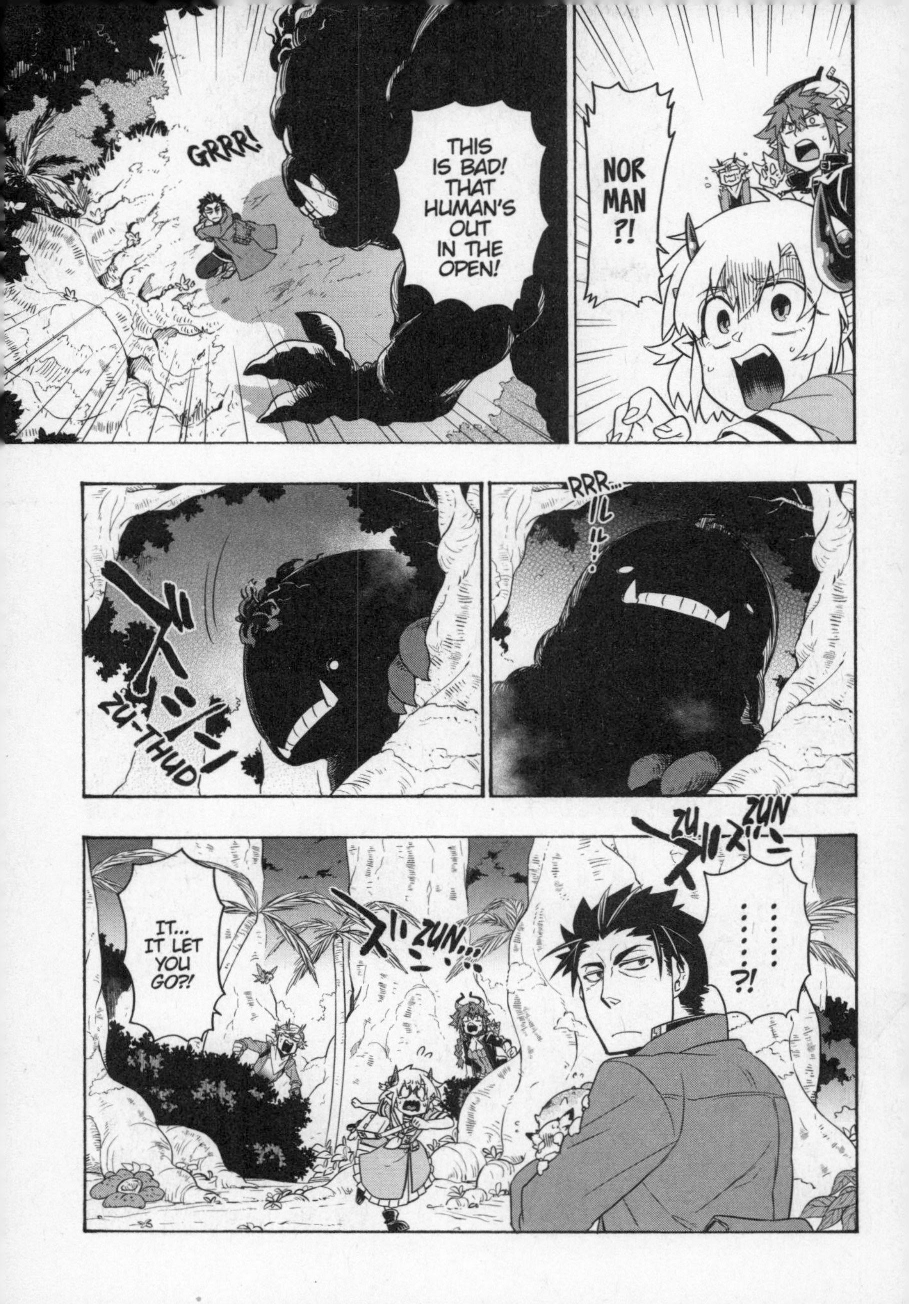
NOR MAN ?!
THIS IS BAD! THAT HUMAN'S OUT IN THE OPEN!
GRRR!
RRR...
ZU-THUD
ZU ZUN
......?!
ZUN...
IT... IT LET YOU GO?!

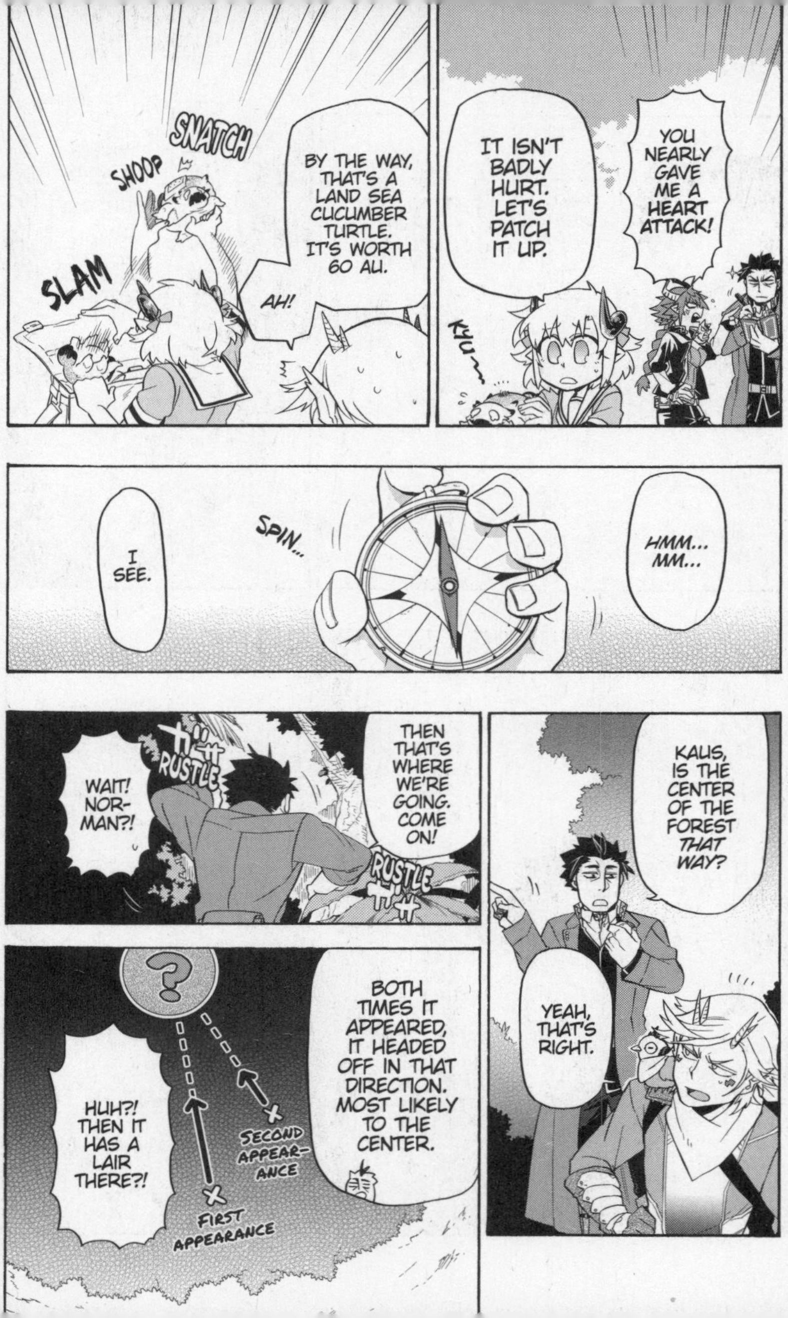
YOU NEARLY GAVE ME A HEART ATTACK!
IT ISN'T BADLY HURT. LET'S PATCH IT UP.
KYU~~
BY THE WAY, THAT'S A LAND SEA CUCUMBER TURTLE. IT'S WORTH 60 AU.
SNATCH
SHOOP
AH!
SLAM
HMM... MM...
SPIN...
I SEE.
KAUS, IS THE CENTER OF THE FOREST THAT WAY?
YEAH, THAT'S RIGHT.
THEN THAT'S WHERE WE'RE GOING. COME ON!
RUSTLE
WAIT! NOR-MAN?!
RUSTLE
BOTH TIMES IT APPEARED, IT HEADED OFF IN THAT DIRECTION. MOST LIKELY TO THE CENTER.
?
SECOND APPEARANCE
FIRST APPEARANCE
HUH?! THEN IT HAS A LAIR THERE?!

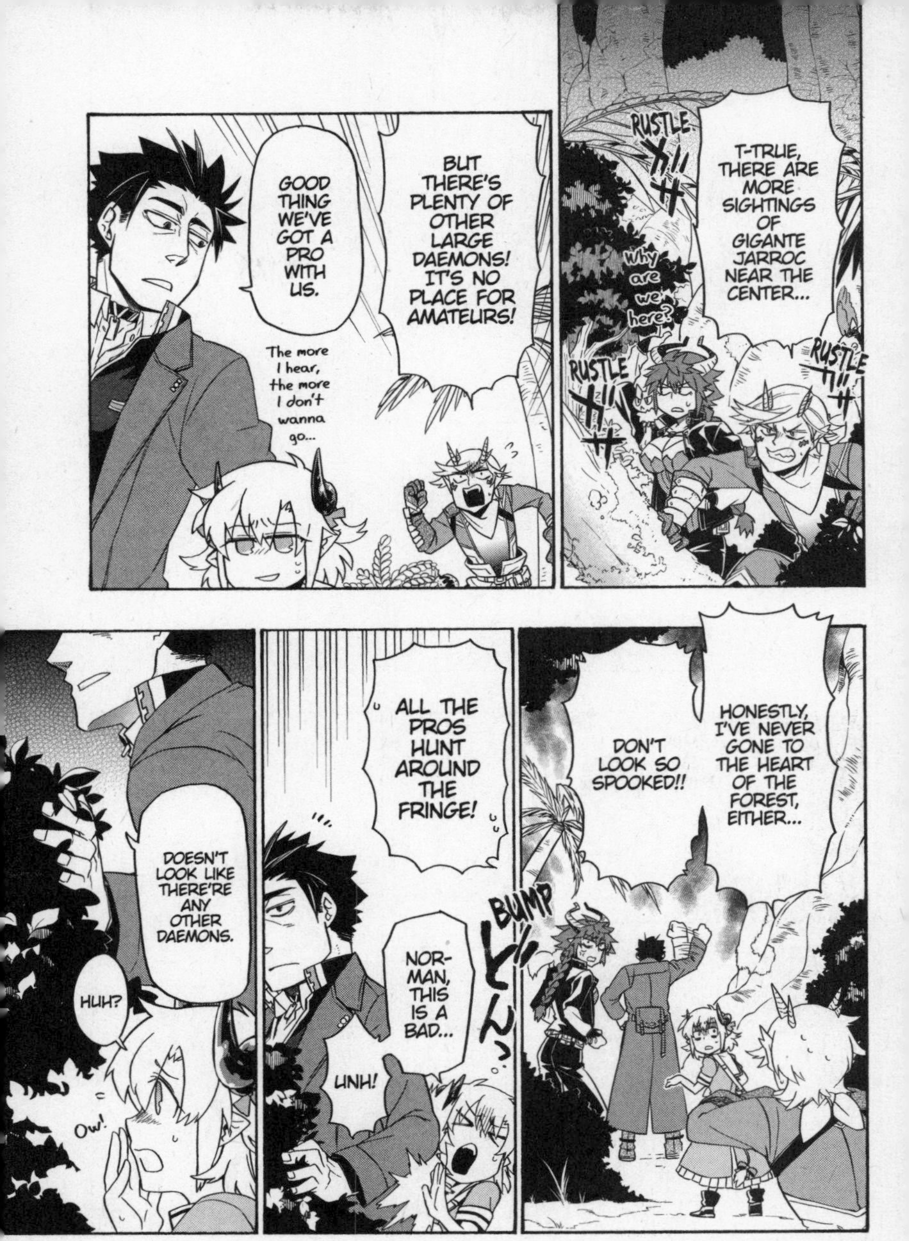
RUSTLE
T-TRUE, THERE ARE MORE SIGHTINGS OF GIGANTE JARROC NEAR THE CENTER...
Why are we here?
RUSTLE
RUSTLE
BUT THERE'S PLENTY OF OTHER LARGE DAEMONS! IT'S NO PLACE FOR AMATEURS!
GOOD THING WE'VE GOT A PRO WITH US.
The more I hear, the more I don't wanna go...
HONESTLY, I'VE NEVER GONE TO THE HEART OF THE FOREST, EITHER...
DON'T LOOK SO SPOOKED!!
BUMP
ALL THE PROS HUNT AROUND THE FRINGE!
NOR-MAN, THIS IS A BAD...
UNH!
DOESN'T LOOK LIKE THERE'RE ANY OTHER DAEMONS.
HUH?
Ow!

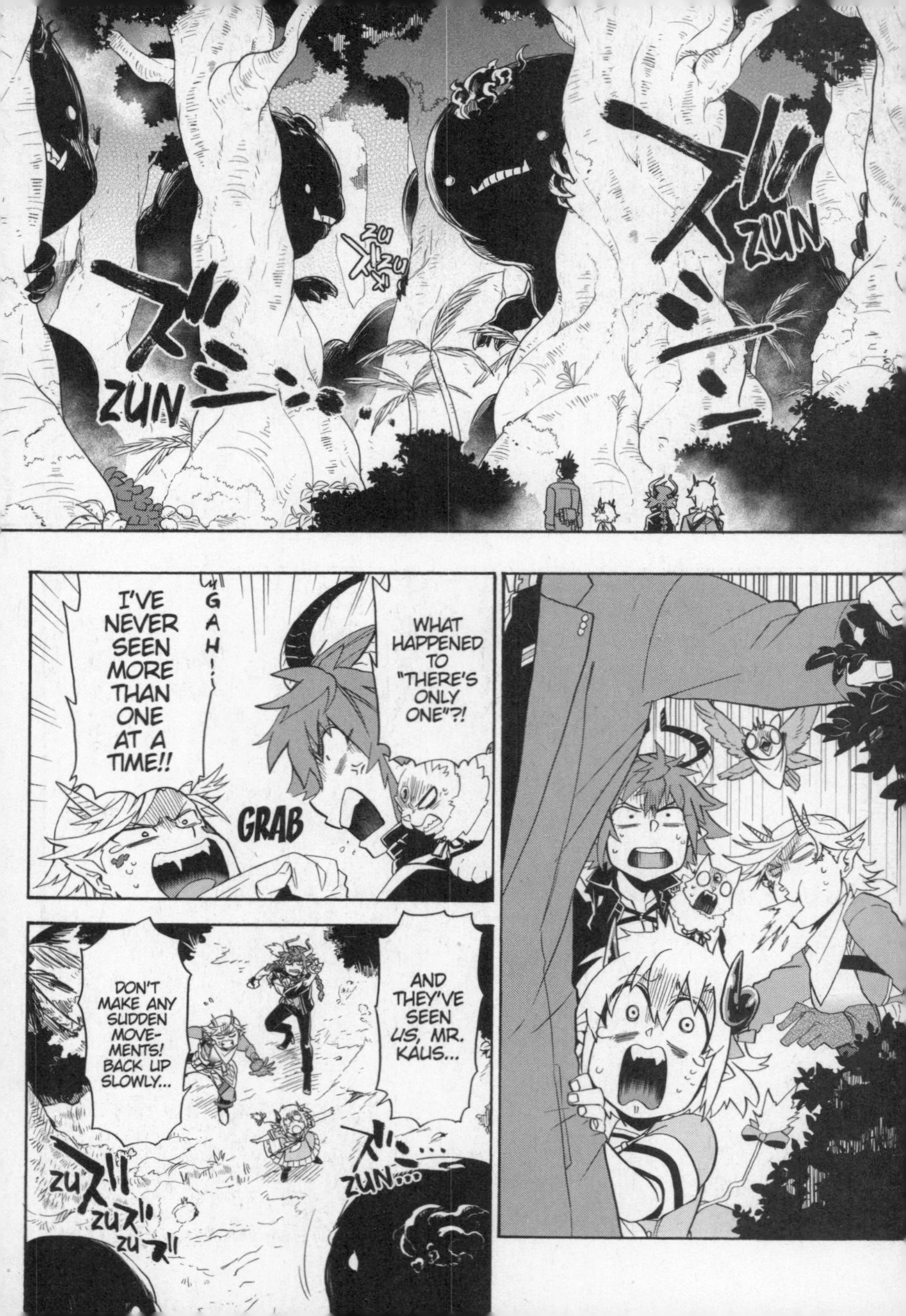
ZUN
ZU ZU
ZUN
WHAT HAPPENED TO "THERE'S ONLY ONE"?!
GAH!!
GRAB
I'VE NEVER SEEN MORE THAN ONE AT A TIME!!
AND THEY'VE SEEN US, MR. KAUS...
ZUN...
DON'T MAKE ANY SUDDEN MOVE-MENTS! BACK UP SLOWLY...
ZU ZU ZU

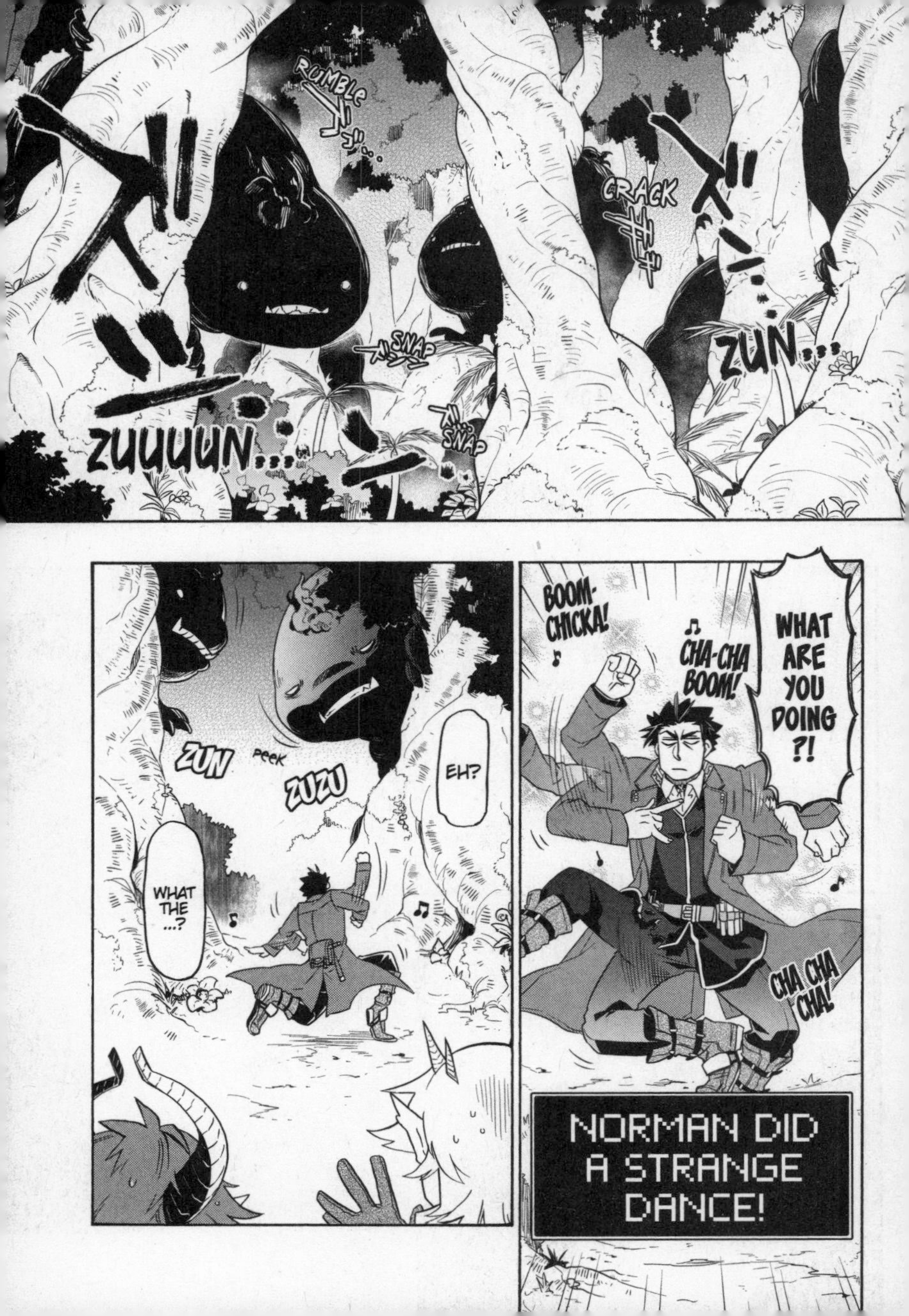
CRACK
ZUN...
RUMBLE
SNAP
SNAP
ZUUUUN...
WHAT ARE YOU DOING?!
CHA-CHA BOOM!
BOOM-CHICKA!
CHA CHA CHA!
NORMAN DID A STRANGE DANCE!
EH?
ZUZU
peek
ZUN
WHAT THE ...?

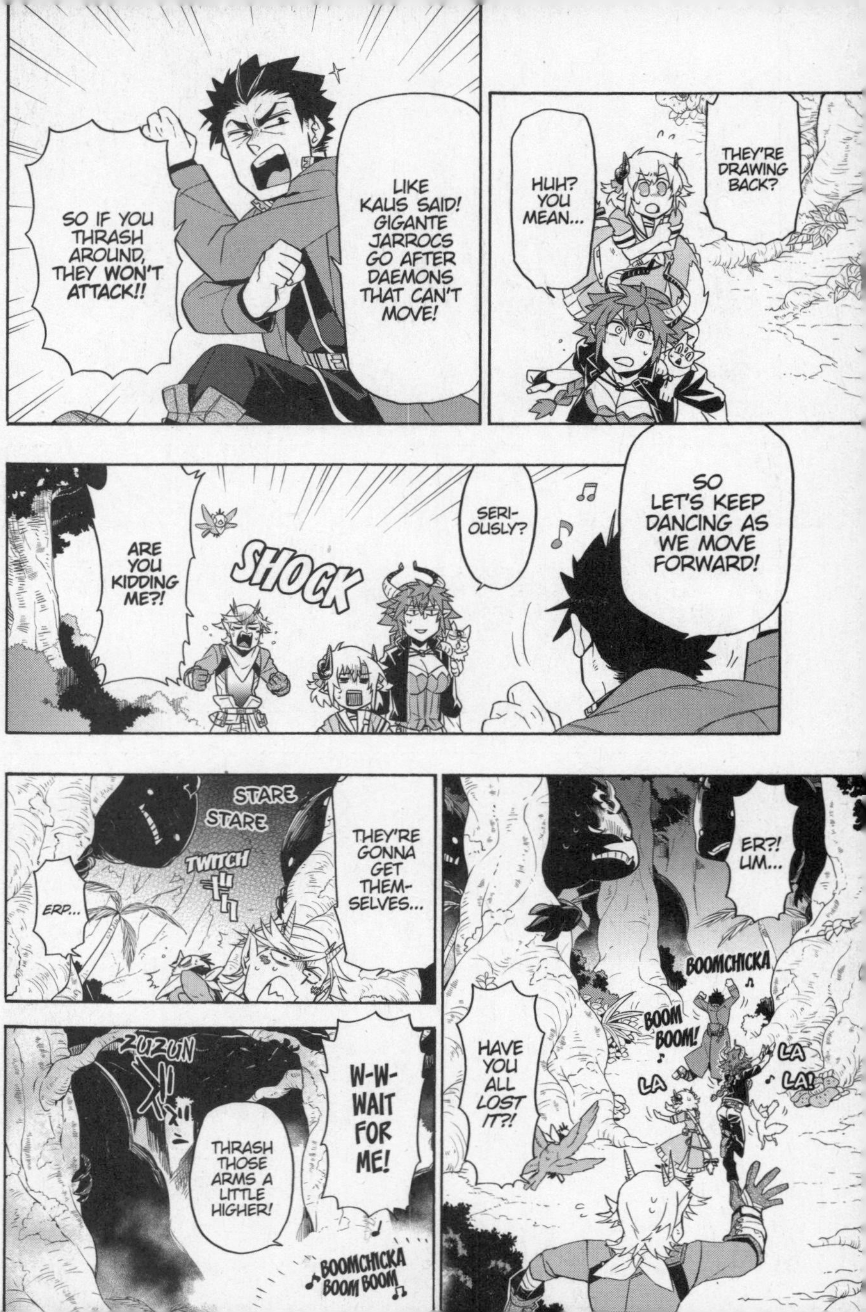
THEY'RE DRAWING BACK?
HUH? YOU MEAN...
LIKE KAUS SAID! GIGANTE JARROCS GO AFTER DAEMONS THAT CAN'T MOVE!
SO IF YOU THRASH AROUND, THEY WON'T ATTACK!!
SO LET'S KEEP DANCING AS WE MOVE FORWARD!
SERI-OUSLY?
SHOCK
ARE YOU KIDDING ME?!
ER?! UM...
BOOMCHICKA
BOOM BOOM!
LA LA LA!
HAVE YOU ALL LOST IT?!
STARE
STARE
THEY'RE GONNA GET THEM-SELVES...
TWITCH
ERP...
W-W-WAIT FOR ME!
THRASH THOSE ARMS A LITTLE HIGHER!
ZUZUN
BOOMCHICKA BOOM BOOM

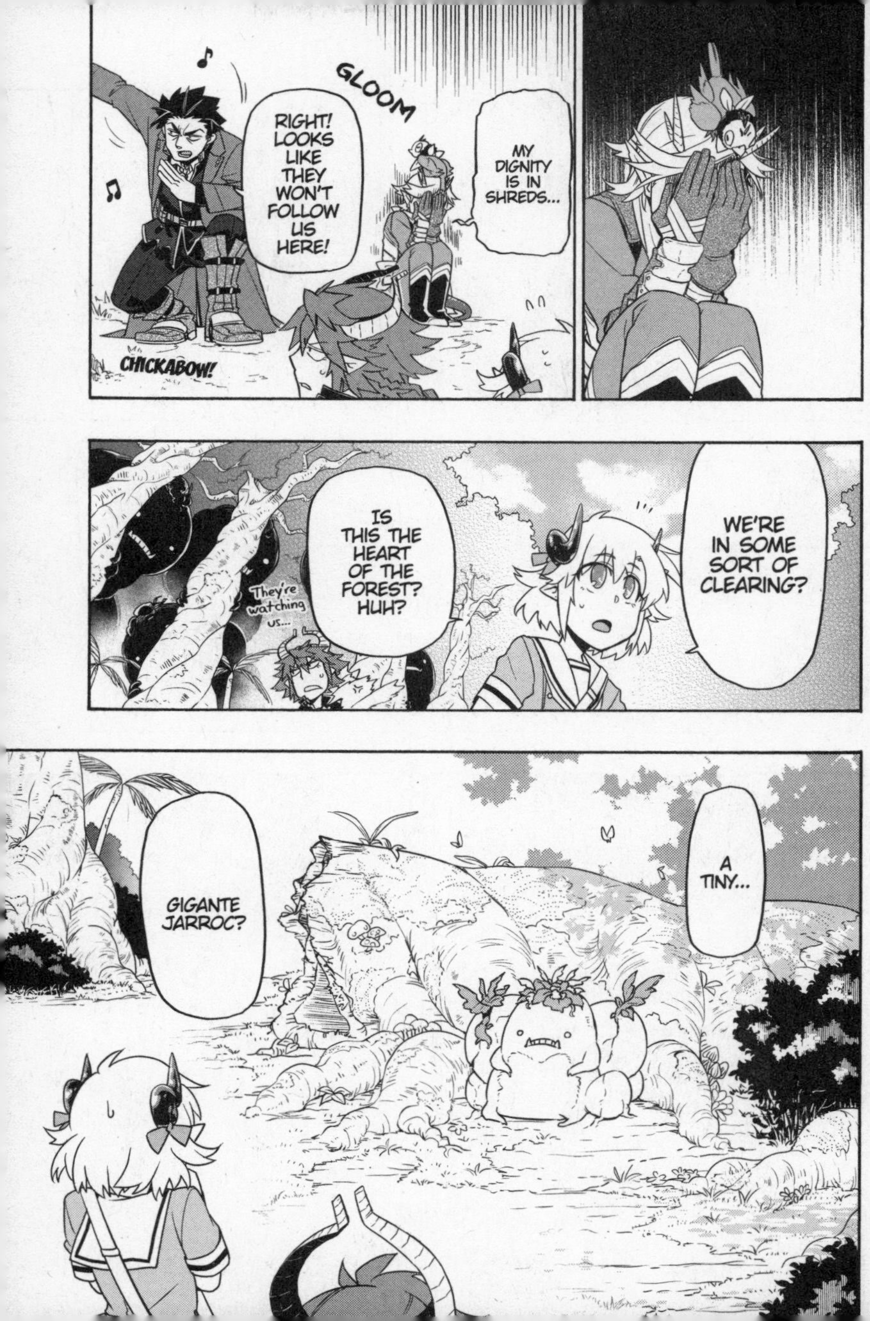
MY DIGNITY IS IN SHREDS...
GLOOM
RIGHT! LOOKS LIKE THEY WON'T FOLLOW US HERE!
CHICKABOW!
WE'RE IN SOME SORT OF CLEARING?
IS THIS THE HEART OF THE FOREST? HUH?
They're watching us...
A TINY...
GIGANTE JARROC?

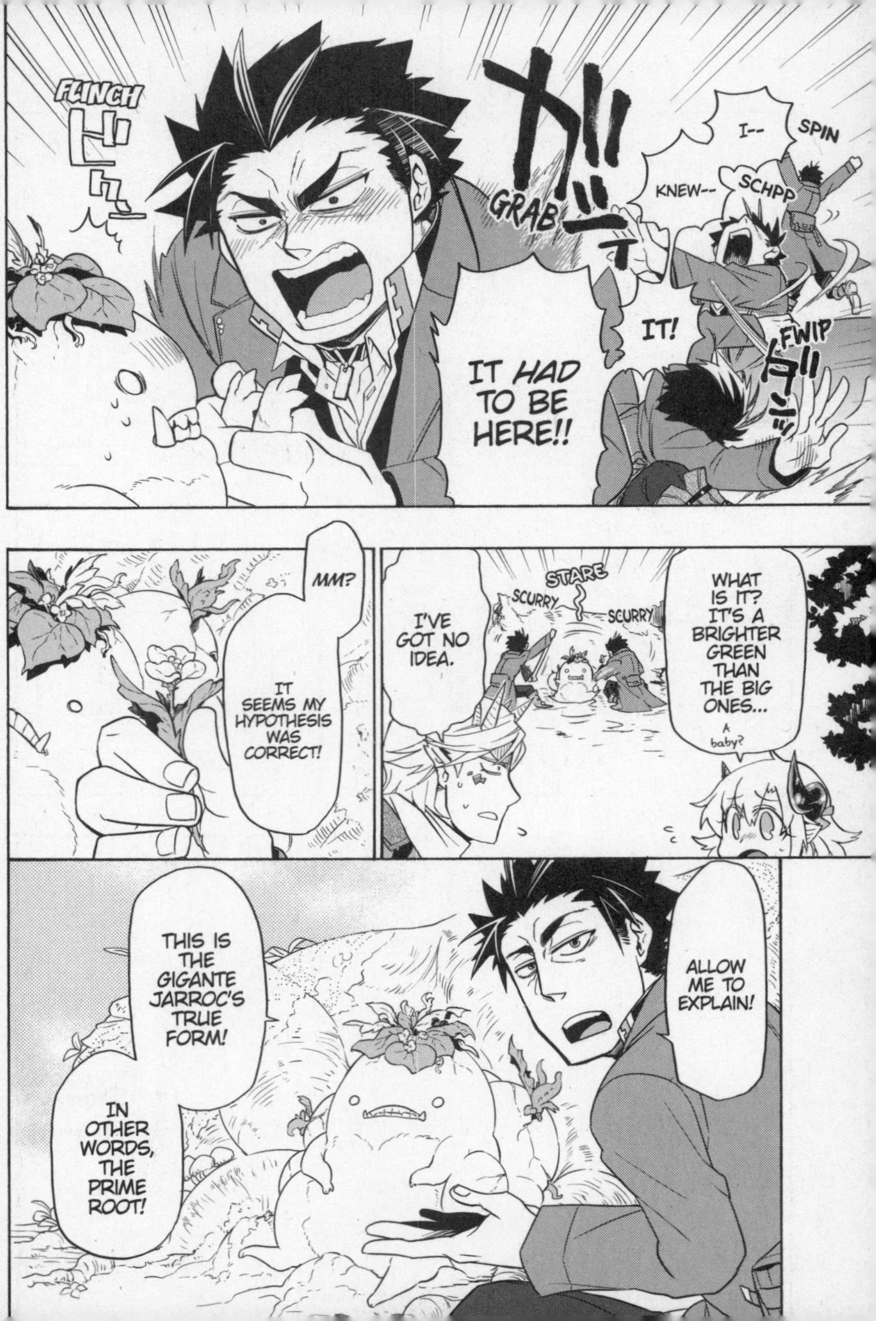
SPIN
I--
SCHPP
KNEW--
GRAB
IT!
FWIP
IT HAD TO BE HERE!!
FLINCH
WHAT IS IT? IT'S A BRIGHTER GREEN THAN THE BIG ONES...
A baby?
STARE
SCURRY
SCURRY
I'VE GOT NO IDEA.
MM?
IT SEEMS MY HYPOTHESIS WAS CORRECT!
ALLOW ME TO EXPLAIN!
THIS IS THE GIGANTE JARROC'S TRUE FORM!
IN OTHER WORDS, THE PRIME ROOT!

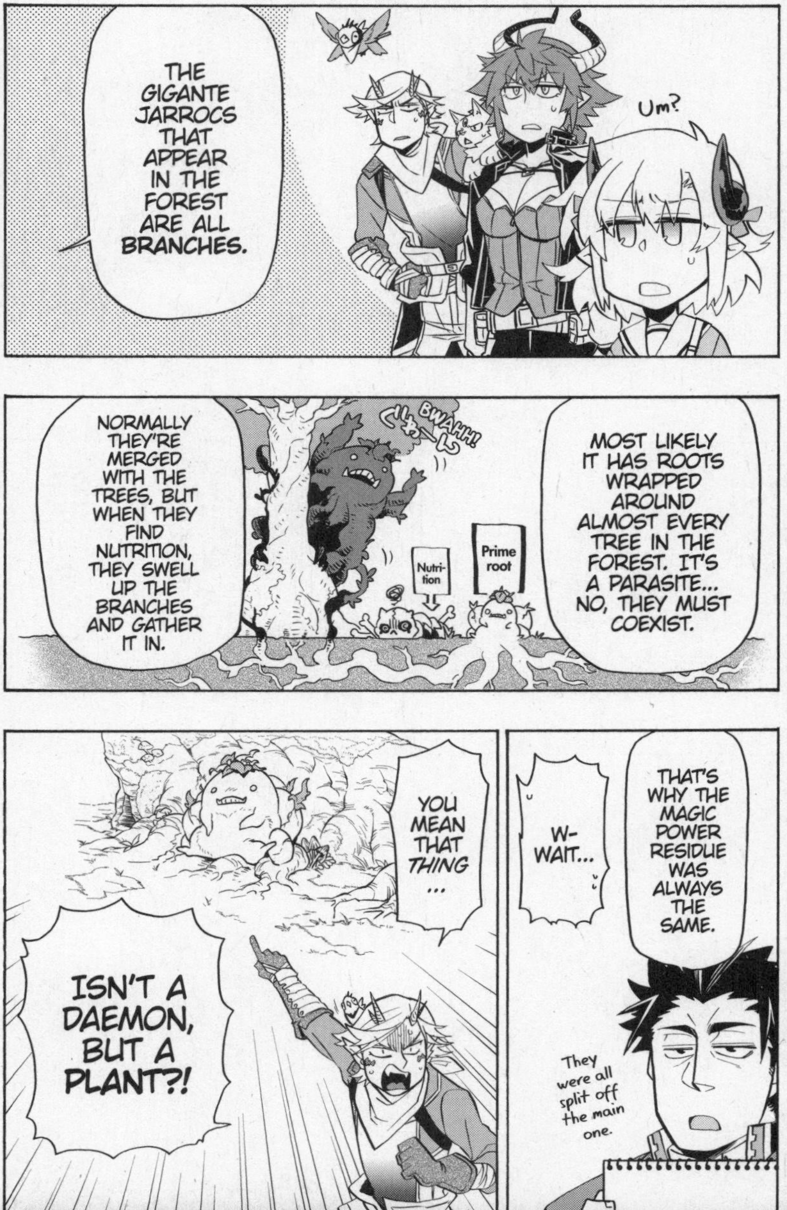
THE GIGANTE JARROCS THAT APPEAR IN THE FOREST ARE ALL BRANCHES.
Um?
MOST LIKELY IT HAS ROOTS WRAPPED AROUND ALMOST EVERY TREE IN THE FOREST. IT'S A PARASITE... NO, THEY MUST COEXIST.
BWAHH!
Prime root
Nutri-tion
NORMALLY THEY'RE MERGED WITH THE TREES, BUT WHEN THEY FIND NUTRITION, THEY SWELL UP THE BRANCHES AND GATHER IT IN.
THAT'S WHY THE MAGIC POWER RESIDUE WAS ALWAYS THE SAME.
W-WAIT...
They were all split off the main one.
YOU MEAN THAT *THING*...
ISN'T A DAEMON, BUT A PLANT?!

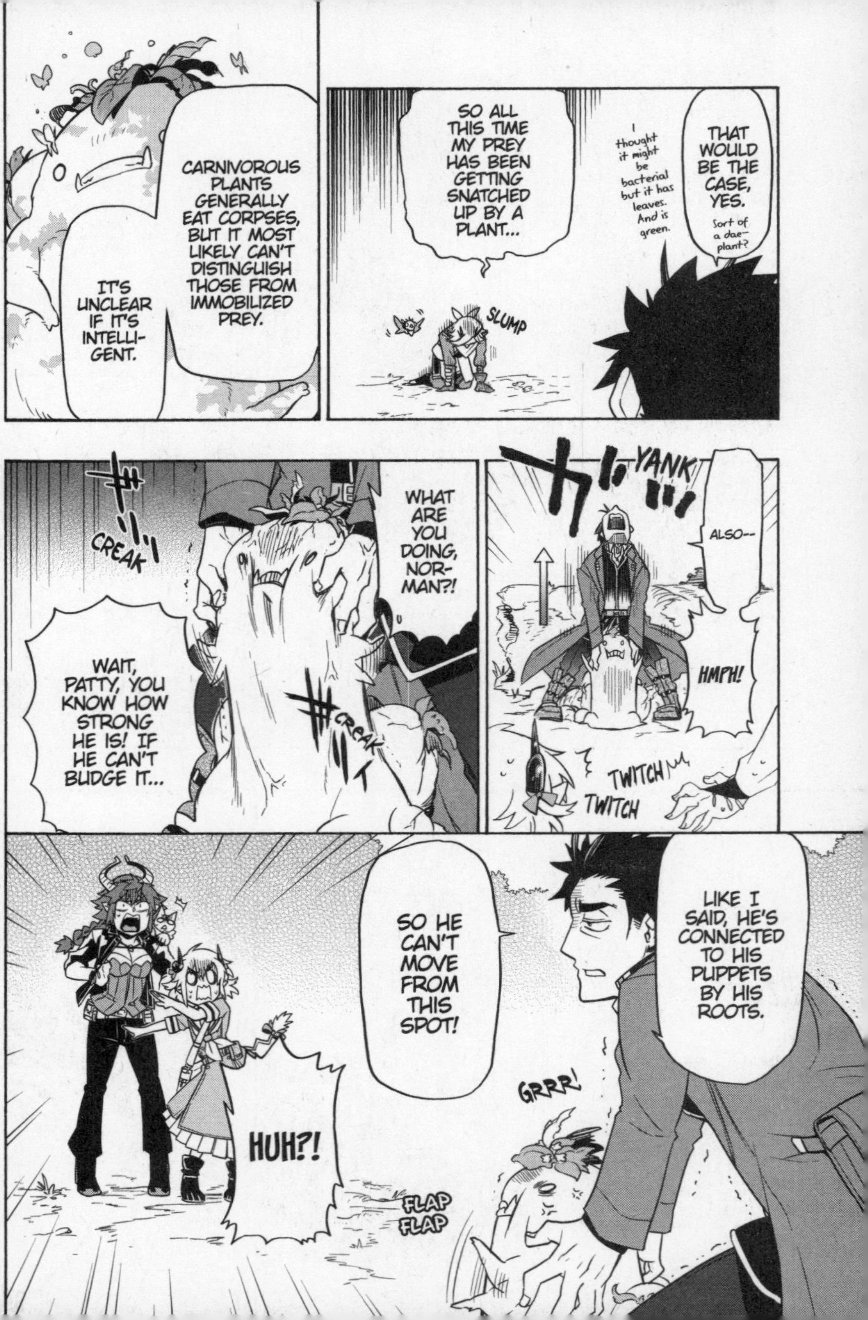
THAT WOULD BE THE CASE, YES.
Sort of a dae-plant?
I thought it might be bacterial but it has leaves. And is green.
SO ALL THIS TIME MY PREY HAS BEEN GETTING SNATCHED UP BY A PLANT...
SLUMP
CARNIVOROUS PLANTS GENERALLY EAT CORPSES, BUT IT MOST LIKELY CAN'T DISTINGUISH THOSE FROM IMMOBILIZED PREY.
IT'S UNCLEAR IF IT'S INTELLI-GENT.
YANK
ALSO--
HMPH!
TWITCH
TWITCH
WHAT ARE YOU DOING, NOR-MAN?!
CREAK
WAIT, PATTY, YOU KNOW HOW STRONG HE IS! IF HE CAN'T BUDGE IT...
CREAK
LIKE I SAID, HE'S CONNECTED TO HIS PUPPETS BY HIS ROOTS.
SO HE CAN'T MOVE FROM THIS SPOT!
GRRR!
HUH?!
FLAP
FLAP

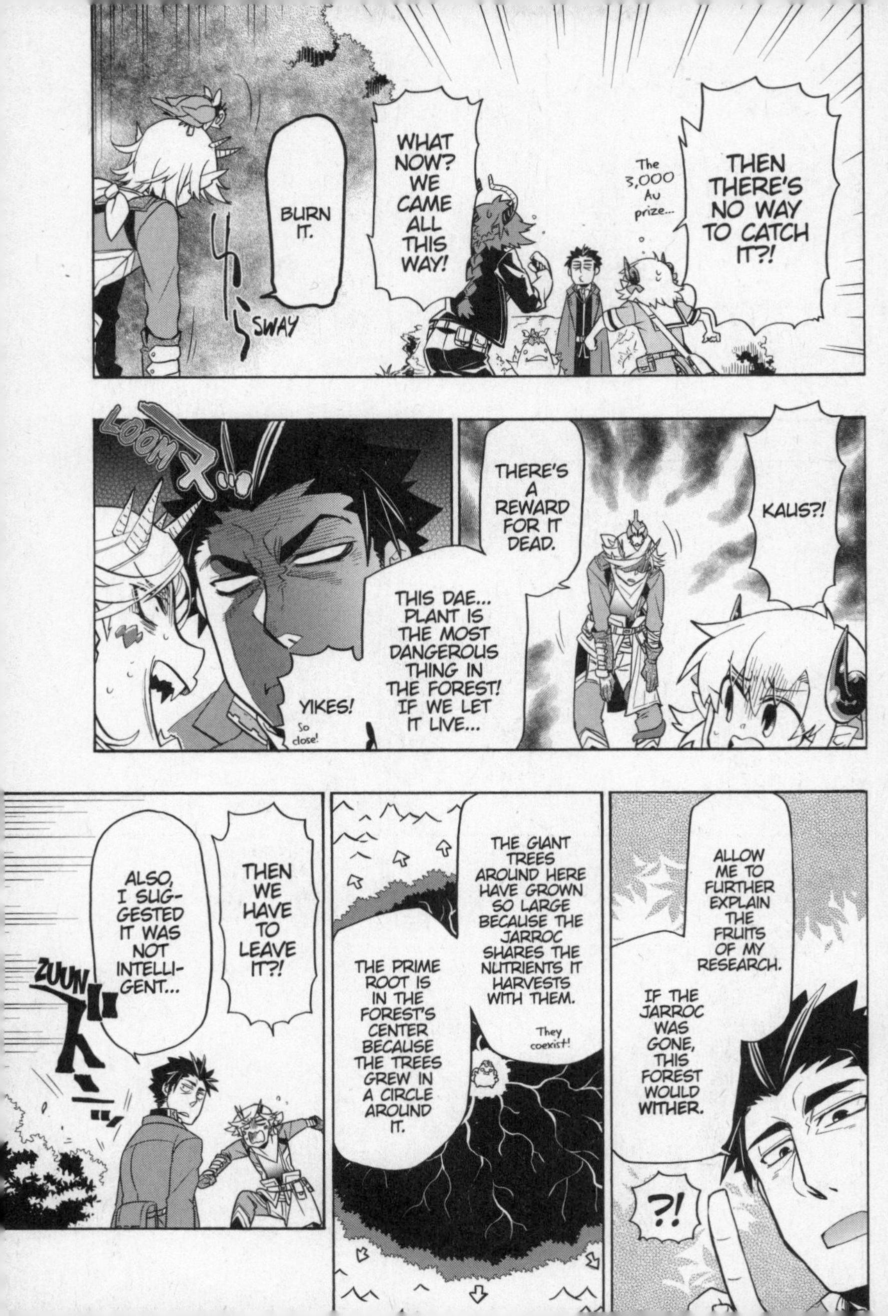
THEN THERE'S NO WAY TO CATCH IT?!
The 3,000 Au prize...
WHAT NOW? WE CAME ALL THIS WAY!
BURN IT.
SWAY
KAUS?!
THERE'S A REWARD FOR IT DEAD.
LOOM
THIS DAE... PLANT IS THE MOST DANGEROUS THING IN THE FOREST! IF WE LET IT LIVE...
YIKES!
So close!
ALLOW ME TO FURTHER EXPLAIN THE FRUITS OF MY RESEARCH.
IF THE JARROC WAS GONE, THIS FOREST WOULD WITHER.
?!
THE GIANT TREES AROUND HERE HAVE GROWN SO LARGE BECAUSE THE JARROC SHARES THE NUTRIENTS IT HARVESTS WITH THEM.
They coexist!
THE PRIME ROOT IS IN THE FOREST'S CENTER BECAUSE THE TREES GREW IN A CIRCLE AROUND IT.
THEN WE HAVE TO LEAVE IT?!
ALSO, I SUG-GESTED IT WAS NOT INTELLI-GENT...
ZUUN

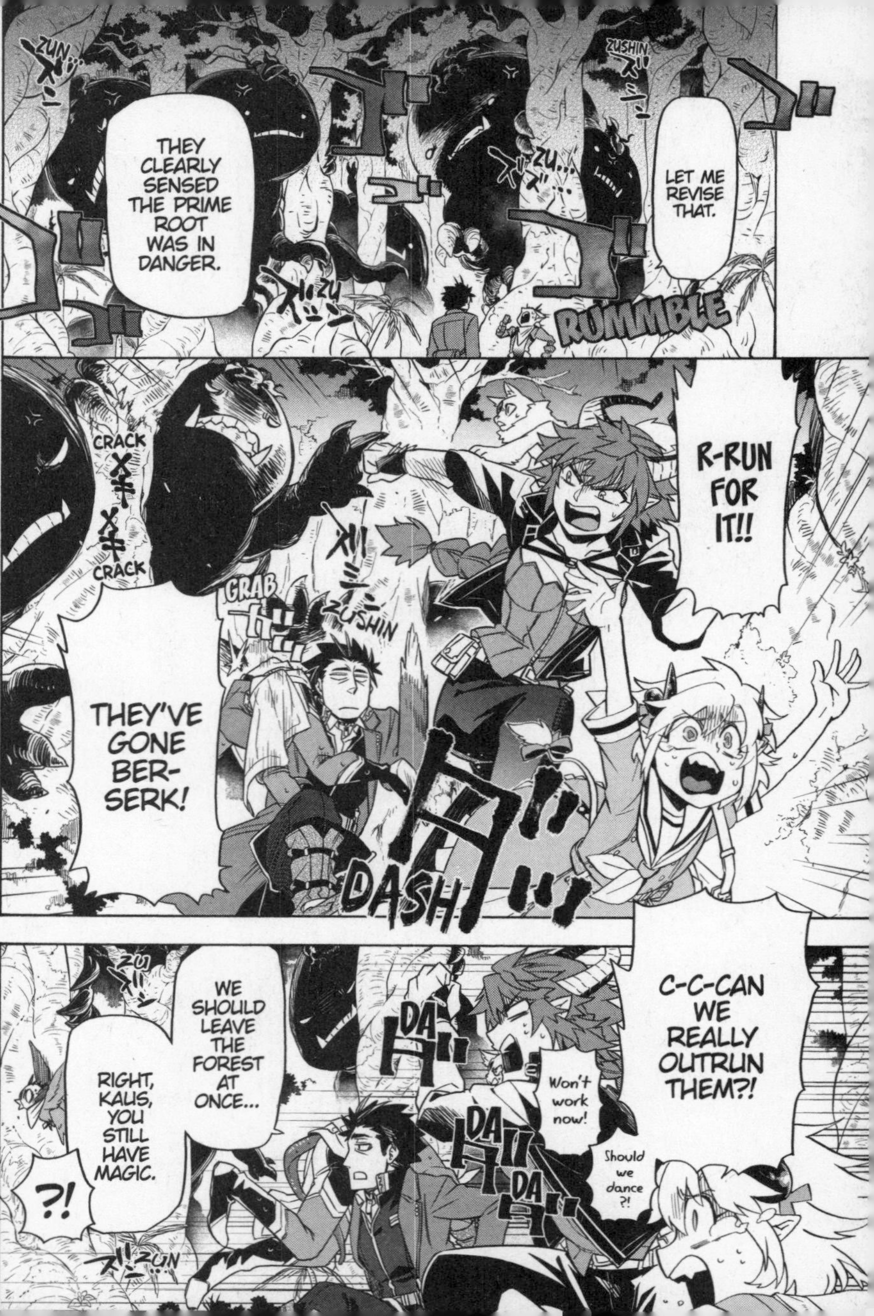
ZUSHIN
LET ME REVISE THAT.
ZU...
RUMMBLE
ZUZU
THEY CLEARLY SENSED THE PRIME ROOT WAS IN DANGER.
ZUN
R-RUN FOR IT!!
CRACK
CRACK
ZUSHIN
GRAB
THEY'VE GONE BER-SERK!
DASH
C-C-CAN WE REALLY OUTRUN THEM?!
Won't work now!
Should we dance?!
DA
DA
DA
WE SHOULD LEAVE THE FOREST AT ONCE...
ZU
RIGHT, KAUS, YOU STILL HAVE MAGIC.
?!
ZUN

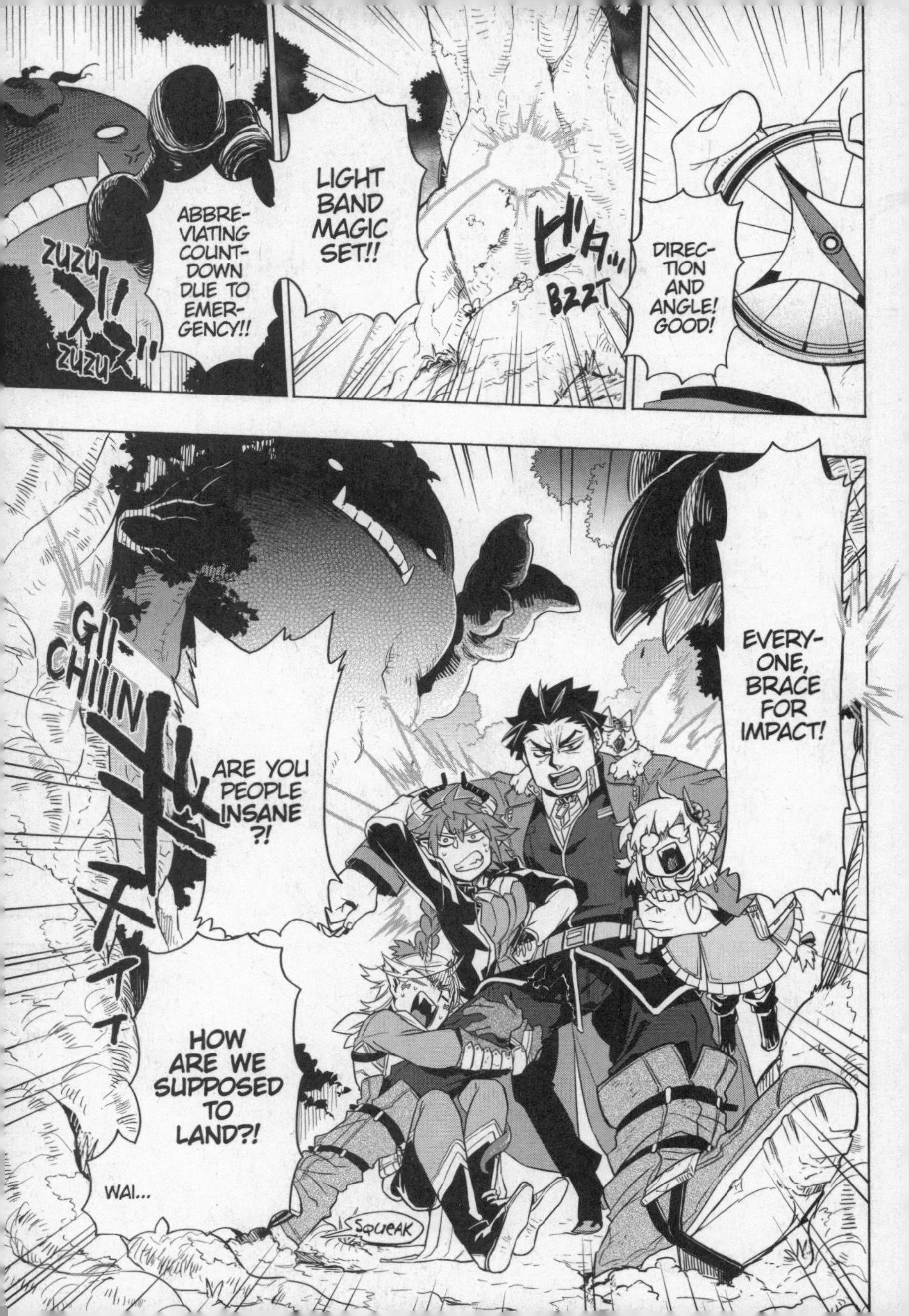
DIRECTION AND ANGLE! GOOD!
LIGHT BAND MAGIC SET!!
BZZT
ABBREVIATING COUNTDOWN DUE TO EMERGENCY!!
ZUZU
ZUZU
EVERYONE, BRACE FOR IMPACT!
ARE YOU PEOPLE INSANE?!
HOW ARE WE SUPPOSED TO LAND?!
WAI...
SQUEAK
GIICHIIIN

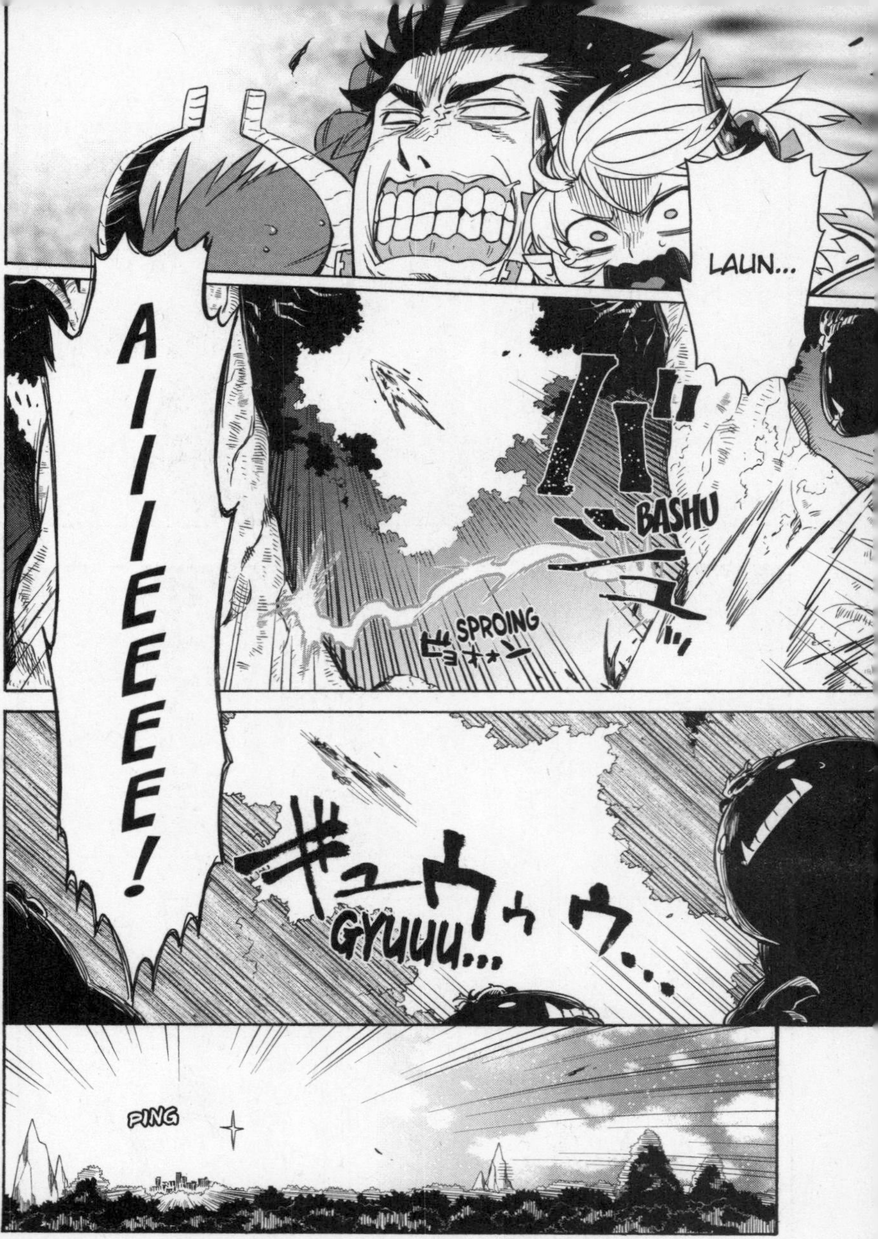
LAUN...
AIIIEEEEE!
バシュ
BASHU
ビョオォン
SPROING
ギュウゥウ...
GYUUU...
PING

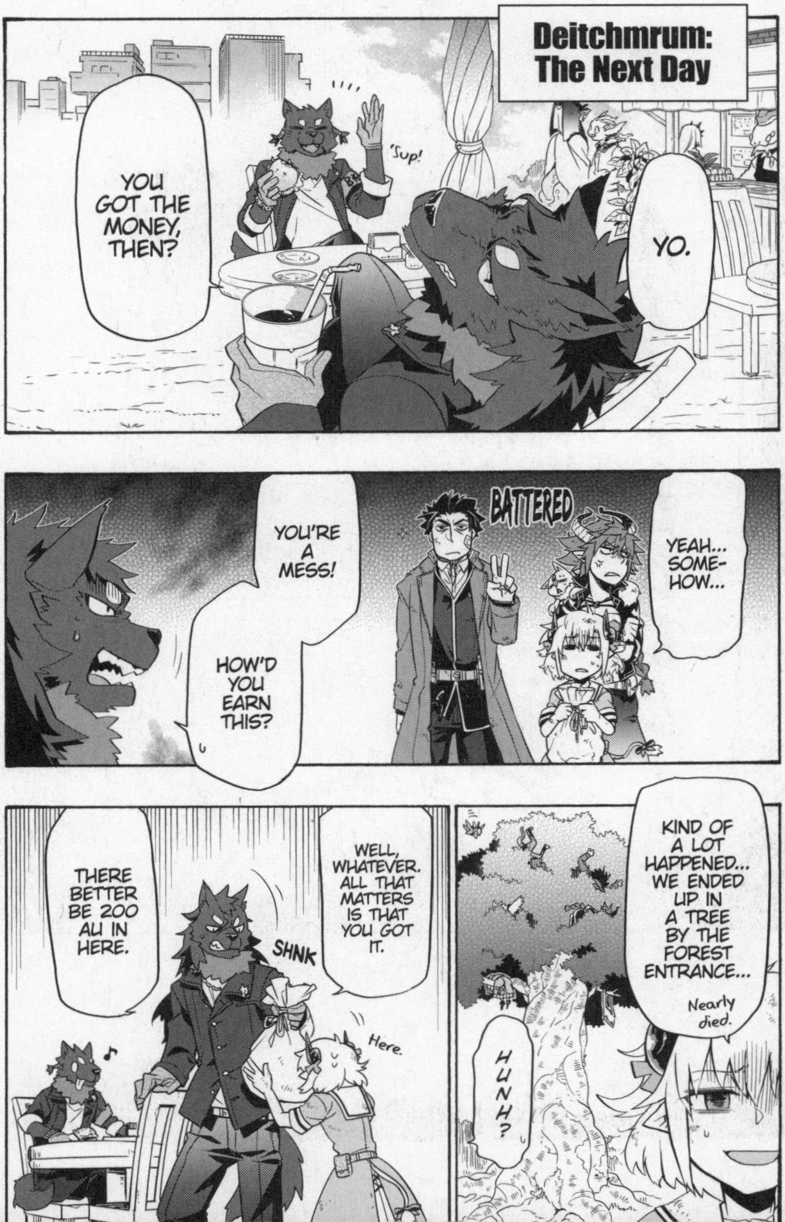
Deitchmrum: The Next Day
YO.
'Sup!
YOU GOT THE MONEY, THEN?
YEAH... SOME-HOW...
BATTERED
YOU'RE A MESS!
HOW'D YOU EARN THIS?
KIND OF A LOT HAPPENED... WE ENDED UP IN A TREE BY THE FOREST ENTRANCE...
Nearly died.
HUNH?
WELL, WHATEVER. ALL THAT MATTERS IS THAT YOU GOT IT.
SHNK
THERE BETTER BE 200 AU IN HERE.
Here.

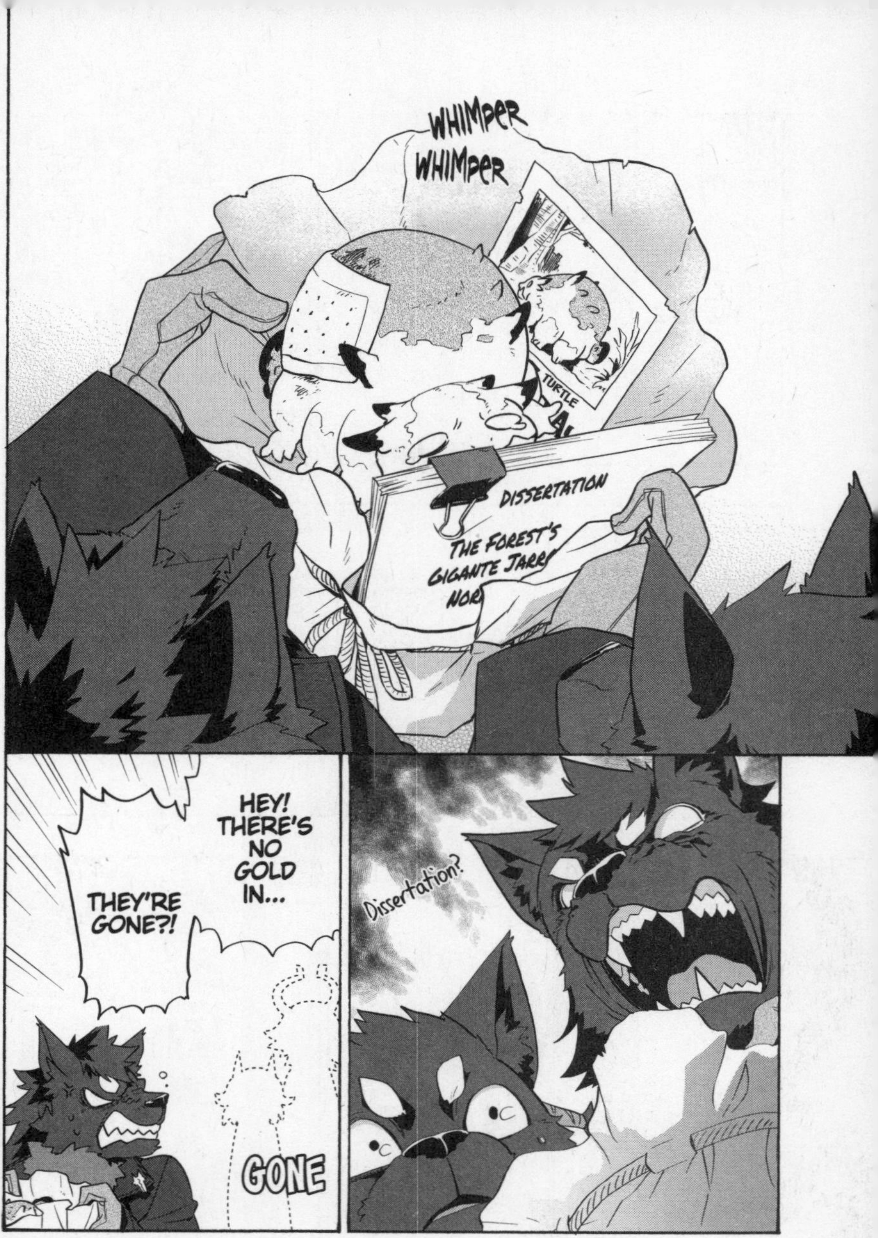
WHIMPER
WHIMPER
TURTLE
DISSERTATION
THE FOREST'S
GIGANTE JARR
NOR
Dissertation?
HEY! THERE'S NO GOLD IN...
THEY'RE GONE?!
GONE

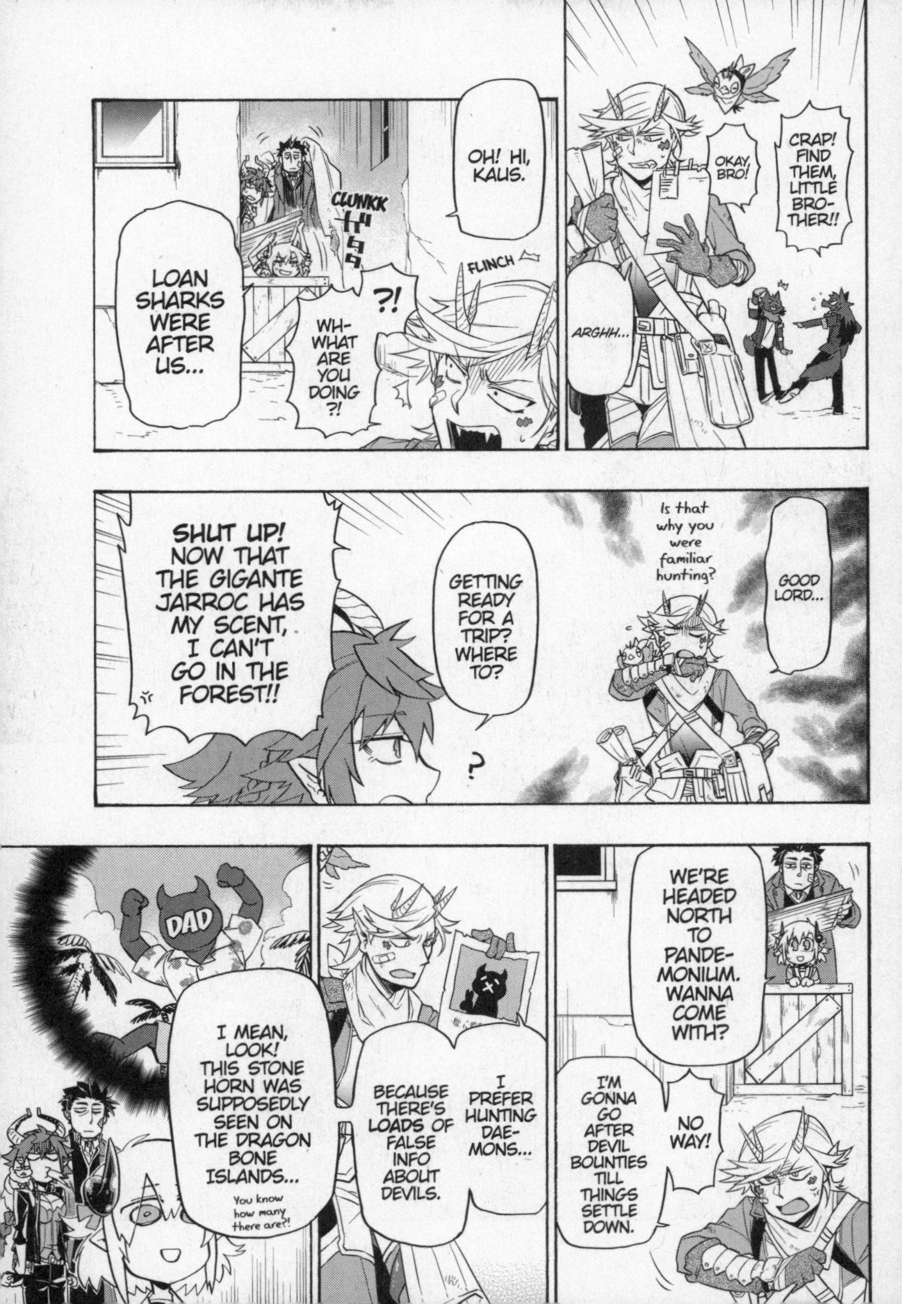
CRAP! FIND THEM, LITTLE BRO-THER!!
OKAY, BRO!
ARGHH...
OH! HI, KAUS.
CLUNKK
FLINCH
?!
WH-WHAT ARE YOU DOING?!
LOAN SHARKS WERE AFTER US...
GOOD LORD...
Is that why you were familiar hunting?
GETTING READY FOR A TRIP? WHERE TO?
SHUT UP! NOW THAT THE GIGANTE JARROC HAS MY SCENT, I CAN'T GO IN THE FOREST!!
?
WE'RE HEADED NORTH TO PANDE-MONIUM. WANNA COME WITH?
NO WAY!
I'M GONNA GO AFTER DEVIL BOUNTIES TILL THINGS SETTLE DOWN.
I PREFER HUNTING DAE-MONS...
BECAUSE THERE'S LOADS OF FALSE INFO ABOUT DEVILS.
DAD
I MEAN, LOOK! THIS STONE HORN WAS SUPPOSEDLY SEEN ON THE DRAGON BONE ISLANDS...
You know how many there are?!

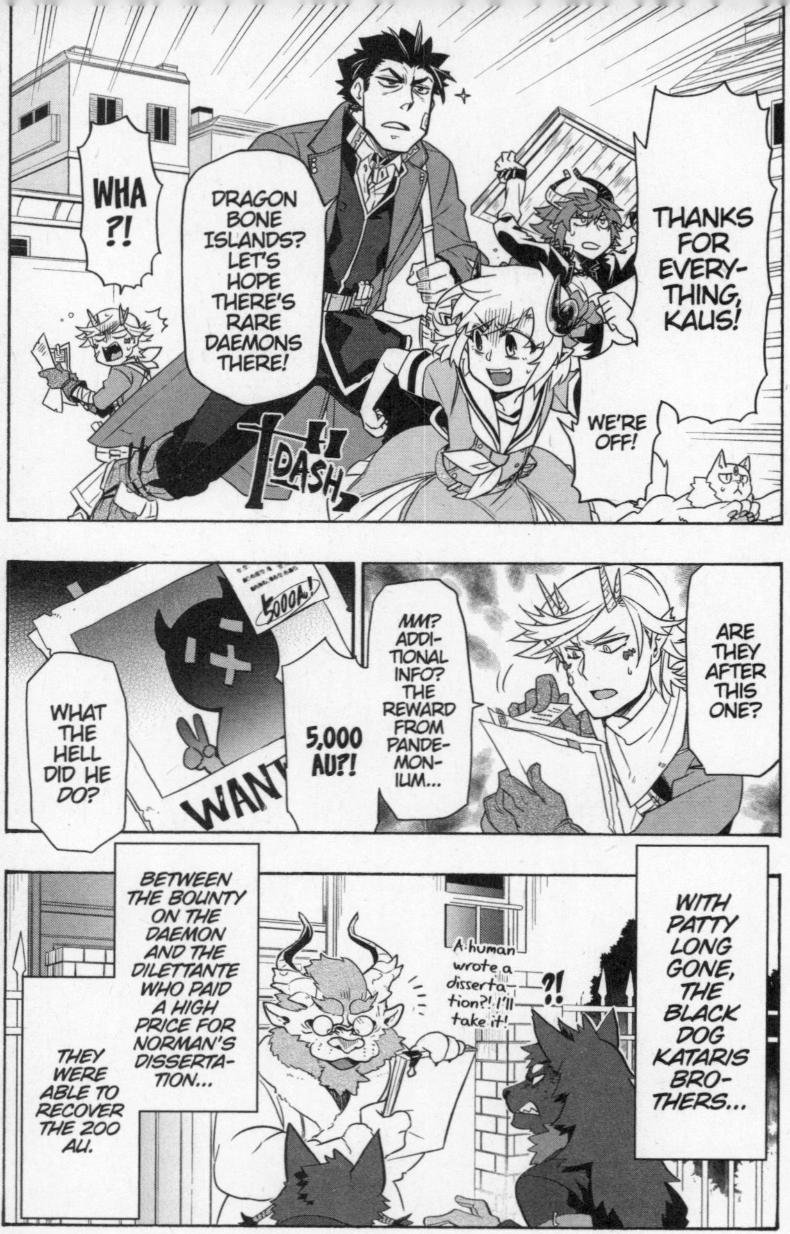
THANKS FOR EVERYTHING, KAUS!
WE'RE OFF!
DRAGON BONE ISLANDS? LET'S HOPE THERE'S RARE DAEMONS THERE!
DASH
WHA ?!
ARE THEY AFTER THIS ONE?
MM? ADDITIONAL INFO? THE REWARD FROM PANDEMONIUM...
5000AU!
5,000 AU?!
WHAT THE HELL DID HE DO?
WANT
WITH PATTY LONG GONE, THE BLACK DOG KATARIS BROTHERS...
?!
A human wrote a dissertation?! I'll take it!
BETWEEN THE BOUNTY ON THE DAEMON AND THE DILETTANTE WHO PAID A HIGH PRICE FOR NORMAN'S DISSERTATION...
THEY WERE ABLE TO RECOVER THE 200 AU.

Sorry For My Familiar

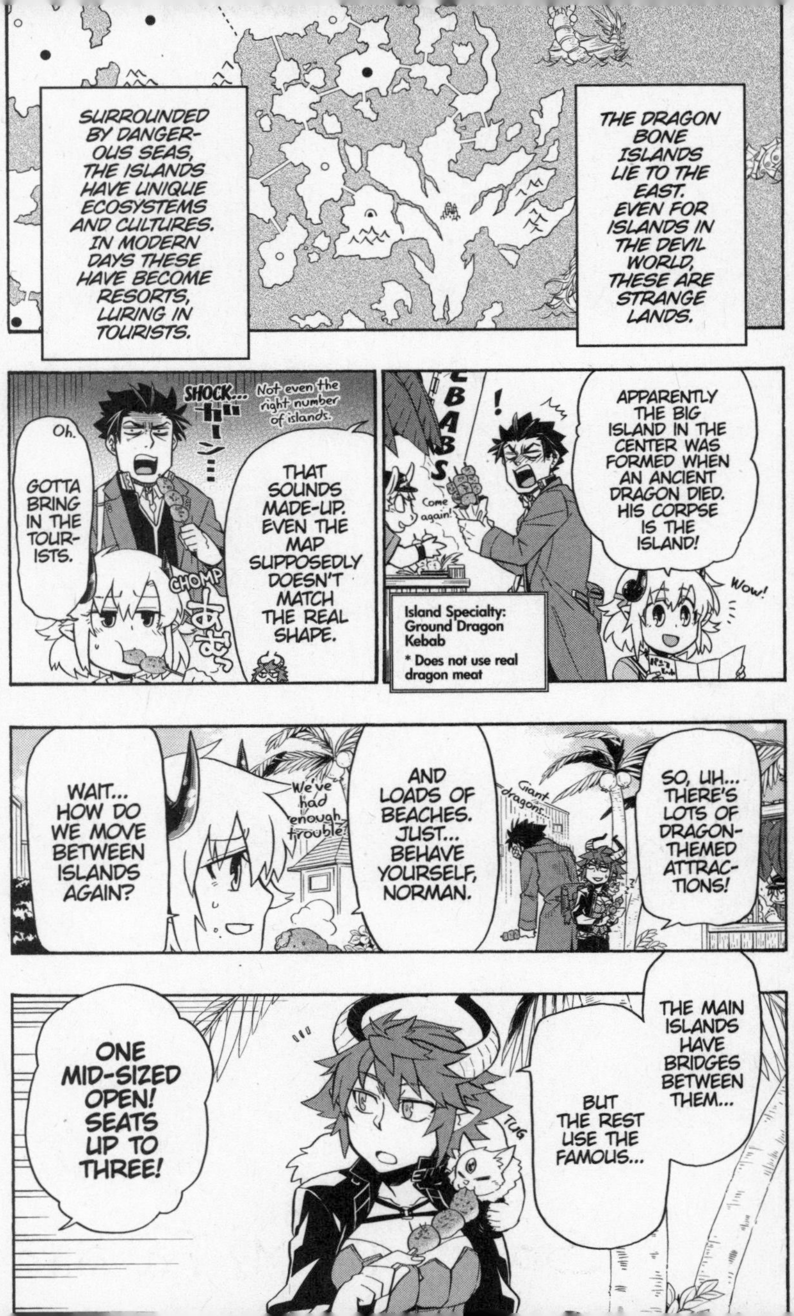
THE DRAGON BONE ISLANDS LIE TO THE EAST. EVEN FOR ISLANDS IN THE DEVIL WORLD, THESE ARE STRANGE LANDS.
SURROUNDED BY DANGEROUS SEAS, THE ISLANDS HAVE UNIQUE ECOSYSTEMS AND CULTURES. IN MODERN DAYS THESE HAVE BECOME RESORTS, LURING IN TOURISTS.
APPARENTLY THE BIG ISLAND IN THE CENTER WAS FORMED WHEN AN ANCIENT DRAGON DIED. HIS CORPSE IS THE ISLAND!
Wow!
!
KEBABS
Come again!
Island Specialty: Ground Dragon Kebab
* Does not use real dragon meat
THAT SOUNDS MADE-UP. EVEN THE MAP SUPPOSEDLY DOESN'T MATCH THE REAL SHAPE.
Not even the right number of islands.
SHOCK...
Oh.
GOTTA BRING IN THE TOURISTS.
CHOMP
SO, UH... THERE'S LOTS OF DRAGON-THEMED ATTRACTIONS!
Giant dragons
AND LOADS OF BEACHES. JUST... BEHAVE YOURSELF, NORMAN.
We've had enough trouble!
WAIT... HOW DO WE MOVE BETWEEN ISLANDS AGAIN?
THE MAIN ISLANDS HAVE BRIDGES BETWEEN THEM...
BUT THE REST USE THE FAMOUS...
TUG
ONE MID-SIZED OPEN! SEATS UP TO THREE!

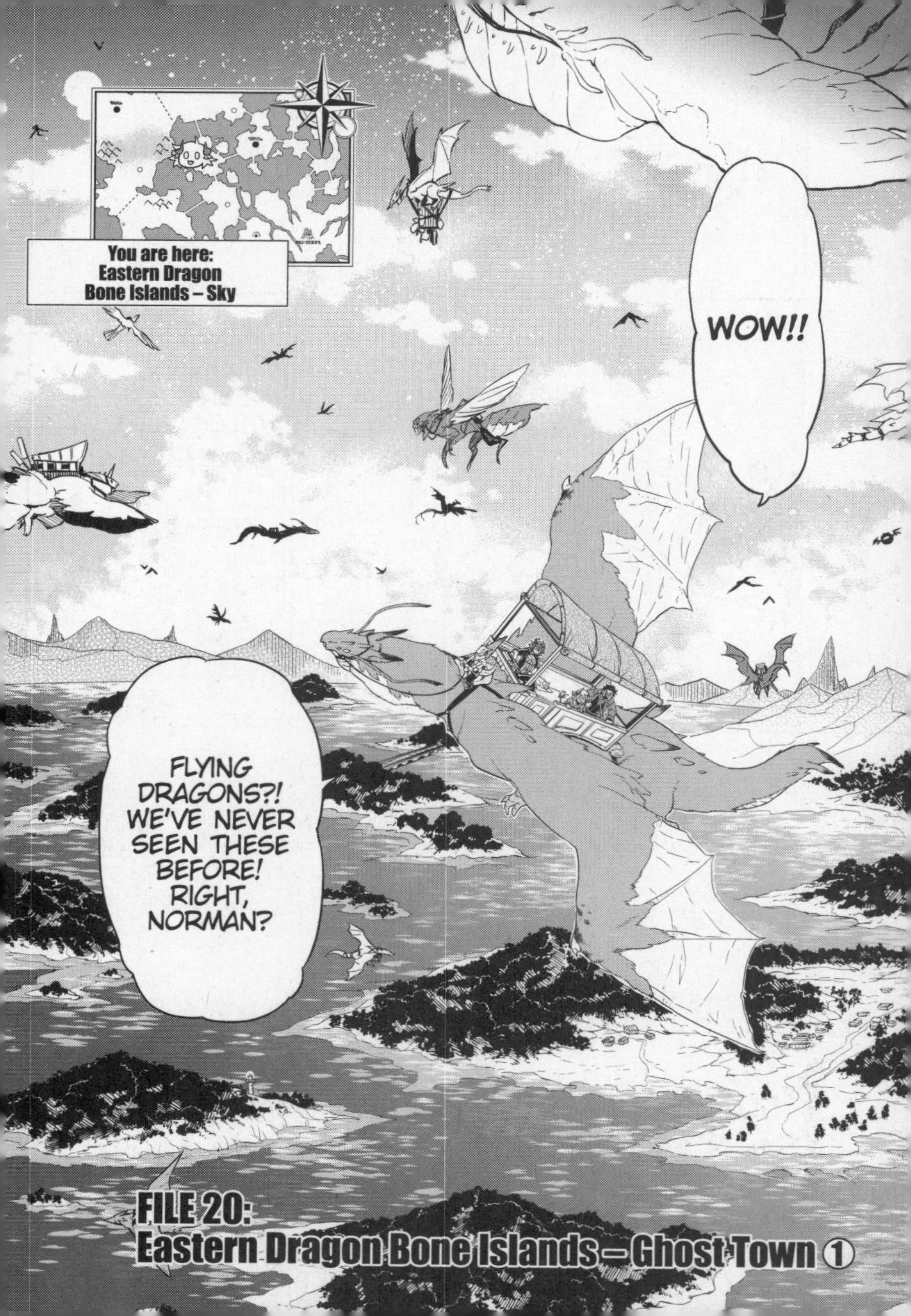
WOW!!
You are here: Eastern Dragon Bone Islands – Sky
FLYING DRAGONS?! WE'VE NEVER SEEN THESE BEFORE! RIGHT, NORMAN?
FILE 20: Eastern Dragon Bone Islands – Ghost Town ①

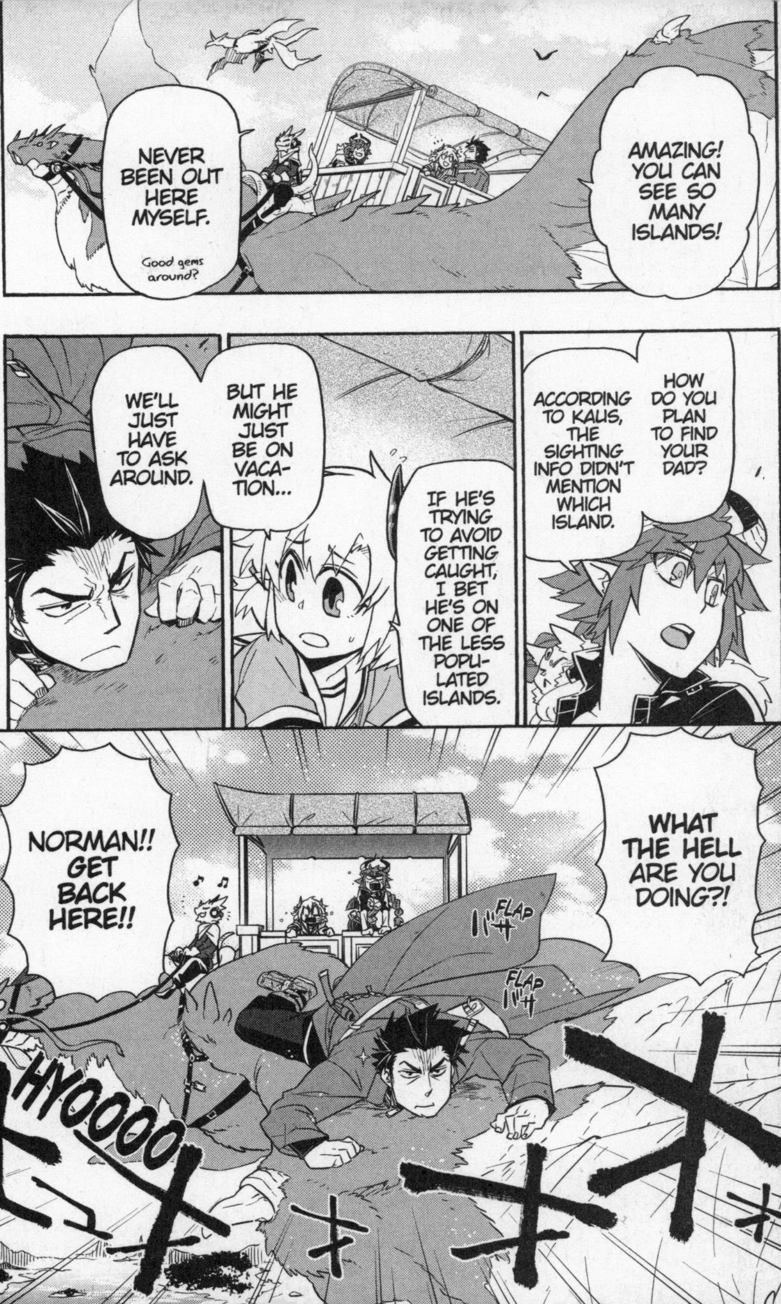
AMAZING! YOU CAN SEE SO MANY ISLANDS!
NEVER BEEN OUT HERE MYSELF.
Good gems around?
HOW DO YOU PLAN TO FIND YOUR DAD?
ACCORDING TO KAUS, THE SIGHTING INFO DIDN'T MENTION WHICH ISLAND.
IF HE'S TRYING TO AVOID GETTING CAUGHT, I BET HE'S ON ONE OF THE LESS POPU-LATED ISLANDS.
BUT HE MIGHT JUST BE ON VACA-TION...
WE'LL JUST HAVE TO ASK AROUND.
WHAT THE HELL ARE YOU DOING?!
NORMAN!! GET BACK HERE!!
FLAP
FLAP
HYOOOO

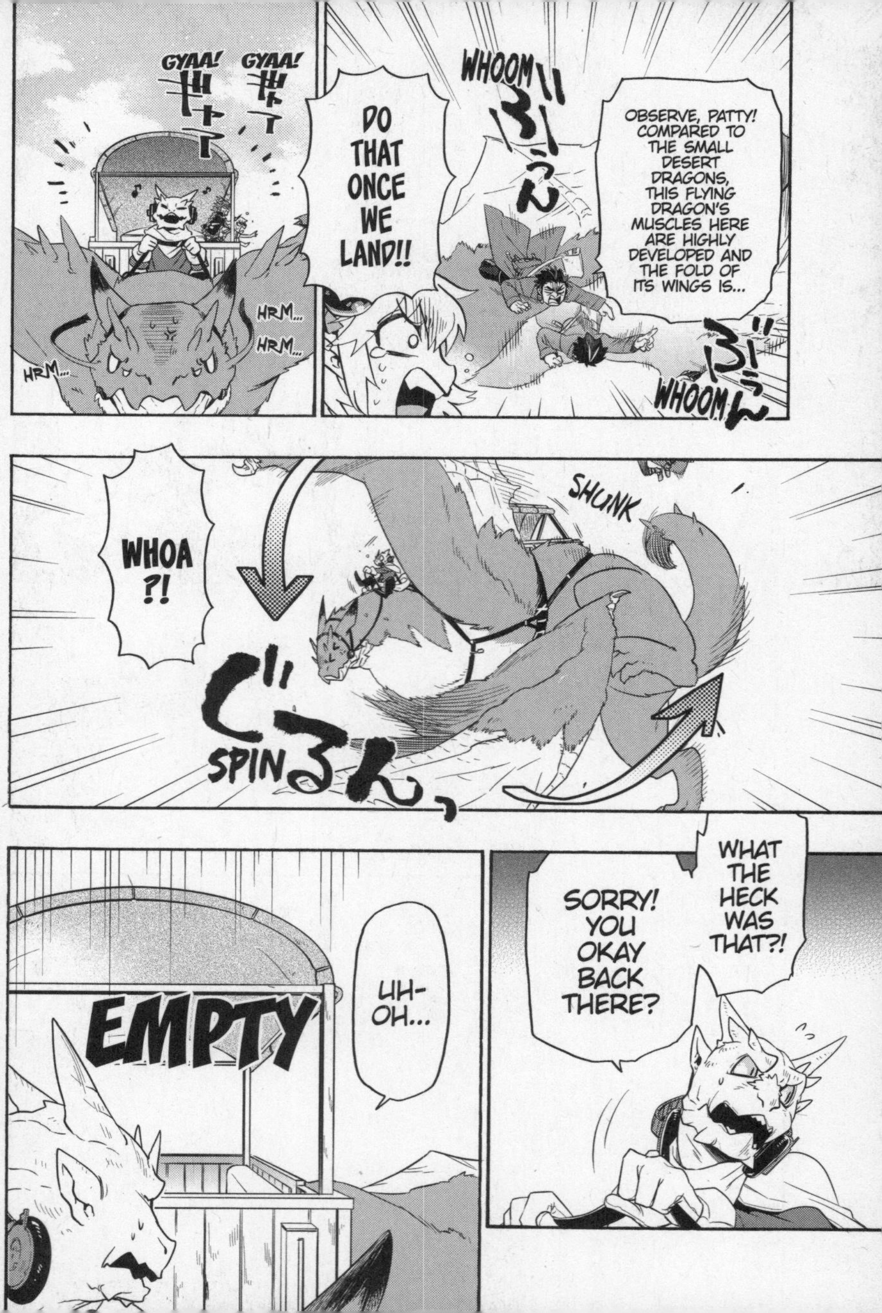
WHOOM
OBSERVE, PATTY! COMPARED TO THE SMALL DESERT DRAGONS, THIS FLYING DRAGON'S MUSCLES HERE ARE HIGHLY DEVELOPED AND THE FOLD OF ITS WINGS IS...
WHOOM
DO THAT ONCE WE LAND!!
GYAA! GYAA!
HRM... HRM...
HRM...
WHOA ?!
SHUNK
SPIN
WHAT THE HECK WAS THAT?!
SORRY! YOU OKAY BACK THERE?
EMPTY
UH-OH...

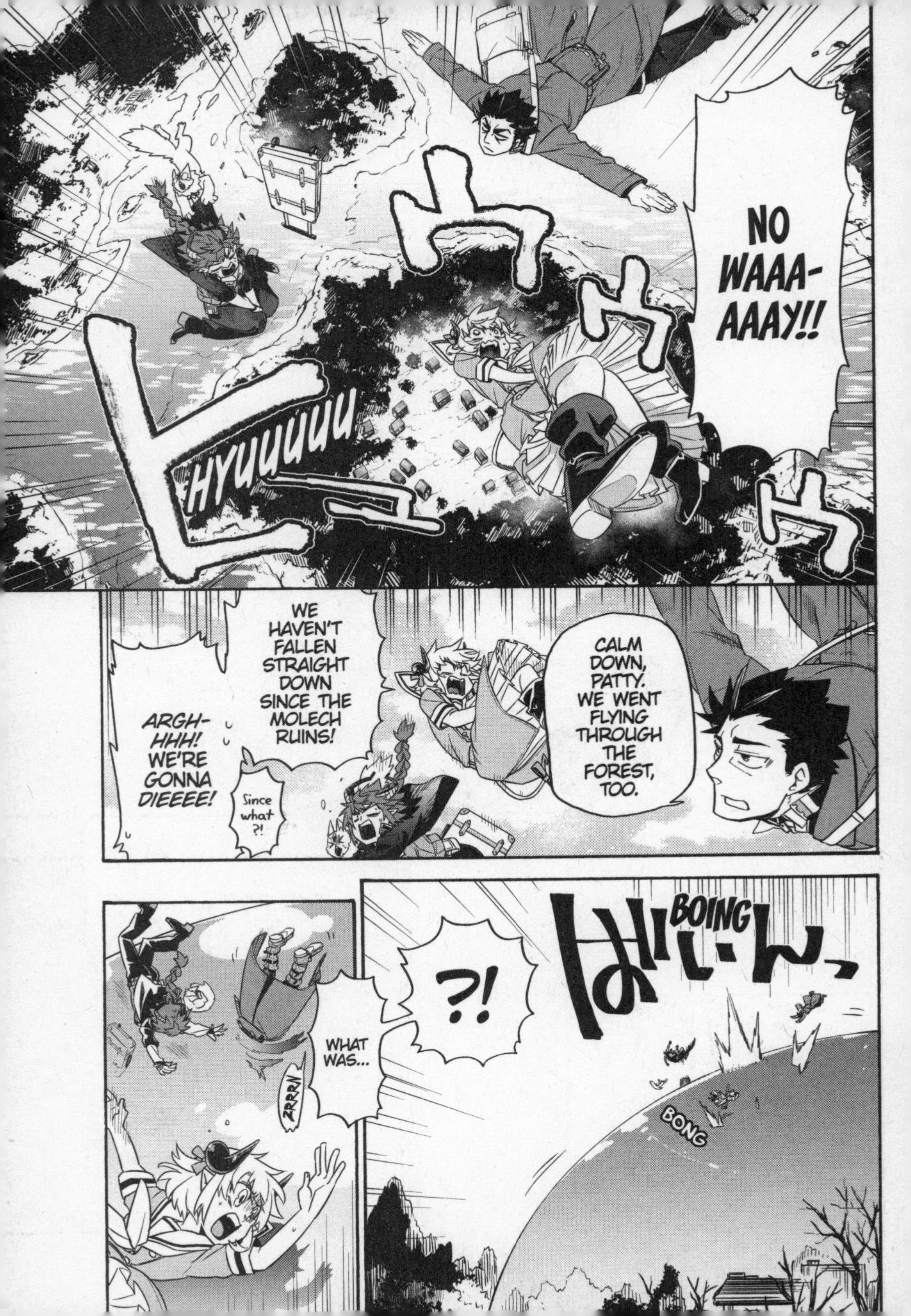
NO WAAAA-AAAY!!
HYUuuuu
CALM DOWN, PATTY. WE WENT FLYING THROUGH THE FOREST, TOO.
WE HAVEN'T FALLEN STRAIGHT DOWN SINCE THE MOLECH RUINS!
Since what?!
ARGH-HHH! WE'RE GONNA DIEEEE!
BOING
BONG
?!
WHAT WAS...
ZRRRN

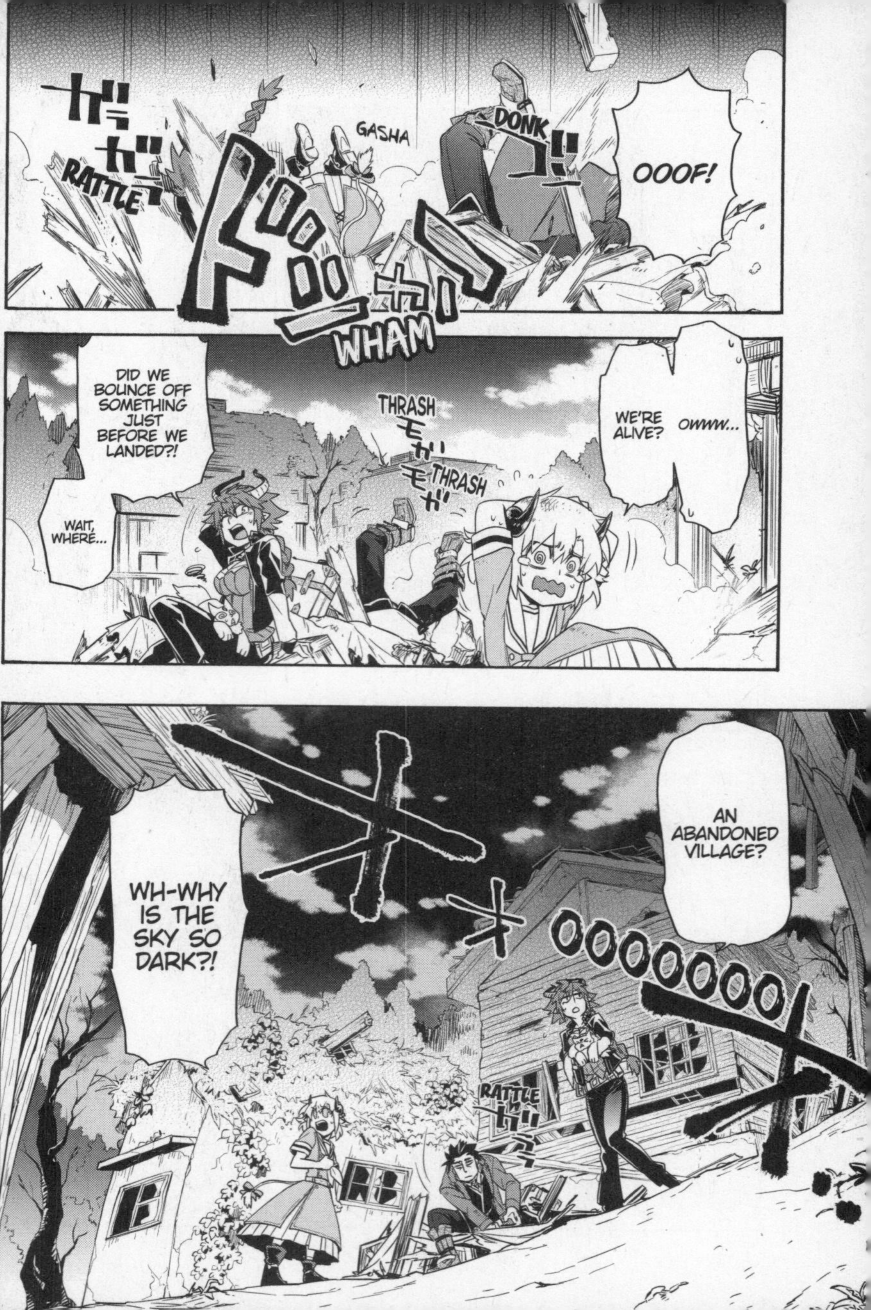
OOOF!
DONK
GASHA
RATTLE
WHAM
WE'RE ALIVE?
OWWW...
THRASH
THRASH
DID WE BOUNCE OFF SOMETHING JUST BEFORE WE LANDED?!
WAIT, WHERE...
AN ABANDONED VILLAGE?
OOOOOOO
WH-WHY IS THE SKY SO DARK?!
RATTLE

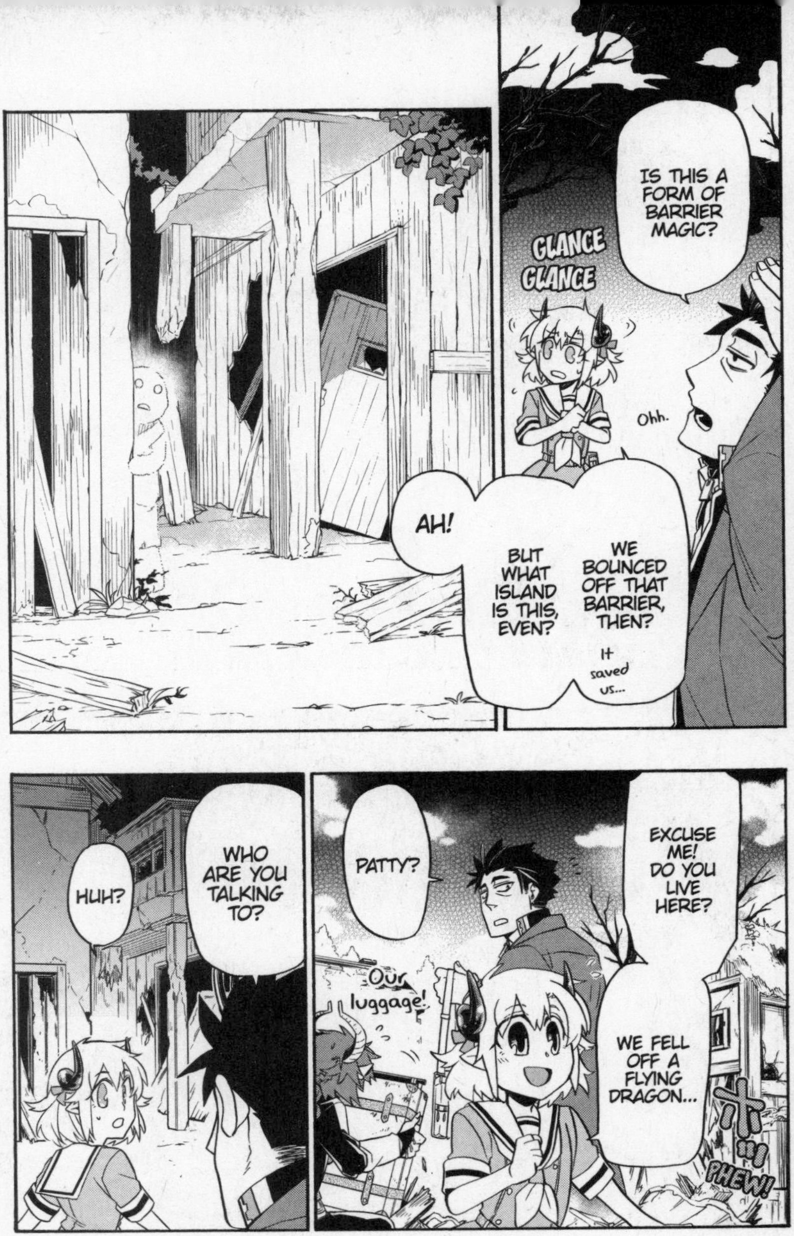
IS THIS A FORM OF BARRIER MAGIC?
GLANCE GLANCE
Ohh.
AH!
WE BOUNCED OFF THAT BARRIER, THEN?
It saved us...
BUT WHAT ISLAND IS THIS, EVEN?
EXCUSE ME! DO YOU LIVE HERE?
WE FELL OFF A FLYING DRAGON...
PHEW!
PATTY?
Our luggage!
WHO ARE YOU TALKING TO?
HUH?

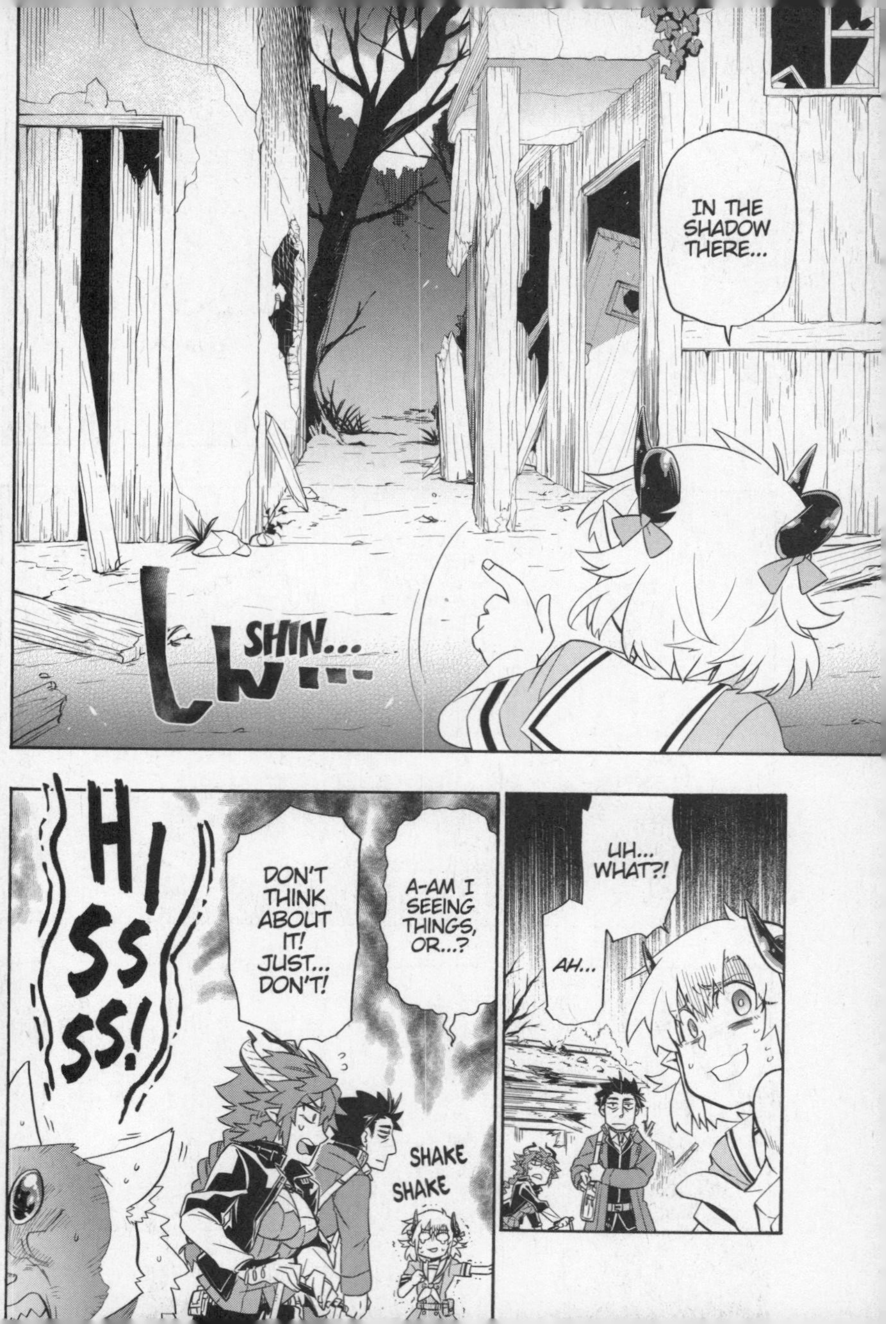
IN THE SHADOW THERE...
SHIN...
UH... WHAT?!
AH...
A-AM I SEEING THINGS, OR...?
DON'T THINK ABOUT IT! JUST... DON'T!
HISSSSS!
SHAKE SHAKE

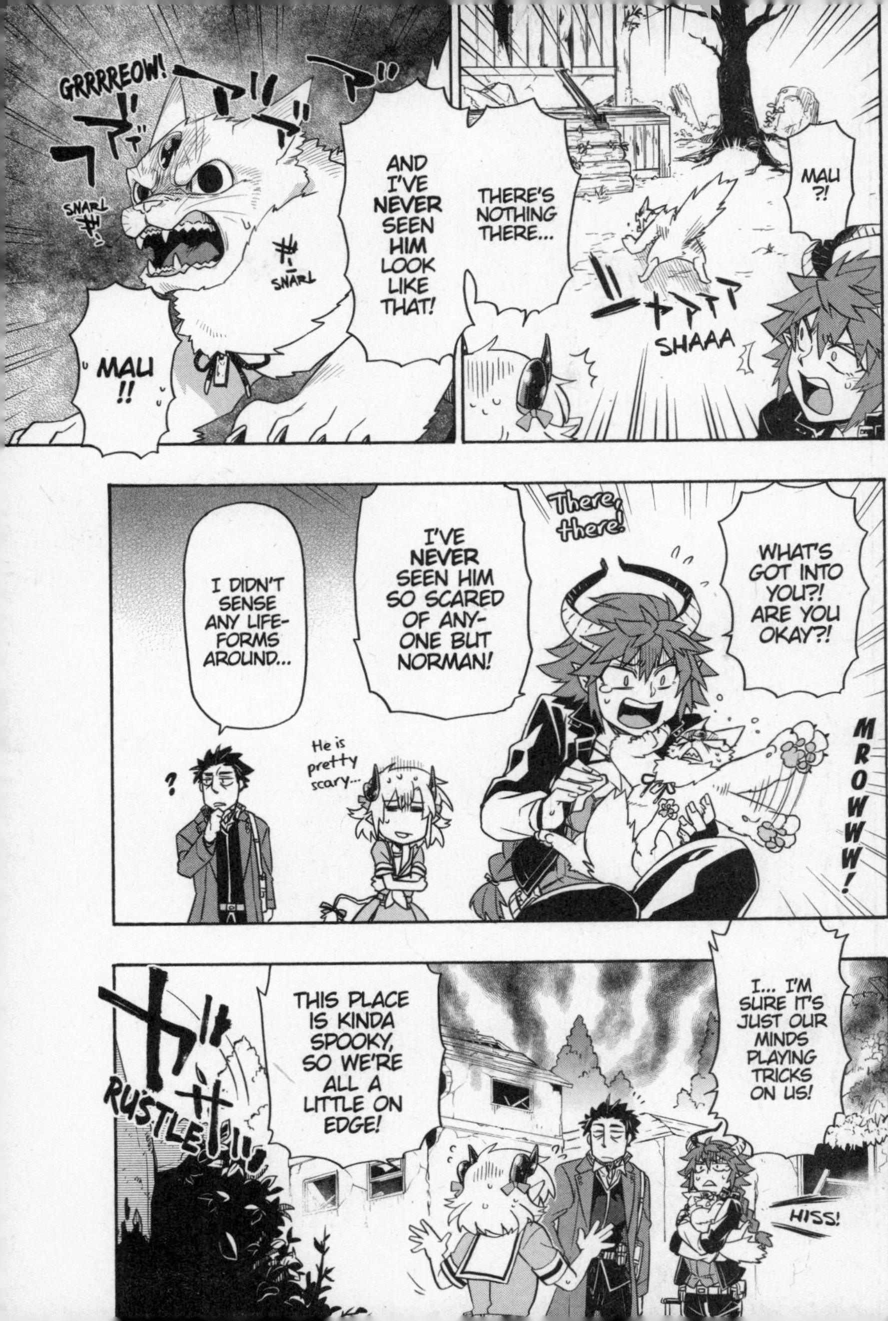
MAU ?!
SHAAA
THERE'S NOTHING THERE...
AND I'VE NEVER SEEN HIM LOOK LIKE THAT!
GRRRREOW!
SNARL
SNARL
MAU !!
WHAT'S GOT INTO YOU?! ARE YOU OKAY?!
MROWWWW!
There, there!
I'VE NEVER SEEN HIM SO SCARED OF ANY-ONE BUT NORMAN!
I DIDN'T SENSE ANY LIFE-FORMS AROUND...
He is pretty scary...
I... I'M SURE IT'S JUST OUR MINDS PLAYING TRICKS ON US!
HISS!
THIS PLACE IS KINDA SPOOKY, SO WE'RE ALL A LITTLE ON EDGE!
RUSTLE!!!

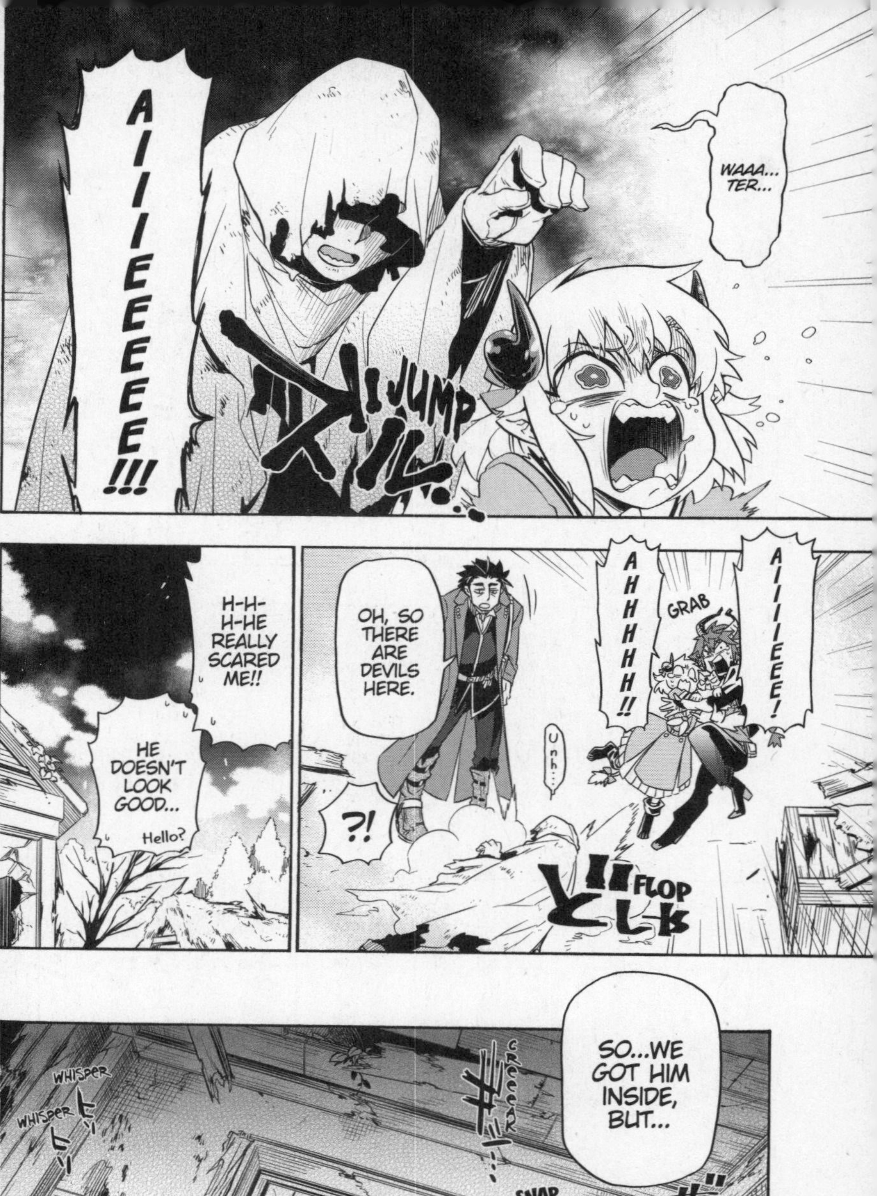
WAAA... TER...
AIIIEEEEEE!!!
JUMP
AIIIIEEE!
AHHHHHH!!
GRAB
OH, SO THERE ARE DEVILS HERE.
Unh...
?!
FLOP
H-H-H-HE REALLY SCARED ME!!
HE DOESN'T LOOK GOOD...
Hello?
SO...WE GOT HIM INSIDE, BUT...
CREEEAK
SNAP
SNAP
WHISPER
WHISPER

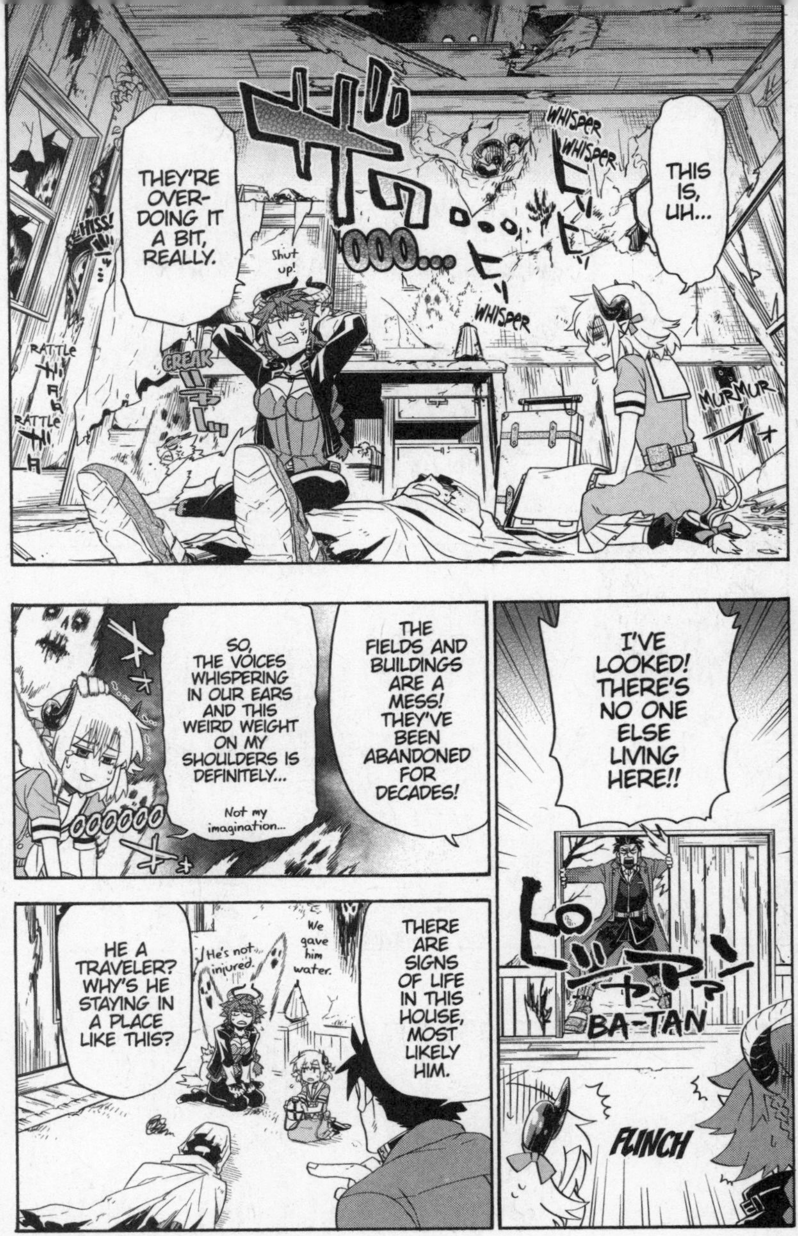
THIS IS, UH...
WHISPER WHISPER
OOO...
WHISPER
MURMUR
THEY'RE OVER-DOING IT A BIT, REALLY.
Shut up!
HISS!
CREAK
RATTLE
RATTLE
I'VE LOOKED! THERE'S NO ONE ELSE LIVING HERE!!
BA-TAN
FLINCH
THE FIELDS AND BUILDINGS ARE A MESS! THEY'VE BEEN ABANDONED FOR DECADES!
SO, THE VOICES WHISPERING IN OUR EARS AND THIS WEIRD WEIGHT ON MY SHOULDERS IS DEFINITELY...
Not my imagination...
OOOOOO
THERE ARE SIGNS OF LIFE IN THIS HOUSE, MOST LIKELY HIM.
We gave him water.
He's not injured.
HE A TRAVELER? WHY'S HE STAYING IN A PLACE LIKE THIS?

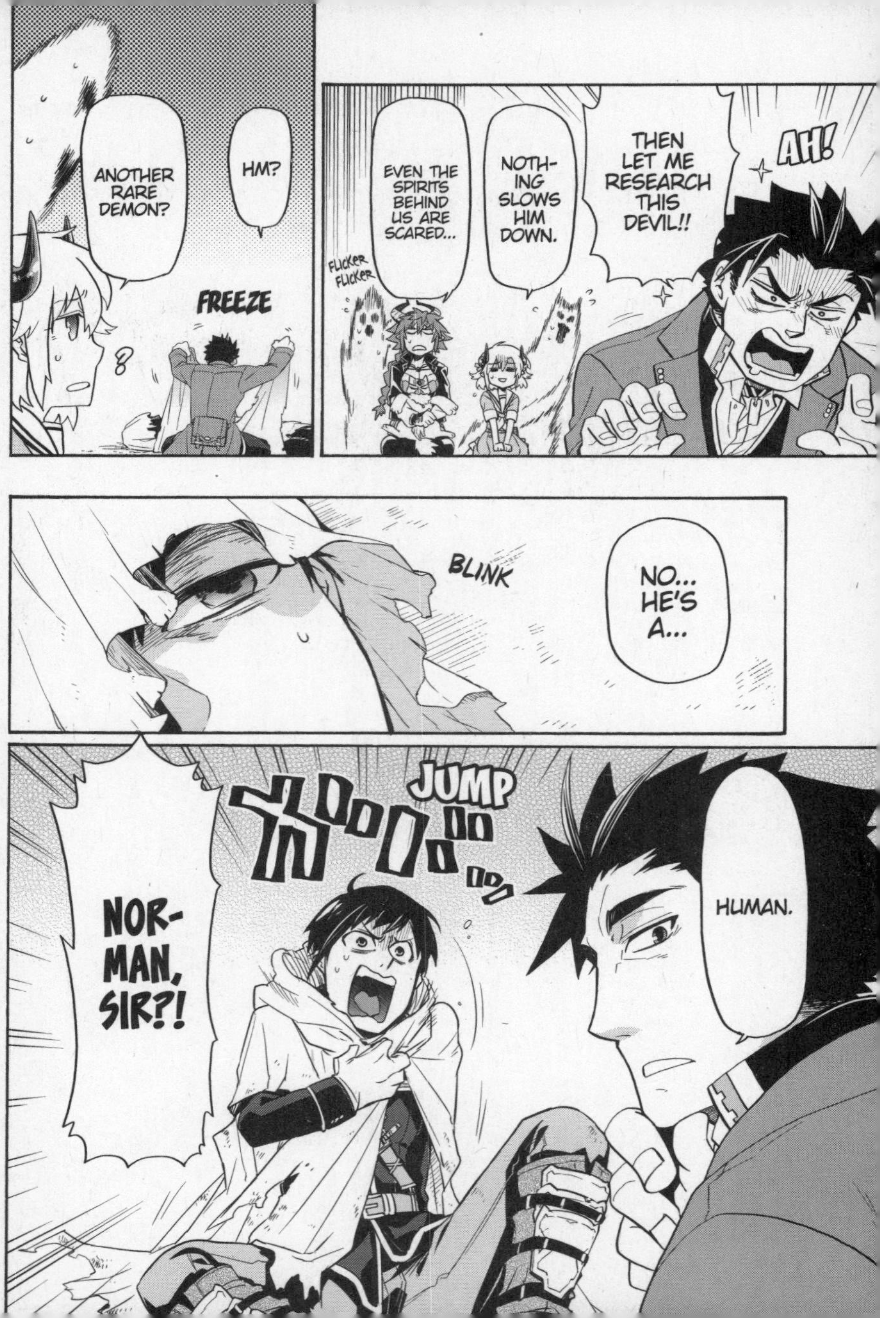
AH!
THEN LET ME RESEARCH THIS DEVIL!!
NOTH-ING SLOWS HIM DOWN.
EVEN THE SPIRITS BEHIND US ARE SCARED...
FLICKER FLICKER
HM?
ANOTHER RARE DEMON?
FREEZE
NO... HE'S A...
BLINK
HUMAN.
JUMP
NOR-MAN, SIR?!

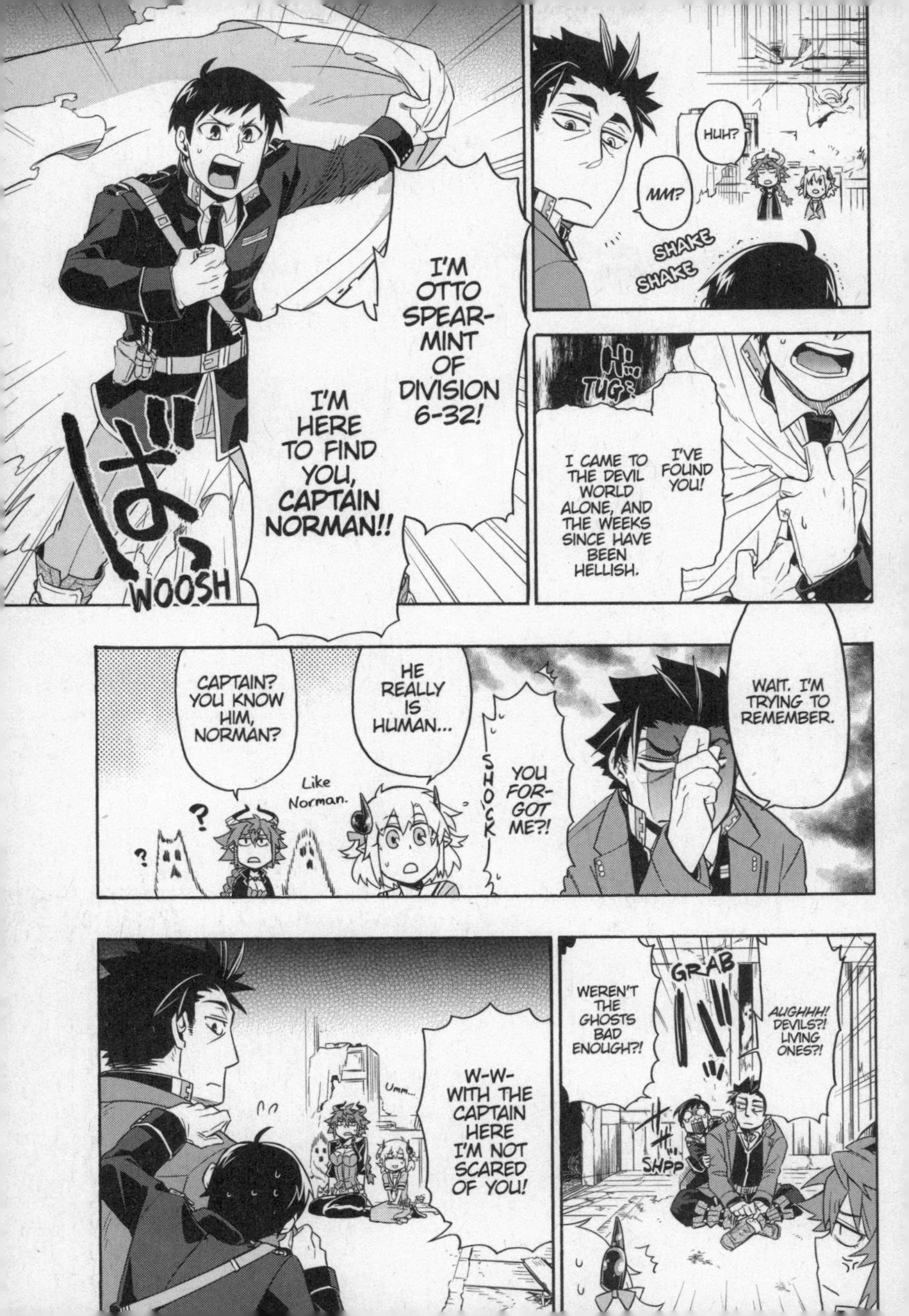
HUH?
MM?
SHAKE
SHAKE
TUG
I'VE FOUND YOU!
I CAME TO THE DEVIL WORLD ALONE, AND THE WEEKS SINCE HAVE BEEN HELLISH.
I'M OTTO SPEARMINT OF DIVISION 6-32!
I'M HERE TO FIND YOU, CAPTAIN NORMAN!!
ばっ
WOOSH
WAIT. I'M TRYING TO REMEMBER.
YOU FORGOT ME?!
SHOCK
HE REALLY IS HUMAN...
Like Norman.
CAPTAIN? YOU KNOW HIM, NORMAN?
AUGHHH! DEVILS?! LIVING ONES?!
GRAB
WEREN'T THE GHOSTS BAD ENOUGH?!
SHPP
W-W-WITH THE CAPTAIN HERE I'M NOT SCARED OF YOU!
Umm...

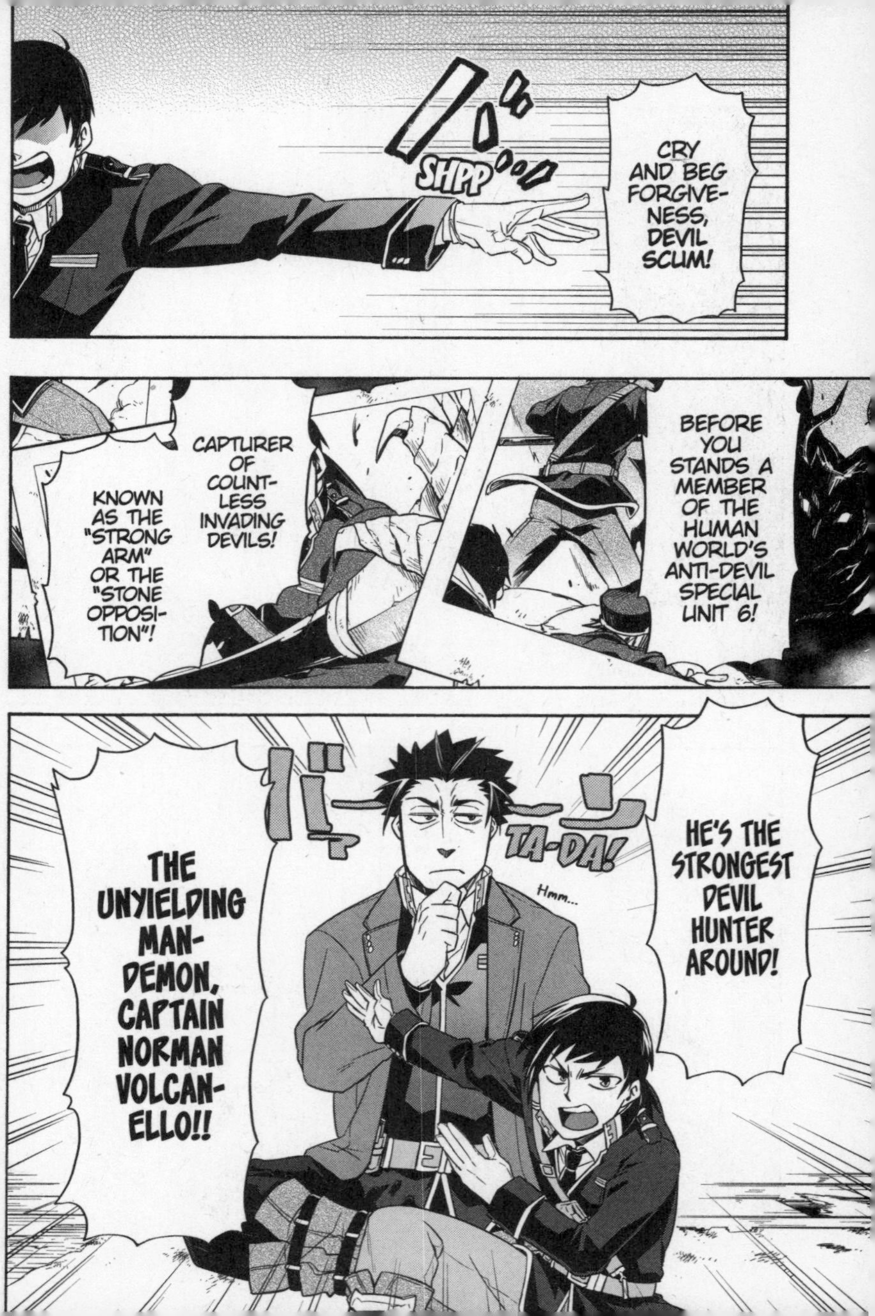
SHPP
CRY AND BEG FORGIVENESS, DEVIL SCUM!
BEFORE YOU STANDS A MEMBER OF THE HUMAN WORLD'S ANTI-DEVIL SPECIAL UNIT 6!
CAPTURER OF COUNTLESS INVADING DEVILS!
KNOWN AS THE "STRONG ARM" OR THE "STONE OPPOSITION"!
HE'S THE STRONGEST DEVIL HUNTER AROUND!
TA-DA!
Hmm...
THE UNYIELDING MAN-DEMON, CAPTAIN NORMAN VOLCANELLO!!

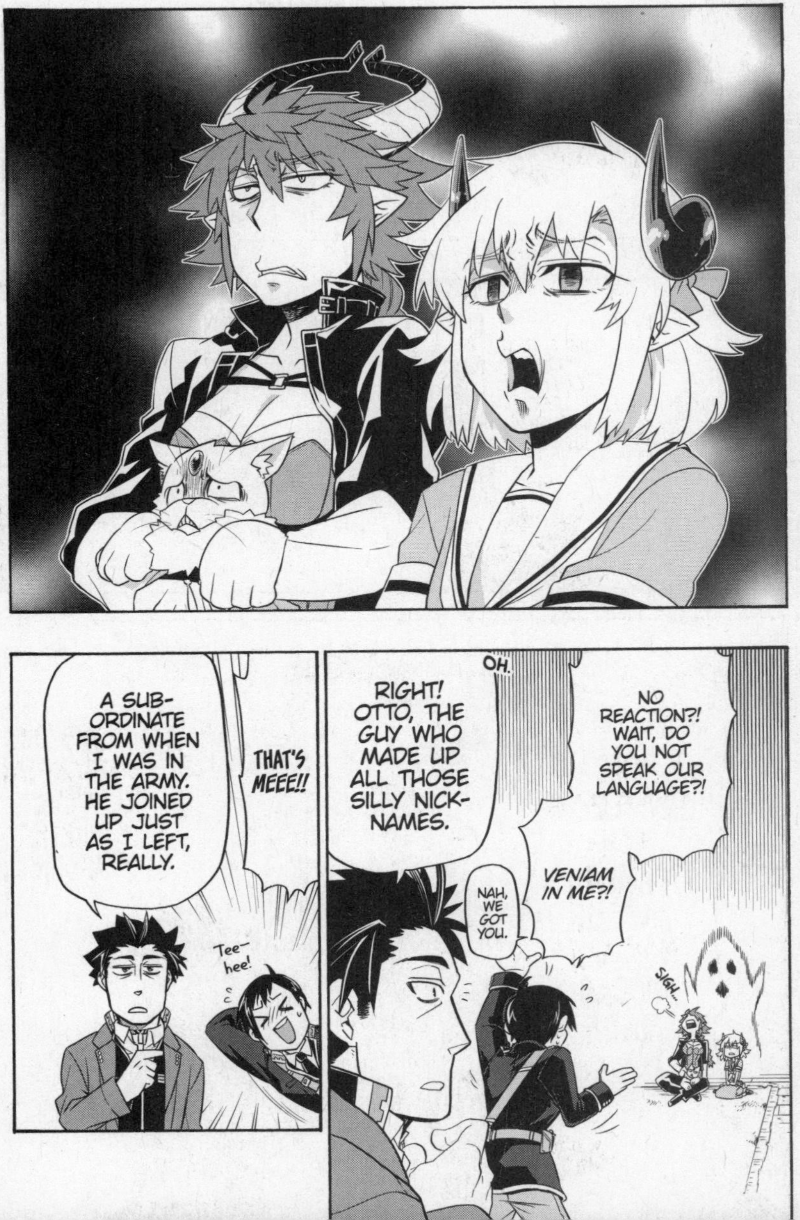
OH.
RIGHT! OTTO, THE GUY WHO MADE UP ALL THOSE SILLY NICK-NAMES.
NO REACTION?! WAIT, DO YOU NOT SPEAK OUR LANGUAGE?!
VENIAM IN ME?!
NAH, WE GOT YOU.
SIGH...
A SUB-ORDINATE FROM WHEN I WAS IN THE ARMY. HE JOINED UP JUST AS I LEFT, REALLY.
THAT'S MEEE!!
Tee-hee!

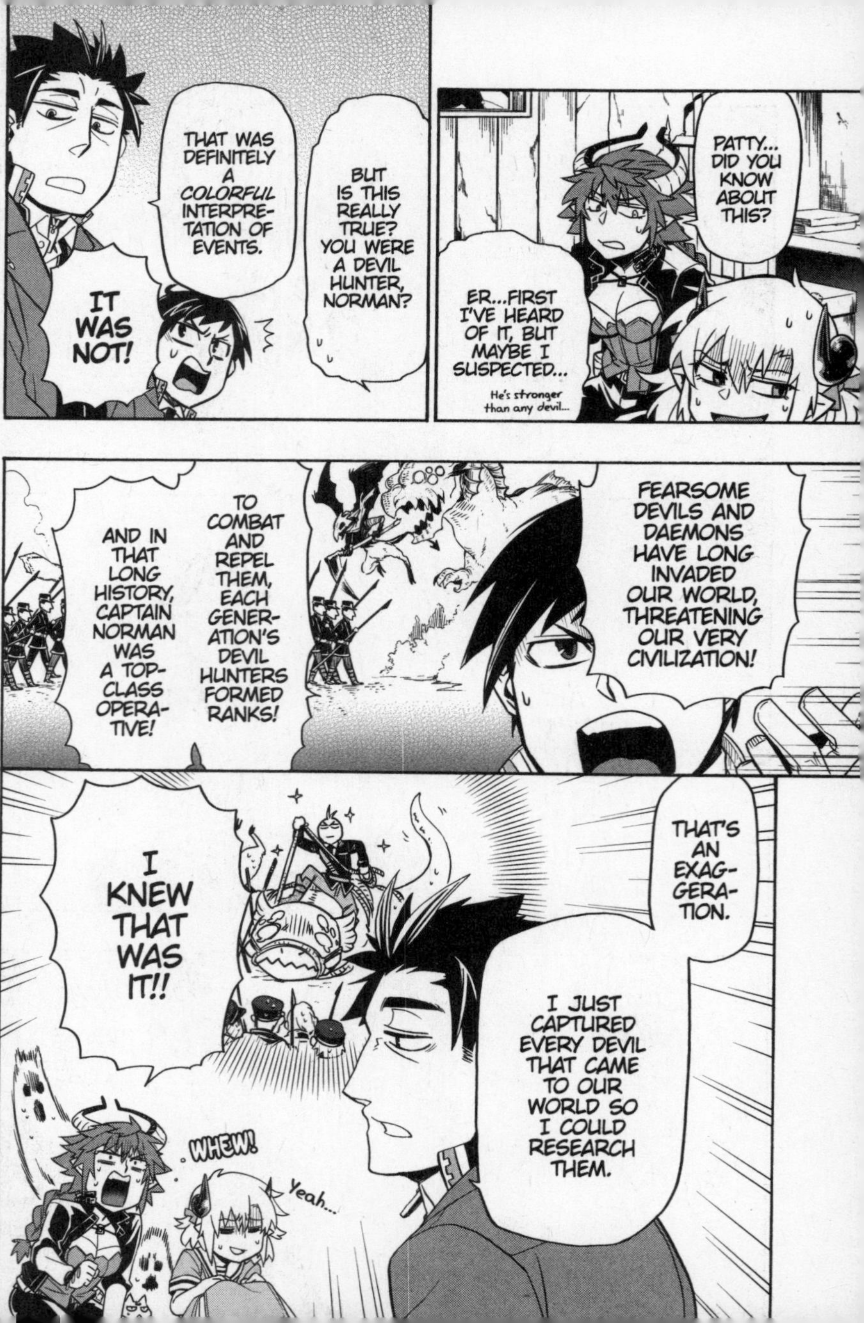
PATTY... DID YOU KNOW ABOUT THIS?
ER...FIRST I'VE HEARD OF IT, BUT MAYBE I SUSPECTED...
He's stronger than any devil...
BUT IS THIS REALLY TRUE? YOU WERE A DEVIL HUNTER, NORMAN?
THAT WAS DEFINITELY A *COLORFUL* INTERPRETATION OF EVENTS.
IT WAS NOT!
FEARSOME DEVILS AND DAEMONS HAVE LONG INVADED OUR WORLD, THREATENING OUR VERY CIVILIZATION!
TO COMBAT AND REPEL THEM, EACH GENERATION'S DEVIL HUNTERS FORMED RANKS!
AND IN THAT LONG HISTORY, CAPTAIN NORMAN WAS A TOP-CLASS OPERATIVE!
THAT'S AN EXAGGERATION.
I JUST CAPTURED EVERY DEVIL THAT CAME TO OUR WORLD SO I COULD RESEARCH THEM.
I KNEW THAT WAS IT!!
WHEW!
Yeah...

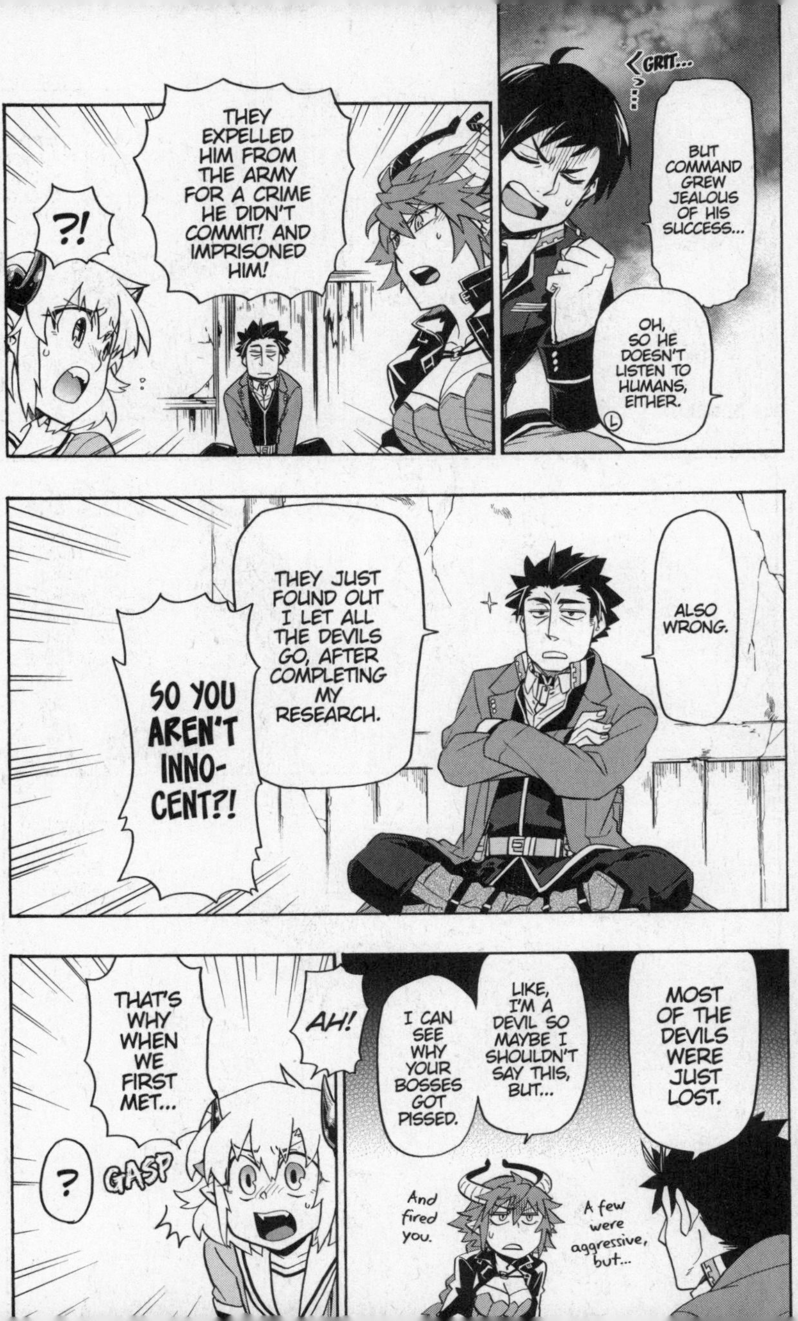
GRIT...
BUT COMMAND GREW JEALOUS OF HIS SUCCESS...
OH, SO HE DOESN'T LISTEN TO HUMANS, EITHER.
THEY EXPELLED HIM FROM THE ARMY FOR A CRIME HE DIDN'T COMMIT! AND IMPRISONED HIM!
?!
ALSO WRONG.
THEY JUST FOUND OUT I LET ALL THE DEVILS GO, AFTER COMPLETING MY RESEARCH.
SO YOU AREN'T INNO-CENT?!
MOST OF THE DEVILS WERE JUST LOST.
LIKE, I'M A DEVIL SO MAYBE I SHOULDN'T SAY THIS, BUT...
I CAN SEE WHY YOUR BOSSES GOT PISSED.
A few were aggressive, but...
And fired you.
AH!
THAT'S WHY WHEN WE FIRST MET...
GASP
?

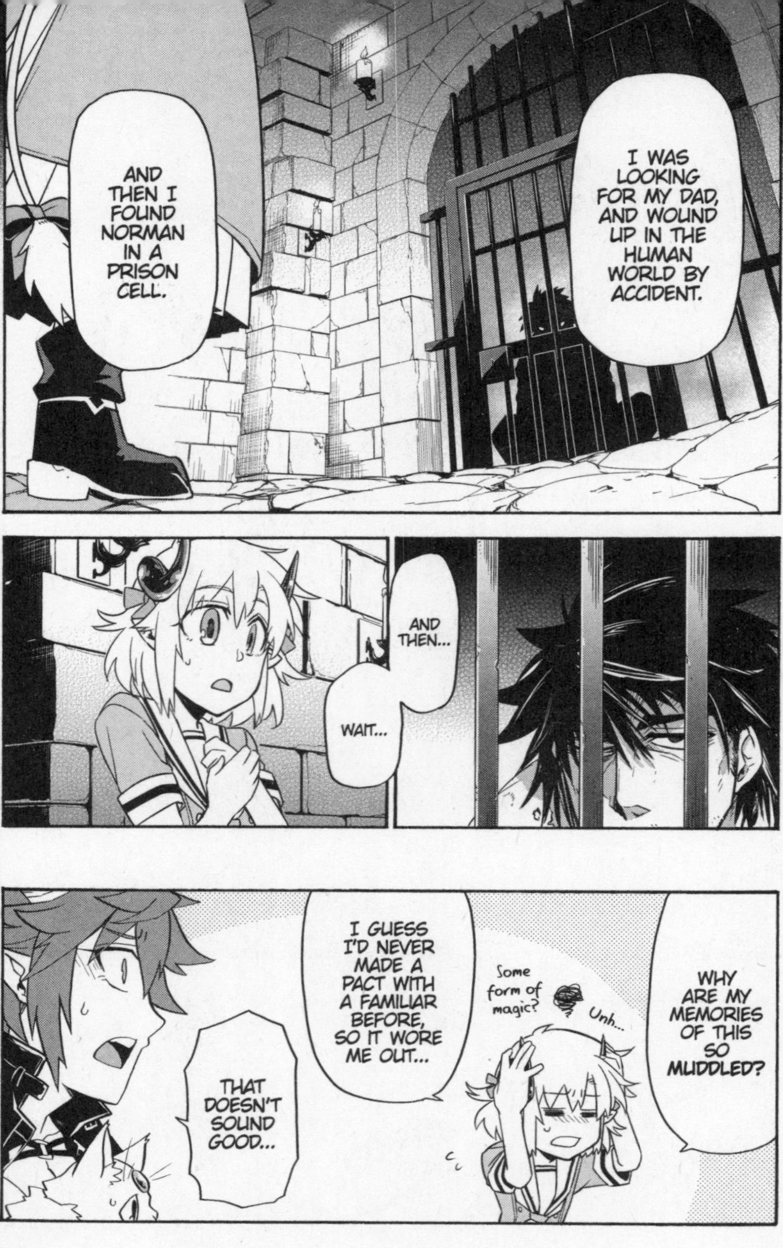
I WAS LOOKING FOR MY DAD, AND WOUND UP IN THE HUMAN WORLD BY ACCIDENT.
AND THEN I FOUND NORMAN IN A PRISON CELL.
AND THEN...
WAIT...
WHY ARE MY MEMORIES OF THIS SO MUDDLED?
Unh...
Some form of magic?
I GUESS I'D NEVER MADE A PACT WITH A FAMILIAR BEFORE, SO IT WORE ME OUT...
THAT DOESN'T SOUND GOOD...

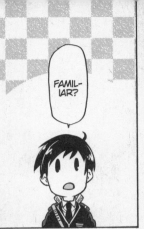

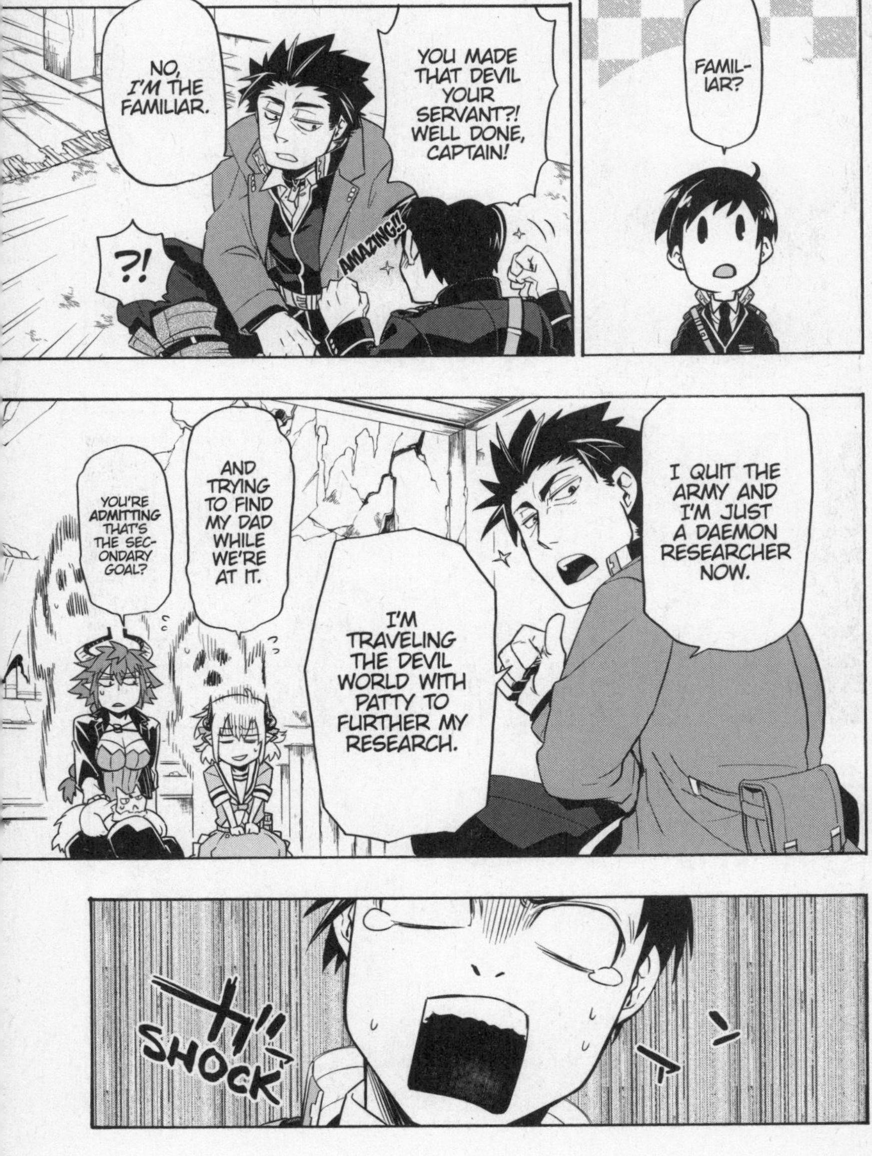
FAMILIAR?
YOU MADE THAT DEVIL YOUR SERVANT?! WELL DONE, CAPTAIN!
AMAZING!!
NO, I'M THE FAMILIAR.
?!
I QUIT THE ARMY AND I'M JUST A DAEMON RESEARCHER NOW.
I'M TRAVELING THE DEVIL WORLD WITH PATTY TO FURTHER MY RESEARCH.
AND TRYING TO FIND MY DAD WHILE WE'RE AT IT.
YOU'RE ADMITTING THAT'S THE SECONDARY GOAL?
SHOCK

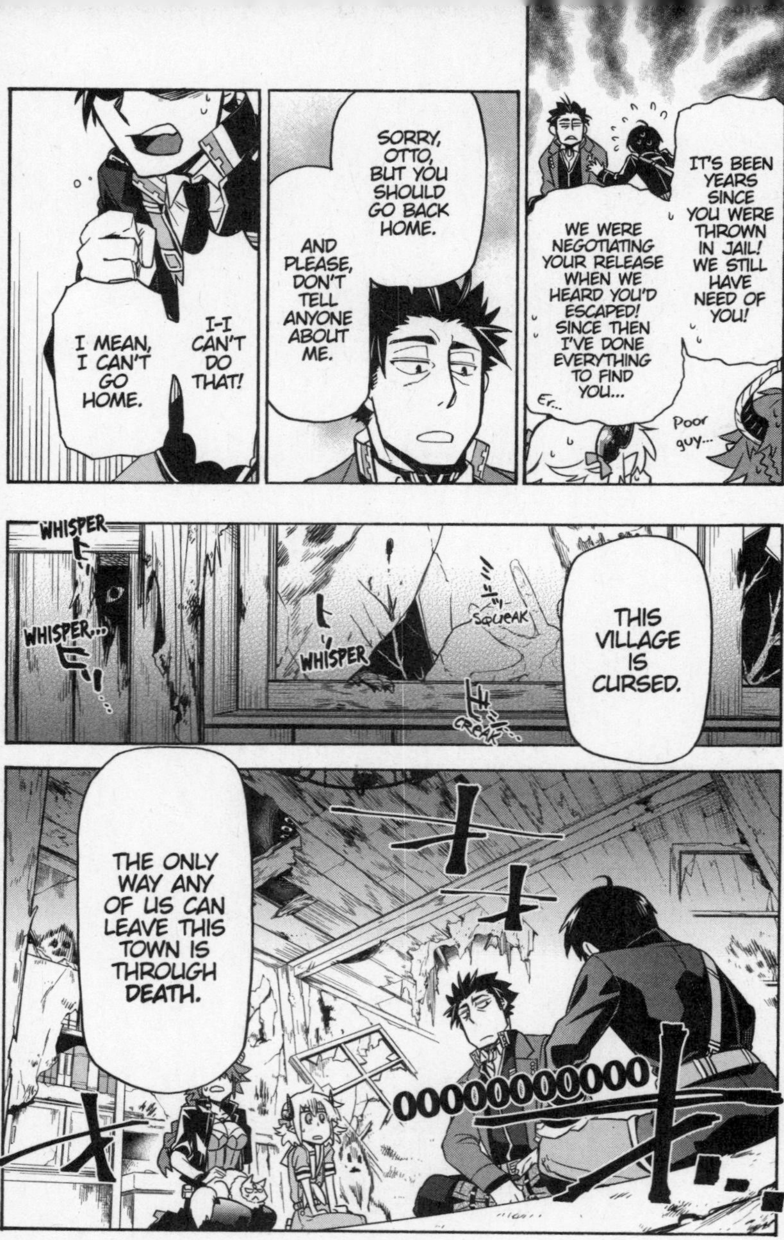
IT'S BEEN YEARS SINCE YOU WERE THROWN IN JAIL! WE STILL HAVE NEED OF YOU!
WE WERE NEGOTIATING YOUR RELEASE WHEN WE HEARD YOU'D ESCAPED! SINCE THEN I'VE DONE EVERYTHING TO FIND YOU...
Er...
Poor guy...
SORRY, OTTO, BUT YOU SHOULD GO BACK HOME.
AND PLEASE, DON'T TELL ANYONE ABOUT ME.
I-I CAN'T DO THAT!
I MEAN, I CAN'T GO HOME.
THIS VILLAGE IS CURSED.
SQUEAK
CREAK
WHISPER
WHISPER...
WHISPER
THE ONLY WAY ANY OF US CAN LEAVE THIS TOWN IS THROUGH DEATH.
OOOOOOOOOOO

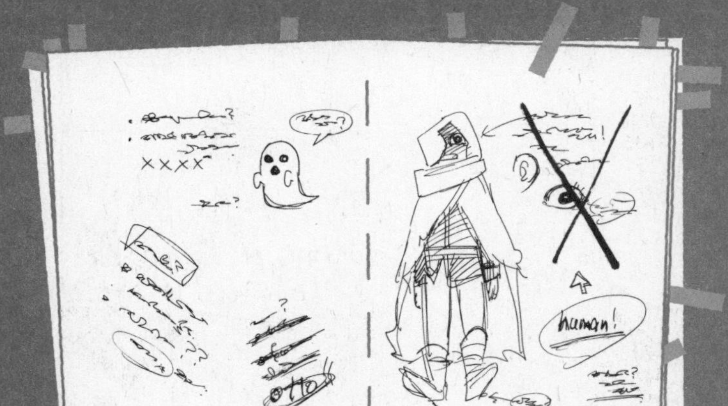
human!

Sorry For My Familiar

FILE 21: Eastern Dragon Bone Islands – Ghost Town ②

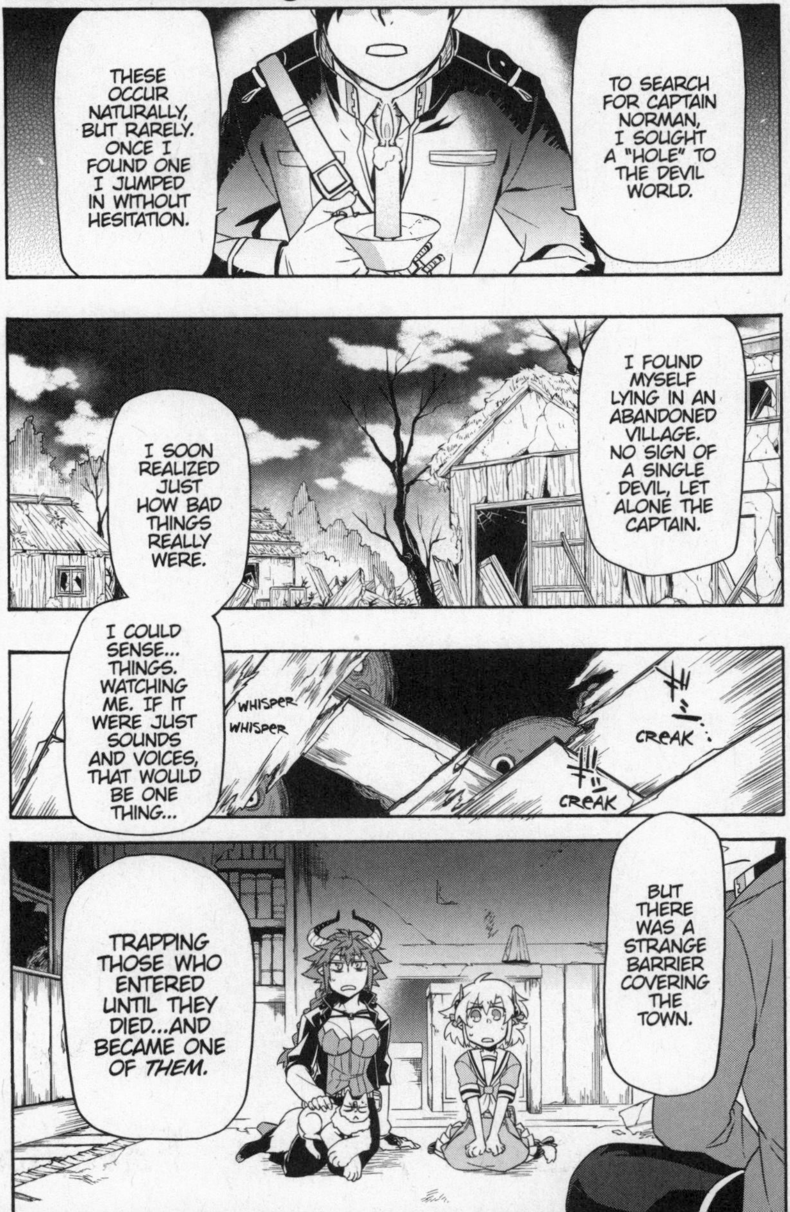

TO SEARCH FOR CAPTAIN NORMAN, I SOUGHT A "HOLE" TO THE DEVIL WORLD.
THESE OCCUR NATURALLY, BUT RARELY. ONCE I FOUND ONE I JUMPED IN WITHOUT HESITATION.
I FOUND MYSELF LYING IN AN ABANDONED VILLAGE. NO SIGN OF A SINGLE DEVIL, LET ALONE THE CAPTAIN.
I SOON REALIZED JUST HOW BAD THINGS REALLY WERE.
CREAK
CREAK
WHISPER
WHISPER
I COULD SENSE... THINGS. WATCHING ME. IF IT WERE JUST SOUNDS AND VOICES, THAT WOULD BE ONE THING...
BUT THERE WAS A STRANGE BARRIER COVERING THE TOWN.
TRAPPING THOSE WHO ENTERED UNTIL THEY DIED...AND BECAME ONE OF *THEM*.

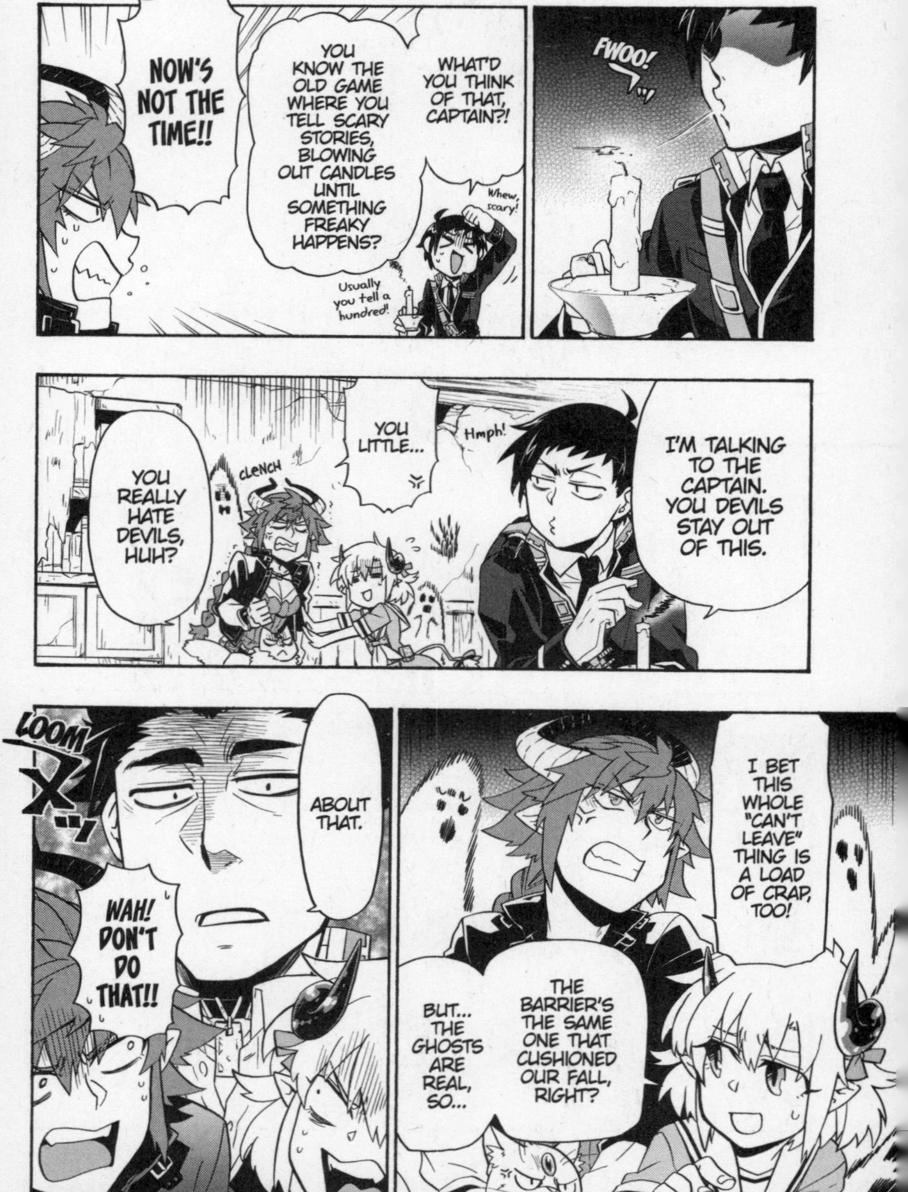
FWOO!
WHAT'D YOU THINK OF THAT, CAPTAIN?!
YOU KNOW THE OLD GAME WHERE YOU TELL SCARY STORIES, BLOWING OUT CANDLES UNTIL SOMETHING FREAKY HAPPENS?
Whew, scary!
Usually you tell a hundred!
NOW'S NOT THE TIME!!
I'M TALKING TO THE CAPTAIN. YOU DEVILS STAY OUT OF THIS.
Hmph!
YOU LITTLE...
CLENCH
YOU REALLY HATE DEVILS, HUH?
I BET THIS WHOLE "CAN'T LEAVE" THING IS A LOAD OF CRAP, TOO!
THE BARRIER'S THE SAME ONE THAT CUSHIONED OUR FALL, RIGHT?
BUT... THE GHOSTS ARE REAL, SO...
ABOUT THAT.
LOOM
WAH! DON'T DO THAT!!

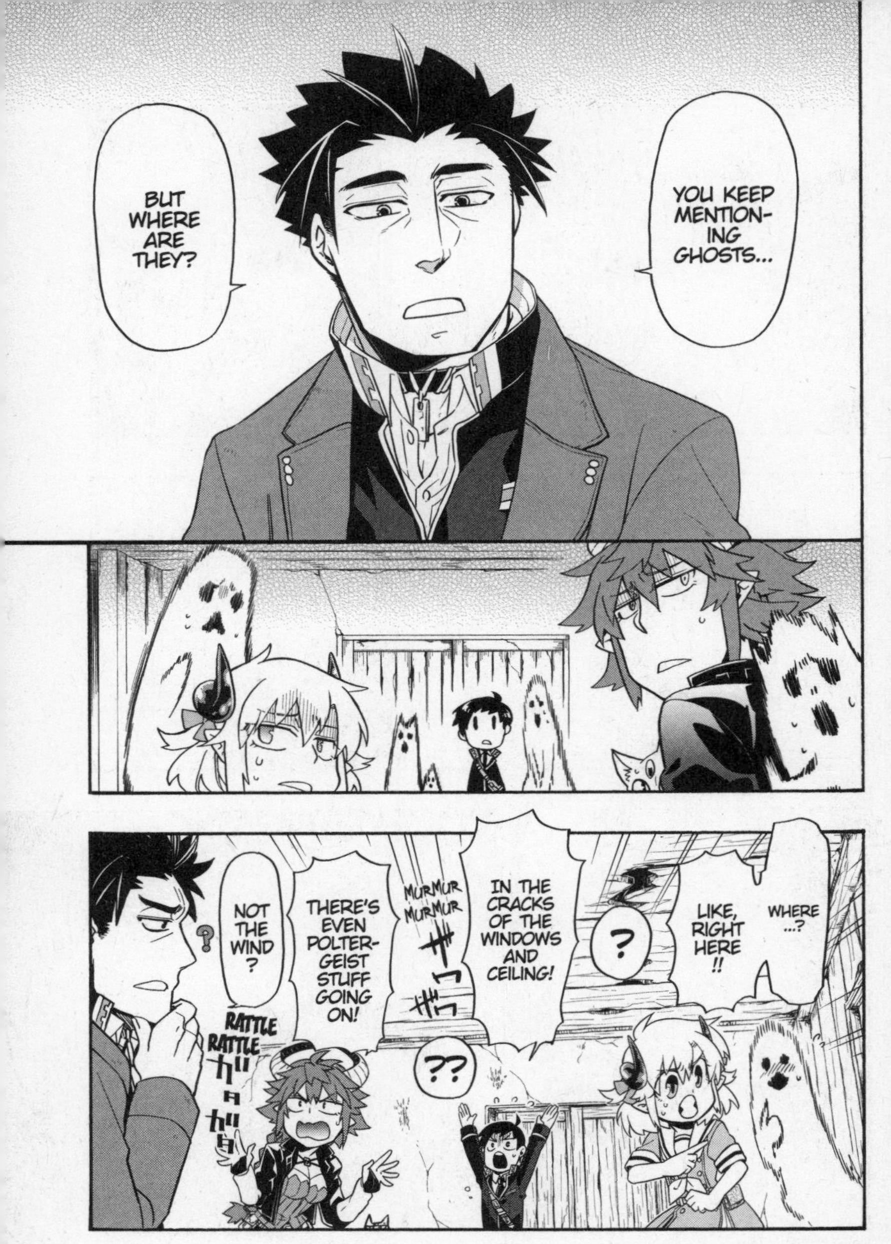
YOU KEEP MENTIONING GHOSTS...
BUT WHERE ARE THEY?
WHERE ...?
LIKE, RIGHT HERE !!
?
IN THE CRACKS OF THE WINDOWS AND CEILING!
MURMUR MURMUR
THERE'S EVEN POLTER-GEIST STUFF GOING ON!
??
NOT THE WIND ?
?
RATTLE RATTLE

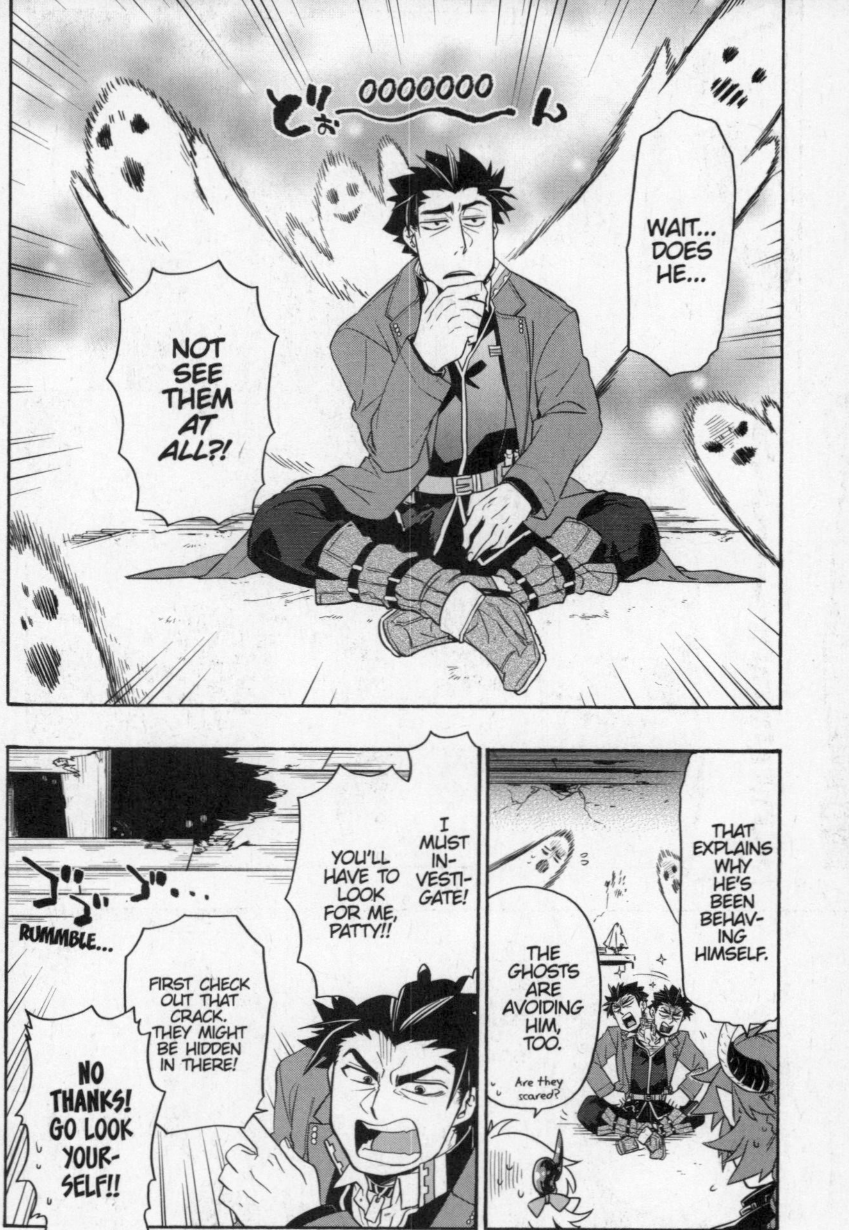
どぉ—OOOOOOO—ん
WAIT... DOES HE...
NOT SEE THEM AT ALL?!
THAT EXPLAINS WHY HE'S BEEN BEHAV-ING HIMSELF.
THE GHOSTS ARE AVOIDING HIM, TOO.
Are they scared?
I MUST IN-VESTI-GATE!
YOU'LL HAVE TO LOOK FOR ME, PATTY!!
ゴゴゴ...
RUMMBLE...
FIRST CHECK OUT THAT CRACK. THEY MIGHT BE HIDDEN IN THERE!
NO THANKS! GO LOOK YOUR-SELF!!

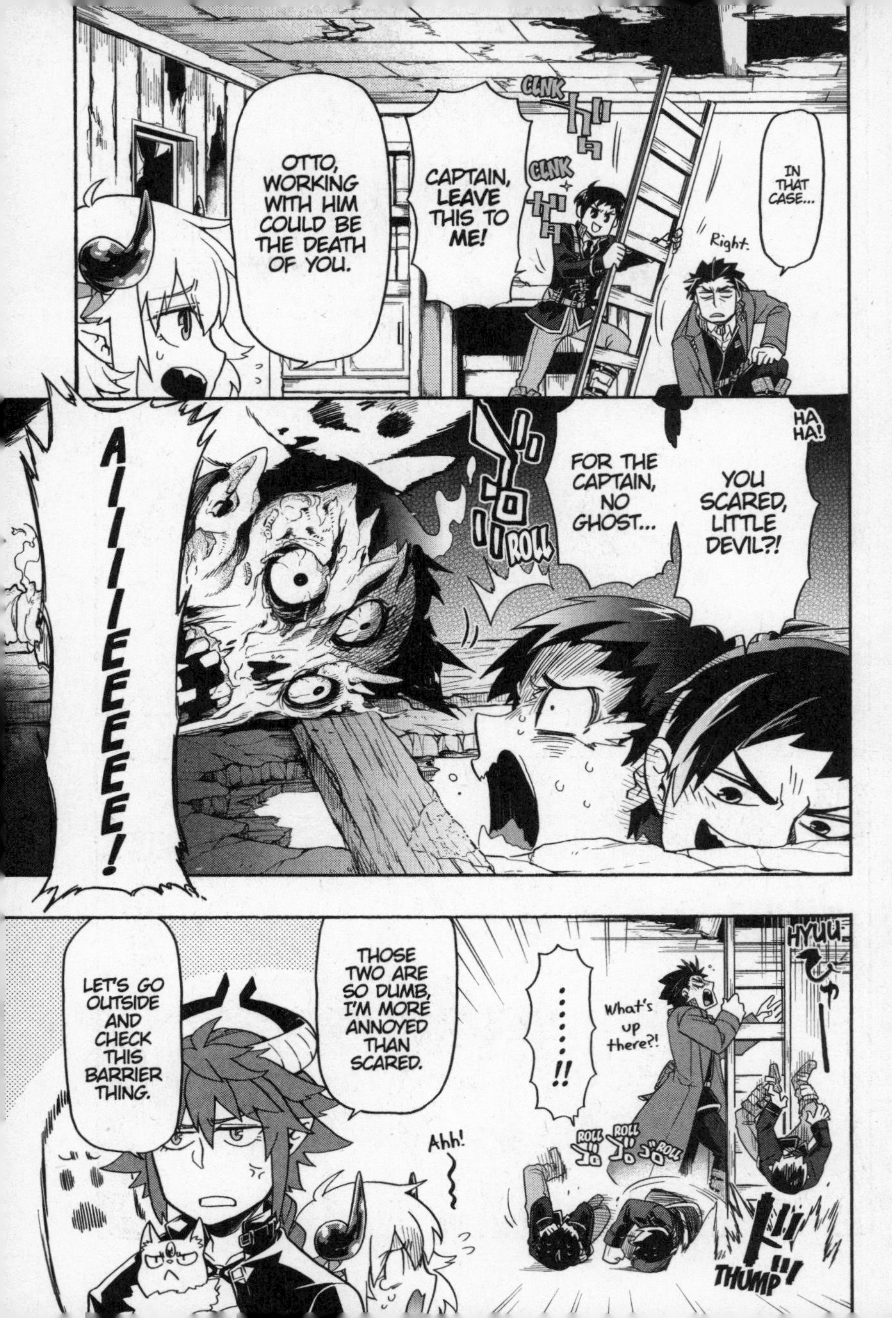
IN THAT CASE...
Right.
CLNK
CLNK
CAPTAIN, LEAVE THIS TO ME!
OTTO, WORKING WITH HIM COULD BE THE DEATH OF YOU.
HA HA!
YOU SCARED, LITTLE DEVIL?!
FOR THE CAPTAIN, NO GHOST...
ROLL
AIIIIEEEEEE!
HYUU
THUMP!!
What's up there?!
......!!
ROLL
ROLL
ROLL
THOSE TWO ARE SO DUMB, I'M MORE ANNOYED THAN SCARED.
Ahh!
LET'S GO OUTSIDE AND CHECK THIS BARRIER THING.

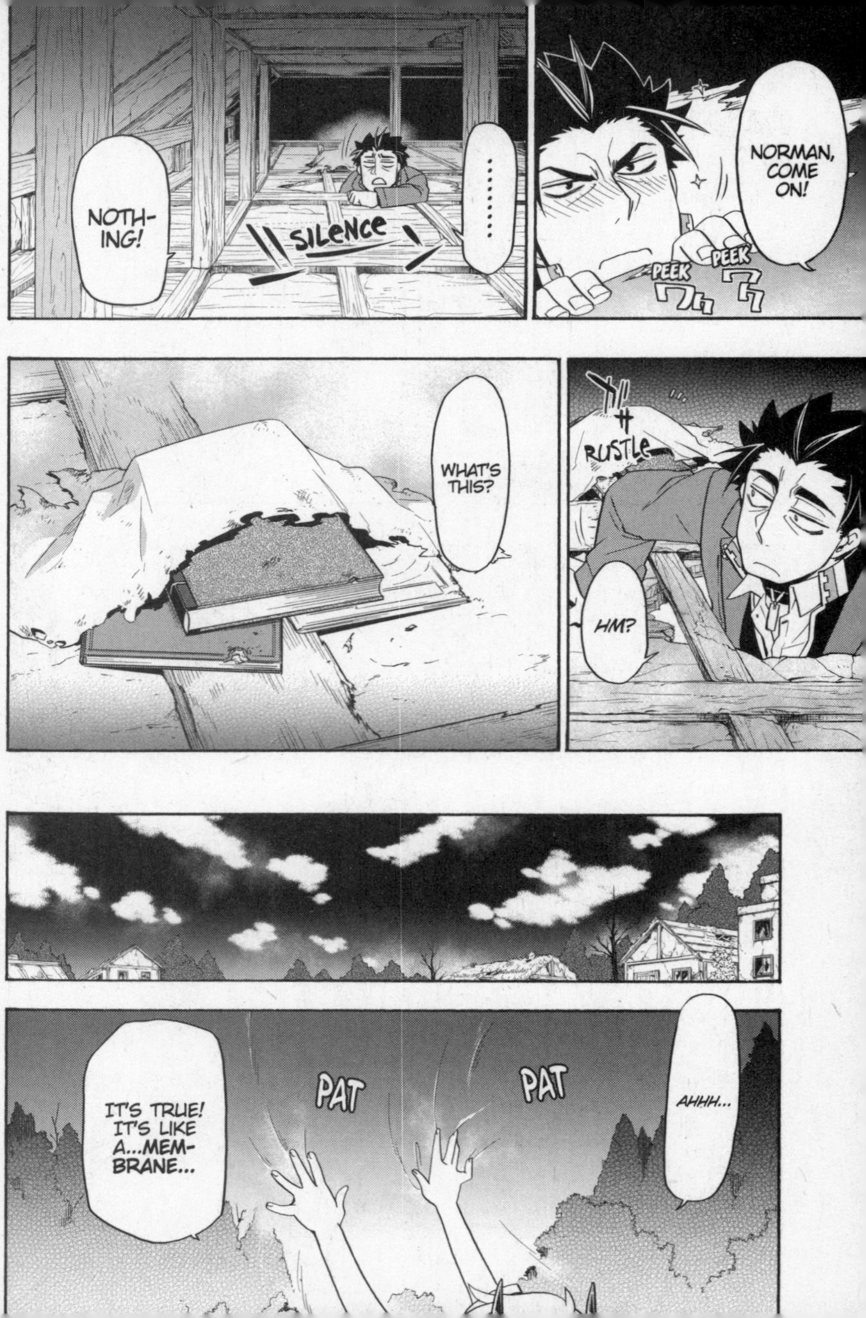
NORMAN, COME ON!
PEEK
PEEK
......
SILENCE
NOTH-ING!
RUSTLE
HM?
WHAT'S THIS?
AHHH...
PAT
PAT
IT'S TRUE! IT'S LIKE A...MEM-BRANE...

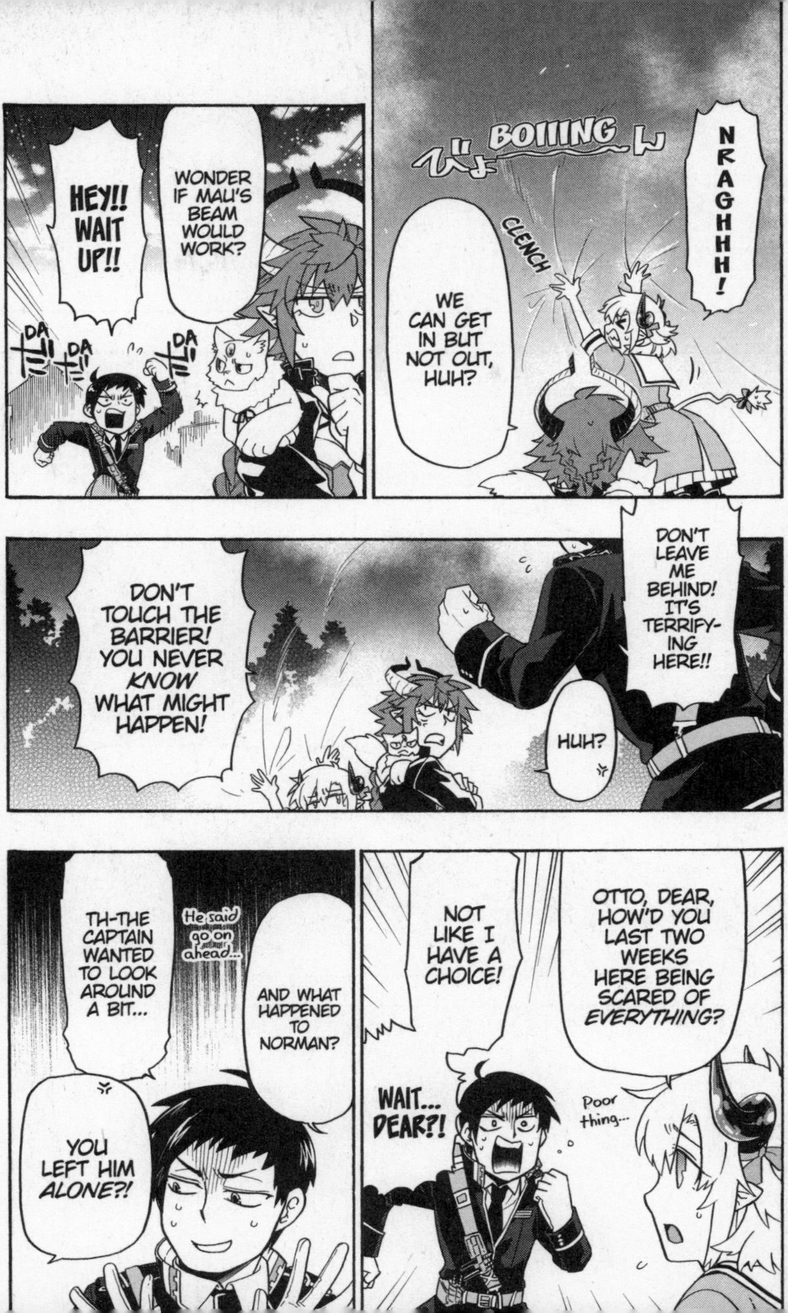
NRAGHHH!
BOIIING
CLENCH
WE CAN GET IN BUT NOT OUT, HUH?
WONDER IF MAU'S BEAM WOULD WORK?
HEY!! WAIT UP!!
DA
DA
DA
DON'T LEAVE ME BEHIND! IT'S TERRIFYING HERE!!
HUH?
DON'T TOUCH THE BARRIER! YOU NEVER KNOW WHAT MIGHT HAPPEN!
OTTO, DEAR, HOW'D YOU LAST TWO WEEKS HERE BEING SCARED OF EVERYTHING?
NOT LIKE I HAVE A CHOICE!
WAIT... DEAR?!
Poor thing...
AND WHAT HAPPENED TO NORMAN?
He said go on ahead...
TH-THE CAPTAIN WANTED TO LOOK AROUND A BIT...
YOU LEFT HIM ALONE?!

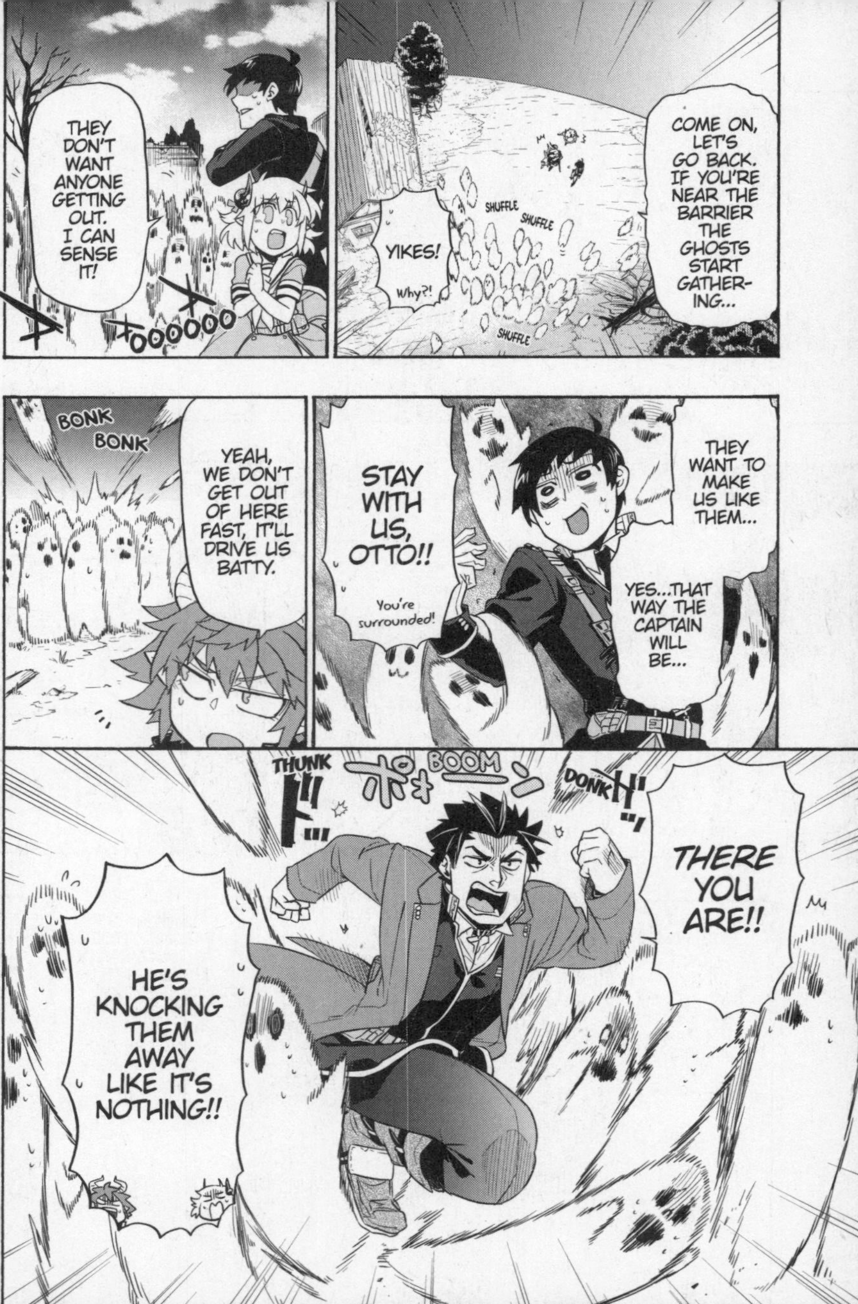
COME ON, LET'S GO BACK. IF YOU'RE NEAR THE BARRIER THE GHOSTS START GATHERING...
SHUFFLE
SHUFFLE
YIKES!
Why?!
SHUFFLE
THEY DON'T WANT ANYONE GETTING OUT. I CAN SENSE IT!
THEY WANT TO MAKE US LIKE THEM...
YES...THAT WAY THE CAPTAIN WILL BE...
STAY WITH US, OTTO!!
You're surrounded!
YEAH, WE DON'T GET OUT OF HERE FAST, IT'LL DRIVE US BATTY.
BONK
BONK
DONK
BOOM
THUNK
THERE YOU ARE!!
HE'S KNOCKING THEM AWAY LIKE IT'S NOTHING!!

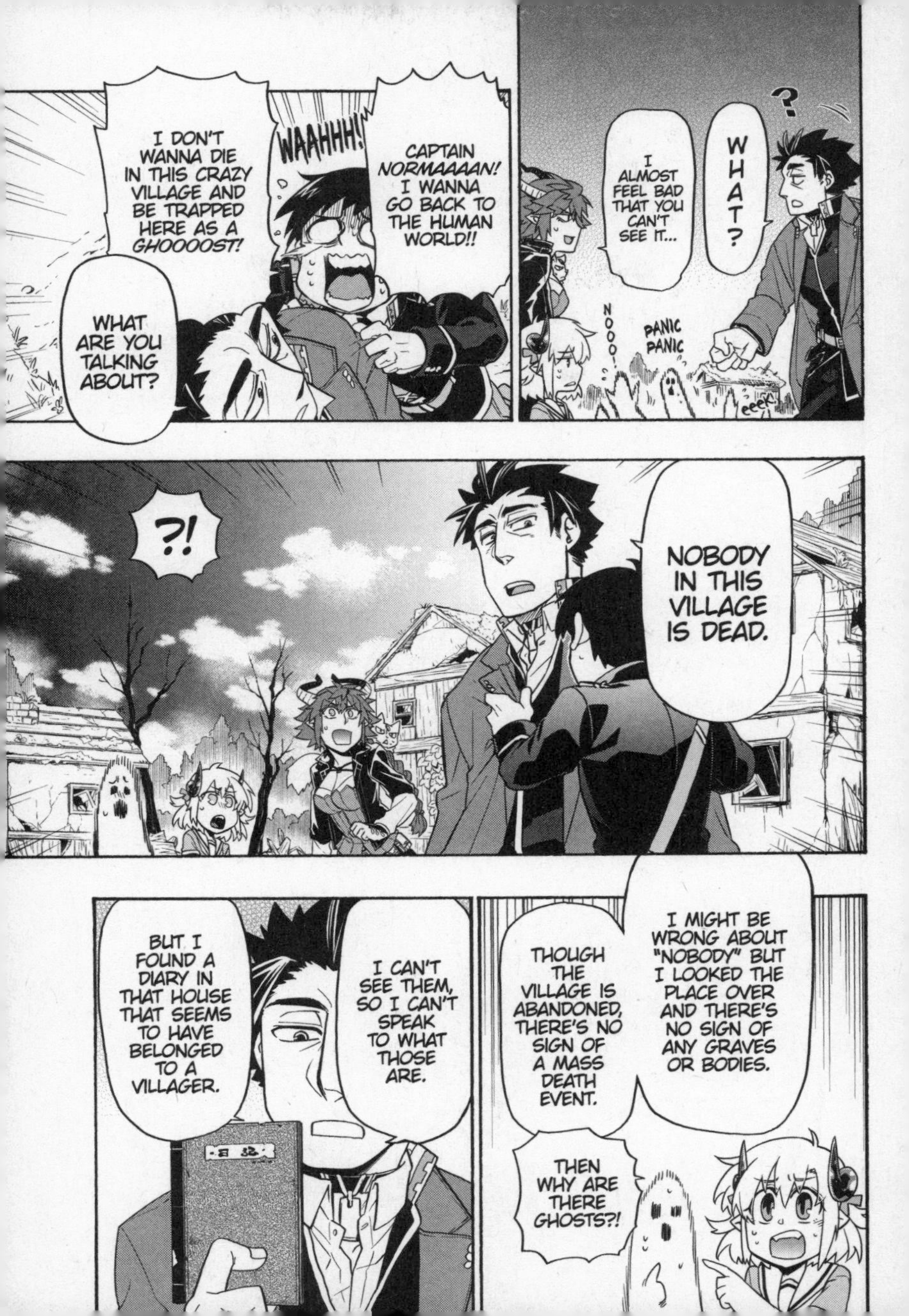
?
WHAT?
I ALMOST FEEL BAD THAT YOU CAN'T SEE IT...
NOOOO!
PANIC PANIC
eeek
CAPTAIN NORMAAAAN! I WANNA GO BACK TO THE HUMAN WORLD!!
WAAHHH!
I DON'T WANNA DIE IN THIS CRAZY VILLAGE AND BE TRAPPED HERE AS A GHOOOOST!
WHAT ARE YOU TALKING ABOUT?
NOBODY IN THIS VILLAGE IS DEAD.
?!
I MIGHT BE WRONG ABOUT "NOBODY" BUT I LOOKED THE PLACE OVER AND THERE'S NO SIGN OF ANY GRAVES OR BODIES.
THOUGH THE VILLAGE IS ABANDONED, THERE'S NO SIGN OF A MASS DEATH EVENT.
THEN WHY ARE THERE GHOSTS?!
I CAN'T SEE THEM, SO I CAN'T SPEAK TO WHAT THOSE ARE.
BUT I FOUND A DIARY IN THAT HOUSE THAT SEEMS TO HAVE BELONGED TO A VILLAGER.

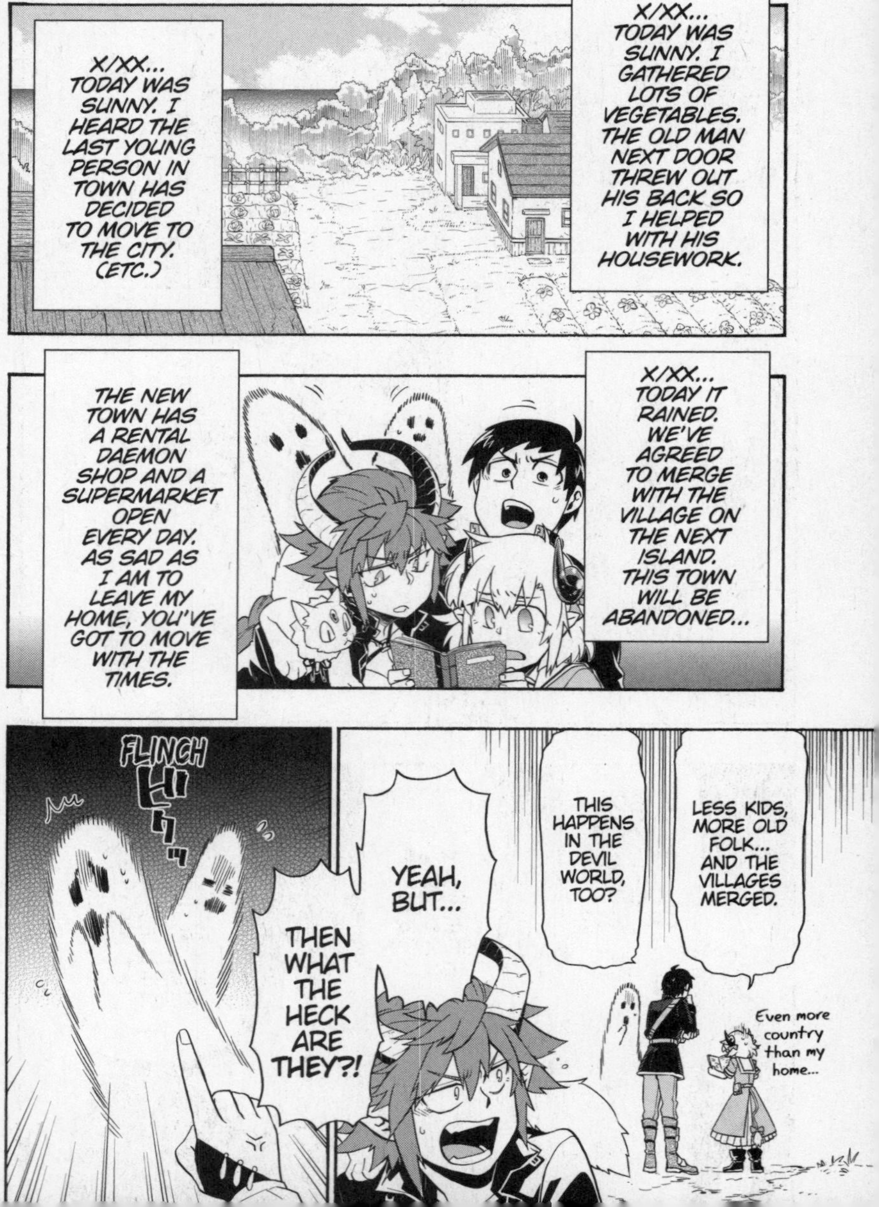
X/XX... TODAY WAS SUNNY. I GATHERED LOTS OF VEGETABLES. THE OLD MAN NEXT DOOR THREW OUT HIS BACK SO I HELPED WITH HIS HOUSEWORK.
X/XX... TODAY WAS SUNNY. I HEARD THE LAST YOUNG PERSON IN TOWN HAS DECIDED TO MOVE TO THE CITY. (ETC.)
X/XX... TODAY IT RAINED. WE'VE AGREED TO MERGE WITH THE VILLAGE ON THE NEXT ISLAND. THIS TOWN WILL BE ABANDONED...
THE NEW TOWN HAS A RENTAL DAEMON SHOP AND A SUPERMARKET OPEN EVERY DAY. AS SAD AS I AM TO LEAVE MY HOME, YOU'VE GOT TO MOVE WITH THE TIMES.
LESS KIDS, MORE OLD FOLK... AND THE VILLAGES MERGED.
THIS HAPPENS IN THE DEVIL WORLD, TOO?
YEAH, BUT...
THEN WHAT THE HECK ARE THEY?!
Even more country than my home...
FLINCH

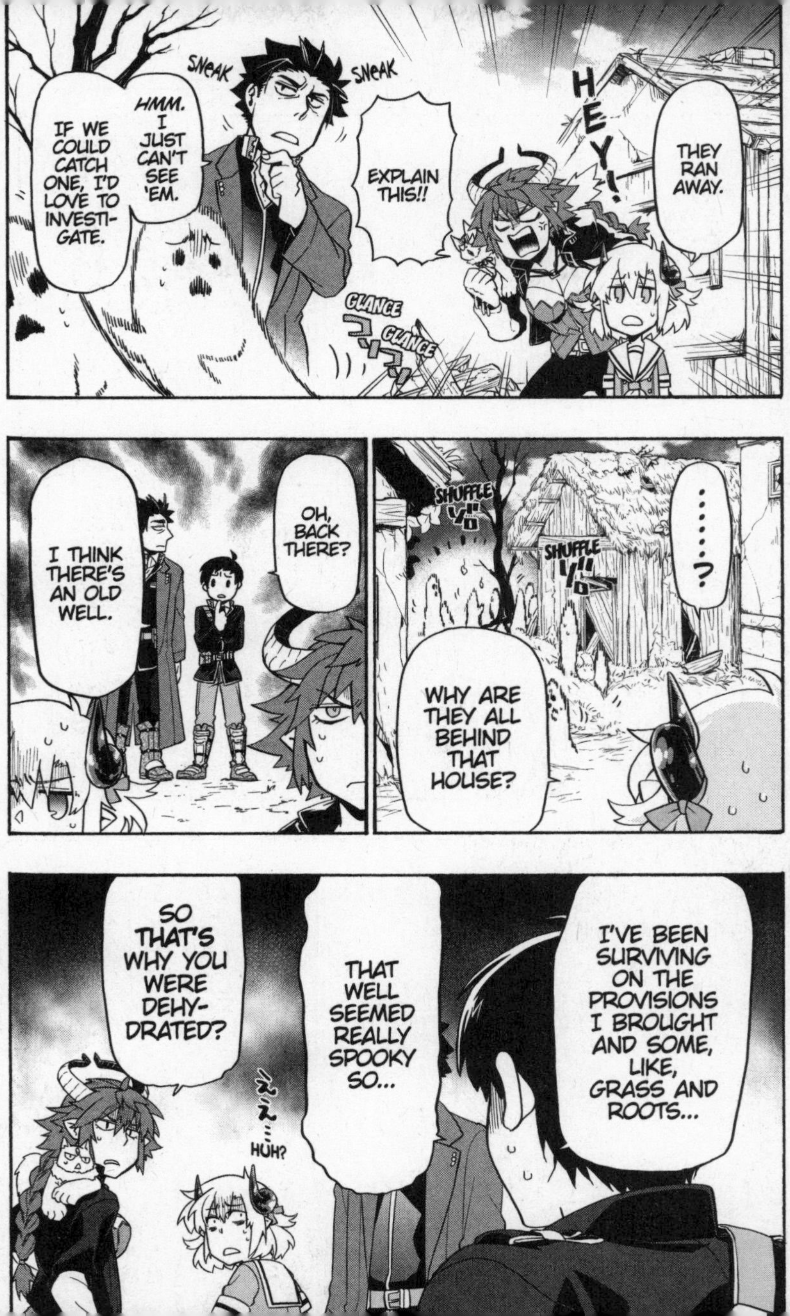
THEY RAN AWAY.
HEY!!
EXPLAIN THIS!!
SNEAK
SNEAK
HMM. I JUST CAN'T SEE 'EM.
IF WE COULD CATCH ONE, I'D LOVE TO INVESTIGATE.
GLANCE
GLANCE
......?
SHUFFLE
SHUFFLE
WHY ARE THEY ALL BEHIND THAT HOUSE?
OH, BACK THERE?
I THINK THERE'S AN OLD WELL.
I'VE BEEN SURVIVING ON THE PROVISIONS I BROUGHT AND SOME, LIKE, GRASS AND ROOTS...
THAT WELL SEEMED REALLY SPOOKY SO...
ええ…
HUH?
SO THAT'S WHY YOU WERE DEHYDRATED?

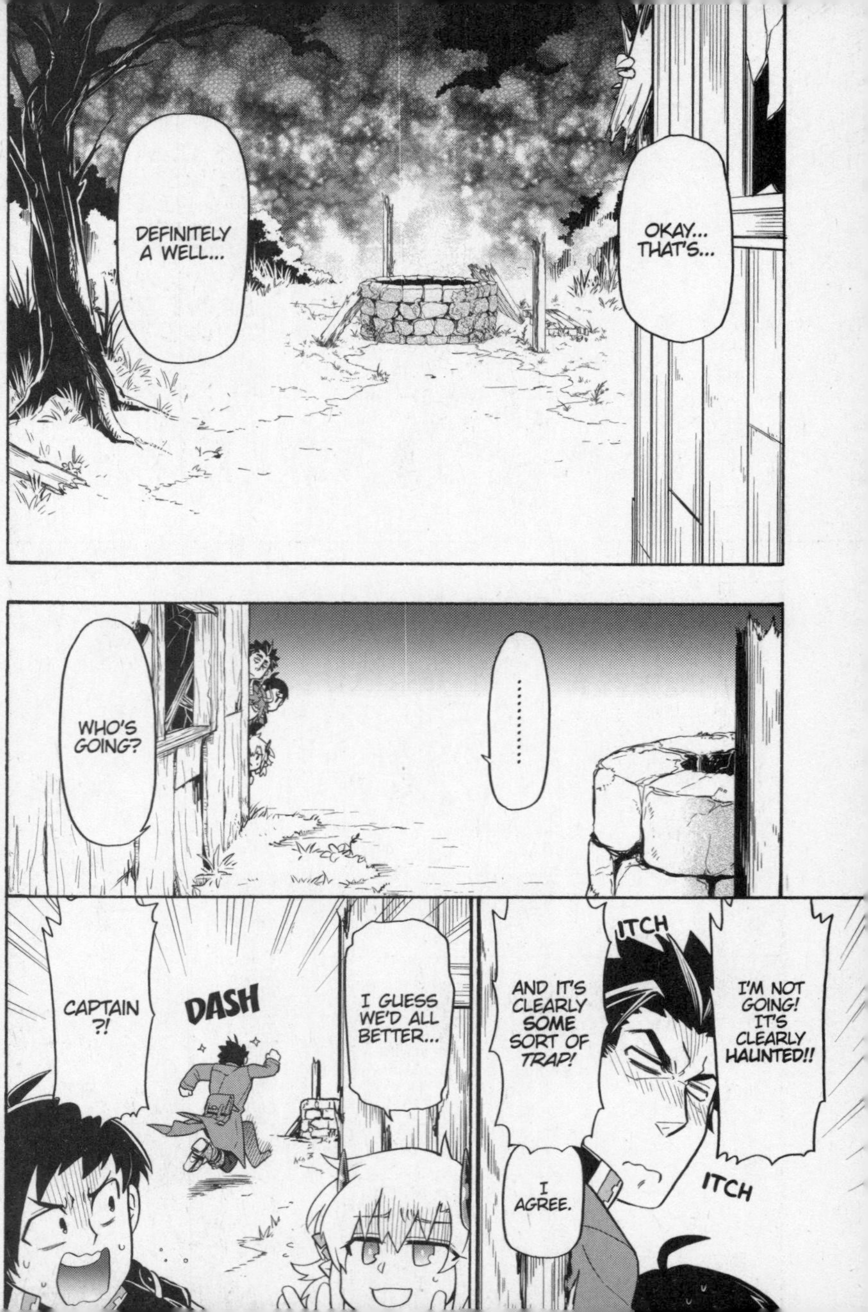
OKAY... THAT'S...
DEFINITELY A WELL...
......
WHO'S GOING?
ITCH
I'M NOT GOING! IT'S CLEARLY HAUNTED!!
AND IT'S CLEARLY SOME SORT OF *TRAP!*
ITCH
I AGREE.
I GUESS WE'D ALL BETTER...
DASH
CAPTAIN ?!

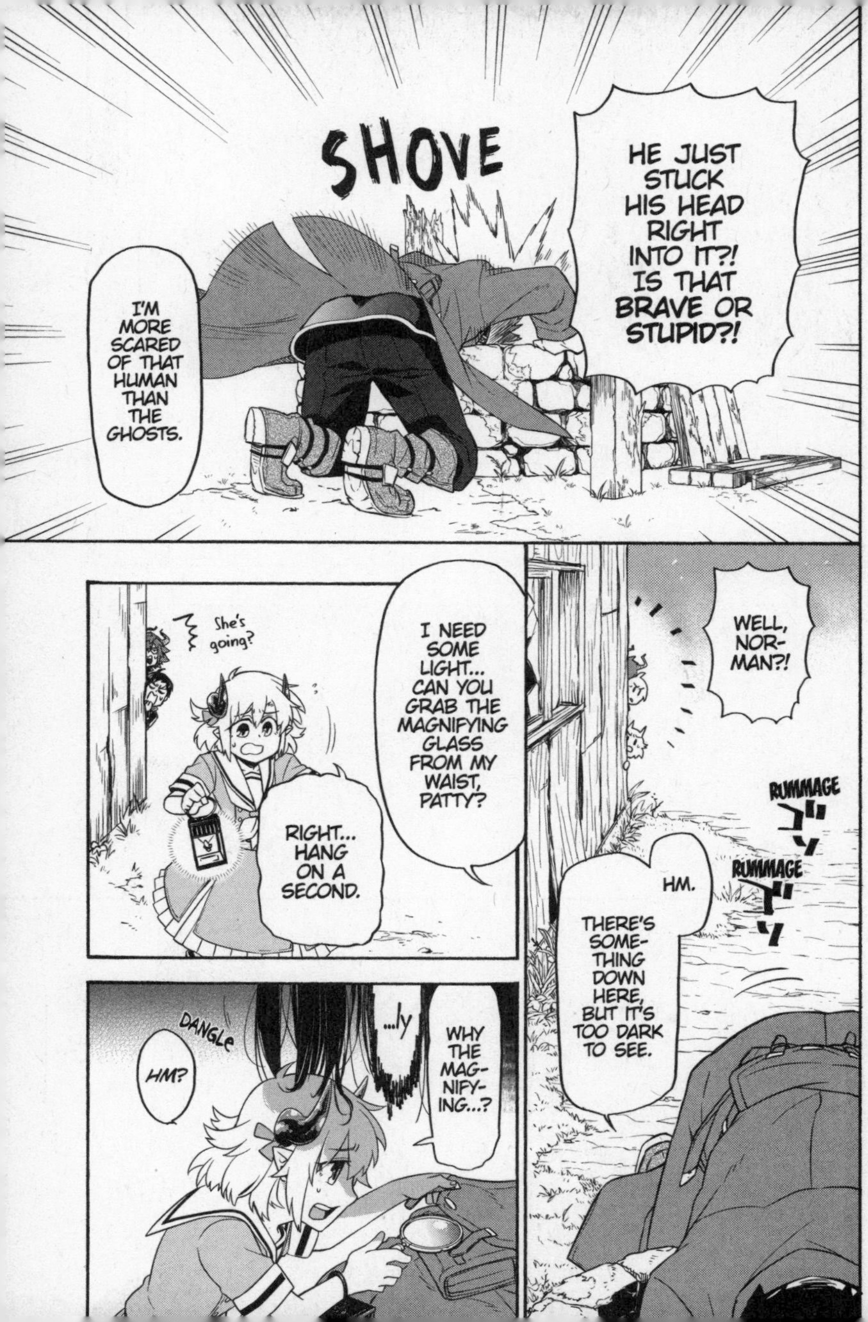
HE JUST STUCK HIS HEAD RIGHT INTO IT?! IS THAT BRAVE OR STUPID?!
SHOVE
I'M MORE SCARED OF THAT HUMAN THAN THE GHOSTS.
WELL, NOR-MAN?!
RUMMAGE
ゴソ
RUMMAGE
ゴソ
HM.
THERE'S SOME-THING DOWN HERE, BUT IT'S TOO DARK TO SEE.
I NEED SOME LIGHT... CAN YOU GRAB THE MAGNIFYING GLASS FROM MY WAIST, PATTY?
She's going?
RIGHT... HANG ON A SECOND.
WHY THE MAG-NIFY-ING...?
...ly
DANGLe
HM?

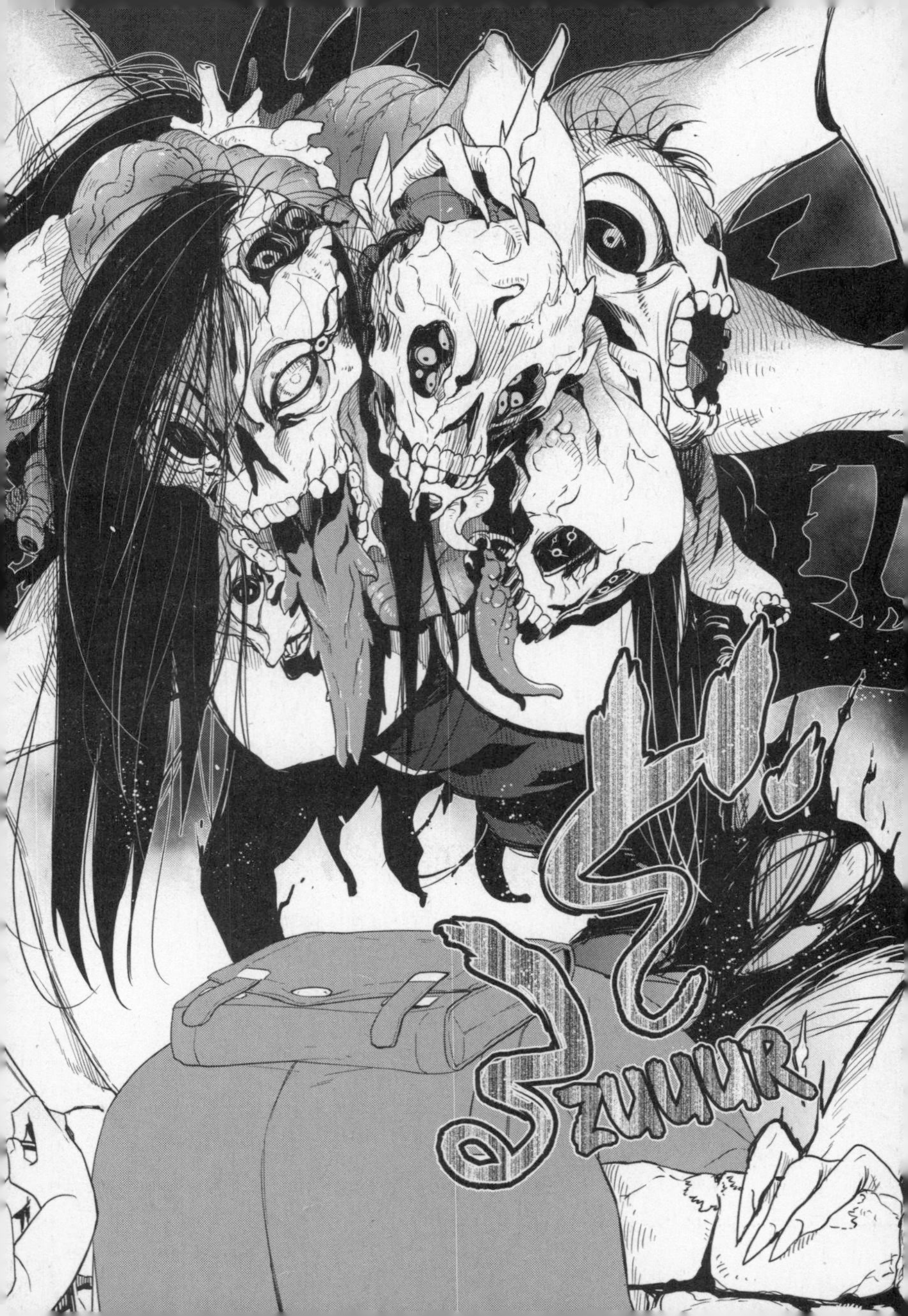
ZUUUR

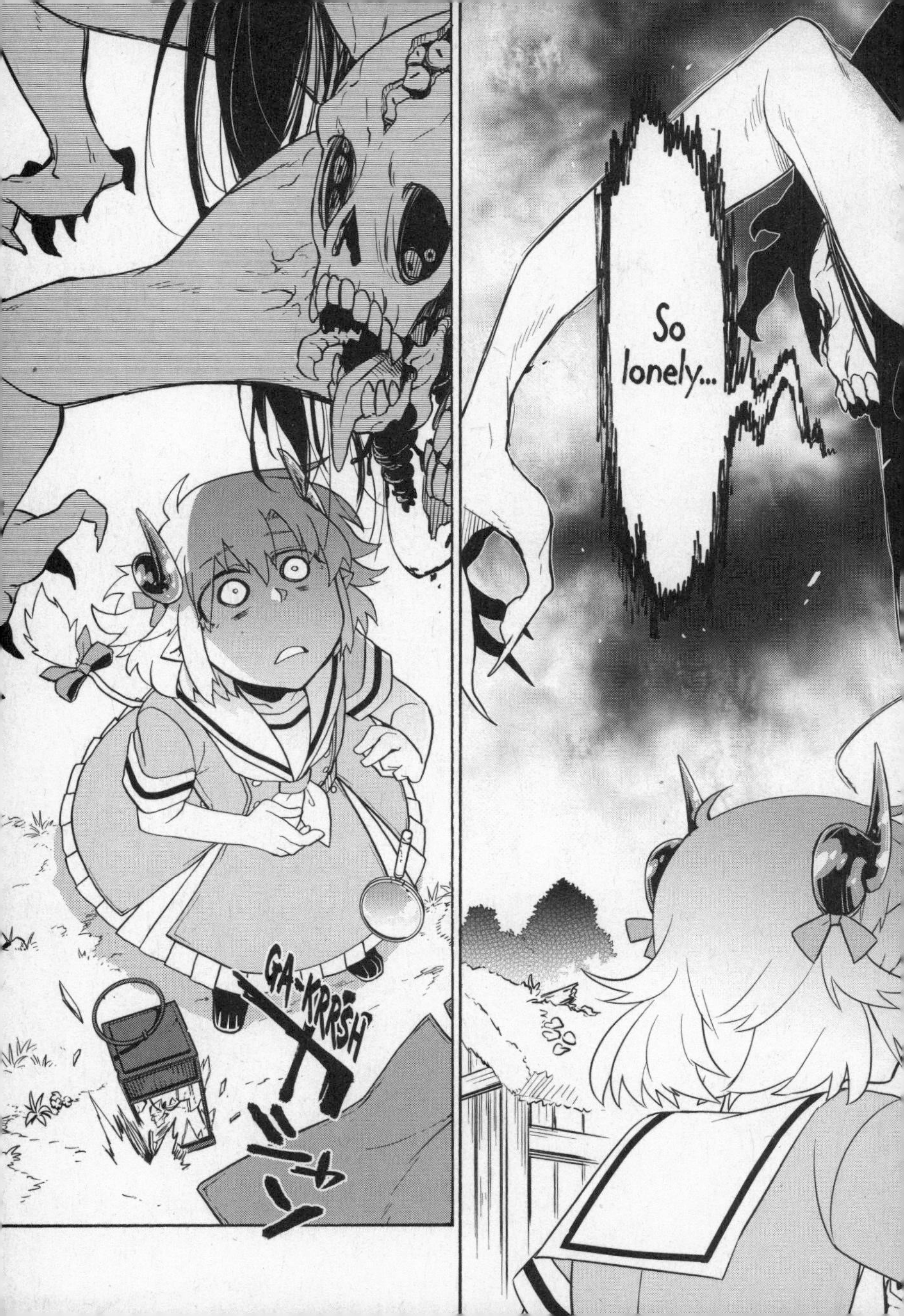
So lonely...
GA-KRRSH

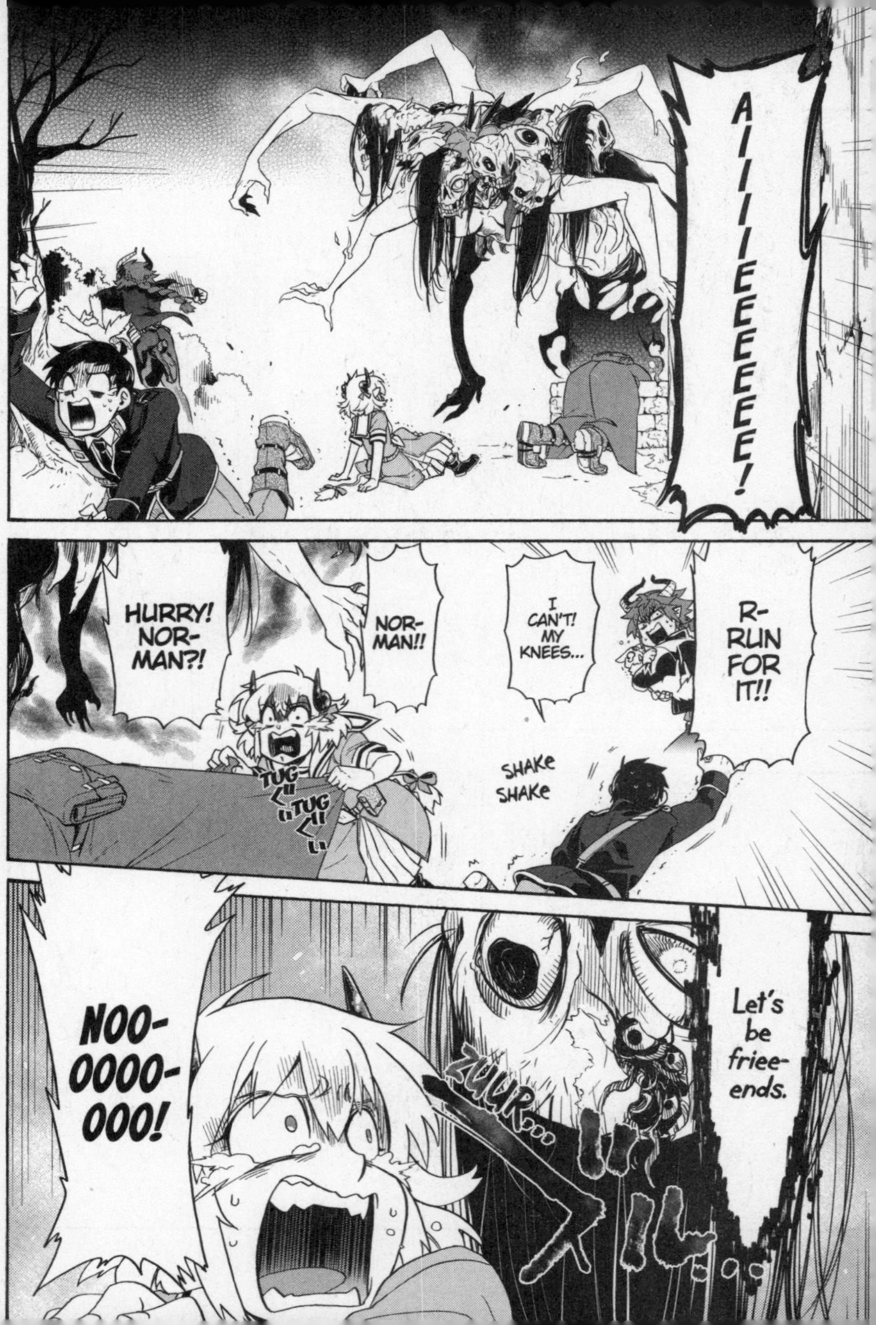
AIIIIEEEEEEE!
R-RUN FOR IT!!
I CAN'T! MY KNEES...
NOR-MAN!!
HURRY! NOR-MAN?!
SHAKE SHAKE
TUG TUG
Let's be frieee-ends.
ZUUR...
NOO-OOOO-OOO!

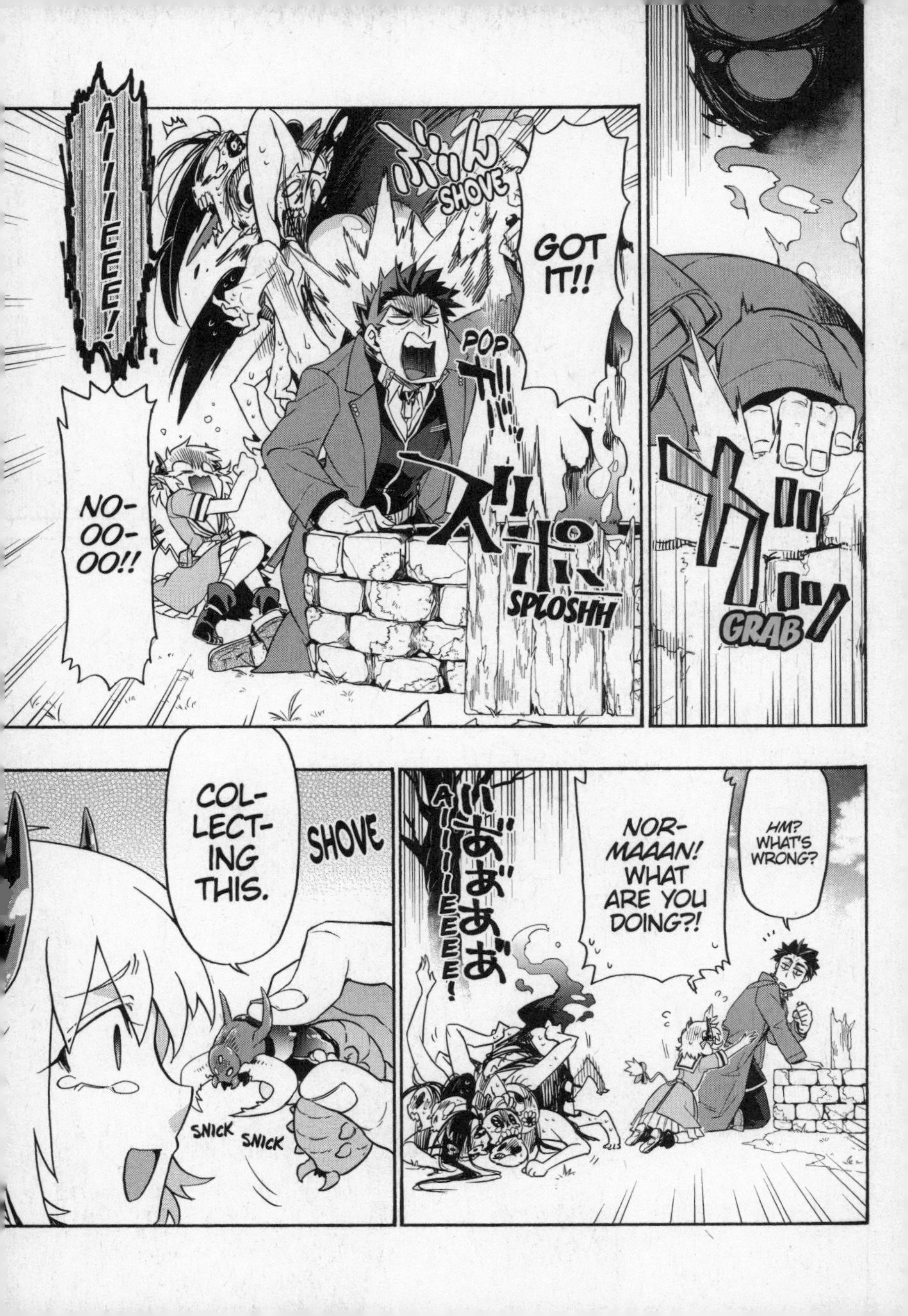
GRAB
GOT IT!!
SHOVE
AIIIEEE!
POP
SPLOSHH
NO-OO-OO!!
HM? WHAT'S WRONG?
NOR-MAAAN! WHAT ARE YOU DOING?!
AIIIIEEEE!
SHOVE
COL-LECT-ING THIS.
SNICK
SNICK

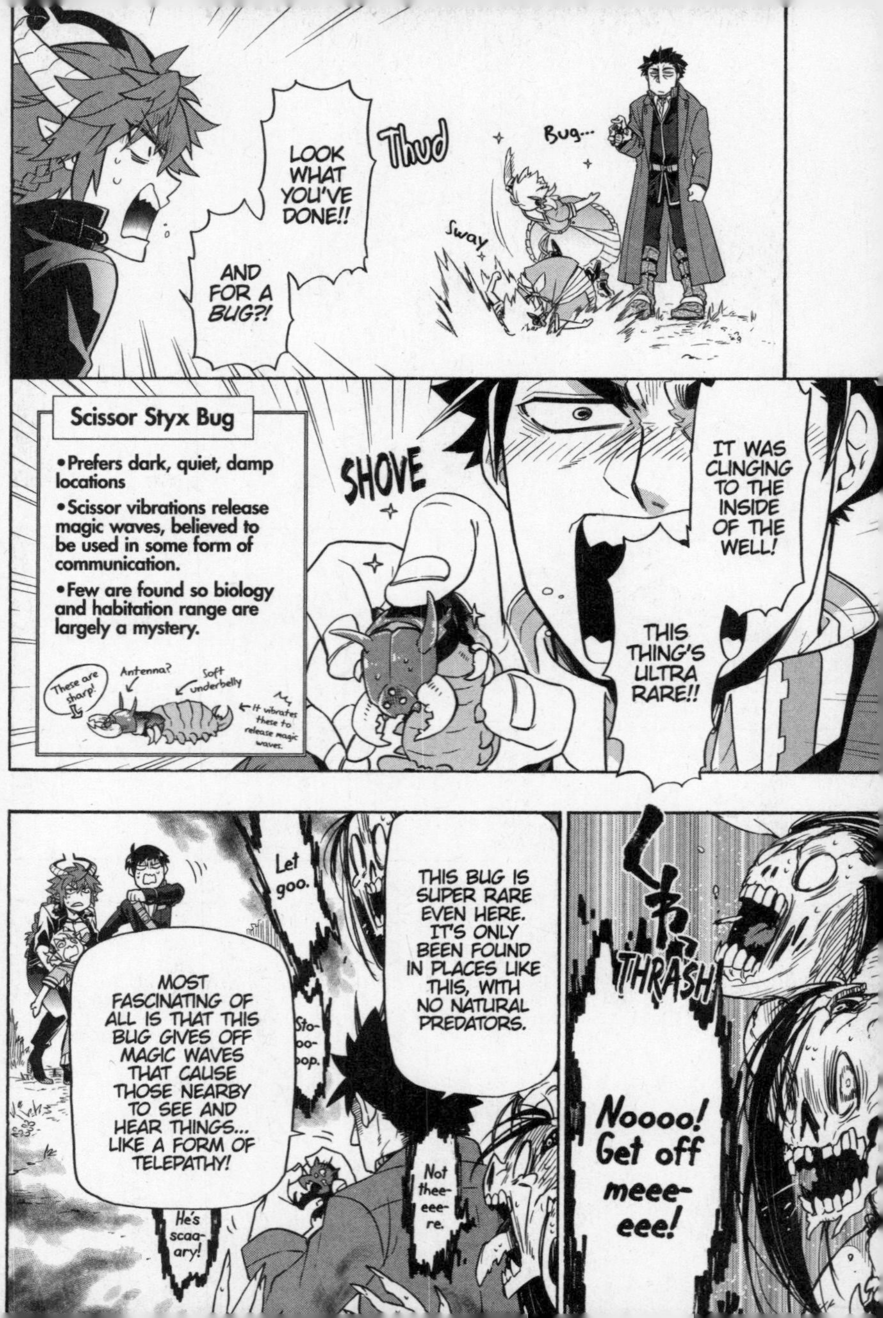
Bug...
Thud
Sway
LOOK WHAT YOU'VE DONE!!
AND FOR A BUG?!
IT WAS CLINGING TO THE INSIDE OF THE WELL!
THIS THING'S ULTRA RARE!!
SHOVE
Scissor Styx Bug
•Prefers dark, quiet, damp locations
•Scissor vibrations release magic waves, believed to be used in some form of communication.
•Few are found so biology and habitation range are largely a mystery.
These are sharp!
Antenna?
Soft underbelly
It vibrates these to release magic waves.
くわ
THRASH
Noooo! Get off meeee-eee!
THIS BUG IS SUPER RARE EVEN HERE. IT'S ONLY BEEN FOUND IN PLACES LIKE THIS, WITH NO NATURAL PREDATORS.
Let goo.
Sto-oo-oop.
MOST FASCINATING OF ALL IS THAT THIS BUG GIVES OFF MAGIC WAVES THAT CAUSE THOSE NEARBY TO SEE AND HEAR THINGS... LIKE A FORM OF TELEPATHY!
Not theee-eee-re.
He's scaa-ary!

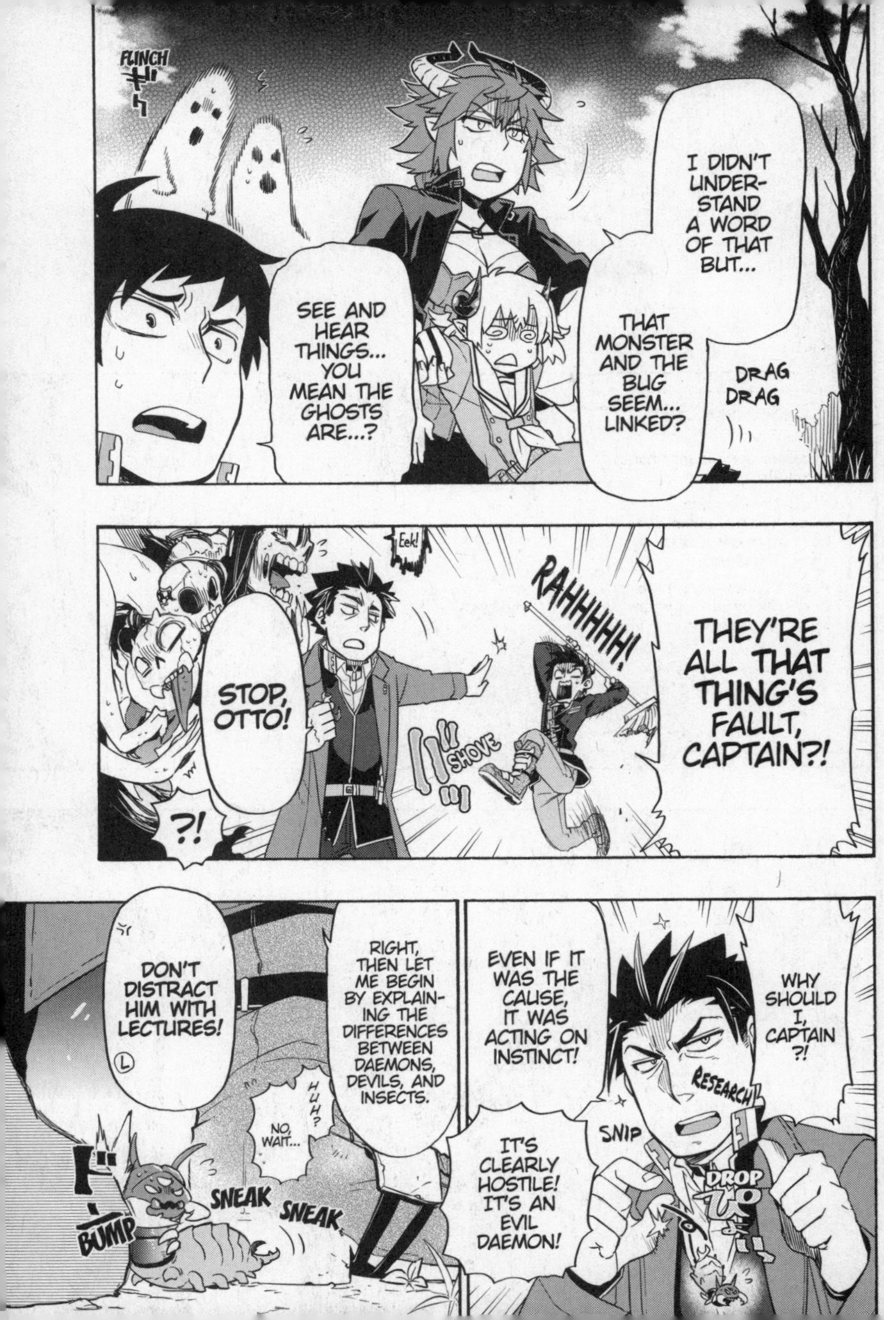

I DIDN'T UNDERSTAND A WORD OF THAT BUT...
DRAG DRAG
THAT MONSTER AND THE BUG SEEM... LINKED?
SEE AND HEAR THINGS... YOU MEAN THE GHOSTS ARE...?
FLINCH
THEY'RE ALL THAT THING'S FAULT, CAPTAIN?!
RAHHHHHH!
Eek!
SHOVE
STOP, OTTO!
?!
WHY SHOULD I, CAPTAIN?!
RESEARCH
EVEN IF IT WAS THE CAUSE, IT WAS ACTING ON INSTINCT!
SNIP
IT'S CLEARLY HOSTILE! IT'S AN EVIL DAEMON!
DROP
RIGHT, THEN LET ME BEGIN BY EXPLAIN-ING THE DIFFERENCES BETWEEN DAEMONS, DEVILS, AND INSECTS.
HUH?
NO, WAIT...
DON'T DISTRACT HIM WITH LECTURES!
SNEAK SNEAK
BUMP

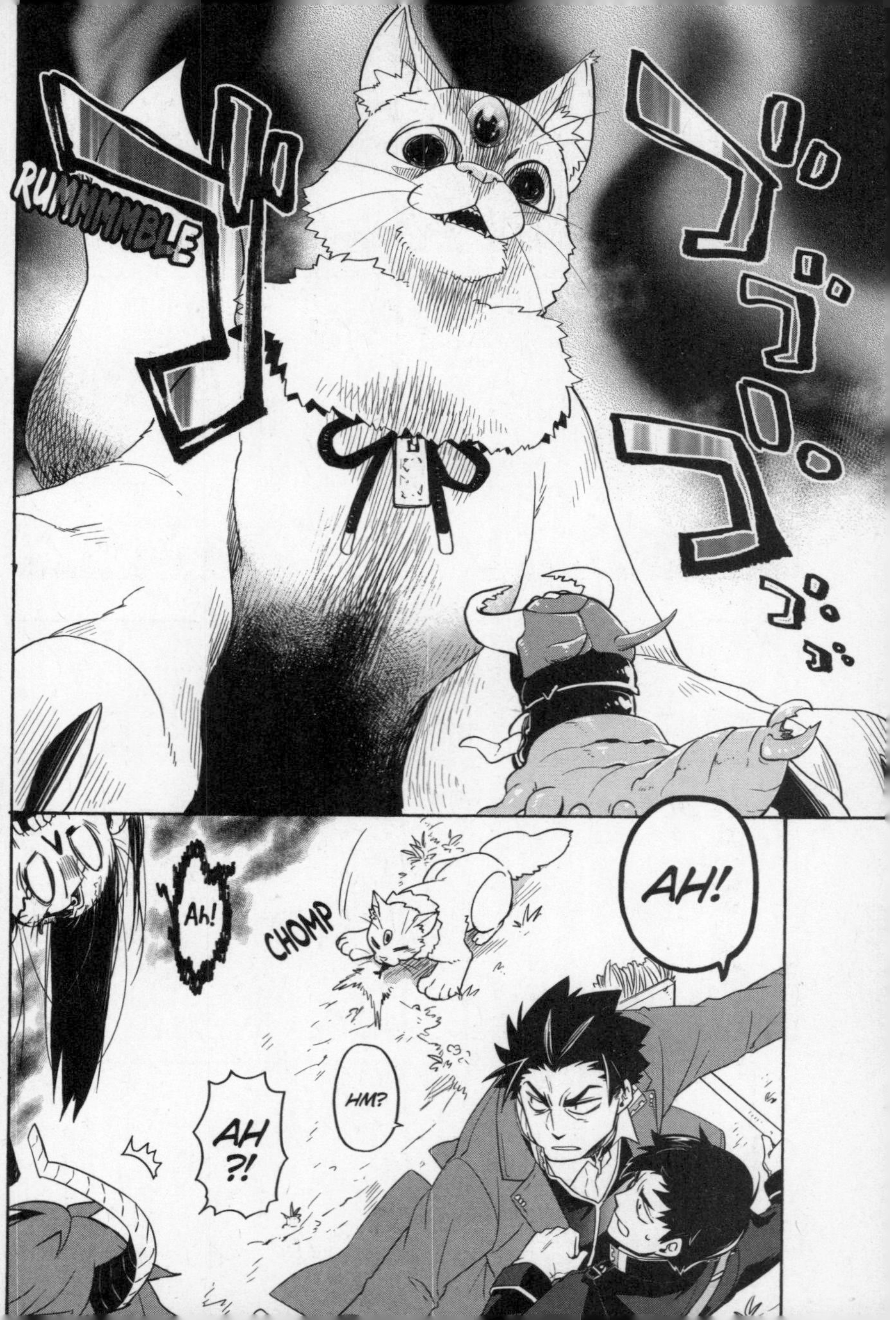
RUMMMMBLE
AH!
Ah!
CHOMP
HM?
AH ?!

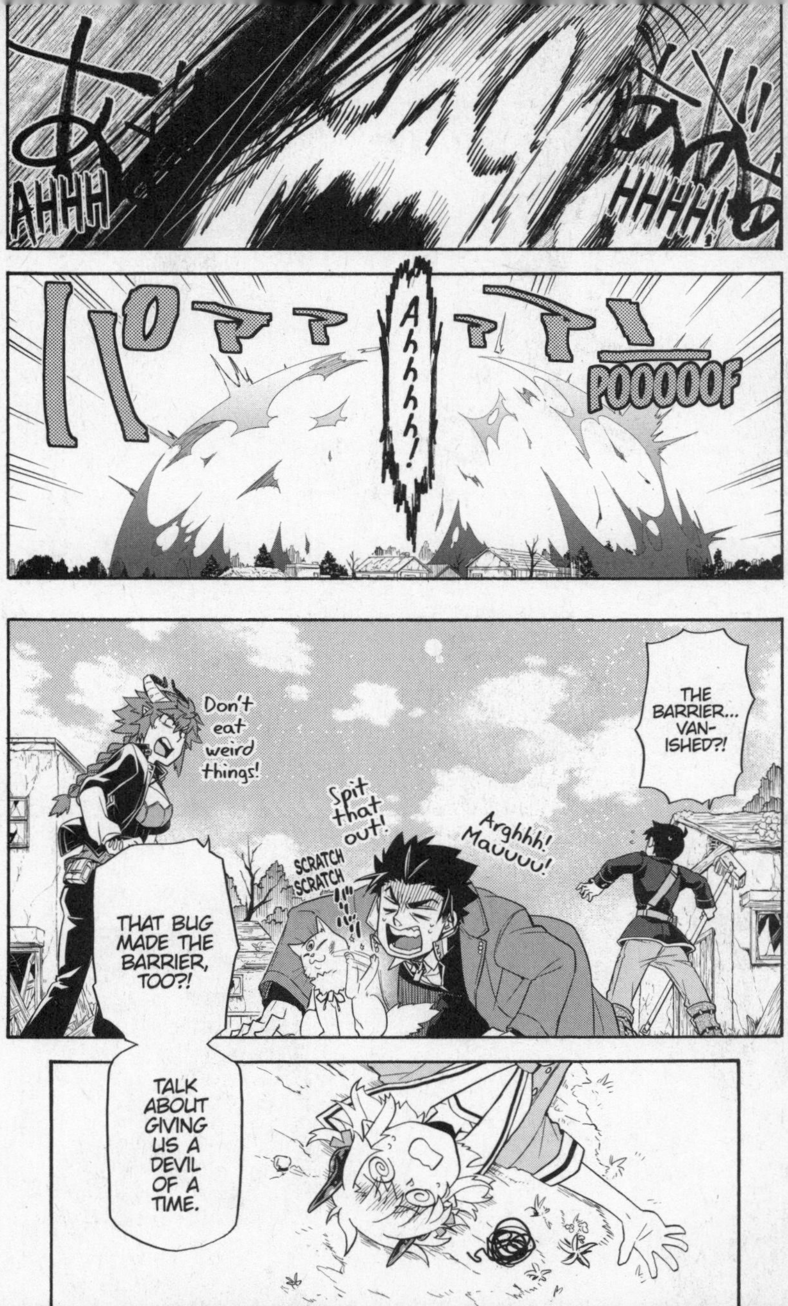
AHHH
HHHH!
POOOOOF
Ahhhh!
THE BARRIER... VAN-ISHED?!
Arghhh! Mauuuu!
Spit that out!
SCRATCH SCRATCH
Don't eat weird things!
THAT BUG MADE THE BARRIER, TOO?!
TALK ABOUT GIVING US A DEVIL OF A TIME.

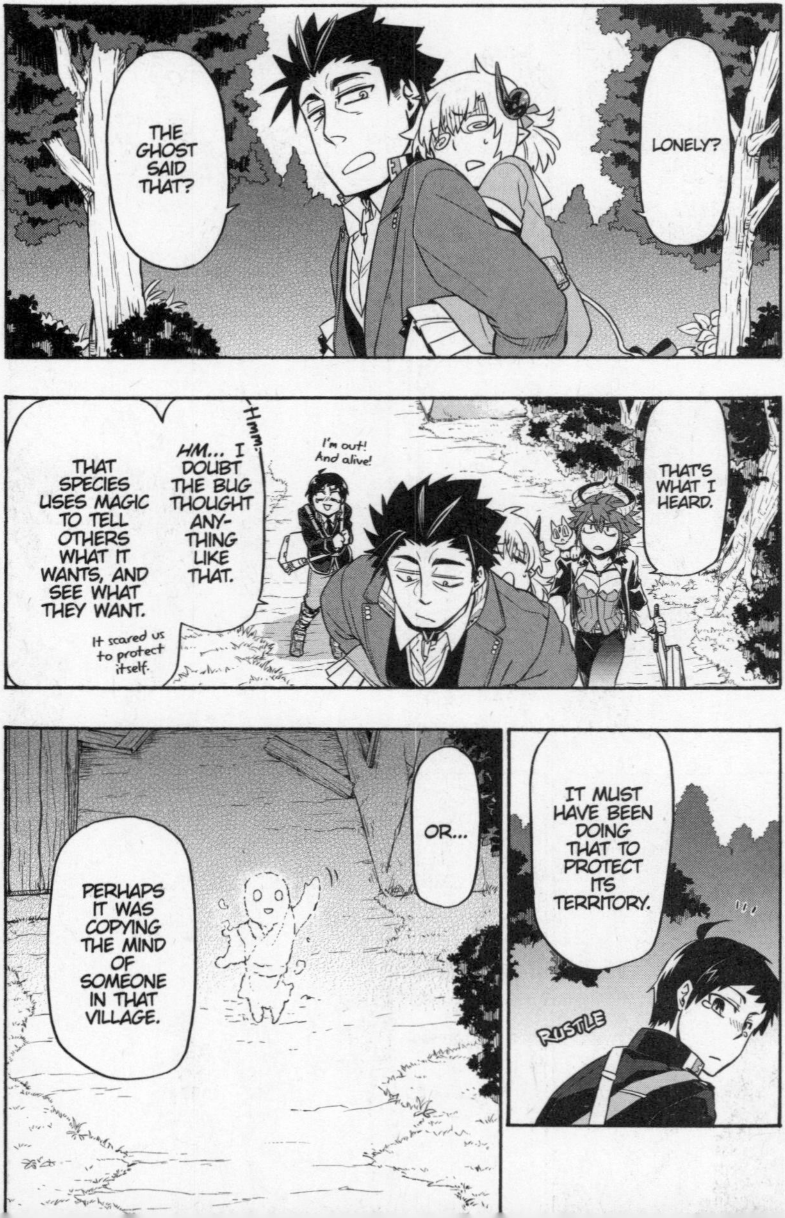
LONELY?
THE GHOST SAID THAT?
THAT'S WHAT I HEARD.
I'm out! And alive!
Hmm.
HM... I DOUBT THE BUG THOUGHT ANY-THING LIKE THAT.
THAT SPECIES USES MAGIC TO TELL OTHERS WHAT IT WANTS, AND SEE WHAT THEY WANT.
It scared us to protect itself.
IT MUST HAVE BEEN DOING THAT TO PROTECT ITS TERRITORY.
RUSTLE
OR...
PERHAPS IT WAS COPYING THE MIND OF SOMEONE IN THAT VILLAGE.

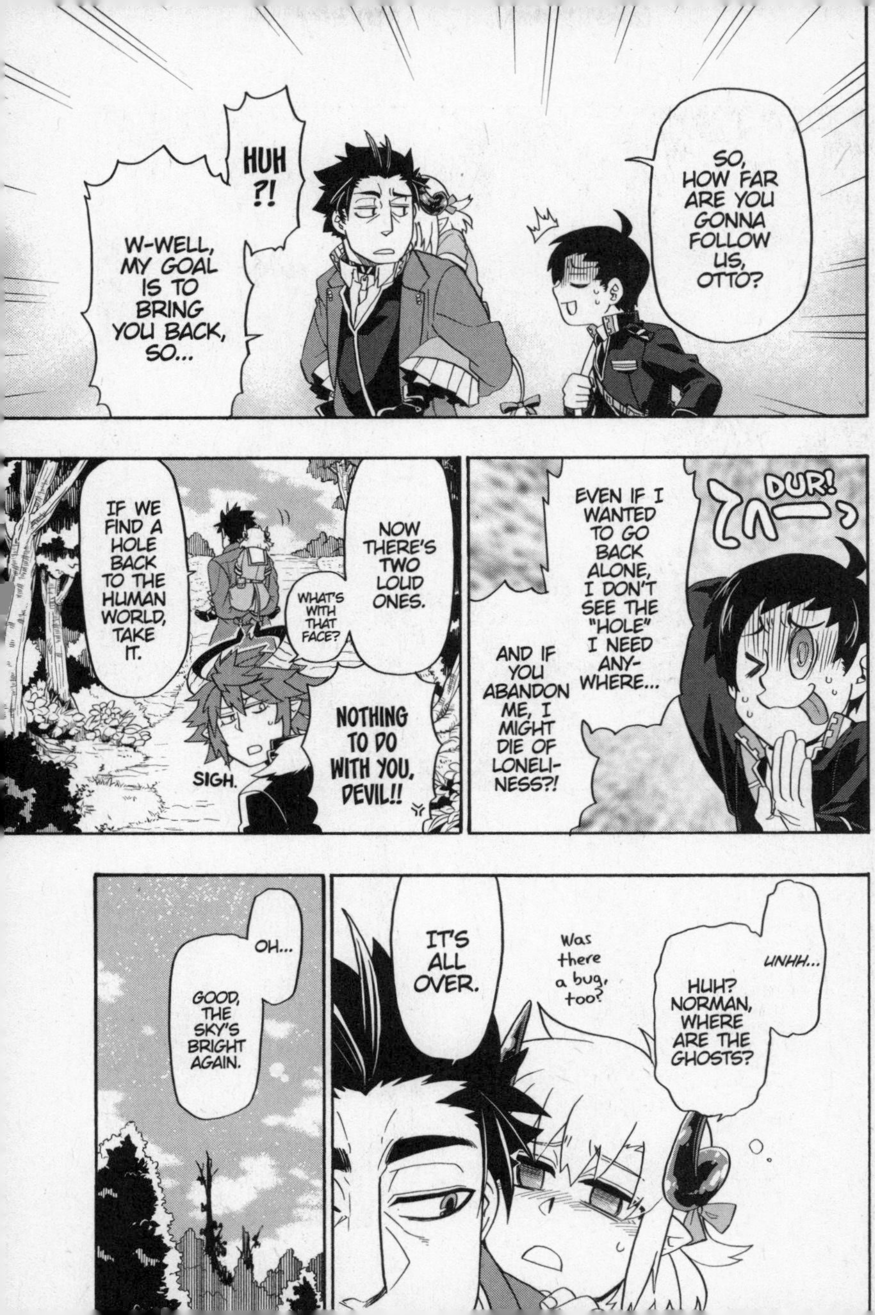
SO, HOW FAR ARE YOU GONNA FOLLOW US, OTTO?
HUH ?!
W-WELL, MY GOAL IS TO BRING YOU BACK, SO...
DUR!
EVEN IF I WANTED TO GO BACK ALONE, I DON'T SEE THE "HOLE" I NEED ANY-WHERE...
AND IF YOU ABANDON ME, I MIGHT DIE OF LONELI-NESS?!
NOW THERE'S TWO LOUD ONES.
IF WE FIND A HOLE BACK TO THE HUMAN WORLD, TAKE IT.
WHAT'S WITH THAT FACE?
NOTHING TO DO WITH YOU, DEVIL!!
SIGH.
UNHH...
HUH? NORMAN, WHERE ARE THE GHOSTS?
Was there a bug, too?
IT'S ALL OVER.
OH...
GOOD, THE SKY'S BRIGHT AGAIN.

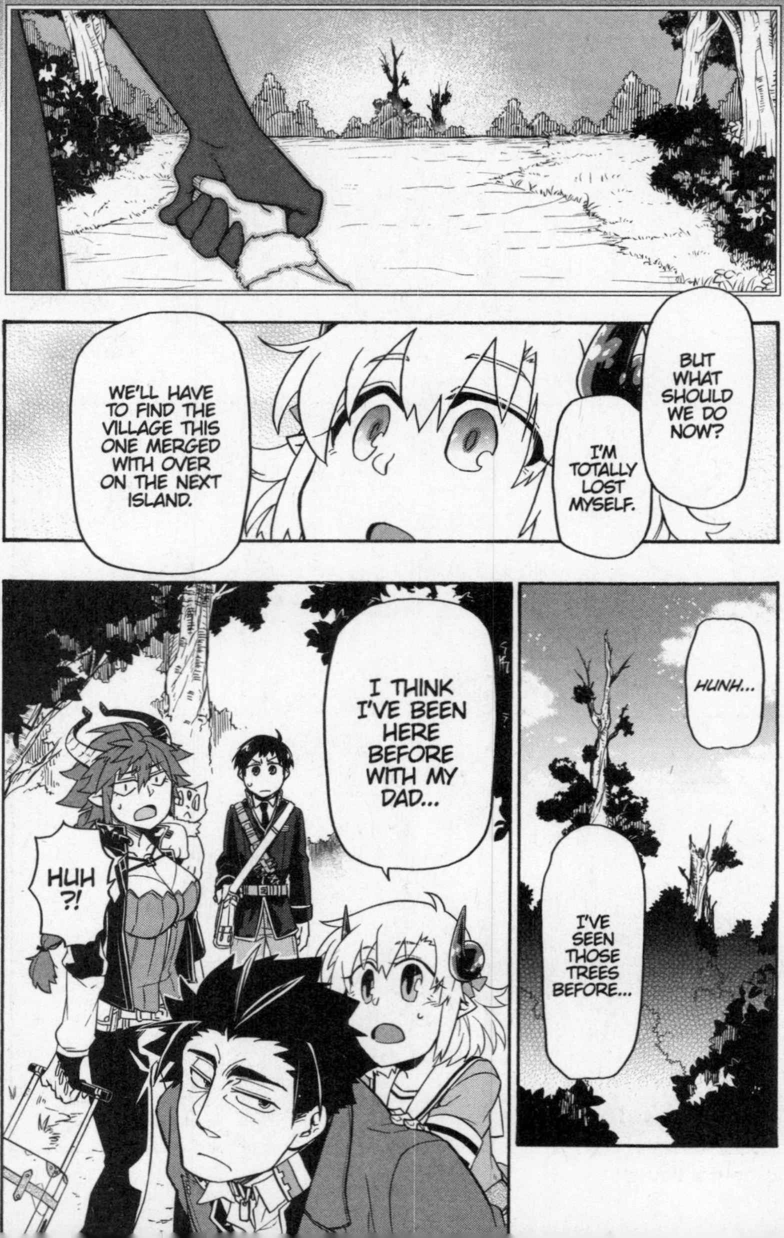
BUT WHAT SHOULD WE DO NOW?
I'M TOTALLY LOST MYSELF.
WE'LL HAVE TO FIND THE VILLAGE THIS ONE MERGED WITH OVER ON THE NEXT ISLAND.
HUNH...
I'VE SEEN THOSE TREES BEFORE...
I THINK I'VE BEEN HERE BEFORE WITH MY DAD...
HUH?!

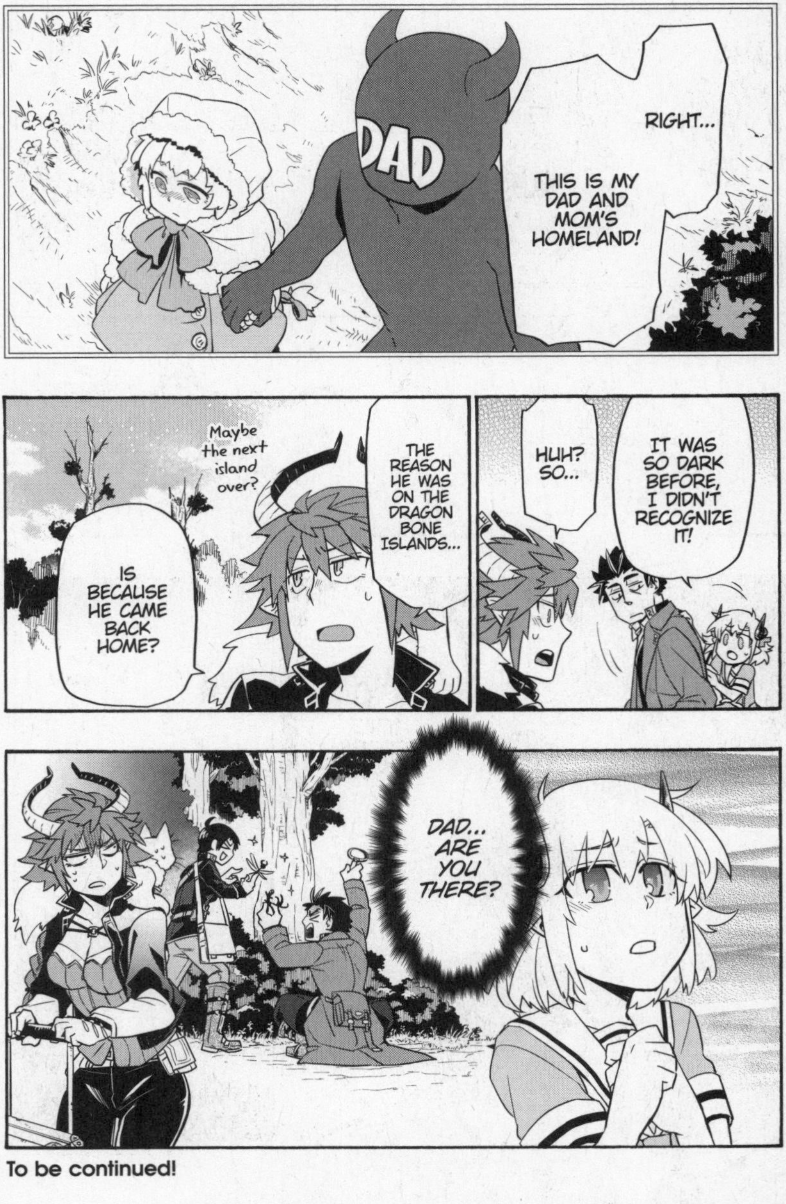
RIGHT...
THIS IS MY DAD AND MOM'S HOMELAND!
DAD
IT WAS SO DARK BEFORE, I DIDN'T RECOGNIZE IT!
HUH? SO...
THE REASON HE WAS ON THE DRAGON BONE ISLANDS...
Maybe the next island over?
IS BECAUSE HE CAME BACK HOME?
DAD... ARE YOU THERE?

To be continued!

Sorry For My Familiar

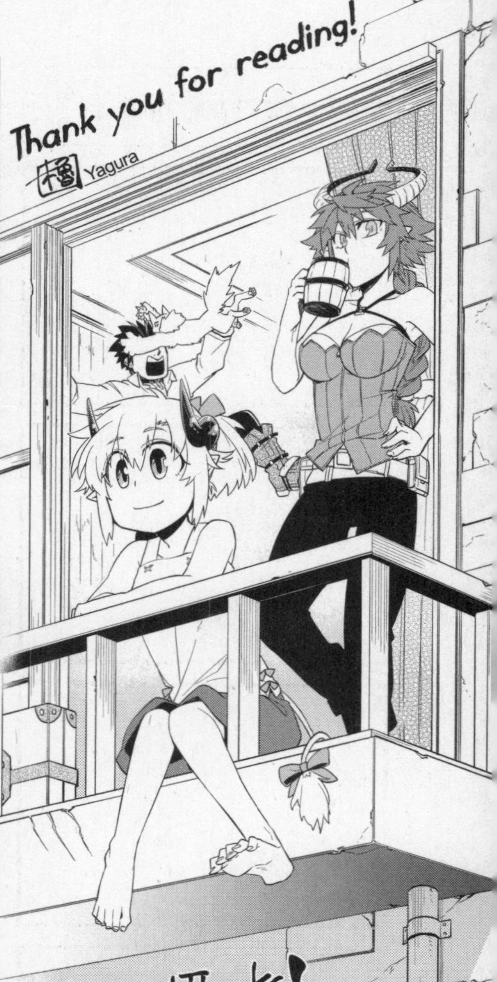

Thank you for reading!
Yagura

Special Thanks!

Assistant: Terada-sensei & Nanami-san

Cover/Logo Design: Sugita-san

Editor: T-san

Thank you all!

FLEHMEN MAU

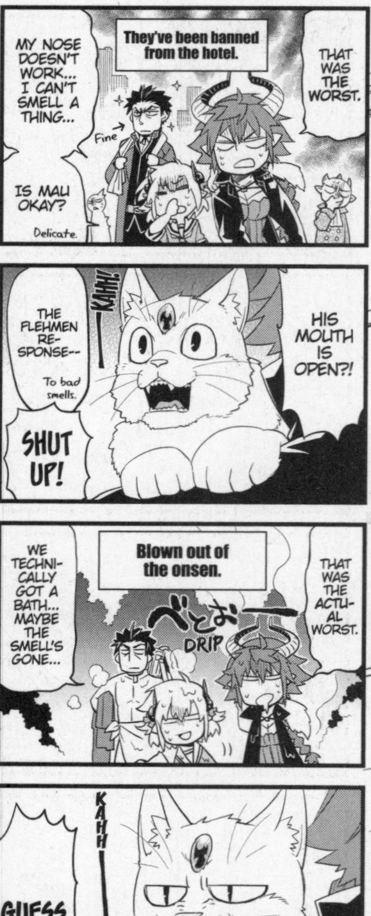

They've been banned from the hotel.
THAT WAS THE WORST.
MY NOSE DOESN'T WORK... I CAN'T SMELL A THING...
Fine
IS MAU OKAY?
Delicate.
HIS MOUTH IS OPEN?!
KAHH!
THE FLEHMEN RE-SPONSE--
To bad smells.
SHUT UP!
Blown out of the onsen.
THAT WAS THE ACTU-AL WORST.
べとぉーー
DRIP
WE TECHNI-CALLY GOT A BATH... MAYBE THE SMELL'S GONE...
KAHH
GUESS NOT!

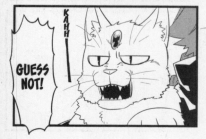

FOREST LUNCH

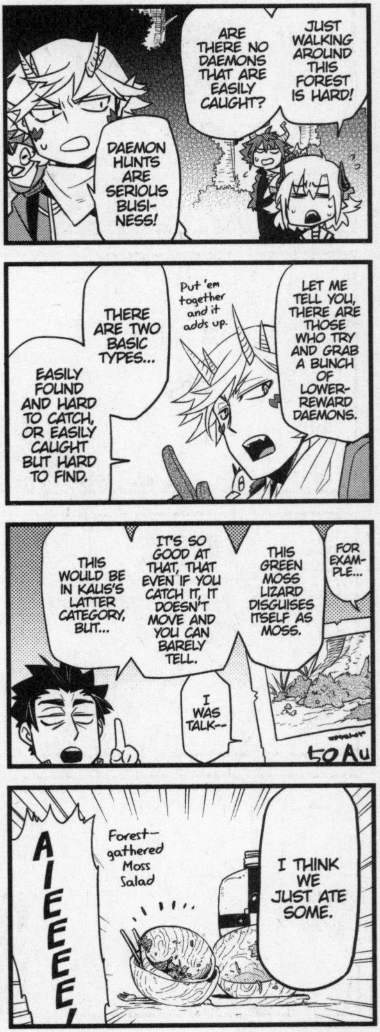
JUST WALKING AROUND THIS FOREST IS HARD!
ARE THERE NO DAEMONS THAT ARE EASILY CAUGHT?
DAEMON HUNTS ARE SERIOUS BUSINESS!
LET ME TELL YOU, THERE ARE THOSE WHO TRY AND GRAB A BUNCH OF LOWER-REWARD DAEMONS.
Put 'em together and it adds up.
THERE ARE TWO BASIC TYPES...
EASILY FOUND AND HARD TO CATCH, OR EASILY CAUGHT BUT HARD TO FIND.
FOR EXAMPLE...
THIS GREEN MOSS LIZARD DISGUISES ITSELF AS MOSS.
IT'S SO GOOD AT THAT, THAT EVEN IF YOU CATCH IT, IT DOESN'T MOVE AND YOU CAN BARELY TELL.
THIS WOULD BE IN KAUS'S LATTER CATEGORY, BUT...
I WAS TALK--
I THINK WE JUST ATE SOME.
Forest-gathered Moss Salad
AIEEEE!

SETTING OFF

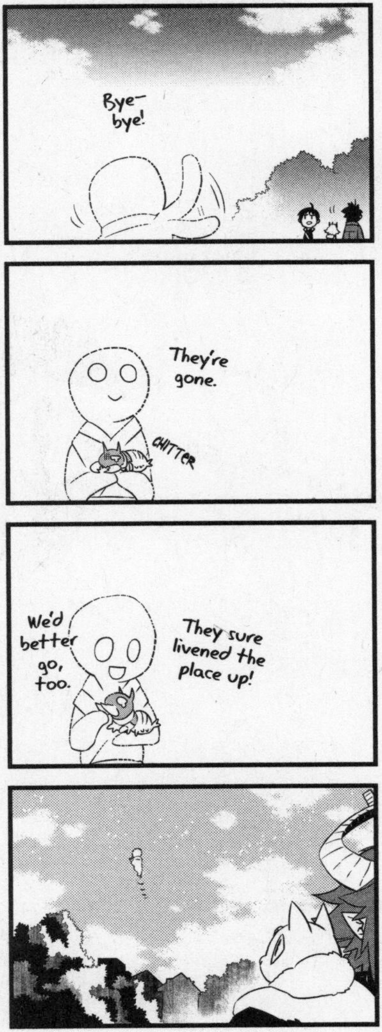
Bye-bye!
They're gone.
CHITTER
They sure livened the place up!
We'd better go, too.

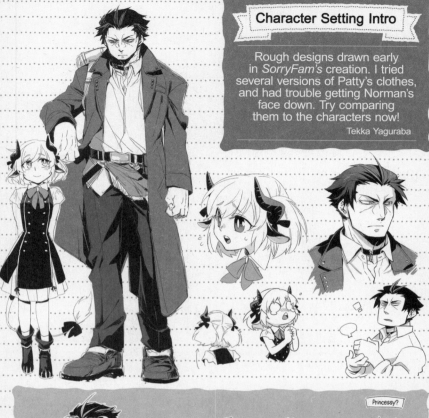

Character Setting Intro

Rough designs drawn early in *SorryFam's* creation. I tried several versions of Patty's clothes, and had trouble getting Norman's face down. Try comparing them to the characters now!

Tekka Yaguraba

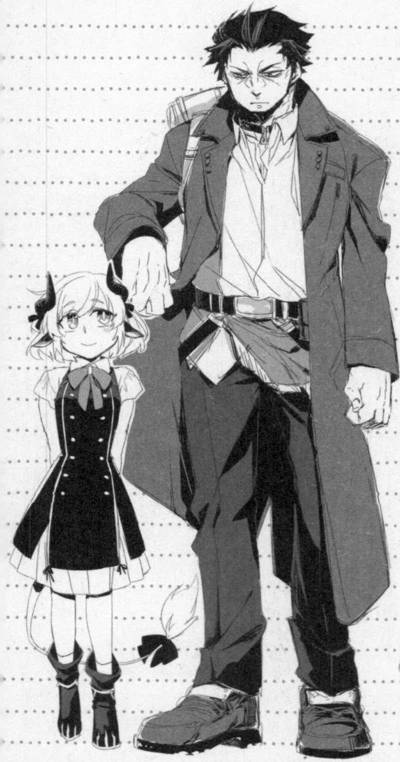

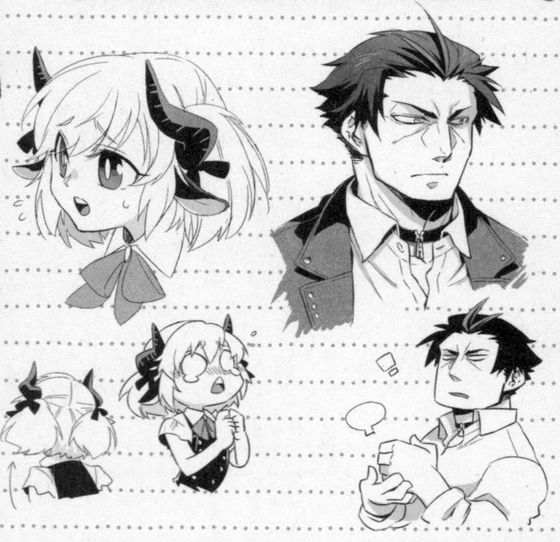

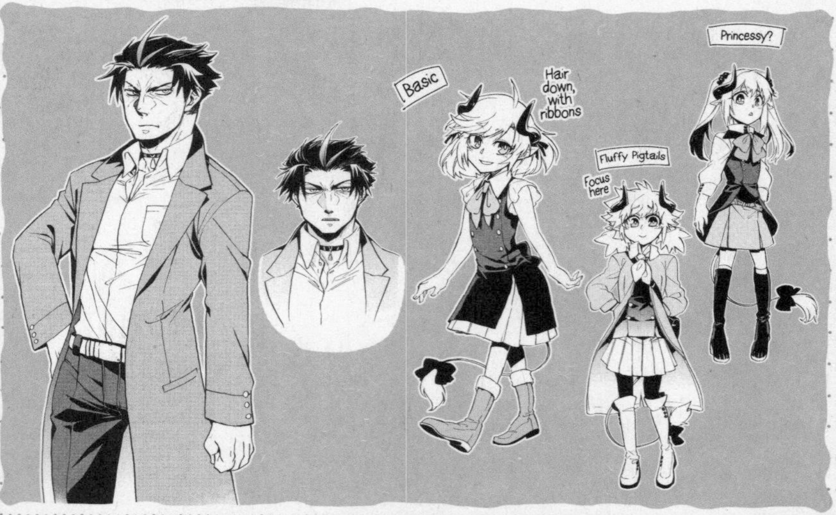
Princessy?
Basic
Hair down, with ribbons
Fluffy Pigtails
Focus here

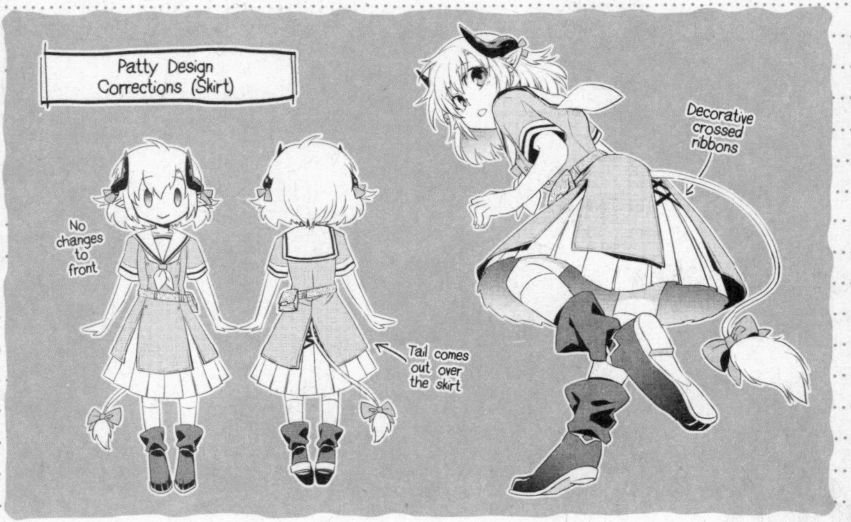
Patty Design Corrections (Skirt)
Decorative crossed ribbons
No changes to front
Tail comes out over the skirt

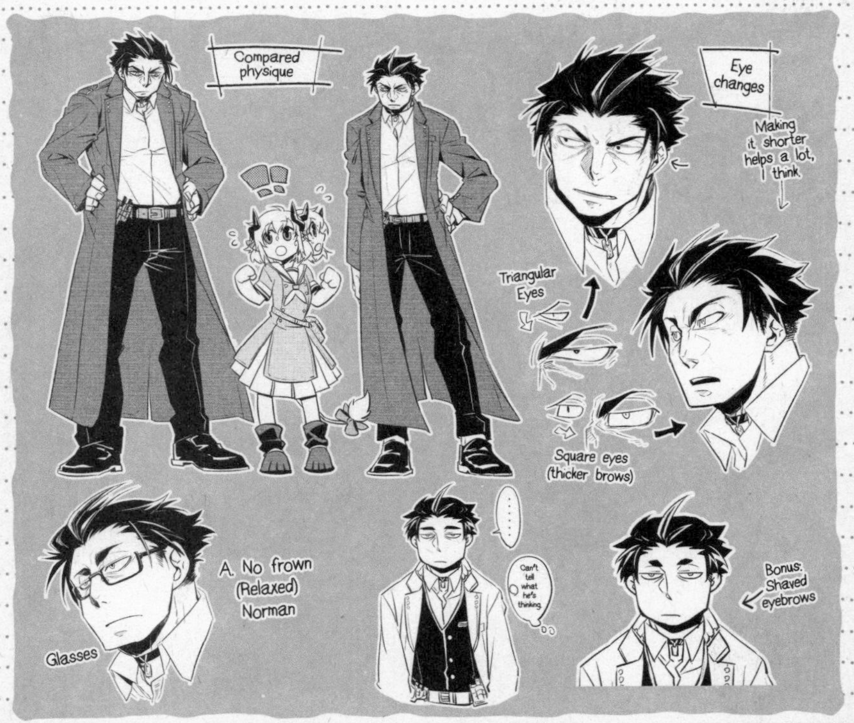
Eye changes
Making it shorter helps a lot, I think.
Compared physique
Triangular Eyes
Square eyes (thicker brows)
Bonus: Shaved eyebrows
.....
Can't tell what he's thinking.
A. No frown (Relaxed) Norman
Glasses

Next Time

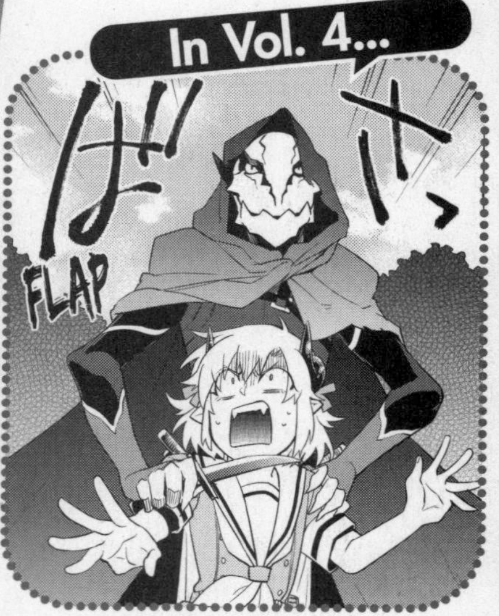
In Vol. 4...
ぱさっ
FLAP

Patty will be in loads of trouble again!!

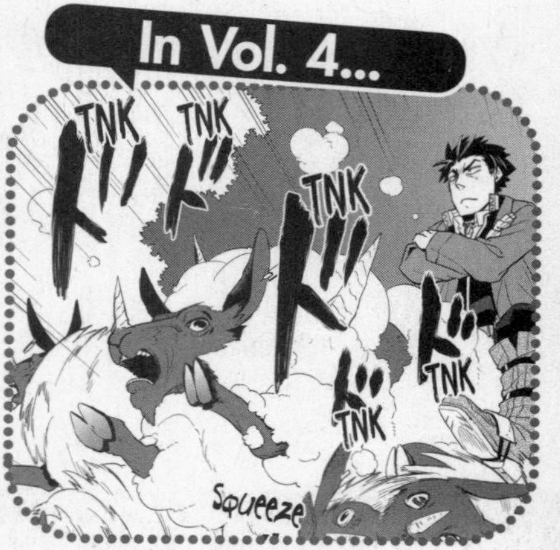
In Vol. 4...
TNK
TNK
TNK
TNK
TNK
Squeeze

Norman will go berserk again!!

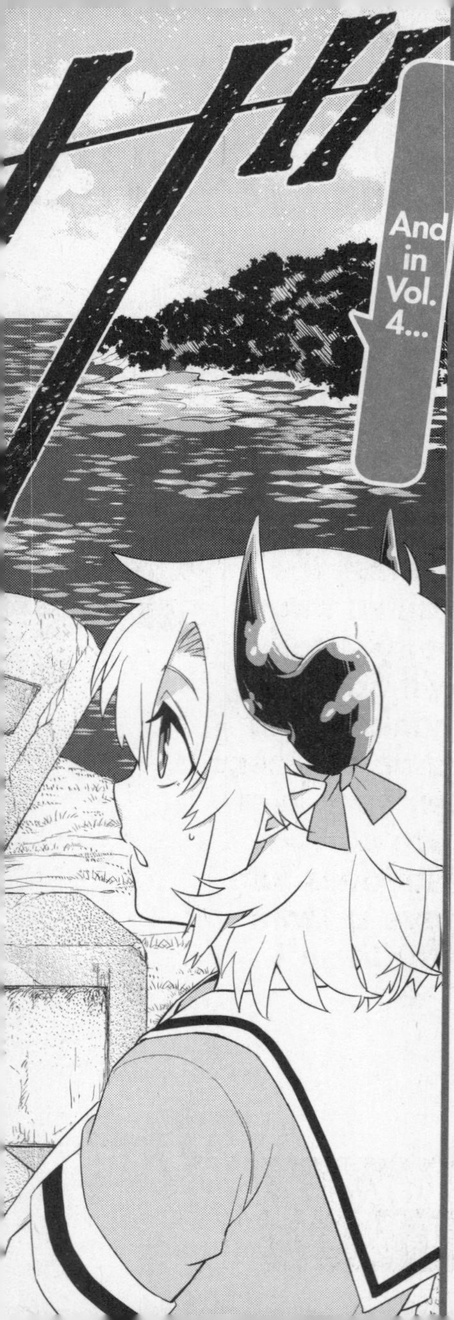
And in Vol. 4...

sorry
for
my familiar!!

vol.3

Tekka Yaguraba

Sorry For My Familiar

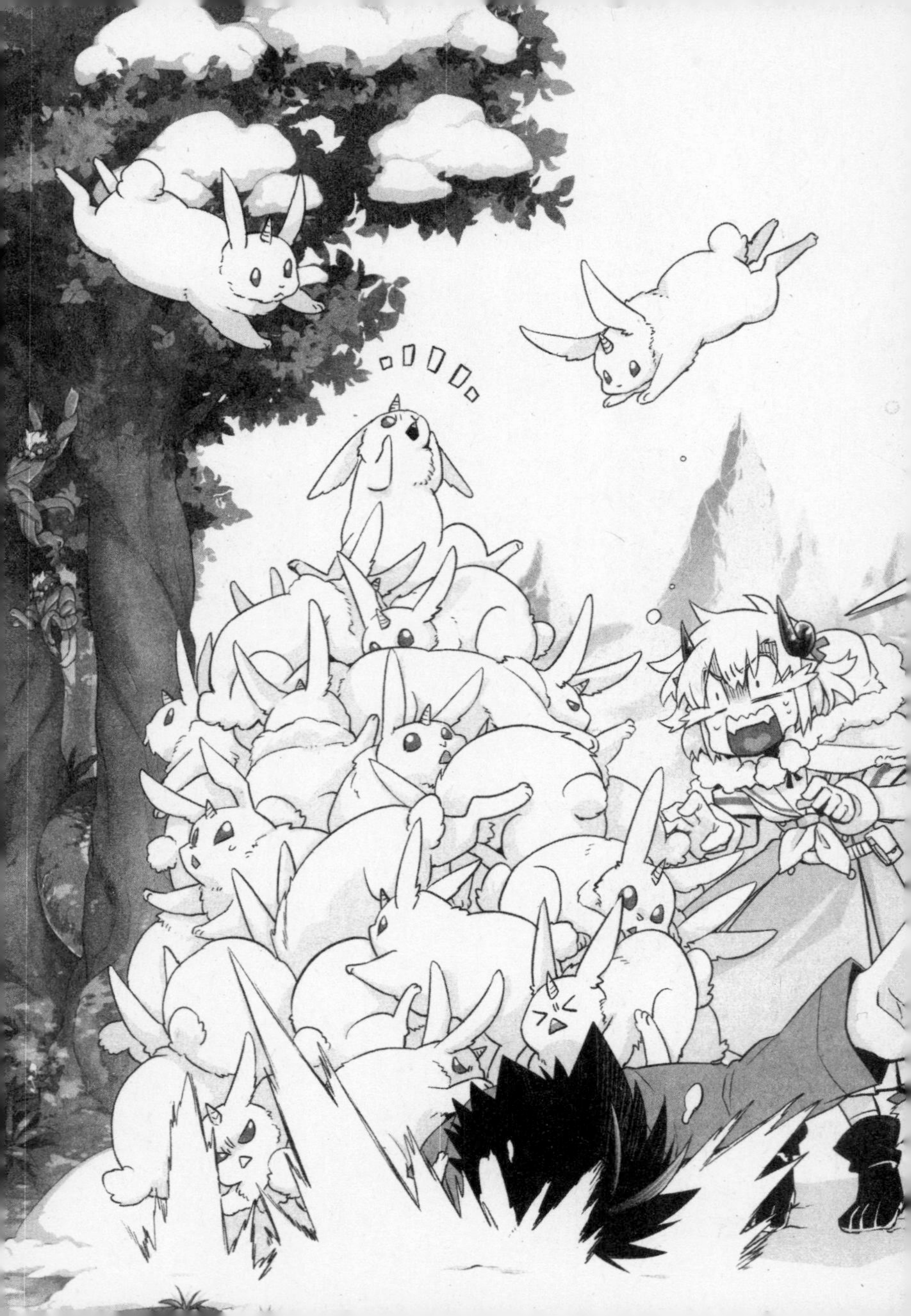

SEVEN SEAS ENTERTAINMENT PRESENTS

Sorry For My Familiar

story and art by **TEKKA YAGURABA**

VOLUME 3

TRANSLATION
Andrew Cunningham

ADAPTATION
Betsy Aoki

LETTERING AND RETOUCH
Kaitlyn Wiley

COVER DESIGN
KC Fabellon

PROOFREADER
Stephanie Cohen
Shanti Whitesides

EDITOR
Shannon Fay

PRODUCTION ASSISTANT
CK Russell

PRODUCTION MANAGER
Lissa Pattillo

EDITOR-IN-CHIEF
Adam Arnold

PUBLISHER
Jason DeAngelis

SORRY FOR MY FAMILIAR VOLUME 3

First published in Japan in 2017 by Kodansha Ltd., Tokyo.
Publication rights for this English edition arranged through Kodansha Ltd., Tokyo.

ISBN: 978-1-626929-47-0

Printed in Canada

First Printing: November 2018

10 9 8 7 6 5 4 3 2 1

READING DIRECTIONS

This book reads from ***right to left***, Japanese style. If this is your first time reading manga, you start reading from the top right panel on each page and take it from there. If you get lost, just follow the numbered diagram here. It may seem backwards at first, but you'll get the hang of it! Have fun!!

1
2
3
4
5
6
7
8
9

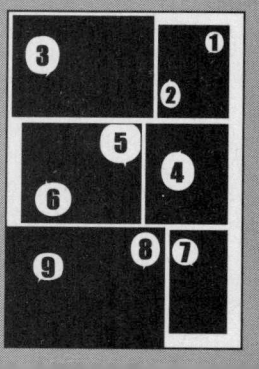